Praise for Emily Sullivan

"One particular gem of a new voice is Emily Sullivan, whose nineteenth-century tales of romance and intrigue are designed to keep a reader on the edge of their seat."

—*Entertainment Weekly*

DUCHESS MATERIAL

"Enchanting…Sullivan delivers sparkling banter, gentle mystery, and plenty of swoon-worthy moments. Historical romance fans will eat this up." —*Publishers Weekly*, starred review

"An exciting Victorian era romance with a down-to-earth Duke and a progressive schoolteacher who tackle issues of privilege, class, and women's rights. A must read for fans of *Miss Scarlet and the Duke*!"

—Alexis Daria, bestselling author of *You Had Me at Hola*

THE HELLION AND THE HERO

"Sullivan expertly exposes her characters' emotional depths and keeps the pages turning with a steady undercurrent of mystery. Series fans are sure to be pleased." —*Publishers Weekly*

"The latest in Emily Sullivan's League of Scoundrels series will satisfy those who yearn for a second-chance romance."

—*Paste* magazine

THE REBEL AND THE RAKE

"*The Rebel and the Rake* will steal readers' hearts before they even realize it's gone, entangling them in the storytelling with much the same stealth as Rafe's investigations." —*Entertainment Weekly*

"After wowing readers with her superb debut, rising historical romance star Sullivan returns with another entrancing addition to her League of Scoundrels series that brilliantly showcases her mastery of deep characterization as well as her gift for crafting a wit-infused plot that effectively threads the needle between desire and danger without dropping a single stitch."

—*Booklist*, starred review

A ROGUE TO REMEMBER

"The literary charms of Sullivan's superbly written debut are many, including a full cast of deftly nuanced characters, an exquisitely evoked Italian setting that would impress E. M. Forster, love scenes that deliver both emotional intensity and lush sensuality, and vivacious writing enhanced by ample measures of wit."

—*Booklist*, starred review

"[A] winning debut... This satisfying love story will especially appeal to historical romance fans looking for a break from the typical English setting." —*Publishers Weekly*

Is This Real or Just Pretend?

BOOKS BY EMILY SULLIVAN

Duchess Material

A Rogue to Remember

The Rebel and the Rake

The Hellion and the Hero

EMILY SULLIVAN

FOREVER

NEW YORK BOSTON

Copyright © 2025 by Emily Sullivan

Cover design and illustration by YY Liak
Cover copyright © 2025 by Hachette Book Group, Inc.

Forever
Hachette Book Group
1290 Avenue of the Americas, New York, NY 10104
read-forever.com
@readforeverpub

First edition: September 2025

Forever is an imprint of Grand Central Publishing. The Forever name and logo are registered trademarks of Hachette Book Group, Inc.

The publisher is not responsible for websites (or their content) that are not owned by the publisher.

Forever books may be purchased in bulk for business, educational, or promotional use. For information, please contact your local bookseller or the Hachette Book Group Special Markets Department at special.markets@hbgusa.com.

Library of Congress Cataloging-in-Publication Data

Names: Sullivan, Emily author
Title: Is this real or just pretend? / Emily Sullivan.
Description: First edition. | New York : Forever, 2025.
Identifiers: LCCN 2025013079 | ISBN 9781538742372 trade paperback |
    ISBN 9781538742396 ebook
Subjects: LCGFT: Romance fiction | Historical fiction | Novels
Classification: LCC PS3619.U4237 I8 2025 | DDC 813/.6—dc23/eng/20250401
LC record available at https://lccn.loc.gov/2025013079

ISBNs: 9781538742372 (trade paperback), 9781538742396 (ebook)

Printed in the United States of America

CCR

10 9 8 7 6 5 4 3 2 1

For the eldest daughters

One

As the train from London came to a screeching halt, Lucien Taylor jerked awake. For one glorious moment he had forgotten where he was, but as he cast a bleary-eyed gaze around the third-class cabin, reality sunk in with sharpened teeth. He shook away the last cobwebs of sleep, peered out the grime-streaked window, and immediately began to have second thoughts. Then third. But it was of little use. Much like this locomotive, he too had reached the end of the line.

Lucien heaved a sigh and reluctantly came to his feet before shuffling off the train onto the deserted platform. He squinted against the golden sunshine and brought up a hand to shield his eyes. *Of course the weather would be perfect today,* he thought bitterly as he scanned the familiar bucolic countryside for the first time in five years. Bunbury was just as he remembered: impossibly lush and adorably quaint. It was the stuff of cozy novels and country house paintings. A prized confection of a village tucked away in the south of England that was impossible not to love—unless you were Lucien.

And he couldn't wait to get the hell out of here.

A pang of guilt immediately followed the unvarnished thought. For though Lucien might have complicated feelings for the village of his birth, he had returned to see his ill father, whom he loved dearly, and who should not have to tolerate his sour mood. The long walk to Atkinson House would be the perfect opportunity to sort out his head.

It was the country retreat of Philip Atkinson, owner of a very lucrative London accounting and investment firm, his wife Edith, who was the granddaughter of an earl, and their three daughters, Alexandra, Phoebe, and Winifred. They were one of the richest and most well-respected families in the area and Lucien's father had been the head coachman for over twenty years. Lucien's late mother had also once been the cook, so Atkinson House was, for better or worse, his childhood home.

He adjusted the strap of his battered satchel, a good-bye present from the staff that had helped raise him, and headed for the stairs. He managed to find some comfort in the knowledge that, while Bunbury might be remarkably unchanged, *he* had changed quite a bit since he left for culinary school in Paris. Lucien was no longer that shy, gawky youth more comfortable with his father's collection of books than actual people. He had experienced life in one of the most exciting cities in the world, with far too many tales to tell—a number of which weren't fit for polite company—along with the veneer of worldly sophistication that came with it.

And yet you are still a complete and utter failure.

Lucien pursed his lips as he raced down the train platform's stairs, as if he could outrun the voice in his head or the regrets that had become his constant companion these last few months. And

Lord knew he had tried. But nothing had silenced that ever-present reminder: not liquor, nor sport, nor the attentions of women. Lucien had taken the biggest gamble of his life and lost. Now he would simply have to live with the consequences.

He reached the bottom of the stairs and turned onto the sleepy village's high street, which amounted to little more than a few shops, and, naturally, a pub. It was the polar opposite of the bustling cosmopolitan life he had been steeped in for years. Paris overwhelmed his senses every single day, effectively silencing those nagging doubts or pestering thoughts. Lucien hadn't realized how very much he had come to depend upon that stimulation. Bunbury felt impossibly flat in comparison.

His shoulders hunched against the sweet country air, as if it were trying to strip him of this hard-won refinement, and he prowled faster toward the main road. Lucien was so fixated on escaping the high street that he failed to notice the elegant young woman exiting the confectioner's shop until he walked directly into her. She let out a shriek as she stumbled back and nearly fell over until Lucien caught her in his arms. As the young lady blinked up at him from under the brim of her wide straw hat, Lucien froze.

"Oh my," she breathed and brushed a stray chocolate-colored curl off her face.

It was none other than Winifred Atkinson, once the object of all his foolish boyhood desires.

Only once? a conniving voice teased as a blush fanned across his cheeks and his heart began to gallop. In truth, she was the paragon against whom he measured all other women. And no one had ever come close. Not once. Not even in Paris.

Lucien cleared his throat and delicately set Freddie, as she was more commonly known, on her feet. Somehow she was even more beautiful than he remembered, with her heart-shaped face, rosy cheeks, and creamy skin—to say nothing of the voluptuous curves encased in her perfectly tailored peach gown.

"I'm so sorry, Miss Atkinson," he sputtered as he stepped back. "Please, forgive my carelessness."

"Entirely my fault, sir," she insisted breezily. "I wasn't watching where I was going at all."

Sir?

Lucien blinked. She stared at him expectantly and the realization suddenly dawned. Freddie didn't recognize him. Though perhaps that shouldn't be such a surprise. After all, it *had* been five years since they had last seen each other. And while she still looked much the same, Lucien had grown a good six inches and gained nearly three stone.

So then tell her who you are.

Lucien opened his mouth but couldn't quite manage the words.

Freddie gave him a warm smile with just a hint of the mischievousness she was known for. *Notoriously* so. "Have we met?"

In truth, Lucien didn't remember meeting Freddie because she had simply always been there. And he forever chasing after her. Little Lucien Taylor, the only son of the coachman and the cook. The skinny boy either with his nose stuck in a book or hiding up a tree. Sometimes both.

"Yes, but it was many years ago," he answered honestly.

She raised a dark brow, intrigued. "And here I thought I knew every handsome man in Surrey."

Her reply pleased him far too much, especially since he very well knew that Freddie was a seasoned flirt. But she had never once directed such attentions toward him. No, she had only ever seen him as a brotherly sort and a convenient playmate. Now, though…now he saw the chance to experience exactly what he had been missing. What he had *ached* for with a painful persistence all those years.

Lucien returned her smile, the one he had finally mastered in Paris, where the ladies praised his boyish charm. "Apparently not, but I suppose I can forgive the oversight."

Freddie's smile turned into a grin. "Well, then we must renew our acquaintance immediately," she insisted, sliding her arm through his. "Though I'm afraid I have to hurry home. Do you live nearby?"

"Yes, just off of Ravenscroft Lane," he replied as they strolled down the high street.

Freddie whipped her head to him. "But that's where I live! Are we neighbors?"

"You could say that."

Oh, but this was *far* too fun.

"Well, then you must be coming to the party tonight."

Lucien nearly stumbled over his feet. He had entirely forgotten. Every September Mr. Atkinson threw his wife an enormous birthday party and invited the entire neighborhood. The whole household was in a tizzy for weeks beforehand, and Lucien always got caught up in the excitement. Then he would watch the festivities from his usual perch on the massive, gnarled oak tree by his bedroom window that conveniently overlooked the back garden, waiting for just a glimpse of Freddie in a beautiful ballgown.

"Are you all right?" she asked as Lucien righted himself.

"Absolutely," he said and flashed her another smile. "You're quite the distraction, Miss Atkinson."

Freddie preened a little and pointed up ahead, where a handsome bay tethered to a shiny black gig waited. "Would you like a ride home?"

He tilted his head. "Please."

Just days before he left for Paris, he had watched Freddie dance with the handsome heir to an earldom during her mother's birthday party, while each guest that passed below him chattered about an impending engagement. Lucien didn't want to believe it—Freddie was barely seventeen at the time and hadn't even had her first season yet—until she strolled right beneath him in the direction of the summer house with the heir in question. After taking a moment to argue with himself, Lucien slid down from his perch and followed a few paces behind, sticking to the shadows. Then he ducked behind a tree and watched as they disappeared into the darkened structure.

No one else saw them, but Lucien knew what would come next. And that he wouldn't be able to bear it. He could still recall the bite of the rough tree bark under his fingertips. How he dug his nails in harder and harder until he drew blood. Until he resolved to get as far away from here as possible.

But as the days turned into weeks, no engagement was announced. It was as if the trip to the summer house had been nothing more than a figment of Lucien's fevered imagination. By then he was across the channel, enrolled in a Parisian culinary school and living with his late mother's family. Too far to do anything other than make a success of himself.

He cast a discreet look at her left hand, but it was bare. No ring. If the beautiful and vivacious Freddie Atkinson was still unattached all these years later, then it was only by her own choice. The idea was undoubtedly intriguing.

He handed her up onto the seat and climbed in beside her. Then Freddie took hold of the reins and off they went.

"Now then," she began as the gig sailed down the tree-lined lane. "Am I ever to learn your name?"

"Certainly," he replied with a smirk. But he intended to put that off for as long as possible.

Freddie tossed her head back and laughed. "Very well. If you won't tell me, then will you at least answer some questions?"

"If you'd like." Now, this would be fun.

"Where were you coming from?"

"London."

She narrowed her eyes. "Beforehand, I mean."

He raised his brows in surprise. "What makes you think that?"

She cast a quick but appraising glance over him. "Your shoes. They were made in Paris. I'd say…three seasons ago."

Lucien didn't know anything about seasons as it applied to shoes. Only that he had purchased them at one of the city's famous outdoor markets. "Impressive."

Freddie shrugged. "The intricacies of fashion occupy a rather large part of my life."

Lucien sensed that there was more behind that little quip, but before he could ask, Freddie continued.

"So, you came here from Paris."

"I never said I did."

"No." Freddie grinned. "But you haven't denied it either. You came here from Paris," she began again. "But it was merely the last leg of a journey that originated in the Far East."

Lucien could only laugh at the yarn she was spinning. "And how exactly did I end up there?"

"You ran away from home as a boy to Portsmouth and stowed away on a ship," she went on, her dark eyes glittering with purpose. "Only you did not realize its destination was Hong Kong. By the time you were discovered, it was too late. Luckily, you were a natural ship hand, so they decided not throw you overboard..."

As Freddie continued to wax on about all the exotic ports he supposedly had visited, Lucien's smile began to fade. Moments before he had felt so worldly and sophisticated, as close to her equal as he had ever been. But now, with just a few sentences, the gap between who he was and who he wished to be had been pushed out of reach once more.

After Freddie decided that he had settled in Bombay for a spell, Lucien cleared his throat. "That is quite the adventure I've had."

"It is, isn't it?" she answered cheerily.

The carriage slowed as she turned onto the long drive that led to the limestone Georgian manor house. It was just visible through the trees and for one aching moment Lucien could imagine they were a couple returning home after a trip away.

"And why have I come back now?"

Freddie quietly considered the question while Lucien held his breath and wondered what dazzling reason she would come up with.

"For the only reason men cross oceans and continents," she softly replied.

"Which is?" he prompted as she fell silent once again. They were nearly at the carriage house now. His little charade couldn't last much longer.

She tugged on the reins and the gig slowly rocked to a stop. Then she turned and met his gaze with a directness that tore through him like an arrow. "Love."

Lucien didn't know how long they sat there, staring at each other. Then he leaned in, just a little bit, until her delicate floral scent filled his nose and her petal pink lips parted.

"That is—"

"*Where* have you been?" A sharp voice laced with disapproval shattered their little reverie. "Mother has been searching high and low for you."

They both slowly blinked, as if waking from a dream. Freddie looked at someone over his shoulder and rolled her eyes.

"The village. I wasn't gone more than an hour."

"Try two," the speaker countered.

"Here," Freddie said as she leaned past him and held out a small pink package. "I got Mother those sweets she likes. Keep it safe for me while I go find her."

Lucien turned around to face the speaker and suddenly he was ten years old again, with the imperious Alexandra Atkinson staring at him with her usual look of disapproval. He had spent most of his childhood absolutely terrified of her and, like most of the staff, tried to avoid her whenever possible.

Her dark brown eyes narrowed slightly. "Hello, Lucien," she said in the same brusque tone she used with everyone. "How was your journey?"

Freddie made some sort of choking sound beside him, but Lucien continued to hold Alex's cool gaze as he smoothly took the package and jumped down from the gig. Though the sisters shared the same dark brown curls and matching eyes, Alex was tall and slim compared to Freddie's curves. She also wore a sober navy suit and matching skirt, like something a severe headmistress would wear, and which was a stark contrast to her sister's frothy peach confection.

Alex had always felt larger than life and so very grown-up, even though she was only about five years his senior. Now Lucien was surprised to find that she was, in fact, a bit shorter than him, though still tall for a woman. It was her bearing, he decided. The way she stalked around the house like the captain of a ship, all while never cracking a smile.

"It was fine," he replied, matching her disinterested tone.

She was just so very *different* from the easygoing Freddie and their other sister, Phoebe, with her approachable eccentricity. It bothered him now for a reason he couldn't quite identify.

As Lucien handed the confectionary box to her, their fingers brushed ever so briefly and the sensation flickered through him. He had to fight against the sudden urge to pull his hand back, as if merely touching Alex was verboten. She was only a woman, he needlessly reminded himself. Not a queen.

Nor a dictator.

While they each continued to silently size the other up, Freddie found her voice.

"You...you can't mean little Lucien Taylor?"

Lucien couldn't help but wince at the description and then was annoyed because Alex noticed. Before her eyes could soften with pity, he quickly turned back to Freddie with an apologetic smile. "I'm afraid so," he said, offering his hand.

She stared at him in disbelief. "My goodness."

As he helped Freddie down, he enjoyed the feel of her warm, small hand in his, while also vaguely noting the absence of the spark he had felt moments before. Perhaps Alex was a witch.

It would certainly explain a few things.

"Thank you," Freddie breathed, still staring at him in wonder.

Lucien basked in her appreciative gaze for another moment as he slowly released her hand. "My pleasure."

Then she hesitated. "And I shall see you tonight, then?"

Lucien's breath hitched. She still wanted him there. Even though he was only little Lucien Taylor. The son of the help. "I wouldn't miss it."

"I believe your father is waiting for you in his quarters," Alex cut in with barely veiled impatience. "Shall I show you the way?"

Lucien's jaw tightened as he released Freddie's hand and shot Alex a glance. She made no attempt to hide her disapproval, which bothered him more than he wanted to admit.

"No need, Miss Atkinson," he replied crisply. "I could never forget my place here."

Lucien didn't wait for her reply as he adjusted his satchel and headed toward the carriage house. Back to where he belonged.

Two

Alex's gaze lingered on Lucien Taylor's figure until he disappeared round the bend toward the carriage house. He had grown considerably since she last saw him, with the kind of broad shoulders and lean form that naturally drew the eye, while his golden-brown hair was just a little too long to be respectable—though given that he had been living among the Bohemians in Paris, that was likely the point. One which was further emphasized by the small gold hoop in his right earlobe. But while his face still retained a hint of chubby-cheeked boyishness, it was tempered by the edge of world-weariness in his hazel eyes. The kind that spoke of experiences one could not find in Bunbury.

"I still don't believe it's him," Freddie marveled as she stared after him. "*Lucien.*"

Alex frowned at the blatant interest in her sister's eyes. This would not do. "I don't see what's so hard to believe."

Freddie turned to her, incredulous. "Are you joking?"

"He's certainly taller now. And bigger," Alex acknowledged. "But I wouldn't go as far to say he is *unrecognizable.* You just never really noticed him before."

Freddie looked offended. "I most certainly did! We were playmates."

"But you never saw him as anything more than that."

And certainly not anyone worth ogling, though Alex kept that thought to herself.

At that moment the memory of young Lucien angrily wiping away stubborn tears surfaced. It had been the night of her mother's birthday party and Alex had come across him en route to the summer house where she was searching for Freddie to stop her from doing something incredibly stupid and inconveniently irreversible. Meanwhile, the shy, sweet boy had been crushed by the actions of her careless and completely oblivious sister.

Lucien's hopeless infatuation had long been obvious even to Alex, who usually didn't concern herself with matters of the heart. For years she had never understood how he could feel so much for a girl who offered him so little in return. Until Alex had been foolish enough to offer her own affections to an unworthy suitor. Until she, too, had been hoodwinked by her own heart.

You need to go somewhere far, far away from here, she had told him that night. *Somewhere you can be whomever you want.*

And, by God, he had done just that.

Only last fall she had learned through servant gossip and her own discreet inquiries that his traveling supper club had been the toast of Paris with a waiting list filled with everyone from artists to aristocrats—until it had fallen quickly, and completely, apart. Still, Alex knew very well just how difficult it was to accomplish what he had. Lucien had managed to create and execute a novel business in the avant-garde capital of the world. Privately, she was convinced it was only a matter of time before he came up with something even better.

Now Lucien had returned to lick his wounds and visit with his ill father. It should be nothing more than a short detour on a promising career path. But if the scene she had interrupted earlier was any indication, he was in great danger of veering off the path entirely and sinking into a Freddie-shaped quagmire.

Meanwhile, *actual* Freddie looked primed to argue before she promptly shut her mouth and turned back toward the direction of the carriage house. The corner of her mouth curved. "Well, then, I suppose I'm seeing him now."

"Freddie," Alex warned. "You know very well that the Ericsons will be in attendance tonight."

They were a wealthy American family interested in investment opportunities in England, and Alex had made it her personal mission to ensure they partnered with Atkinson Enterprises. That would help the company make greater inroads in New York society and be a huge coup for her professionally. That Hank Ericson Jr., the eldest son and heir apparent, had been pursuing Freddie since the spring also weighed heavily in their favor, but the man was beginning to grow impatient with her laissez-faire approach to courtship. It seemed as though everyone except Freddie was waiting on their engagement. But in the years since her debut, she had left a trail of broken hearts that stretched from Bunbury to the Continent. And since she had no interest in joining the family business, that left the business of getting married. Freddie would not charm her way out of this one. At least, not without a more compelling reason than *boredom.*

"Not to worry, dear sister," she said sweetly, albeit with a thick layer of sarcasm. "I know very well that nothing is more important to you than maintaining your business relationships, and I won't do anything that could possibly jeopardize them."

"That's not what I—"

But the rest of Alex's protest was lost as Freddie marched toward the house. She sighed and stared at the little box of sweets still clutched in her hand. Leave it to Freddie to wait until the day of the party to buy Mother a gift. She ran a finger along the edge of the familiar pink box. When they were children and particularly restless Mother would take them on long walks into the village, always with a stop at the sweet shop, where she would buy a bag of lemon drops for herself. Alex lifted the box and inhaled the fragrant notes of citrus. A smile touched her lips as her heart warmed with old memories.

Perhaps…perhaps it wasn't such a bad present after all. The Sèvres porcelain vase Alex had spent months tracking down suddenly seemed gauche in comparison. She never got gifts right. It seemed like the more effort she put in, the more she failed.

Because you lack all sentimentality.

It was a barb her sisters frequently lobbed at her. And they weren't wrong. But there were other areas where she excelled *because* she wasn't swayed by menial emotions. Like business, for example. Freddie could act the martyr as much as she wanted, but it was Alex's commitment to her *business relationships* that had allowed her youngest sister to spend the last five years swanning around London without a care. Freddie would do well to remember that. Alex shoved the box into her skirt pocket and headed inside. As always, there was work to be done.

❧

Lucien did his best to outrun Alexandra Atkinson's disapproval, but he could feel her sharp-eyed glare at his back until he turned the corner. He let out a breath as the carriage house came into view.

It was the only place on the property where he could never be dismissed. The one place where he was always welcome.

His parents had met while working in service for the family, his father the coachman and his mother an apprentice to the Parisian chef the Atkinsons had poached from a London hotel. Lucien's mother, Celeste Laurent, had worked hard to earn her position and until she became a head chef, she had no interest in the distraction of a romance with *anyone*—not even the very persistent Englishman who became a coachman in large part because it allowed him time to read. It was only once the Parisian chef returned to France and Celeste took his place that she allowed true love to prevail. They settled in the cozy flat above the carriage house and filled it with secondhand books and handwritten recipes. Lucien came along a few years later, an unexpected but happy surprise for the older couple, who assumed they had missed the chance to be parents, and he was doted on accordingly.

Lucien climbed the stairs that led to the flat two at a time, suddenly eager for the safe confines of home, and let himself in. There he was greeted by the comforting scent of dusty paper and tea leaves.

He inhaled greedily and scanned the front room. "Father?"

"I'm in here, Lucien!"

His father's quavering voice carried from the back of the flat. Lucien frowned in concern as he made his way toward the bedroom. It was nearly the afternoon. His father would *never* be abed at this time of day unless something was very wrong.

You may find him much changed.

He recalled the dire warning in a letter from Mrs. Holloway, the housekeeper. The one that had compelled him to spend his last francs on a ticket home instead of a final, desperate attempt to save his business. Lucien had only seen his father once since he'd left for Paris during a brief visit to London after he finished culinary school. Lucien was interviewing at several hotels in Mayfair and managed to fit in lunch with his father in a pub not far from the Atkinsons' London residence. Over a simple shepherd's pie and two pints of bitter, Lucien confessed his dread about working in a professional kitchen before tentatively mentioning the idea for the supper club. His father's response had been short and salient:

Now is the time for big leaps, my boy. Before life gives you reasons to look first.

It was just the push he needed.

As Lucien entered the room, his father reclined in an over-stuffed armchair with a thick book on his lap. He took off his reading glasses and smiled. "There he is! Come here, my boy. Let's have a good look at you."

Though he was dressed for the day, his father wore slippers and an old dressing gown over his shirt and trousers. As Lucien drew closer, he noticed the hollows beneath his father's cheeks. He had battled a nasty bout of pneumonia over the winter and Lucien saw that he was still alarmingly gaunt months later.

In his letters, his father had minimized his illness, of course, so it wasn't until the housekeeper wrote to Lucien directly that he learned just how close to death his father had been. And how weak he still was. Even now, he wasn't able to resume his full duties. The Atkinsons had been very accommodating of his illness, but their goodwill wouldn't last forever. If his father didn't fully recover, he would have to be replaced.

Lucien was filled with a sudden, piercing regret. His father had spent a considerable part of his own savings helping him go to culinary school. He should have taken the London hotel job and paid his father back first. Then he could have tilted at windmills all he wished without imperiling anyone but himself.

"Please, don't get up," Lucien said as he approached.

"Nonsense," his father groused and slowly came to his feet. "I'm hardly the invalid Mrs. Holloway made me out to be." Then he wrapped Lucien in a tight embrace, as if to emphasize the point.

"Glad to hear it," Lucien replied, while noting the small brown medicine bottle on the nightstand by the bed. Yet another reminder that sickness still lingered here.

His father pulled back and pressed a hand to Lucien's cheek. "I'd forgotten how much you look like her," he murmured in surprise. "You didn't used to. But as you've grown older…"

There was no need to finish the thought. Lucien glanced away from the sheen in his father's eyes and cleared his throat. The likeness to his mother had been a frequent topic of conversation among his French relatives. And he had long grown tired of it.

"The aunts all send their regards," Lucien said with a tight smile.

His father let out a sharp laugh and moved to sit back down in his chair. "Oh, I'm sure." This time he allowed Lucien to help him. "They all blame *me* for why she never returned home."

Lucien pressed his lips together. It was true. "I did tell them she was very happy here."

"Good." Then he gave Lucien a searching look. "But they *were* nice to you, weren't they?"

"Yes. Very." That was also true.

His father relaxed and let out a sigh. "Good," he repeated. "And the language wasn't too much trouble?"

"It was an adjustment at first, but I got on well enough."

"Thank the Lord your mother was so insistent on you learning French."

En Français, mon petit chou.

Lucien smiled at the memory of this near constant refrain. She had been insistent almost to the point of obsession at times, speaking to him nearly exclusively in French when they were together, while his hapless father, who could only retain a handful of words, mostly food-related, looked on in bemusement. "I am very grateful."

Lucien decided not to mention how mercilessly his Gallic cousins had teased him about his pronounced English accent when he first arrived. Even five years later, he still hadn't managed to convince anyone that he was a native speaker.

"Here, I brought you something." Lucien pulled out a book wrapped in paper from his satchel. Aside from a few items of clothing, it was the only thing he had brought with him from Paris. And he had stubbornly held on to it while he sold off everything else.

"*The Count of Monte Cristo*!"

"It's a first edition," Lucien said proudly.

His father looked appropriately shocked and that alone made all those sacrifices worth it. "My goodness. How on earth did you afford it?"

Lucien shrugged. "I got a good price."

In truth he had spotted the book in a shop window and spent an irresponsibly large sum. But that was back when his little business was thriving. When the whole city seemed to fall at his feet and there was no limit to his success. How quickly things changed.

His father rightly gave him a skeptical look but didn't press the issue and began to flip through the pages with reverence. "How you loved this book as a boy. We must have read it half a dozen times over the years."

Indeed, the story of Edmond Dantès and his lifelong devotion to Mercedes had sparked something inside Lucien, and laid out a path for him to follow. That despite seemingly insurmountable obstacles, in the end true love could prevail.

"Come," his father said, rising once more. "Your room is all ready for you."

Lucien dutifully followed him down the short hall to his old bedroom, which was really more of a glorified closet and barely big enough to fit the narrow bed. Still, his chest fluttered as he entered the tiny space, as if the last five years hadn't happened and he was that lonely, heartsick boy once again.

His father looked him over from top to toe before turning to the bed with a wince.

"You might not fit in there anymore."

"I'll be fine," Lucien insisted.

"We can switch. I'll sleep in here and you—"

"Father, *no*. This is fine. More than fine," Lucien added. "Besides, it's only for a few nights." After which he intended to go to London. For as much as he wished to linger by his father's side, Lucien needed money and he would not find a profitable future here in Bunbury.

His father relented with a short nod. "You have a place to stay in the city?"

"My friend Alain from culinary school is a concierge at the Linden. He offered the use of his sofa until I get on my feet."

Like Lucien, Alain found professional kitchens too chaotic. But his Gallic charm served him quite well in the hospitality service.

Alain had generously offered to use his connections to find Lucien something and Lucien intended to take him up on it. Even if it meant washing dishes, Lucien was no longer in a position to turn down work.

His father was quiet for a moment as he mulled this over. "I'm sorry there isn't more here for you," he said abruptly. "And that I couldn't help you more when you needed it."

Lucien let out a sigh. They had been over this, both before he left and in many, *many* letters afterward.

"You paid for my school," Lucien said. "That was more than enough." His father began to reply but Lucien continued. "And I wouldn't have accepted a penny more from you anyway."

"A parent should be able to help his only son—only *child*," he insisted. "I wasted so many years piddling about," his father continued mournfully. "Just looking after myself. Never thinking about the future. I could have worked harder. Earned more."

Lucien pressed a hand to his father's shoulder and held back his shock at how narrow it felt. "But then you wouldn't have met Maman and I wouldn't even *be* here," he pointed out.

His father rubbed a hand down his haggard face. "Let me have this regret, Lucien. Please. Besides, what kind of parent would I be if I didn't feel some guilt?"

Lucien smiled at the twinkle in his eye. "A fair point, I suppose. Just don't ruminate on it too much. I admire the life you created for yourself. You found a way to be paid to read."

His father let out a weary laugh. "Yes, well. It seemed like a good idea at the time."

"It's *still* a good idea."

Lucien set his satchel on the narrow bed and began unpacking his few possessions. He shook out his only evening jacket and frowned. "This will need a good pressing."

"Why?" His father asked absently. "You have somewhere to be?"

"Yes. The party tonight," Lucien replied, deliberately keeping his eyes on the piece of clothing. "Miss Winifred invited me."

He didn't need to see the disapproval on his father's face.

"Lucien," he cautioned. "I thought you were done with all that."

"She's a friend. Miss Alexandra, too," Lucien added, though that wouldn't stand up under questioning. He could already picture her frown of disapproval at the mere idea.

"Miss Winifred is engaged to an *American*," his father said. "And I'm sure he'll be there tonight."

Lucien stiffened, then recalled her bare ring finger. She certainly hadn't behaved like an engaged woman. "Then I will offer my congratulations," he said casually.

"Well, they haven't announced anything yet," his father amended. "But I'm told it's as good as done."

Lucien turned around. "I understand perfectly. And not to worry. I have no intention of coming between the happy couple."

"It's not *them* I'm worried about."

Lucien's shoulders tightened and he met his father's sympathetic gaze head on. "The iron is in the cupboard, then? I'll need to start now if I'm to have any chance of smoothing out these wrinkles by tonight."

"Yes." His father relented with a nod. "The same place it always was."

"Thank you." Lucien then left the room before anything more could be said. He would not be dissuaded from this. Not by anyone.

Three

My goodness, the staff have outdone themselves this year," Phoebe marveled as she took in the ballroom, which was covered in pink flowers, gauzy matching bunting, and glimmering tea lights.

"It looks like the den of some particularly louche fairy king," Alex remarked.

Phoebe laughed. "It does, rather. Mother must be delighted."

As if to punctuate the point, the sound of their mother's laugh carried across the space and the sisters exchanged a knowing look. At least the guest of honor was enjoying herself.

"I'm going to take a turn," Alex said. It was time to get back to work.

"Don't forget to have a little fun," Phoebe called to her retreating back. "It *is* a party, after all."

She shrugged off the comment and began patrolling the perimeter of the dance floor, taking note of who was here—as well as who wasn't. Though officially this might be her mother's birthday party, it was also a useful measure of Atkinson Enterprise's influence and the most interesting part of the evening by far.

Alex had begun unofficially working for her father while still in the schoolroom after she had exceeded the limits of her governess's admittedly limited knowledge. Back then, Atkinson Enterprises was still known as Atkinson and Son, the accounting and invest-ment firm her grandfather had started. Alex loved spending long afternoons in her father's office, looking over the books searching for errors or finding new ways to increase profit margins. There it was calm and quiet. No constant distractions from her demanding sisters or interruptions from her well-meaning but overattentive mother. Where she didn't have to explain what she was thinking about (*Books, usually*) or why she was frowning (*Really? She hadn't noticed*). Where she could just…be. But best of all was her father's unmitigated joy whenever she presented him with one of her findings.

My brilliant girl.

Her father dutifully opened a savings account in her name and deposited a sum every time she made him money, but it was his approval that she valued the most. It wasn't until she went to Oxford, first to Lady Margaret Hall and then to the more broad-minded Somerville College, to study mathematics and economics, that Alex realized there was good money to be made in investing in new businesses in exchange for a share of any future profits. She wrote up a proposal and presented it to her father the day after she graduated. And the day after that, she began working at the newly christened Atkinson Enterprises.

Since then, she and her father had been partners of sorts. Alex had her own office, met with employees, and looked over every single business proposal the company was considering investing in. She also sought out potential businesses on her own. And though she rarely met with clients herself, her father took her advice seriously. Alex knew that, to much of society, she was nothing but an odd little spinster whose father had given her the job out of pity. But they both knew the truth, and for a long while that was enough for

Alex. Until their trip to New York a few months before had made it very clear that Alex's unmarried status was hindering her future at the very company she had helped build. Now she was determined to do whatever was necessary to prove that she was perfectly capable of running the company to the board of Atkinson Enterprises.

Even something as ghastly as *socializing.*

Alex nodded at an older man with a ridiculously large mustache. He also happened to be the owner of one of England's largest shipping companies. "Mr. DeWitt, lovely to see you here. Enjoy your evening."

The man stared back at her in shock. "Oh, yes," he said after a moment. "You as well, Miss Atkinson."

And to think, *she* was supposed to be the odd one.

Alex continued on, noting the presence of three more titans of industry, a handful of influential MPs, a member of cabinet, a viscount, and even a minor German prince. England's youngest duke was also in attendance, but it was only Will Margrave and he didn't really count.

She found her parents happily enmeshed in their little circle of friends and leaned toward her father's shoulder. "I spotted Lord Hughes and the home secretary, as well as Mr. DeWitt."

"Excellent." He took a sip of champagne. "This might be our best turnout yet."

"I know what you two are whispering about," her mother cut in. "I told you: no *work* tonight."

Alex and her father exchanged sheepish looks. "Sorry, Mother."

"Yes, my love."

Her mother then placed a hand on Alex's arm. "Do try to enjoy yourself, darling."

"I *am* enjoying myself."

Her mother narrowed her eyes. "With something besides plotting your next deal. I want to see you dance."

Alex balked. "Absolutely not." She hadn't danced since Phoebe's coming-out ball and still hadn't recovered from the experience.

Before her mother could harangue her any further, she was saved by Lady Westmoor and her inability to follow any conversation she hadn't started. "And what did your lovely girls get you for your birthday?"

"Now's your chance," her father whispered and Alex began to slowly back away.

"Alex found me the most beautiful vase. Oh! And dear Freddie!" Her mother laughed as she clasped her hands to her chest in delight. "She gave me a box of…"

Alex walked faster until she was out of earshot. She didn't need to hear about how charming and thoughtful Freddie's little gift was. Unfortunately, that put her right in the path of her sisters. Their backs were to her and their heads bent together conspiratorially. Alex couldn't ignore the childhood instinct to eavesdrop on their conversation.

Phoebe gasped. "And you just bumped into each other on the street?"

"I had no idea who he was though until we returned home and Alex greeted him. Cheeky man." Freddie let out a dreamy sigh. "It's like something out of a novel."

"But where on earth has he been all this time?"

"Paris." The sisters turned to Alex at her abrupt answer. "He went to culinary school there," she added.

Freddie narrowed her eyes. "How do you know that?"

"Because I take an interest in other people's lives."

Phoebe gave her a pleading look. "Alex…"

Since childhood she had played the part of peacemaker between her and Freddie with limited success.

"No, she's right," Freddie said. "I'm afraid I didn't give much thought to Lucien after he left." Then she paused to make sure Alex was looking directly at her. "Thankfully, we've both grown since then. *Considerably*." Without another word, she sauntered straight toward Lucien, who had just entered the ballroom.

As he caught sight of Freddie, Lucien broke into a dazzling smile and Alex felt a strange tug low in her belly. He was attractive, she could admit. And perhaps under different circumstances, Alex might even welcome a union between him and Freddie but there was too much at stake.

Alex crossed her arms. "Now she's trying to irritate me. The Ericsons will be here any moment."

Phoebe tilted her head. "You don't think it's possible she's genuinely interested in him?"

"Who's interested in who?" Will Margrave, more formally known as the Duke of Ellis and Phoebe's newly minted fiancé, asked as he joined them.

"Freddie and that young man," Phoebe replied as she gestured across the room. "You'll never guess who that is."

Will squinted in consideration. "I've no idea." Before he had unexpectedly inherited a dukedom, he was their neighbor, and Alex's closest friend. Last month she had even asked him to pretend to be her fiancé before it became very clear his heart belonged to Phoebe. Alex was genuinely thrilled for them, but that still left her in need of a temporary faux beau to help silence her father's nagging about improving her position with the board.

"It's *little Lucien Taylor*," Phoebe said gleefully.

"Is it now?" Will squinted a little harder. "Not so little anymore, is he?"

"No, he's just returned from Paris and Alex is *convinced* that Freddie is only paying him attention to annoy her," Phoebe continued. "But I say she's simply interested in renewing their acquaintance."

"Nothing with her is ever that simple, Phoebe," Alex replied. "That's the trouble. And then I'm left to clean up whatever mess she's caused."

Will hummed, his gaze still on Lucien and Phoebe. "Ericson won't like it, that's for sure."

Phoebe bit her lip in consideration. "You still think of her as our coddled younger sister," she began gently. "But you underestimate her, Alex. She's a grown woman now."

Alex forced her shoulders to remain in place. "I know that. But she could try harder to *act* like one."

As if to punctuate her point, Freddie let out a loud laugh that carried across the dance floor and caused several heads to turn.

Phoebe winced. "Perhaps," she acknowledged. "I just don't think your business concerns should dictate her personal happiness."

Alex arched a brow. "The only one getting in the way of her own happiness is Freddie herself."

As the orchestra struck up a waltz, Lucien extended a hand to Freddie, which she readily accepted. His broad shoulders flexed as he swept her into her arms. Every eye in the room seemed captivated by the handsome pair as they moved across the gleaming floor.

"Goodness," Phoebe breathed. "I didn't know he could dance like that."

"Must have picked it up in France," Will quipped and held out his hand. "Shall we join them, my dear?"

Just as Phoebe flashed him a treacly smile, Alex caught sight of the Ericsons entering the room. She let out a curse under her breath as Hank Jr.'s gaze immediately fixed on Freddie and he scowled.

"Excuse me," she said. "It appears I already have a mess to clean up."

Alex left the lovebirds behind and drew up alongside her parents, who had just greeted their new guests. But Mrs. Ericson wasted no time.

"Who is Winifred dancing with?" she asked with barely veiled suspicion.

"Ah…" Father shot her a panicked look. He probably couldn't even *tell* that it was Lucien.

"Oh, that's the coachman's son," Alex said with a dismissive wave. "He recently returned from Paris. We all grew up together."

"*That* is little Lucien Taylor?" her mother unhelpfully put in. Alex shot her a quelling look, which she quickly noted. "Freddie is like a sister to him," she added.

But Hank Sr. did not look convinced. "I have a sister," he said. "And we don't dance like that."

"No? It's quite normal here," Alex replied in a strangled tone. She didn't even know what she was saying anymore, only that she had to fix this. *Now.*

Mercifully, the waltz ended and they were forced to break apart. But as Lucien escorted Freddie toward the refreshment table, they whispered to each other just a little too intimately for a pair of old friends.

Hank Jr. cleared his throat. "Perhaps we should leave."

"Please, do stay—" her father began.

"You have it wrong, sir," Alex interrupted. "I assure you."

Hank Jr. arched a brow. "Oh? And how *exactly* am I wrong,

Miss Atkinson? Because from here it appears your sister has a new suitor. And I don't appreciate being made to look like a fool."

Alex's throat suddenly went bone dry as she frantically seized on an explanation. It was outrageous. Unbelievable, even. But it just might work…

"Mr. Taylor isn't courting Freddie," she said, managing to regain some degree of control. "Because he's courting me."

The silence that followed was, in a word, deafening. Alex held his gaze, almost challenging Hank Jr. to contradict her. But he was still a gentleman and she a lady. He wouldn't dare.

"I see," he finally said, though he still looked far more suspicious than convinced. "Forgive me."

"No apology necessary," Alex gritted out.

Then she felt her father's hand on her elbow. "If you'll excuse us for a moment."

"And I'll go fetch Freddie," her mother trilled.

The ballroom passed by in a blur as Alex was guided into her father's study. But as she entered the room, the full weight of what she had said hit her.

Oh God.

She pressed her hands to her face as an embarrassed flush heated her cheeks. Behind her, she heard her father shut the door. Alex whirled around.

"I'm sorry. I don't know what came over me. I just—"

But she stopped short. Father was looking at her rather strangely.

"Is it true?"

Alex couldn't help frowning at the disbelief in his voice. "No," she huffed. "Of course not," she couldn't help adding. "But I didn't know what else to say to convince Hank Jr."

Father nodded slowly, as if he were mulling over something. "I think he believed you, though. Or he could, with a little more encouragement."

"What does that matter? It *isn't* true," she said, hating that she sounded just a touch pitiful.

As he stepped toward her the light from the wall sconce caught the gleam in his eye. "But what if it was?"

Alex's mouth opened and closed a few times. She felt like a lost goldfish. "I'm not sure what you mean," she said carefully, though that was a lie. Sometimes it felt as if she had a direct line to her father's mind, which made their working relationship feel so effortless.

And this was no exception.

"It is an *unusual* situation to be sure, given his parentage," her father began. "But Lucien has shown his business acumen. We can spin that into something. And besides, stranger things have happened in this family, have they not?" He punctuated this with a little laugh then turned serious once more. "Regardless, we can't let the Ericsons walk away now. Otherwise these last few months will have been a complete waste of time. And you need this deal to help win over the board, Alex."

Never mind the genuine friendship that had blossomed between Father and Hank Sr. Men like that put business before nearly everything else.

"I *know* that," Alex huffed as she crossed her arms.

"Then find out what that boy needs to feign a courtship with you and give it to him. Pay him whatever he wants. No price is too high," he added offhandedly.

Alex managed to lift her chin while the hot bite of humiliation sank into her neck. "Am I truly so displeasing that you would need to offer him carte blanche merely for the pretense of a courtship with me?"

Though this was very nearly the scenario she had been searching for herself, it still stung to have it laid out so plainly by someone else.

Her father's gaze softened. "My dear. That isn't what I meant at all. Money just makes things…cleaner." Alex wasn't sure she agreed with that. "Try to think of it as a business arrangement," he continued. "And I've told you before that you'll have a much easier time with the board if you have a partner. Not because you aren't capable," he said over her objection. "But because our clients won't trust a lone woman with their money."

Alex gritted her jaw. They had gone over this for months now. Her father was getting older and wanted to hand off Atkinson Enterprises to her, but the board was skittish about having a woman in charge—especially an unmarried one.

"And yet they seem to have no problem spending the dividends I've earned them," she grumbled.

Father took her hand in his. "I want you to succeed in this world, Alexandra. I *know* you can. Don't let your pride get in the way. Do whatever it takes."

That was easy for him to say when he didn't have to hide his abilities to protect the fragile egos of men. But trying to explain that to him hadn't worked before, so Alex simply nodded.

"Fine. I'll speak with him."

"That's my brilliant girl," her father said proudly. "And Lucien's a smart lad. I'm sure he'll accept whatever you offer."

"Yes," Alex said with a distracted nod. For she had seen the look on Lucien's face as he danced with Freddie. And asking him to give up what he wanted most would not come easily—nor cheaply.

Four

Alex returned to the ballroom and scanned the crowd for Lucien. She needed to get this business settled as quickly as possible. But she hadn't managed more than a few steps before Phoebe glided over with a too-wide smile and took her arm.

"Come take some air with me and Will."

"I can't right now. Have you seen Freddie? I need to speak to her."

"Well, *I* need to speak to *you*."

Alex raised an eyebrow at her sister's schoolteacher tone. But before she could tease her for it, she noticed that people kept looking over at them and whispering. There seemed to be a hum in the air. Something had happened.

"Just act normally," Phoebe murmured before she could ask.

Well, that never worked for Alex as people seemed to find her version of normal incredibly off-putting. Instead, she tried to follow Phoebe's lead and forced a smile, nodding at various guests, who only stared back in wonder.

When they finally reached the back terrace that led out to the garden, Phoebe tugged her over to a secluded corner where Will was waiting for them. As usual, the garden had been decorated to match the ballroom.

"Tell me what is going on," Phoebe demanded without preamble. "Is it true about Lucien? How on earth did that happen? And *when?*" Her sister grew more agitated with each question.

Alex's pulse raced. Her careless remark had already begun to spread. She needed to put her plan in action before it reached Lucien's ears.

"The way it usually does," she said flatly. "We saw each other this afternoon and that was that."

Will let out a kind of choking sound, while Phoebe looked incredulous. "*That* was *that?* Come now, Alex. There has to be a fair bit more to it."

She let out an impatient huff. "Why? Isn't that how it was with the two of you? You saw each other and just *knew.*"

Phoebe and Will exchanged a sheepish look.

"In a way, perhaps," she admitted. "But it certainly took longer than a few *hours* for us to be together."

"Only because we were both being hopelessly stubborn," Will said, giving Phoebe a fond smile. She grinned back at him and Alex rolled her eyes.

She had no desire to stand here while they mooned over each other. "Well, I'm simply more efficient. My time is valuable and I can't spend months denying my very obvious feelings for no good reason."

Phoebe pointedly ignored the dig. "But you barely *know* each other," she protested. "Freddie was at least playmates with him once. But you—"

"I know enough," Alex insisted. This was met with skeptical looks and Alex's chest began to tighten. If she couldn't convince Phoebe and Will, there was no hope of convincing the Ericsons.

"And we…I…we've been corresponding," she spat out. "Though we hadn't settled things until today." There. That sounded like a somewhat more reasonable explanation. Even still, her mouth twitched. She was a terrible liar but managed to hold Phoebe's incisive gaze.

"Oh." Her sister's eyes softened with understanding. "So earlier, when you were so cross with Freddie for taking an interest in him, it was because you were…"

Alex squeezed her eyes shut. She knew what Phoebe was implying.

Jealous.

A base, childish emotion she had rarely indulged in even when she *was* a child, as it served no real purpose and indicated an appalling lack of self-control. And yet, in this scenario it aligned perfectly with her current needs. So Alex swallowed her pride and opened her eyes.

"Yes," she finished. "I was…jealous." The word felt sour on her tongue and her lip curled in distaste, but this only added an air of authenticity to her performance. "We weren't yet ready to discuss our relationship, as it is still very new, but Freddie's behavior has forced our hand."

Phoebe and Will exchanged another look. She was certain they had bought it.

"Now then," Alex said primly. "If you'll excuse me, I need to find Lucien."

"Of course." Phoebe nodded, now full of sympathy and understanding. "But perhaps you should talk to Freddie first before she hears it from someone else."

If she hasn't already.

Alex could picture her younger sister's riotous laughter over the news, which could ruin everything.

"I saw her slink upstairs not long after her waltz with Lucien ended," Will said. "Though he is nowhere to be found."

Alex's mouth twisted as she analyzed the situation. She would bet the entire company that Freddie was preparing to rendezvous with Lucien in the summer house and she had to put a stop to *that* as soon as possible.

"Thank you," she replied and hurried back into the ballroom without waiting for Will's response. They would forgive her rudeness, as usual.

Alex then picked her way through the crowd as quickly as she could manage without bothering to acknowledge anyone else. There wasn't a moment to waste on pithy small talk or empty *hello*s. Once she had reached the other side, Alex avoided the main staircase and the assorted people milling about the entry hall and headed up the back stairs instead. Then she practically bolted down the hallway and had just put her hand on the knob to Freddie's bedroom when her sister opened the door and immediately looked disappointed.

"Oh. It's you. What do you want?"

"I need to speak with you."

But as Alex moved to enter the room, Freddie blocked her. "I don't have time—"

"*Now*, Freddie," she demanded. "Lucien can wait."

They eyed each other for a moment until Freddie let out a resigned sigh and stepped aside.

"Very well. Do come in," she said with an exaggerated wave of her arm.

Alex generally avoided her sister's bedroom, as it was decorated in a shade of pink that made her eyes ache. Freddie also seemed to have acquired every piece of lace in England.

"Go on. Out with it," Freddie said from behind her as she closed the door. "I can practically *hear* your disapproval."

Alex gingerly sat down on a shapeless lump swathed in frothy fabric. She wasn't quite sure if it was meant to be a chair or a footstool.

"You've managed to find even more things to cover in lace. Somehow."

Freddie rolled her eyes. "I wasn't referring to my room, which everyone else loves."

Alex shot her a dubious look. She could already feel the headache coming on. Time to get to it. "Hank Jr. was not amused by your little display downstairs with Lucien."

Freddie lifted a shoulder. "We were only dancing. I'm allowed to *dance* with other men."

"What about meeting them in the summer house?" Alex challenged.

Freddie didn't even try to deny it. She simply crossed her arms and sat down hard on the lace-trimmed bed. "We aren't even engaged yet," she protested. "And he certainly hasn't stopped gallivanting around London. It isn't my fault he gets jealous so easily."

Alex paused. She hadn't known that about Hank Jr.—not that it was terribly surprising. Men seemed to have expectations for women that they would never apply to their own behavior.

"It isn't," she agreed. "But even still, no one likes being embarrassed. And you know how sensitive men can be."

"I suppose," Freddie grumbled.

"Besides, you can't really be considering throwing him over

because of one waltz with *Lucien Taylor?*" Alex infused the name with a mixture of horror and disbelief. It wasn't very kind, but she had to get through to Freddie quickly.

"It's not only because of him," she said. "I...I have my doubts about Hank Jr."

Alex narrowed her eyes. "What kind of doubts?"

But her sister merely shrugged. "You wouldn't understand."

Though Alex could certainly challenge her on that point, this wasn't the time to pick apart her past. And while she could sympathize with Freddie to an extent, it would not be at Lucien's expense. He would fall back in love with her while she moved on to whatever or whoever caught her eye next.

"You can have as many doubts as you like," Alex began. "But don't drag Lucien into it just because you're having a wobble. He deserves better than to be someone's distraction."

Freddie raised her eyebrows. Alex had spoken with more feeling than usual. "I'm sorry. I didn't mean—"

"No, you're right," Freddie said on a sigh. "He is more than that."

Alex's shoulders sagged in relief. "Good."

"Which is why I think I'm falling in love with him."

"*What?*" Alex shot to her feet.

"Well, maybe not *in love*," she hastily amended. "But I do *like* him. Very much—"

"Freddie," Alex warned, but her sister wasn't listening.

"—he's so handsome. And interesting. Did you know he had his own supper club in Paris?"

"Yes."

Freddie looked surprised. "Oh. Well, it's quite a brilliant idea, isn't it?"

"It is," Alex nodded. "But you aren't in love with him, Freddie. You—you just aren't."

"You don't know what I *feel*," Freddie protested and dramatically flopped back onto the bed.

"Perhaps…perhaps you should take a nap," Alex said as she moved toward the door.

Freddie scoffed. "As if I could sleep after that waltz!" Then she sat up on her elbows and tilted her head. "Where are you going?"

Before her sister could catch on, Alex scurried out of the room and closed the door behind her. Then she pulled out the skeleton key she always wore around her neck and locked the door. Freddie let out a muffled cry and began to pound on the door.

"I'm sorry!" Alex called out. "Get some rest!" she added, though there was no chance of that happening.

Freddie shouted something in response. It was too muffled for Alex to understand, but she guessed it wasn't particularly flattering. "You'll thank me later!"

Then Alex picked up her skirts and hurried down the hall. She would pay dearly for this, so she had better make it worth it.

As she returned to the ballroom, she spotted Will near the terrace.

"I locked Freddie in her room," she murmured when she reached his side. "Please don't let her out for another ten minutes. And *don't* let her near the summer house."

"What?" Will whirled around. "Alex, wait!"

But then she slipped out onto the terrace and headed toward her destination.

It was time to make Lucien Taylor's wildest dreams come true.

Five

*S**he was late.***

Lucien shoved his hands in his trouser pockets and began to pace. He had been lurking in the back of the summer house for more than fifteen minutes now. Well past the time Freddie had whispered in his ear just before she slipped away.

A creeping sensation ran through him. Perhaps he had misunderstood her. Or perhaps his fevered imagination had invented the entire scene. After all, the evening thus far had been the stuff of countless boyhood fantasies: attending one of the Atkinsons' parties, dancing with Freddie, and holding her full attention. But even his most vivid fantasy was nothing but a pale imitation of the real thing. She had looked absolutely breathtaking in a lush, pink gown that brought out the natural blush in her cheeks. And while Lucien had certainly enjoyed waltzing with her, it went beyond the physical. Freddie was witty and charming and just so very *lively*.

He gave his arm a hard, desperate pinch and let out a yelp.

Definitely awake, then.

Besides, he would never have imagined the glowers Alex had not so subtly been casting at them from across the room. If Freddie noticed, she said nothing. She simply laughed louder and smiled wider. So much so that, if Lucien was being very honest with himself, there were moments when it almost felt like she wore a mask. That the entire scene was part of a performance. One that had been tailored for someone other than Lucien…

No.

He shook his head and forced the thought from his mind. He had wanted this woman for half his life, if not longer. He would not ruin this evening with useless nitpicking. At least, not prematurely, anyway.

But as the minutes dragged on, only two possible options remained: Either Freddie was late, or she had changed her mind. Just as Lucien's spirits began to sink dangerously close to the floor, the door of the summer house creaked open. It might as well have been a trumpet blast from the angel Gabriel himself, for the rush of joy that swept through him.

There. All that worrying was for naught.

And yet, his neck still prickled with a strange sense of awareness. Something about this wasn't right.

Lucien cleared his throat as a dark figure came into view. "I'm back here."

A few floor lanterns provided some light, but he couldn't see her face. Freddie made no response as she slowly moved farther into the room, gliding nimbly around the furniture. Dozens of potted plants and exotic shrubs filled the space, lending it something of a fantastical quality. One could almost imagine they were in a villa on the Riviera, not landlocked in the English countryside. It was also warm in here. And seemed to grow even warmer as she approached with the steady, regal bearing of a queen. Lucien tugged on his collar and forced his nerves to settle as much as he could manage.

You're a grown man now. And she wants you. So take what is yours.

Just as Lucien set his shoulders back and stood a little straighter, Freddie stepped into a shard of moonlight. But instead of the impish smile he was expecting, her face looked drawn. And serious.

Much too serious.

Lucien reared back in confusion.

"I can see you are disappointed," she began in a clipped voice laced with disapproval. "But hear me out first."

It was *Alex.* What the hell was she doing here?

"Where…where is Freddie?" He hated how desperate he sounded. How weak. Like the pitiful boy he had once been.

"Freddie isn't coming," she said. That usual maddening disinterest in her voice only made him sound hysterical by comparison.

"But she—"

Alex stepped closer. "I know what she told you, but I'm afraid that isn't possible," she said with cool formality, as if they were discussing a missed appointment rather than a clandestine meeting.

From a distance it was easier to mistake her for her sister, but now there was no confusing the two of them. Whereas Freddie's gown had made her stand out, Alex had taken the opposite approach and was swathed in a shade of green so dark she practically blended in with the shrubbery. Still, he couldn't help skimming over her figure. She was taller and less shapely than Freddie, but the gown still accentuated her full bust and narrow waist, while the color provided a pleasing contrast to her porcelain skin. As she stared directly at him, her large brown eyes looked nearly black.

Lucien's gaze traveled over her face, far longer than it ever had before, ever *dared*, and he suddenly blinked in astonishment. Good Lord, Alexandra Atkinson was *attractive*. It was Freddie who was always hailed as beautiful and vivacious, whereas words like *spinster*, *ice queen*, and, occasionally, *termagant* were applied to her sister. But if he had passed Alex on the street, he certainly would have turned his head. Maybe even touched the brim of his hat if he was feeling particularly bold.

Her beauty was quieter. More mysterious. And Lucien liked it very much. He felt the unmistakable twinge of lust deep in his belly.

The realization was as horrifying as it was confounding.

She raised a haughty eyebrow at his silence. "Well? Aren't you going to say anything?"

Lucien gave himself a shake. He had been standing there this entire time just staring at her like a dolt. "Of course I am," he blustered, which didn't do much to help. Then he straightened his lapels in a bid to gather his scattered thoughts. *Freddie. Right.* "Why isn't it possible for her to see me?"

"Because she is attached to another man."

Lucien let out a snort. "Didn't seem that way to me."

Alex narrowed her eyes. And damn it all if he didn't like that too. "Nevertheless, the connection remains. His name is Hank Ericson Jr. and he is the son and heir of a multimillion-dollar American manufacturing magnate. We are also hoping to take the family on as clients."

"Ah, I see. And you don't want me interfering in any potential business opportunities."

"I think 'interfering' may be too strong a word," Alex replied with a shrewd look. "But Freddie is feeling a little nervous about her future, and she is easily distracted at the moment."

Lucien leaned forward, determined not to be cowed by this woman. "Then perhaps she shouldn't be marrying someone who makes her nervous."

Alex smiled at that, but it only reminded Lucien of a shark. Something cold and sinister. And ready to strike. "Forgive me, but you have been gone a long time and know nothing about the situation or my sister," she said. "I want what is best for her, and you are simply a novelty."

He took a step forward. "I am her *friend*."

"And yet we both recall how that turned out for you," she murmured.

The searing flush of embarrassment engulfed Lucien's body. Damn her for remembering that night. And damn her for bringing it up now. He had only been a boy, then—a miserable, heartbroken one at that.

Alex let out a sigh and for a brief moment a flash of weariness cross her face. "I'm only trying to protect you, Lucien. She *will* hurt you again."

"I don't need your protection. In case you haven't noticed," he said darkly, "I'm not that boy anymore."

Then he stepped closer in an attempt to emphasize his height. But rather than move back, Alex simply lifted her chin and held his gaze. Of course this woman wouldn't be easily intimidated. She probably made grown men cry for fun. Now why did that make him want to smile?

"I noticed," she said quietly, her dark eyes shining in the moonlight.

Somehow they had moved even closer together, though Lucien couldn't recall taking any more steps. He couldn't smell any perfume on her either. Only the faint scent of ink and paper. If he leaned forward just a little more, their chests would touch. The thought sent an unexpected thrill through him.

"Have you?" he said roughly.

She still held his gaze, those dark doe eyes boring into his own while the moment stretched between them, as thick and slow as golden syrup.

But rather than answer, Alex inhaled and took a step back. And then another. Until she was firmly out of reach and the invisible tether between them was unceremoniously snipped. Lucien blinked. It felt like he had just woken from a dream—and a damned strange one at that.

Then she clasped her hands tightly in front of her and cleared her throat. It called to mind a schoolteacher about to issue a particularly boring lecture.

"In any case," she began, "I've come to make you a proposition of sorts. In exchange for keeping away from Freddie."

He let out a surprised laugh. "And why on earth would I agree to such a thing?"

"Because you're a businessman."

"I *was* a businessman," he corrected her.

She let out a huff. "Pity doesn't suit you, Lucien. Your supper club was an excellent idea and was wildly successful—for a time, at least. Now you've had a setback and need to start again. And I can help."

He raised an eyebrow, reluctantly intrigued. "How?"

"As I'm sure you're aware, we run an investment firm," she drawled. "I specialize in identifying business ideas that have the potential for great success. I will introduce you to my contacts in London and help you secure investors."

"I'm sorry, but investors for what?"

"To reopen your supper club, of course," she said. "In London."

Lucien immediately shook his head. "No. I don't do that anymore."

She tilted her head, perplexed. "Then what *are* you planning to do?"

"Quite literally, anything else? The supper club was a massive failure. I have no wish to repeat the experience."

But Alex only waved a hand, unconcerned. "So you clashed with your business partner and parted ways. It's hardly unheard of, especially for your first try. I wouldn't call that a massive failure."

Lucien rubbed the back of his neck. "It involved a tad more than that, I'm afraid."

Just a little embezzlement, intimidation, and threats of bodily harm.

Not that he wanted to explain any of it, least of all to her.

Alex stared at him expectantly, but Lucien looked past her toward the main house. The ballroom glowed in the near distance like a beacon in the dark. So much had felt within his reach only a few months ago. What would he give to feel that way again? Or to finally have it for himself?

He glanced back and found Alex still watching him intently. Or like a panther stalking its prey.

"Do you really think it could work?" he asked, despising the note of hope in his voice. "In London, I mean."

"I think it would take the city by storm." She said it with such certainty, such conviction, that he was sorely tempted to believe her. "And with enough capital, it could be even bigger than before."

God, she *was* serious about this.

"All in exchange for simply staying away from Freddie?"

He hated himself a bit for even considering this, but he could always agree to it for now and then pursue Freddie in earnest later—especially if he did become a success. Then he would actually have something to offer her. More than his measly little heart, anyway. Lucien couldn't deny his growing excitement at the thought.

Alex hesitated. "Well, no. There's something else I need from you. To help convince Hank Jr. that you aren't really a threat."

She looked rather nervous all of a sudden and Lucien found himself intrigued. What could possibly make *this* woman nervous? "All right. What is it?"

She closed her eyes. "You'll need to court me. Publicly." Lucien could only stare at her in shock until she was finally forced to look at him. "Well?"

"You can't be serious," he blurted out, regretting the words as soon as he spoke. For Alex was *always* serious.

As expected, she looked incredulous. "Am I ever not?"

"Yes. I mean, no. Sorry. It's only—" Lucien paused and put his hands on his hips. "You want me to *court* you?"

"This was a terrible idea," she muttered and raised her hands. "Forget it. Forget everything."

But as she turned to leave, his arm shot out to grasp her elbow before he had time to think. "Wait."

She glanced back and stared at the spot where he touched her. She must have felt it too, then. That strange frisson of awareness. Something dancing on the edge of heat. Their eyes met and that nervousness flashed across her face once again. Just for a moment.

"It . . . it would only be for show," she murmured.

It took a moment for his muddled mind to understand what she was referring to.

The courtship. She wanted him to *pretend* to court her. But why?

She gently tugged on her arm once, twice, before he remembered to let go. Then she looked away and began to absently rub the spot where he had touched her.

"Father thinks it would help our clients and the board have confidence in me. In my leadership," she continued, as if she had heard the question.

"If you have a man at your side," he added.

Alex nodded. The faintest blush stained her pale cheek.

His heart clenched at this rare display of vulnerability from her. "That's absurd."

She turned back to him then, her expression as impenetrable as steel once again. "That's business."

As Lucien tilted his head in consideration, Alex shifted on her feet. His lips curved in a slow smile. She was clearly uncomfortable not being entirely in control of the situation, which meant Alexandra Atkinson might have a heart after all. And if that were the case, he just might be able to do this. Hell, he might even enjoy it.

"Tell me the terms again."

<h1 style="text-align:center">Six</h1>

⁓

Alex suggested Lucien take the evening to think things over before they parted ways. Then she went back to the main house, but he had no desire to linger at the edges of the party any longer.

After checking on his father and finding him fast asleep, Lucien collapsed onto his old bed. But despite his exhaustion, he spent most of the night in a restless haze, dozing off only to wake again moments later. It wasn't until close to dawn that he eventually drifted to sleep. And when he finally dreamed, it was of her. Of Alex.

You need to go somewhere far, far away from here.

It was another night. Another birthday party for Mrs. Atkinson. Only Lucien was five years younger and his heart was breaking. As he sat in the oak tree outside his window, he watched Freddie lead a man into the summer house. Then he waited as long as he could stand to, praying with a fervor he didn't know he possessed. But they didn't come out.

Half blind with tears and sorrow, he clambered down the tree and fell to his knees in a wretched heap. Lucien always knew there was little chance that Freddie would ever love him back, but he hadn't realized how fiercely he had clung to that little sliver of hope until it was wrenched from his arms. Now it was over and he was lost. He was so mired in his own misery that he didn't hear the sound of footsteps. Only felt a hand on his shoulder.

Alex's stern face, ghostly pale in the moonlight, stared down at him while humiliation burned his skin. It wasn't enough to watch the girl of his dreams abscond with another man. No, he had to be caught *crying* over it in the dirt beside a hedge. But he hadn't needed to breathe a word of it to Alex. Somehow she just knew.

Where you can be whomever you want . . .

He had forgotten the glimmer of sympathy in her dark eyes. His anger began to slowly fade then, replaced by understanding. By possibility.

"Wake up, my boy." His father's voice echoed through his mind, as if it came from a great distance. It seemed to drag him to the surface of consciousness, but the realization came along with him.

Alex had seen something in him that night. Seen him in a way Freddie never had. Lucien slowly blinked awake and winced. The curtains had been thrown back and the room was awash in morning sunlight. His father hovered in the doorway staring at him anxiously. Before he could ruminate on the strangeness of the situation, alarm shot through him.

Lucien sat up. "What is it? What's happened?"

But his father crossed his arms and raised an eyebrow. "I was hoping you could tell me."

"What?" He squinted, both in confusion and because the room was so damned *bright*.

"Oh, Leonard. Give the boy a moment, will you?" Mrs. Holloway called out from the kitchen. "I've brought over some breakfast. Come when you're ready, Lucien," she added.

His father gave him a warning look. "Mrs. Holloway has to get back to the house. *Some* of us can't lay abed all day."

Lucien rubbed his face. Judging from the sunlight, it couldn't be much later than nine o'clock. But to a man like his father, it might as well be noon. "I'll be right there."

"Five minutes," he warned, then closed the door and shuffled back down the hall.

Lucien rushed through his toilette and threw on the crumpled trousers and shirt he'd worn the night before. When he entered the kitchen, his father was sitting at the table with Mrs. Holloway, an impressive spread of breakfast items before them while they whispered to each other and shared an intimate smile. The tender scene filled him with unexpected warmth. When Lucien's mother had died nearly ten years before, his father had been so broken for so long. But now it was a relief to see him happy again and to know that he had someone to watch over him when Lucien would inevitably leave once more.

They both looked up and his father immediately frowned. "Sit, please," he said sternly and pointed to the chair across from him. Lucien automatically lowered his head, as if he had been caught in an act of boyhood mischief. Still, he dutifully obeyed. But Mrs. Holloway was all smiles as she poured him a cup of tea and passed him a plate loaded with teacakes and currant buns.

Lucien murmured his thanks and took a sip.

"So," his father prompted. "How long have you two been carrying on?" Lucien set down the teacup, genuinely puzzled, but before he could answer, his father continued: "Is that why you came back? It's fine if it is, but I don't understand why you never *said* anything. Did you think I couldn't keep it to myself?" His agitation grew with each word until Mrs. Holloway placed a gentle hand on his arm.

"Leonard. Let him explain. You'll work yourself into a fit." Then she fixed Lucien with a pleading look. "Go on, love."

His eyes darted between them. "I'm sorry, but I haven't the faintest idea what you're talking about."

They fell into a stunned silence until his father could take no more.

"You're courting Alexandra Atkinson!"

Lucien went still. "Where did you hear that?"

His father made a chortling sound. "Where *didn't* we hear it? My God, the whole estate has been twittering about it since last night."

Lucien's hands tightened on the hard edges of the chair. So much for having the evening to think it over. Alex certainly worked quickly. She must have spread the news herself so he wouldn't have the chance to back out. Or explain himself to Freddie first. He let out a huff. The woman was *diabolical*. The vulnerability. The nervousness. The hesitation. It had all been an act. And one that he had completely fallen for.

Lucien would not make that mistake again.

"Well? Aren't you going to say anything?" his father pressed. "At least tell us how it happened."

"I…I can't really explain it," Lucien said with a strange little laugh and shook his head. There. That was the truth, at least.

A kind of understanding flickered in his father's eyes as he sat back in his chair. "Then it's true," he murmured.

Lucien stared at him. He hadn't really considered all that this agreement would require of him.

I will introduce you to my contacts in London and help you secure investors.

It could be even bigger than before.

You'll need to court me. Publicly.

And in exchange, he would have to lie to everyone in his life.

Lucien released a breath. He could end this right now. Claim it was only a silly rumor. A misunderstanding that had gotten out of hand. But then he would be back where he started. With nothing. And as much as he would have liked to deny Alex and her underhandedness, he needed this more.

He nodded. Just once.

His father slowly inhaled then broke into a dazzling grin and playfully batted his arm. "You knave! And here I was all worried over Miss Winifred."

"Oh, but this is a much better match," Mrs. Holloway unhelpfully added.

Lucien cleared his throat and managed to swallow the urge to demand just what the hell *that* meant. "It's very early days," he said instead. "I'd rather not say too much right now." And certainly not before he spoke with Alex herself.

However, his father and Mrs. Holloway were far too excited to be deterred by something so reasonable as prudence.

"It is *highly* unconventional, of course," Mrs. Holloway said diplomatically. "But given Miss Alexandra's lack of suitors, I can't imagine the master and mistress will be too much concerned."

His father laughed. "They're probably breaking out the champagne as we speak!" Then he shot Lucien a sheepish look. "Oh. Sorry, my boy. I didn't mean—"

"It's fine," he replied tightly. "I am aware of our respective places in society as well as her…reputation. And as far as I know, her parents are supportive."

Mrs. Holloway and his father exchanged looks of relief, then launched into a discussion of his and Alex's various attributes as well as the compatibility of each.

"They are both so clever," Mrs. Holloway began. "Though she is quite serious."

"But that's just it, my dear. Perhaps our Lucien brings out her lightheartedness," his father replied thoughtfully.

"Oh, excellent point, Leonard! And Miss Alexandra could use that. Poor thing spends most of her time at the office." Then she addressed Lucien. "You *must* take her out dancing. And to the theater. A musical review!"

"Yes," he said placidly, fighting the urge to laugh at the absurdity of this situation. *Did* Alex dance? He certainly couldn't remember ever seeing her in the arms of a man. Any man. Briefly, he wondered if she even liked men. In Paris he had met a number of women who openly preferred the company of other women. But truthfully, Alex didn't seem to have a preference for either sex. Or people in general.

He turned his attention back to the conversation and, to his alarm, found that Mrs. Holloway had broached the subject of potential wedding dates.

"It would have to be next spring," she pronounced. "As there is far too much to do for Miss Phoebe's December nuptials." Then she cast him an appraising look. "Unless, of course, it becomes a double wedding."

Lucien shot to his feet. "I'm going for a walk."

Not exactly subtle, but he had listened to enough of their nonsense.

He left them planning a wedding that would never happen to a woman he was only pretending to court and headed for the one spot on the estate where he could enjoy some privacy at this hour. Lucien had a hell of a lot to think about.

Seven

Usually Alex rose with the dawn, as it was far easier to get things done without her mother, sisters, or even her father interrupting every few minutes. Apparently no one in the Atkinson household could make their own mundane decisions, or remember who had come to supper last month, or when the British Museum opened. At times she wondered if they coordinated who would approach her in which order, but it seemed far more likely they were simply unaware, as they all seemed quite surprised when she inevitably grew snappish from their constant demands. Everyone always wanted something from her, but no one ever concerned themselves with what *she* wanted.

But today she rubbed her bleary eyes, retrieved her pocket watch from the bedside table, and sat up with a start. Goodness, it was nearly nine o'clock. But then, she had retired much later than usual. Before she could think better of it, her duplicitous mind conjured the image of Lucien Taylor in the summer house with his hazel eyes fixed upon her as he leaned in close.

Tell me the terms again.

A shiver ran down her spine at the memory, just as it had last night. For one ridiculous moment, Alex had actually thought he would *kiss* her, and in the resultant confusion, she blurted out that he should take the night to think things over. It was a terrible negotiation tactic, and a hot flush washed over her at the amateur blunder. Of *course* he didn't want to kiss her. But far more important, the more time someone had to think over a deal, the more they asked for.

Alex shook her head, but Lucien's inviting image stubbornly lingered. She let out a sigh and flopped back onto the pillows. There was nothing to be done about it. She had no leverage in this situation and must give him whatever he wanted. Her only concession was that Lucien didn't know just how desperate she was to make this work.

After indulging in another moment of indolence, Alex forced herself out of bed. If she hurried, she could nip downstairs for a light breakfast and head to Father's study before the rest of the household even began to stir. She needed some time to herself. Time to think.

After washing up, Alex donned a light blue day gown and arranged her hair in a simple Psyche knot. It was more untidy than she preferred, but this was a country morning, not an afternoon meeting in London. Here she did not need to prove her acumen to a roomful of arrogant men.

The thought was strangely depressing. Usually Alex *loved* any opportunity to subvert expectations, but today she only felt tired. Perhaps because after spending the last seven years doing just that, it still wasn't enough.

You'll feel better after you eat, she reasoned.

But as she headed for the stairs, the weariness only grew until it felt like something far more than a simple bowl of porridge could fix.

After gulping down a cup of black coffee in the breakfast room, Alex impulsively decided to pocket a warm crumpet and head directly outside. As she stepped onto the back terrace, the strange ennui began to slowly dissipate. The morning was bright and the air was crisp with the faint scent of early autumn, which she inhaled by the lungful. Back in London she would have already been at her desk for at least an hour, if not more. For once, she was glad not to be there.

Alex wandered past her mother's tidy flower beds toward the ancient forest that surrounded the property. As she walked along the footpath that wound through the woods, she idly chewed on pieces of crumpet and forced herself not to think of work. Unfortunately, that didn't leave much else to ruminate on.

Other than Lucien, of course, offered the cheeky voice in her head.

No. He is also *categorized under work.*

Alex then smiled to herself, as Lucien might object to that description. But before she could pursue this dangerous line of thinking any further, Alex glanced up and came to a halt.

Though she didn't have any particular destination in mind, it was still something of a surprise to find herself on the path that led to the pond. She hadn't been over this way in many years but was gripped by a sudden urge to sit on the mossy bank and look out over the tranquil water. As this morning seemed to be made for frivolity, she decided to follow the impulse and walked faster.

She rounded the bend just someone was emerging from the pond—a *naked* someone. Without thinking, she ducked behind a tree just off the path and prayed she hadn't been spotted. The rough bark dug into her back, but she would have given anything to melt completely into the surface at this moment.

It was a man. Probably some local farmhand, as the pond was a popular swimming spot with the villagers. Alex slowly peered out from behind the tree. Only a few yards away stood the man. He faced the water and was leisurely wrapping a towel around his lean waist. As he was obviously occupied with drying himself, now was the perfect opportunity to sneak away. But just as she resolved to run off, something caught her eye. The man appeared to have a tattoo on his upper left shoulder. She squinted, trying make it out, when she noticed the small gold hoop glinting in the early morning light amid the strands of wet, golden brown hair clinging to his neck. As a droplet of water slid down between his well-formed shoulders, her breath caught in recognition. *Oh God.* The man wasn't some farmhand. It was *Lucien.* Alex quickly darted back behind the tree just as he turned around. If he saw her now, she would never recover. And he certainly wouldn't want anything to do with her. Not when it looked like she was *spying* on him!

Alex peeked around the tree as far as she dared. His back was to her once more while he now dried his hair with the towel—which left the rest of him entirely uncovered. She forced her gaze away from his bare backside and muttered a curse. This situation was growing worse by the second. She needed to get out of here. *Now.* With great care, she took a step, then another. But every dried leaf and twig underfoot sounded as loud as an elephant crashing through the jungle. Perhaps it was better if she just made a run for it and hoped he couldn't tell it was her. But just as Alex took a lunging step forward, the hem of her dress snagged on a jagged branch sticking out of the ground and she fell to her knees in a loud crunch. She froze in terror and in the silence that followed, Alex was able to delude herself into believing that, actually, she hadn't been *that* loud. Then, the blissful moment came to an end.

"Is someone there?" Lucien's sharp voice rang out through the forest.

Alex snapped to attention and began to furiously tug on her skirt, but the blasted thing wouldn't come loose. She glanced back to see that Lucien was pulling on his trousers and cursed again. Then pulled harder.

"Show yourself!" he bellowed, now throwing on his shirt.

She decided to rip the hem to free herself and was very nearly there when Lucien stormed over, an impressive look of menace on his face. But once he registered who she was, the menace turned into shock.

"Miss Atkinson?"

Alex cleared her throat and slowly came to her feet, trying her best to look unperturbed. As if this was a perfectly normal situation that she was entirely in control of.

"I think you can call me Alex now."

Lucien only stared back at her, dumbfounded.

He hadn't buttoned the shirt. Or put on shoes. Alex dearly wished she didn't know how shapely his chest was.

Or his backside, for that matter.

Alex pursed her lips as she tried to marshal her ridiculous thoughts, then decided it would have been far better to have left her skirt entirely behind if it meant she could have avoided this conversation.

"I'm sorry," she said with all the formality she could muster. "I didn't mean to intrude on you. Truly. I was taking a walk and decided to come to the pond."

"Of course," he replied with a confused frown. "I didn't think anyone would—"

"There's no need to explain yourself," Alex said haltingly as she tried to look anywhere but at him.

He *really* should button his shirt.

Lucien appeared to have the same thought as he glanced down. "Excuse me for a moment," he said as he turned away and began to button his shirt.

"I should go."

But he threw her a look over his shoulder. "Please don't."

Alex cleared her throat. "Fine."

Then she clasped her hands against her waist and averted her gaze while he hurriedly buttoned his shirt.

After a few painfully awkward moments, he finished. "There. Much better."

Then he swiftly bent down and freed her hem with embarrassing ease.

"Thank you," she murmured as he stood.

"Not a problem," he said. "No need to ruin a perfectly good dress."

Alex could have sworn his gaze darted over her figure. But that was absurd.

"I'd rather have my pride, actually," she admitted.

To her astonishment, he smiled. "That makes two of us, I suppose."

Alex pressed her hands against her eyes as she suddenly blushed. "Oh God, I'm so embarrassed."

Lucien chuckled. "It's all right. Really. It's nice to know even you can bungle things up now and then. It makes you seem more…"

Alex dropped her hands and arched a brow. "Human?"

It would hardly be the first time someone questioned her sentience.

But Lucien ignored her dry tone and gave her a thoughtful look. "I was going to say approachable."

"Oh." That felt worse, somehow.

Lucien furrowed his brow. "Sorry." Then he cupped the back of his neck with one hand and shoved the other in his pocket. "I only meant that you can be rather…intimidating." He glanced at her through his lashes as he said the last word, as if trying to gauge her reaction.

"I see." She had been told as much before by other people and still hadn't the slightest idea what to do about it. "I suppose that would make it rather difficult for you to pretend to court me, then," she added, steeling herself for disappointment.

"About that," he began. "You said I would have the night to think things over, but news of our"—he waved a hand as he searched for the word—"*situation* has spread through the household staff."

Alex's mouth dropped open. "Already?" Though she knew it had begun to spread among the guests, she hadn't realized the staff would take such an interest. Though perhaps that was understandable, given Lucien's connection. She would need to be better prepared to anticipate all eventualities if they moved forward with this arrangement.

"Yes. My father asked me about it this morning." Lucien's eyes narrowed in suspicion. "But that can't be much of a surprise to you."

Understanding dawned on her. "You think *I* did that on purpose?"

Lucien shrugged. "Well, it rather forced my hand in the moment."

"I am not quite so desperate as that, thank you," she said primly.

"Wait," he said as she turned to leave. "I'm sorry. I wasn't trying to imply—"

Alex turned back to face him. "What? That I am so undesirable that not only would I need to find a fake suitor but would also have to *force* him into it?"

Lucien's face fell. "I didn't think—"

"No," she snapped. "You most certainly did not." She took a few steps before Lucien caught up with her.

"Alex. *Please.*"

It was the pleading note in his voice that brought her to a halt. No man had ever begged for her before. It seemed to trip something within her. A scenario she had never once considered.

And Alex found she rather liked it.

⁓

As Alex slowly turned around and crossed her arms, the movement had the unintended effect of drawing attention to her chest. Even still, Lucien made sure to keep his eyes firmly on her face. The woman might dress like someone's dowdy aunt, but her clothes were still expertly tailored to accentuate every curve. This gown in particular had a neckline just below her collarbones. Lucien had never given a thought to collarbones before, but since she was usually buttoned up to her chin, this was…distracting.

When Lucien first found Alex behind the tree tugging helplessly at her skirt, she had looked up at him with such desperation that it brought to mind a scene out of some horrible Greek myth, wherein he was the lusty god and she the flailing wood nymph.

But since this *was* Alex, the moment quickly passed before she resumed her usual stoicism. Still, the feeling had lingered even through his anger over her duplicity and any embarrassment over being caught without a stitch on.

He fully believed that she had inadvertently stumbled upon him because the idea that she might have *intentionally* followed him there was simply too silly and her own embarrassment far too obvious. However, it was harder to accept that she hadn't deliberately spread the news of their courtship for her own advantage. Until he saw pain flash across her face. It was perhaps the truest emotion he had ever seen from her. As those fathomless dark eyes stared once again, betraying nothing, Lucien began to have an inkling of what lay beneath the mask she showed the world.

"I didn't mean it like that."

She scoffed. "You most certainly did."

"Only that you did it with *intention*." He ran a hand through his damp hair in frustration. "Nothing about you has ever struck me as desperate."

Alex stared at him intently for a long moment, then seemed to conclude he was telling the truth. "Fair enough." Then she lifted her chin. "So then, what have you decided?"

It was back to business as usual. He should have known their little moment of shared vulnerability wouldn't last, and yet he still felt disappointed.

"I can put an end to all of this within an hour, if you wish," she added at his silence.

Lucien took a breath. He didn't know why he was even hesitating about this. He needed a path forward, and right now Alex offered him the best option. The *only* option. All he had to do was play the doting beau for a few weeks until Alex was satisfied. That also meant he could be closer to Freddie than he would ever be allowed otherwise. And if she really *did* decide not to wed that American fellow, Lucien would be in a prime position to declare himself to her. He would have to explain his little arrangement with Alex, of course, but they would have a good laugh over it. And Freddie would understand completely. As if anyone would ever choose *Alex* over her.

And yet, something about this entire scenario remained vaguely unsettling.

Perhaps because you're still a little frightened of Alexandra Atkinson.

He pushed the ridiculous feeling aside and extended his hand. "That won't be necessary."

Alex stared at it and looked up. "Excellent. I look forward to working with you." But instead of taking his hand, she pulled something out from her pocket and placed it in his palm. "You'll need to stay in London, of course."

"That won't be a problem," he said as his fingers closed over the card. "I already planned to go there as soon as possible."

"Good." She gave him a stiff nod. "Come and see me on Monday. First thing."

As she brushed passed him, Lucien turned over the business card she had given him. It was made of expensive cardstock, but otherwise quite plain, with just her name and the address of Atkinson Enterprises embossed in black ink. My God, the woman walked around her own home with *business cards* on her person.

"And Lucien," she began as she looked over her shoulder. "You'll need to make it look real."

He drank in the hint of uncertainty in her gaze and tucked the card into his breast pocket. "I think I can manage that."

She swallowed in response, another subtle betrayal of nerves, and his eyes were hopelessly drawn to the movement of her pale throat. Then she turned back and headed into the woods. Lucien watched until she disappeared from view.

No, he thought as the sense of unease returned. *That won't be a problem at all.*

Eight

It was still rather early when Alex returned to the house. Since Mother's party had gone on into the wee hours of the morning, she hadn't expected to see anyone else until closer to noon, but there was Aunt Winifred, her sister's namesake and her mother's favorite aunt, tucking into a plate of kippers at the breakfast table. "Ah, good morning, Alexandra," she said brightly. The previous evening's festivities had clearly not dampened the older woman's usual vivaciousness. "Join me, will you?" She held up a forkful of fish.

Alex managed to hold back a grimace. No one else in the family dared touch the stuff, but her mother always made sure to have them on hand whenever Aunt Winifred stayed with them.

"I'm afraid I have work to do."

Aunt Winifred raised an imperious eyebrow. "At *this* time of the day? No, I don't think so. At least have a Bath bun."

Given that it would take longer to convince Aunt Winifred than consume the bun, Alex relented and took a seat.

"Are you enjoying your visit?"

"Oh, yes," Aunt Winifred said with an easy smile. "I love my solitude of course, but it's always great fun coming here."

She lived on a rambling estate in Cornwall and had largely retired from society since the death of her husband nearly a decade ago. "As a matter of fact, I've decided to extend my visit. Last night your mother asked me to come to London to help with planning Phoebe's engagement ball next month."

"It's to be a *ball* now?" Alex groused as she slathered her bun in butter. "So much for a small family party."

"Well, she is marrying a duke, dear," Aunt Winifred said gently. "Even if it is only William. Still, society will expect something rather grand."

Alex avoided balls whenever possible. Unfortunately, her usual excuses would not work here. "I suppose."

"We'll find you something beautiful to wear. And you can even borrow my sapphire necklace," her aunt said. "The one my dear husband gave me when I turned forty, bless his soul. It will go quite nicely with your coloring."

Gowns and necklaces weren't exactly motivators for her, but Alex still appreciated the gesture. "Thank you."

"Amanda will be furious," Aunt Winifred said gleefully. "She *never* misses the chance to ramble on about the importance of living a virtuous life, but I see the covetous look in her eye when I wear it. That woman is just as insufferable as her husband."

Alex smiled. "You mean your son?"

Aunt Winifred had married Mr. Terrence Bailey, a wealthy older gentlemen who was regarded as something of a libertine. At the time of their marriage there had been a good deal of whispers regarding his ability to remain faithful but, by all accounts, he absolutely doted on his wife and together they made their mark in both London and the burgeoning arts scene in Paris. But while Aunt Winifred and her husband enjoyed being the vanguard, their only son, Mortimer, had rebelled by becoming a tiresome country vicar—and a spectacularly judgmental one at that. He and his wife, Amanda, took great pleasure in looking down on every person they met, but especially his Atkinson cousins, whom he regarded as god-forsaken hoydens.

"He really is the most *ungrateful* child," Aunt Winifred huffed. "But I am looking forward to helping Phoebe with the ball and the wedding, seeing as my own daughter-in-law refused any such assistance." She punctuated this with a roll of her eyes. From what Alex recalled, Mortimer and Amanda had wed in a very small, very simple ceremony in his own parish, to which neither she nor any members of family had been invited. Aunt Winifred had been terribly embarrassed by the entire ordeal.

"It is their loss," Alex said honestly. Aunt Winifred was one of the most generous people she knew and had always doted on her and her sisters.

Aunt Winifred reached across the table and patted her hand. "Thank you, my dear." Then she hesitated and gave her a searching look. "Your mother also mentioned that you might need a chaperone, as she rather has her hands full with Freddie."

Alex balked. Lucien was right. Word *had* spread. "That won't be necessary."

Aunt Winifred didn't look convinced. "I know you're used to going about on your own, but things will be different now that you are being courted."

Alex's stomach sank. As a spinster who spent most of her time working while ignoring society, she had enjoyed a certain amount of freedom. But her aunt was right. Courting couples were supposed to follow a strict set of rules. Alex didn't even *know* all of them.

Aunt Winifred must have read the terror on her face. "It's all right," she began. "I have an excellent reputation. I was Cecily Beauford's chaperone years ago when she was being courted by three different men, including Earl Havisham's son. The chit didn't even make it to Ascot before he proposed to her. And I also know when to give couples a little privacy. *That* is the key to bringing about a quick engagement," she added with a wink.

Alex's stomach sank even further. "We aren't getting engaged," she blurted out. This was quickly turning into more than she could manage.

Her aunt blinked in confusion. "Don't you want to? Lucien Taylor is such a handsome young man. And the coachman's son! It will cause the most delightful stir," she added with a waggle of her brows. "Oh, if my dear Terrence was still with us he would be beside himself with excitement. You *know* how he loved to rile up those stuffy society matrons."

Alex didn't, given that she had still been in the schoolroom when the man died, but she certainly had no desire to mix with society or rile matrons.

She pushed her chair back and stood. "I have to go." Because she couldn't discuss this anymore. Luckily, her family was used to her abrupt exits.

"We'll talk more later," her aunt called out as Alex hurried from the room.

Unfortunately, this put her straight into Freddie's path. And her sister was ready to pounce.

"Is it true?" she demanded. "This absolute *rubbish* about you and Lucien?"

This morning had been filled with a number of irritations,

which made Freddie's scornful tone particularly grating. But Alex carefully hid her anger behind a mask of indifference and crossed her arms. "I'd thank you not to refer to our courtship as rubbish."

Freddie let out a huff of disbelief. "What on *earth* did you do to get him to agree to this? Are you blackmailing him?"

"No." Alex drew the word out in a bid to control her temper. "He simply enjoys my company."

She managed to say this with a straight face, but Freddie narrowed her eyes and stepped closer. The sudden resemblance between them caught Alex off guard. If this was what she usually looked like, no wonder people found her so intimidating. The effect was unnerving.

"You're just doing this to put me off Lucien so I don't ruin your little deal with the Ericsons. That blasted *business* is all you ever care about."

"Freddie—"

"No," she snapped. "This is low. Even for *you*."

Alex pursed her lips. Her sisters were forever criticizing her ambition, but not once had they ever lobed the accusation at their father. And they seemed to have no issue spending the money Alex brought in. Well, she was damned tired of their hypocrisy.

"If you're so convinced that I'm standing in your way," she began coolly, "then why don't you end things with Hank Jr.? Go knock on his door right now and tell him it's over. That you will *never* marry him."

Predictably, Freddie balked.

Alex huffed. "See? You don't even know what you want. But *I* do. So stay out of my way," she tossed off as she stormed down the hallway.

"Whatever is really going on here, it won't matter," her sister called out just before she turned the corner, not sounding the least bit cowed. "No one will ever believe he wants you."

Alex didn't stop. She outran the cresting wave of anger that nipped at her heels until she reached her bedroom. Then she shut the door soundly behind her and pressed her back against it.

It was the absolute certainty in Freddie's voice that rankled the most. Along with the faint whisper in her own mind.

She's right.

But before Alex could be swallowed up by doubts, she pushed away from the door and stalked over to her closet. Then she pulled out her valise and tossed it onto the bed. If she hurried, she could be back in London for tea, where she wouldn't have to answer any insipid questions or explain her behavior. Where she was gloriously invisible—until someone wanted something from her.

She threw in clothes, stockings, and shoes without really seeing them. All that mattered was getting out of here. The country had grown tiresome. And she had a train to catch.

Nine

Not two days after striking a tentative agreement with Alex, Lucien found himself in the frigid hallway of a London apartment building, cold, tired, hungry, and *very* late. He had not spent much time in London apart from a few days here and there over the years and had gotten properly lost on his way from the train station. Then it began to rain, which quickly turned into a downpour. For a brief moment Lucien considered popping into a pub to wait the storm out but decided to save his coin and make a run for it instead.

Now he was a few shillings richer but absolutely soaked to the bone. Just as another tooth-rattling shiver came over him, Alain Fournier threw open the door, handsome as ever and the very epitome of French refinement.

"There you are, Lucien! I was just about to man a search party for you," he said in heavily accented English before kissing both of Lucien's cheeks. Then he drew back and his dark eyes skimmed over Lucien's dripping clothes in horror. "Come inside right this instant! You'll catch your death out there. The landlord keeps this building as cold as a nun's tit, but the hearth is blazing."

Lucien chuckled through his chattering teeth as he crossed the threshold. "Thank you."

He had forgotten that Alain had a tendency to fuss over people he cared about. Luckily, Lucien could use a little fussing at the moment. The flat was small but cozy, just two rooms from what Lucien could see, and the hearth was indeed blazing with the comforting glow of lit coals.

"Welcome to my humble abode," Alain said with a grand sweep of the hand.

"Sorry I'm so late," Lucien said as Alain took his coat. "And wet."

But Alain clucked his tongue. "Do not apologize for your country's abysmal weather. But please stay here while I fetch you a towel. Though you are my dear friend, that does not mean I want you ruining my carpet."

Alain was not serious about much apart from textiles and good chocolate. With his eye for detail and penchant for sweets, he could have easily become a master pâtissier. But instead he had chosen hospitality services.

Lucien did his best not to drip on the floor while Alain disappeared into the bedroom. "A lovely place you have here," he called out.

Despite the small size, the flat was elegantly decorated.

"Ah, thank you," Alain replied in a slightly muffled voice. "I have become friendly with the hotel's very handsome designer and he always gives me the best castoffs."

"Oh, that's convenient."

Alain reentered the main room carrying a towel with a robe draped over his arm. "It is, rather. Though I won't tell you what I had to do for that armchair in the corner," he added with a saucy wink.

Lucien laughed again and accepted the towel. "Your ingenuity never fails to impress me."

"One day I will not be this beautiful," Alain lamented with a dramatic sigh as he brushed a hand through his thick dark hair. "So I must make the best of it while still I can."

Lucien let out a muffled snort while he rubbed the towel over his damp hair. "I'm sure you will make a very lovely older gentleman one day."

"Ugh! Do not even *speak* of such things." Alain then thrust the robe at him. "Take off your clothes and put this on."

It was one of the softest things Lucien had ever held. "Very nice. Is it also from the designer?"

Alain looked offended *"Non!* I took it myself from the hotel." Then his sharp gaze fell on Lucien's satchel. "Is that all you brought?" Alain clucked his tongue before he could answer. "Then Rene really did clean you out."

"To nearly my last franc," Lucien admitted plainly as he unbuttoned his wet shirt. Alain had known Lucien's former business partner even longer than he had, yet he too had been shocked by their mutual friend's duplicitousness.

"That *swine.* Where is he now?"

"Somewhere on the Riviera with Madame Deveraux," Lucien said with a casual shrug that probably did not fool Alain.

Indeed, his friend's eyes filled with sympathy. "I am sorry, Lucien. Rene has always been impulsive. He could have built an empire with you but instead he chose to follow his heart—or rather his…" Alain motioned below his waist. "But the money will run out soon enough and Madame Deveraux will certainly leave with it."

Lucien believed as much, but it was cold comfort given that he was still broke either way.

Alain brightened. "And in the meantime, I have plenty of things you can borrow." Then he gestured for Lucien to hand him his wet shirt and trousers.

He complied and pulled on the robe, which indeed proved to be one of the softest things he had ever worn. "Thank you, Alain. I promise I will be out of here very soon."

But Alain simply waved a hand and moved to drape the clothes over a drying rack set up before the hearth. "There is no rush at all. I am busy at the hotel most days anyway and am hardly ever here."

Still, Lucien did not want to impose on his friend any more than necessary. "I have a meeting tomorrow morning, actually. Do you know the Atkinsons? They run Atkinson Enterprises."

"Oh, yes," Alain said. "Mr. Atkinson often comes to dine at the hotel with his clients. Shall I make us tea?"

"Please."

Alain disappeared into the small kitchen and Lucien moved closer to the hearth and let the heat wash over him. As he slowly warmed up, he grew more drowsy and had almost dozed off on his feet when Alain bustled in with the tea tray.

"Here we are! Make sure you have a financier. I made them only yesterday," he said, setting the tray down on the small table beside Lucien. "I am impressed that you already have a meeting with Atkinson Enterprises."

"I grew up on the family's country estate, actually," Lucien explained as he joined Alain on the sofa. "My mother was the cook and my father is the head coachman."

"How funny!" Alain said as he poured Lucien's tea. "And now he wants to hire you?"

"Well, not exactly," Lucien began, accepting both the teacup and a financier. "Do you know his daughter?"

Alain fell quiet for a moment as he considered the question. "She has dined with him before, I believe. A very elegant young woman."

"Not Winifred," Lucien said automatically. "The eldest one. Alexandra."

Alain raised an eyebrow. "That was who I meant."

Lucien's cheeks began to heat. "Right. Of course."

He felt embarrassed to have made such an assumption, which made him no better than everyone else.

"You're blushing," Alain said unnecessarily. "Do you *like* Miss Alexandra?"

Lucien opened his mouth to deny it, like a petulant schoolboy, but he was supposed to like Alex. He cleared his throat instead. "Ah, that is a rather complicated question at present," he said instead, which naturally only heightened Alain's interest.

"Explain."

"We are…in a manner of speaking…courting."

"What!" Alain cried out and threw up his hands. "But this is wonderful!" Then he immediately sobered. "Why aren't you more excited? You look like you ate some bad fish and I know it is not because of my baking."

"It is still new. *Very* new."

Alain gave him an understanding look. "Does her father not approve?"

"That is something we will discuss tomorrow," Lucien said carefully. That was true enough given that he had yet to see Mr. Atkinson since Alex's proposition. Who knew how the man would take the news, fake or not.

Alain nodded as he considered this. "Well, he would be a fool to reject you simply because of your family. And besides, he seems rather unconventional himself if he lets his daughter work for him."

"A fair point."

"I have even heard a few whispers that she is actually behind his greatest successes," Alain said as he waggled his eyebrows and took a sip of tea.

"It's more than just whispers," Lucien replied. Though he had his quibbles with Alex, her competence was not one of them. One only had to have a single conversation with her to see that she was incredibly intelligent. Was it really that much of a stretch to imagine her behind a desk undertaking the same tasks that plenty of other men across the city performed daily?

It would help our clients and the board have confidence in me.

He grimaced a little as he recalled her words from the other night. A lack of imagination was at the very heart of her little proposition, after all. "That is, she is quite capable of the work," Lucien added.

Alain was still giving him that thoughtful look. "Hmm. I can see it," he said after a moment.

"See what?"

But Alain only smiled at his petulant tone. "Let me make you something to eat. Then you should rest for your important meeting tomorrow."

That was at least something Lucien would not object to.

Ten

The next morning, after a good long sleep and a hearty breakfast of boiled eggs, toast, and the most delicious strawberry jam, Lucien felt restored. As his jacket and trousers were still a touch damp, Alain insisted he borrow a brown town suit. They weren't exactly the same size, as Lucien was a bit taller. Even still, it fit far better than anything he had ever worn before.

"And was this a castoff from the hotel's designer as well?" he quipped.

Alain shot him a sly smile as he smoothed the back of the jacket. "*Non*. But I do have a good friend who works for a tailor on Savile Row. And sometimes gentlemen do not pick up their wares and I can get them for much less. They are still outrageously expensive, mind you, but I would sacrifice much more for excellent tailoring."

As Lucien looked at his reflection in the floor-length mirror, he could understand the reasoning.

"Now hurry up," Alain said with a clap of his hands. "I am done playing valet. There is a grand duchess checking in today and I need to make sure her room is filled with fresh-cut roses beforehand or else she will be very put out."

"Good lord. That almost makes me miss the list of demands we would get ahead of our private events." He and Rene hadn't held very many of those, but they were a good moneymaker when funds were short—as well as a massive headache. He didn't know how Alain could stand catering to the ridiculous demands of the very wealthy all day long.

"Keep that up and I'll bring you to work with me," he threatened.

"All right, all right." Lucien raised his hands with a smile. "I'm going."

Before Alain left for the hotel, he patiently explained the best route to take to get to the Atkinsons' office and even drew up a little map. And for a short while, it worked.

Lucien left the flat with plenty of time and made it to the station but was then hustled onto the wrong omnibus by a hoard of impatient passengers, and when he managed to push his way off and board the right one, it broke an axle. Lucien then gave up on London's transportation system and decided to walk the rest of the way. However, once he reached the narrow streets of the City, his progress slowed to a glacial pace.

Lucien tried his best to weave through the office workers filling the pavement but it was of little use. He would be late for his appointment with Alex. And she was *not* the kind of woman one wanted to keep waiting. He let out a sigh of defeat and fell in step behind two men in nearly identical black suits and matching bowler hats. As much as he lamented his current precarious state of unemployment, the thought of being another cog trudging off to the same office every day to push papers or add numbers for some faceless owner who reaped most of the profits was even worse. Lucien had loved the satisfaction of running his own business, albeit with a partner.

He had met Rene in culinary school, where they both discovered their knife skills were sorely lacking and their tolerance for the

insanity of a professional kitchen nonexistent. When Lucien mentioned the idea of running a private supper club that changed loca-
tions and themes each week, Rene's enthusiasm for the idea gave
him the push he needed. And Rene was happy to let Lucien take
the lead and enact his vision, while he stayed behind the scenes and
kept the books. For the first time in his life, Lucien found something he was good at—or so he had thought. It turned out that having Lucien act as the face and brains behind the business had been
an excellent distraction while Rene robbed him blind before running off with Madame Deveraux, the wife of one of their investors.

But because that wasn't nearly enough duplicitous behavior for one
man, shortly before the business collapsed, Rene had spread the word
to customers and their other investors that it was actually *Lucien* who
had been embezzling, but that, if they gave their money directly to
Rene, he would reopen the supper club. Instead, he had taken the
entire lot and absconded to the Riviera, leaving Lucien to deal with
their creditors and swindled customers. When Lucien eventually
managed to sort everything out, he had been left with next to nothing.

What a waste it all had been.

As the familiar taste of bitter regret began to fill Lucien's mouth,
Alex's stern voice echoed in his mind:

Pity doesn't suit you.

No. And he was so bloody *tired* of going over the past. Of rumi-
nating over things he hadn't done and certainly couldn't fix now.
Lucien wouldn't let it define him. He couldn't. Just then he spotted Atkinson Enterprises up ahead, and he moved a little faster.
This was his chance. And he wouldn't let anything stop him. Not
a broken-down omnibus or an unfamiliar metropolis or even the
assured disapproval of a slightly terrifying woman.

But as he entered the lobby, Lucien stopped short and took a breath. It was cavernous, with marble floors and gold accents that brought to mind a particularly ostentatious Catholic church. Lucien was so busy marveling at the architectural details that he barely noticed the secretary right in front of him until she loudly cleared her throat.

"May I help you, sir?"

He snapped to attention and smiled at the young lady. "Yes, sorry. I have a meeting with Miss Atkinson. I'm Lucien Taylor."

She scanned a sheet of paper on her desk and then pointed down a hall. "Take the stairs to the third floor."

He nodded politely and followed her instructions while still taking in glimpses of the impressive, imposing space. A trio of smartly dressed men were just ahead of him on the stairs and in the middle of a hushed conversation that sounded rather dire.

"I was here 'til all hours last night," one lamented.

"Did you make any progress?" another asked.

The third snorted. "That is for *her* to decide."

Then they all fell into a gloomy silence as they appeared to ponder this while Lucien hung back a bit to make his eavesdropping less noticeable. But the men were too consumed by their thoughts to pay him any mind as they all trudged up the stairs and disappeared through an entryway that led to the third floor. Could they be talking about Alex?

I have even heard whispers that she is actually behind his greatest successes.

Though Lucien had readily supported the idea, in truth he didn't exactly know what Alex did here. When he mentioned this visit to his father, he had been surprisingly dismissive.

Do you know she goes in every morning at eight sharp? And most days she doesn't leave 'til half six. Even her *father doesn't keep those hours.*

Lucien had raised an eyebrow. *You think she isn't really doing any work?*

Well, I know she's clever for a lady and all, but come now, he said. *I've heard it's just a lark. Something to keep her busy since she has no real marriage prospects.* Then his eyes widened. *Oh. Sorry, Lucien. I didn't mean—*

It's fine, he said quickly, not wanting to say any more about this courtship than necessary.

But if any lady could have a head for business, his father began. *I'd say it'd be her.*

Lucien couldn't help smiling as he pictured Alex's barely veiled contempt at such a backhanded compliment. But his father was hardly an outlier, as most people held the same opinion. And if someone had asked Lucien a week before, he might have even made the same assumption. Now, though, he wasn't so certain. Alex was clearly competent—*terrifyingly* so—but the world of business was still largely the domain of men. Once in a while a woman managed to breach its walls, but not without snide whispers undermining her accomplishments.

Perhaps that is the case here.

Lucien's stomach tightened as he reached the third-floor landing and moved down the hall. Time to find out. This floor was even nicer than the lobby, with fine Turkish carpeting in tones of red and blue and walls papered in matching red brocade. Golden wall sconces with electric light gave off a warm, sumptuous glow. But unlike the churchly feeling of the lobby, the atmosphere was far more bustling up here, with people flitting back and forth. Raucous laughter could even be heard from a nearby room. Lucien managed to flag down a passing woman.

"Excuse me, I'm looking for Miss Atkinson's office."

"Round that corner and at the end of the hall," she replied briskly, pointing behind her. "You'll see her secretary, Mr. Potts."

A male secretary? Interesting.

Lucien thanked her and continued on. This part of the floor was a little quieter and he passed an office with a gold-plated sign bearing Mr. Atkinson's name and title.

Farther down at the end of the hall, a pale, thin-faced man in spectacles sat behind a desk. As Lucien approached, Mr. Potts paid him no attention. His fine blonde hair was combed and parted to the side and he was frowning down at a piece of paper, pen in hand. After a moment, Lucien cleared his throat and Mr. Potts glanced up momentarily before returning his gaze to the paper.

"And *you* are?" he drawled in a voice laced with disapproval.

Lucien suddenly felt like a naughty schoolboy in front of the headmaster. "Lucien Taylor. I have an appointment with Miss Atkinson."

Mr. Potts finally looked directly at him and his frown deepened. "You're late."

"Yes, I—I'm very sorry about that," Lucien stammered, "but I—"

"You'll need to wait," Mr. Potts said and flipped through an appointment book. "Miss Atkinson is extremely busy this morning and doesn't have time for you at the moment."

Lucien blinked. "Of course."

The man gestured to a chair against the wall and Lucien obediently took a seat. Alex's office door was closed and he couldn't tell if she was in there with someone.

After a moment, Lucien leaned forward. "Do you know *when* she might have time to meet with me?"

Mr. Potts cast him an arch look. "No."

Lucien blew out a breath and sat back in the chair. Surely she had *some* time available this morning to see him. If only so he could explain his lateness.

Fifteen excruciating minutes passed, and just as Lucien was considering getting up to stretch, the office door swung open and two men he recognized from the stairs walked out looking defeated.

"There now, Perkins. Good show," one said, clapping a hand on the other man's shoulder. "Better luck next time."

But Perkins could only manage a weak nod as he stared off into the middle distance with a vacant expression.

As the men passed down the hall, Lucien craned his neck to catch a glimpse of Alex just as Mr. Potts entered the office and blocked his view. He shot Lucien a glance as he closed the door behind him.

All right. *Now* he would see her. Lucien straightened his jacket and adjusted his cuffs in preparation. Another few minutes passed before the door finally opened. Lucien rose, but just as Mr. Potts exited the office, another man came rushing down the hall. They nodded at each other and he slipped into the room, closing the door soundly behind him.

Lucien cast a bewildered look at Mr. Potts. This time he smiled and shrugged before taking his seat behind the desk.

"Should I come back later?"

Mr. Potts arched a brow. "Do you have somewhere you need to be?"

"Well, not right at the moment," Lucien said, trying to look at least a *little* important.

"Miss Atkinson should be able to see you after her meeting with Mr. Farnsworth."

"Oh. If that doesn't take too long, I should be able to manage," Lucien replied airily, but Mr. Potts did not look the least bit convinced that he had any other pressing engagements.

Another quarter hour passed before the door opened again. Somehow this Mr. Farnsworth looked even more devastated than the other two. He trudged down the hall staring at the floor and muttering to himself. What on earth *happened* in there?

Just as Lucien began to rise, Mr. Potts nipped in yet again and shut the door behind him. This was getting ridiculous.

When Mr. Potts finally exited the office, Lucien stood and put his hands on his hips. "Now listen here. I can't be kept waiting all—"

But the rest of his little rant was lost as Alex herself appeared in the doorway.

"My apologies, Mr. Taylor," she said smoothly. "I didn't mean to keep you from your business. Do you still have time to meet?"

She held his gaze, one dark brow arched, and Lucien could feel the blush staining his cheeks.

"Ah, yes. For a little while," he added.

Alex looked amused. She very well knew that was a lie, but instead of calling him out, she simply gestured for him to enter. "Then please do come in."

As Lucien passed Mr. Potts, they exchanged glares. The nosy secretary then hovered in the doorway.

"Would you like me to take notes, Miss Atkinson?"

"That won't be necessary."

Lucien smiled at the man and then promptly closed the door in his face.

Eleven

"harming fellow," Lucien said as he stepped farther into the office, then came to a halt as he took in the space. It was, in a word, stark—especially when compared to the rest of the building. The walls were plain white, the wood floors clean but bare, and the only furniture was a large desk with two grossly mismatched chairs.

Alex had already taken her seat behind the desk and was shuffling some papers around. She glanced up, distracted. "Who, Potts? I hired him specifically because he *isn't* charming. That way people only come to see me if it is absolutely necessary. He also has excellent penmanship," she added and returned her gaze to her desktop.

"A vital quality in a secretary," Lucien quipped as he sat down on a hideous wooden chair that would not have been out of place in a Tudor torture chamber. Somehow it managed to be even more uncomfortable than it looked, but he gathered that was the point. Between the odious Mr. Potts, the sterile room, and the spasm-inducing furniture, Alex clearly didn't want anybody hanging about. Fair enough.

She hummed in response and continued her reading while Lucien took the opportunity to openly look at her. She wore a sober navy-blue gown with a high neckline trimmed in white lace at her throat and her hair was pulled back in a tight bun. Back in Bunbury Lucien had thought she dressed rather plainly, especially compared to the other women of her class, but apparently that had been her partywear. Leave it to Alex to dress for a ball like she was organizing a church rummage sale.

She let out a sharp tsk and for one brief, terrifying moment Lucien worried that somehow she had heard the unkind thought. But then she opened a small black case and put on a pair of dark-rimmed spectacles.

"I hate wearing these," she grumbled.

Any other woman would have resembled a dour old school-marm, but on Alex the effect was . . . distracting.

Lucien cleared his throat. "I take it you just delivered some bad news to Mr. Farnsworth?" he asked in an attempt to make conversation, as it appeared Alex was in no hurry to do so.

"Not that it's any of your business," she scolded without looking up. "But no, I wouldn't say that."

"Really? The man looked like you had just killed his dog."

Alex finally met his gaze then and, as her deep brown eyes stared at him intently from behind her spectacles, Lucien regretted engaging her in conversation. He crossed his legs but that provided little relief.

"Did he?" She seemed genuinely surprised. "Huh. I can't imagine why."

Lucien shifted in his seat. "Well, what did you say to him?"

As she said, it wasn't any of his business and certainly not related to their arrangement. And yet he couldn't contain his curiosity. It was also preferrable to have something to focus on besides his unruly cock.

Alex shrugged, bewildered. "I simply gave him my notes on a project he is working on. Nothing out of the ordinary."

Lucien's mouth curved. "I see."

Alex huffed. "This isn't a nursery school. It is a place of business," she said with a frown, tapping her desk for emphasis. "And I'm not one to sugarcoat things, *especially* when it is clear that the other person has not put in very much effort."

"You don't need to defend yourself to me," Lucien said, raising his hands. "It's perfectly reasonable to have high standards."

But Alex did not take this as the intended compliment. "I hold everyone to the same standards I set for myself," she said coolly. "Now if you're done inquiring about the emotional state of my colleagues, I'd like to get started. I *do* have other appointments today."

"Right. Of course." Lucien cleared his throat. "But first please allow me to apologize for being late. I got lost on the way over, and the morning rush slowed me down even more."

Alex steepled her fingers. "I see. And where are you staying?"

"Hackney."

She sat back in her chair. "Well, no wonder. That's very far. You should have found something closer."

Lucien's jaw tightened. If only it were that simple. "I'm staying with a friend." He would not add that he couldn't bloody well afford anything closer.

But Alex simply shrugged again. "Suit yourself. But most of our activities will take place around here or closer to Mayfair."

Lucien nodded. He assumed as much. The city's elite tended to congregate in a rarified enclave of neighborhoods. Anything else was considered déclassé.

"And if you do get tired of the travel, I can find something for you. A flat in The Albany, perhaps?"

He smiled tightly. The Albany was one of the most sought after addresses for wealthy bachelors. And far, *far* out of his budget. But like hell would he admit it. "Perhaps."

She took off the spectacles and rubbed the bridge of her nose. For a very brief moment she looked tired and Lucien wondered if she had come to the office even earlier than eight. Just as he began to feel a touch of sympathy for her, Alex set the spectacles aside and straightened in her chair. Back to business.

"Now then, I've taken the liberty of drafting a proposal for you." She passed him the papers she had been reading. "Have a look. I'm sure I missed some details, but the most important pieces are there.

"Thank you," Lucien said, amazed. "You didn't need to do that."

But she swiftly brushed off his appreciation. "It's best to move things along."

Lucien held back a frown. "Right." God forbid he mistake her business acumen for something as pedestrian as, say, thoughtfulness. Then he skimmed through the pages but came to a halt at a very large number. "Is . . . is this the initial investment?"

It was more than double what he and Rene had barely managed to scrape together in Paris.

Alex looked concerned. "Is that not enough? I might have been too conservative. We can certainly increase the amount if—"

"No, no," he said quickly. "I think this is manageable."

With this kind of money, he could enact all of the ideas they hadn't been able to afford back in Paris. Though some customers had found their ragtag approach novel, it had been born out of necessity rather than design. Now he could afford things like individual menu cards and matching silverware. Even tablecloths! But then, Lucien was getting ahead of himself. He didn't have any investors yet. And this was still just a number on a piece of paper.

"Good," Alex said, relieved. "Take that home and look it over. I'm happy to hear your thoughts."

"Even if I don't sugarcoat them?"

The corner of her mouth lifted just a smidge at his teasing. "I would expect you not to." Then the smile vanished. "On Thursday evening there is a monthly salon held at Mr. Peter LaSalle's townhouse in Russell Square that is attended by a number of business-minded people. I thought it would be a good place to start making introductions."

Lucien nodded. Back to it, then. "Who is Mr. LaSalle?"

"Officially, he's an economist and lecturer at King's College, but most of his ideas come from his wife," Alex said matter-of-factly. "She studied philosophy at the Sorbonne."

Lucien smiled. He was beginning to appreciate her bone-dry sense of humor.

"And she's French, of course, so the two of you have something in common," she continued. "In any case, he's popular and usually serves good wine. There will be people there that you should meet."

"Then we should go."

"Good." She held his gaze for a moment before handing him another piece of paper. "I also thought it would be helpful if we had a contract of sorts."

Lucien gave her a skeptical look as he accepted the paper. "Is that really necessary?"

"Necessary? No," she said. "Useful? Absolutely."

Lucien began to read. It sounded straightforward enough.

Both parties agree to a minimum of two public engagements per week for a duration of six weeks, at which time the contract can be renegotiated or terminated by either party…

…Miss Atkinson will introduce Mr. Taylor to the attached list of contacts and negotiate on his behalf…

…Mr. Taylor will not engage in a romantic or physical relationship with another woman for the period outlined above.

Lucien glanced up and found Alex watching him closely. "Why does this last condition only mention me? Shouldn't it apply to you as well?"

Alex let out a sharp laugh then quickly sobered. "That won't be needed. I assure you."

But Lucien slid the contract across the desk. "Still, I'd feel better if the language included the both of us."

If she was going to make him sign something that insinuated he was a cad, then by God she'd have to do the same.

Alex stared at him for a moment. "Fine," she said primly. "I will change it."

"The rest of it works."

She avoided his gaze and focused on tapping the pages together. "Glad to hear it."

Had he upset her? "Alex—"

But before he could continue, Mr. Potts knocked on the door before entering.

Lucien shot him a glare that the man completely ignored.

"Your father is here, Miss Atkinson."

But Mr. Atkinson did not wait to be summoned and bustled into the room. "Lucien," he said with a jovial smile and stuck out his hand. "Wonderful to see you again."

Lucien stood and took his hand. "You as well, sir."

Unsurprisingly, Mr. Atkinson had a firm, confident handshake. "I'm glad you were able to come by today." Then he looked back at the hovering secretary. "That is all, Potts."

The man obediently slunk away and shut the door behind him.

"Now then," Mr. Atkinson began conspiratorially. "Has Alexandra gone over everything with you?"

Lucien stared back at him, dumbstruck. Not once had it occurred to him that Alex would tell her father, well, *everything*. Then again, why wouldn't she? After all, this arrangement involved their business. Maybe it had even been Mr. Atkinson's idea in the first place. Regardless, Lucien rather wished Alex had mentioned this to him. And it didn't seem fair that he was expected to lie to his own father while hers acted as a confidant.

"Of course I have," she said impatiently, but Mr. Atkinson didn't seem to notice.

"And you can agree to the terms?" he asked eagerly.

Lucien nodded just as Alex said, "Most of them."

Mr. Atkinson raised an eyebrow at her.

"I have to change the language a bit," she explained and shot Lucien a glance. "At Mr. Taylor's request."

"It's very minor," Lucien explained.

But Mr. Atkinson still looked apprehensive. "Good. Because Hank Jr. was in a fine snit at the party," he explained, casting Lucien a look. "And I'd hate to go back on my word about your little courtship."

Alex bowed her head. "Yes, Father."

"That won't be necessary, sir," Lucien added. Something about the way he said *little courtship* niggled at him.

Mr. Atkinson stared at the both of them rather dubiously. "But remember, nothing I say will matter if you can't convince other people."

A muscle tensed in Alex's jaw as she glanced at Lucien. "We know."

Mr. Atkinson crossed his arms. "So, what have you planned?"

"We're going to attend the LaSalle salon on Thursday."

"And?" Mr. Atkinson prompted after an uncomfortable pause. "What else?"

Alex let out an irritated huff. "Nothing. People will see us together and hear that we are courting and in the meantime I can introduce Lucien to potential investors."

"Oh, that's very romantic," Mr. Atkinson said, rolling his eyes.

"It is convenient," she said tightly. "And I am *busy*."

Lucien bit back a grimace, suddenly feeling like an imposition on her valuable time.

"No," her father drew out the word. "You are courting, remember? So you need to do something much sooner than Thursday. What about this afternoon?"

Alex balked. "I have work to do. Our meeting with Mr. Finch is at three and—"

"Oh, you don't need to be there. I can handle Finch," Mr. Atkinson said with a dismissive wave.

"But I wrote the brief and need to explain my changes," Alex insisted.

Her father's eyes softened. "My dear. I'm sure what you wrote up is brilliant as usual, but you know very well that he will accept whatever I suggest."

The subtext being that Alex's presence at the meeting was of little consequence. Lucien couldn't help feeling a flicker of sympathy for her.

Alex's body tensed but after a moment she relented with a single nod. "Fine. Just make sure you actually read it beforehand this time."

"I will. I promise." Then Mr. Atkinson turned to Lucien. "Are you free this afternoon?"

"Yes, sir."

"Good, good." Then Mr. Atkinson tilted his head. "It doesn't need to be anything elaborate, mind you. Just something where you are both seen enjoying each other's company."

Lucien couldn't help glancing at Alex, but she was too busy staring at the desktop.

"A walk around Hyde Park, perhaps?" Mr. Atkinson continued. "I'll send over a note to see that Aunt Winifred is available to chaperone."

"Don't be ridiculous," Alex huffed. "It's only a walk."

But her father shot her a chiding look. "Yes. And she'll need to be there, Alexandra, if people are to think this is real. Is that going to be a problem for you? Because if it is, we should just call the whole blasted thing off now."

Alex's dark gaze met Lucien's and he saw the flash of panic in her eyes.

"It won't be a problem," he said. Then before Lucien could think it through, he came around the desk and stood before her with his arm outstretched. She stared at his open palm for a moment before taking it. Lucien helped her to her feet and smoothly tucked her arm beside his. He gave her an encouraging smile that she hesitantly returned and together they turned to Mr. Atkinson.

Unfortunately, his frown only deepened. "Heaven help us," he muttered. "It will be a miracle if this works."

Twelve

Not long after luncheon and after her father practically shooed her out of the building, Alex reluctantly left the office—though she had every intention of returning later in the day. Her presence at the meeting with Mr. Finch might be considered de trop by the attending parties, but she had a great deal of work to catch up on if she was going to be larking about the park all afternoon.

But first she needed to collect Aunt Winifred from Park House, her family's Belgravia mansion. It had once been two connected townhouses occupying the top of a crescent, but her parents combined them to create one larger home. At the time, it had been considered rather gauche of them to do this, which Alex couldn't understand given that many of their neighbors occupied far larger and often far more gauche mansions themselves. But apparently it was perfectly acceptable if one merely inherited an obscenely ugly mansion.

The carriage pulled up outside the house and Alex sent Markham the coachman inside for Aunt Winifred. Then she pulled out Lucien's contract from her satchel and began to make the necessary revisions, grumbling to herself all the while.

She still didn't understand why he had looked so offended. After all, he was a young man in London and she knew very well what young men in London got up to. When her colleagues weren't actively avoiding her, she could usually pass by unnoticed. And so she learned an awful lot about what happened outside the office. Married, engaged, unattached—it didn't seem to matter. They all reveled in the same frivolities. Alex didn't much care as long as it didn't affect their work, but she wasn't some moon-eyed clodpoll, either. Why Lucien insisted that *she* be included in the decorum clause was another matter entirely.

Alex rarely mingled in society of any kind, and then usually only under duress. She preferred her own company most of all, but enjoyed Will, Phoebe, and her parents in measured doses. Freddie was only tolerable under very specific circumstances, usually when the rest of her family was present. Alex had lived her life that way for years now. Happily. Productively.

And, on occasion, just a little bit lonely.

She grimaced at the thought. Perhaps that was true, but it was a small price to pay for the luxury of predictability.

Alex had let her emotions rule her once and the tumult that followed had been at far too high a cost for her.

"Good afternoon, Alexandra," a voice cut through, startling her from her thoughts. "A fine day for a walk, I think."

Alex lifted her gaze as her aunt climbed into the carriage and sat down across from her.

Blast.

She had let her mind wander and had barely gotten through the first sentence of the contract. That wasn't at all like her.

"Hello, Aunt Winifred. Thank you for accompanying me today on such short notice."

"Oh, it's no trouble," she replied. "Happy to help. Though your mother is rather frazzled. The responses for Phoebe's wedding have begun to arrive and she may need our help going through the rest of them this evening."

Alex held back a sigh. The wedding wasn't for another three months and she was already sick to death of hearing about it. "Of course," she said dutifully.

So much for returning to the office, then. Perhaps she could send Phoebe and Margrave an invoice for all the working hours she had missed as a wedding present. Only as a joke, of course.

"What is that?" Aunt Winifred asked, pointing to the contract in Alex's hand.

"Nothing. Work," she said, hurriedly stuffing it back into her satchel.

"My goodness. Do you take it everywhere with you?"

Alex stiffened a little at the disapproval in her aunt's tone. "My work doesn't end when I leave the office, Aunt."

"I'm not sure your father even lives by that dictate," she said with a laugh.

"Yes, well, he doesn't have to anymore," Alex grumbled.

Aunt Winifred's gaze softened a little. "He owes a great deal to you, doesn't he?"

Alex looked out the window as London passed by in a soot-tinged whirl. "We owe it to each other," she replied honestly.

She very well knew that most men in his position would not have let their daughters step foot inside their place of business, let alone work there. Yet Philip Atkinson had only too readily brought her into his world after she had left Oxford. But though Alex might be been allowed to come to the office, meet with his mediocre employees, and turn their proposals into something that would actually turn a profit, it never felt like enough. Even the men she worked with didn't quite take her seriously. They always seemed to find a way to undermine her suggestions, if not to her face then at least to each other. Or convince themselves that it had actually been her father who had such brilliant insights rather than Alex herself. *Never* Alex.

She knew very well that if any of them had found themselves in such a position they would have left, in loud protest, in fact. But Alex didn't have that luxury. For there was nowhere else for her to go as no other firm would hire her. So instead, she worked harder for longer and found some degree of satisfaction in that.

Until she came up with a plan to win the board's unanimous approval as her father's heir and take over the company herself one day. And for that she would write a dozen decorum clauses if it got her what she wanted.

Aunt Winifred cleared her throat.

Alex blinked. Her aunt had said something but her mind had wandered *again*. "Sorry?"

"I was saying that I don't understand why you couldn't come inside the house and change," Aunt Winifred began. "As you have several lovely walking gowns in your possession."

Alex was tempted to ask exactly *how* her aunt knew this, but the answer would likely only annoy her. Aunt Winifred and her mother had probably taken an inventory of her wardrobe in preparation for this blasted courtship business.

"Because there wasn't any time," Alex replied. "And walking gowns are the stupidest thing I've ever heard of, given that I am perfectly able to walk in what I am wearing now."

Aunt Winifred raised a brow. "You very well know that the

purpose of a walking gown is to show off your figure to the greatest advantage while allowing for ease of movement during a promenade." Her disapproving gaze skimmed down her figure. "Alas, I cannot say the same of what you are currently wearing."

Alex lifted her chin. "I don't care."

"But what about Mr. Taylor?"

"He saw me in this earlier and didn't seem to mind."

Aunt Winifred huffed. "Well, he certainly wouldn't *tell* you. My goodness, Alexandra. You have a lot to learn about men."

"I doubt that, given I work with them every day," she replied dryly.

As she hoped, Aunt Winifred didn't have a response to that remark and they traveled the rest of the way to Hyde Park in blessed silence.

They were to meet Lucien by the monstrous Albert Memorial and then walk along the path by the Serpentine. It was a popular route that should give them plenty of time to be observed by the gossipmongers of the ton. The carriage came to a stop and they disembarked not far from the memorial. As they walked along the pavement, Alex spotted Lucien first. He was idly pacing around, hands shoved in his trouser pockets. He hadn't yet noticed them, so Alex took the opportunity to look him over freely. Lucien still wore that brown town suit from earlier—the one that fit him remarkably well, though it was just a bit too short. She was curious when he had acquired it, given that his evening suit had not been of equal quality. But though Alex did not move about much in society, she very well knew that it was *not* the sort of thing one could discuss with a gentleman, so her curiosity would remain unsated.

"Oh, there he is," Aunt Winifred cut in. "My, he is looking *very* well today."

Alex made a noncommittal hum, though her eyes never left his figure.

He looked directly at her then, as if he had sensed her presence, and as their eyes met Alex felt a strange jolt of awareness, even at this distance. He smiled and raised a hand in greeting and Alex did the same, though she felt horribly awkward, like an old forgotten automaton in need of oil.

As they approached, her aunt leaned in by her ear. "There is a little path not far from here that offers some privacy," she murmured. "I will conveniently get lost, if you like."

"No," Alex gritted out, keeping her smile. "That will not be necessary."

Aunt Winifred huffed. "Oh, you are no fun," she teased.

The comment had been playfully meant, and yet Alex couldn't help bristling. It was true, after all. Freddie was fun. Phoebe was fun too, when she wasn't worried about that school of hers. But Alex? No one would ever call her fun. And even when she *was* having fun, people criticized her for not having fun in the right way. In *their* way. She was told to smile. To talk more. To laugh louder. Since continually failing to meet other people's expectations was exhausting, Alex removed herself from such situations as much as possible. But as she stared at the handsome young man waiting for her, Alex understood that she wouldn't have that luxury anymore. And a pit formed in her stomach.

"Are you all right, my dear?" Aunt Winifred murmured.

Alex gave herself a shake, but the feeling that had begun to coil in her belly did not dissipate. "Yes. Only I…I…" she struggled to explain herself. Luckily, her aunt's eyes softened and she patted her arm.

"It's perfectly natural to feel nervous."

Nervous.

Alex nearly laughed. That was it. She was nervous. And more than a little worried that she wouldn't be able to do this. Before she could check the impulse, she covered her aunt's hand with her own and gave it a squeeze. "I'm glad you're here," she said honestly. Just as a look of surprise crossed her aunt's face, Alex turned to Lucien. "Good afternoon. I see you managed to find the place," she quipped.

Lucien laughed. "Yes, and I only got lost once on the way. I suppose that counts as progress."

Alex's smile grew as they stared at each other for a moment. His eyes really were the most beautiful shade. In this light they looked more green than hazel. Her aunt cleared her throat then and Alex blinked. Goodness, she had actually *forgotten* about Aunt Winifred. "Oh, my apologies," Alex said abruptly. "Do you remember my aunt, Mrs. Winifred Bailey? Perhaps you met at the party the other night."

Lucien took Aunt Winifred's offered hand and bowed with perfect politeness. "Yes, we did. A pleasure to see you again, Mrs. Bailey."

"You as well, Mr. Taylor," her aunt preened. "And don't worry. I won't interfere too much. I know how young people are these days." Then she turned to Alex. "Shall we move on to the park?"

Alex nodded and together they walked toward the nearest entrance. After a moment, Aunt Winifred pried Alex's hand off of her own and tilted her head toward Lucien, who was a few steps ahead. Alex had been gripping her aunt's hand rather tightly and immediately released her.

"Sorry," she murmured.

"It's fine," her aunt gently replied. "But go on. I'll hang back and give you a bit of privacy."

Alex swallowed and nodded, then she moved next to Lucien, who waited for her by the entrance. She flashed him a small smile as she was beset by nerves once more, but Lucien looked perfectly at ease as he offered her his arm.

"Shall we?"

Alex stared at it for a moment as the strangest sensation washed over her. It felt as if she stood at the edge of some great precipice and, once she stepped forward, she would not be able to return.

She glanced up at Lucien and found him watching her intently. Briefly, she wondered if he felt it too but something in his gaze set her at ease.

And then, she took it.

Thirteen

$\mathcal{L}$ucien and Alex walked along in companiable silence for a few minutes. He sensed that Alex was far more comfortable behind her desk than on his arm, so rather than force her to talk, he let her take the lead. Meanwhile, he was perfectly happy to enjoy their quiet stroll. It was a lovely afternoon. One of those rare moments when the English weather was close to perfect. A light breeze ruffled his hair and Lucien closed his eyes and tilted his head toward the sky, enjoying the faintly warming rays of autumn sun.

"What did you do after you left the office?"

Lucien blinked at the abrupt question and glanced down at Alex, but she was still looking ahead. "I went to the British Museum."

She turned toward him in surprise. "What did you see?"

"The Anglo-Roman Gallery. I didn't have time for much more than that. I've been wanting to visit since I was a boy, but I never had the chance before now."

Her mouth curved in a small, delighted smile. "I'm glad you were able to go. That's one of my favorite places," she added shyly.

"It is?"

Alex nodded. "I try to visit at least once a week." Then she turned back toward the path and for one wild moment Lucien considered asking her to keep looking at him. He liked when she looked at him, he realized.

"It's quiet," she continued hesitantly. "I like that. I like that I can simply go and look at things and no one expects me to talk. I can just…be."

Something twinged in his chest at this admission. "Yes, it seems like an excellent place to do just that."

Alex turned to him once more then, her dark eyes full of surprise, and the twinge deepened. She swallowed and his eyes were drawn to the movement of her pale throat. "Perhaps we…we could go there. Together."

Lucien forced his gaze to meet her own and nodded. "I would like that," he answered honestly.

But Alex frowned and looked away once more. "No one would see us there, though. Not the right sort, anyway."

It took a moment for her meaning to penetrate his woolly brain. *The courtship. Right.*

Lucien had forgotten about that.

We could still go, you and I.

He had just gathered the courage to say those words when two finely dressed ladies emerged from a curve on the path just up ahead. Alex subtly stiffened beside him but she said nothing as they continued on. After a few more steps, the two women took notice of them and whispered to each other. As they grew closer, Lucien could see that one of them was staring at Alex in recognition.

"I *thought* that was you, Alexandra," she said with a broad smile that reminded Lucien of a tigress. Or perhaps an eel. She wasn't pretty, exactly, but she carried herself with the kind of confidence Lucien had recognized among the very wealthy.

"Hello, Mildred," Alex replied evenly.

"Oh, you know it's *Millie*," the woman said with a humorless laugh. "Millie Henderson now, actually. And this is my cousin Mrs. Bates." She waved a hand toward the mousy woman beside her.

Alex nodded in greeting and then the two women turned expectantly to Lucien. "This is Mr. Taylor," Alex said after a moment. "And my aunt, Mrs. Bailey." By then her aunt had come beside them. They all exchanged polite greetings, and while Alex's expression remained neutral, the tension never quite left her body.

"And you are still Miss *Atkinson?*" Mrs. Henderson asked, emphasizing her last name with brows raised.

"Yes," Alex said.

When it was clear that she would say nothing more, Mrs. Henderson addressed her cousin. "Alexandra and I were at Oxford together. Though I left as soon as Mr. Henderson proposed. Ghastly place, Lady Margaret Hall, though I suppose it was better than Somerville. Filled with nothing but godless *bluestockings*," she said, referencing Oxford's other women's college. She then turned to Alex with a pinched look. "But you had a much more interesting experience, if I recall."

Something about her tone set Lucien on edge, but Alex's expression didn't change. "I found it very educational. Especially once I moved over to Somerville."

"Oh," Mrs. Henderson said, surprised. "That must have been after I left."

"Yes."

The woman let out a soft huff at this but said nothing more. Then they forced out a bit of small talk before the quota for propriety was reached.

"Well, it was *lovely* to see you," Mrs. Henderson said at last. "Perhaps we will meet again this season?"

"Perhaps."

Before things could turn even more awkward, Mrs. Bailey made some excuse and they continued on down the path.

"Well, that was unpleasant," her aunt remarked once they were out of earshot. "What on earth happened between you, Alex?"

"Nothing," she said far too quickly. "Mildred is a silly woman. She only bothered with Oxford in the first place to make her beau jealous or some other nonsense and caused naught but trouble while she was there."

Her aunt arched a brow. "What *kind* of trouble?"

Alex's lips pursed. "The distracting kind," she said firmly. Then she moved ahead of them, signaling that the subject was closed.

Mrs. Bailey stared at her retreating back with a look of concern mixed with irritation. "Are you open to a little friendly advice, Mr. Taylor?"

"Certainly," he replied.

"I've never met anyone quite like our Alexandra. I'm sure you could say the same." Lucien nodded at her expectant look. Then her aunt sighed a little. "That girl carries so much on those slim shoulders of hers and hides it all from the world. She is a tough nut to crack, to be sure. And not many are up to the task." Lucien couldn't help glancing at Alex's stiff form marching up ahead. "But I truly believe it is worth the effort," her aunt finished.

"As do I," Lucien replied, mainly because it was the kind of thing a suitor would say. But as her aunt gave him an approving smile and gestured for them to follow in Alex's wake, Lucien recognized that it was also the truth. Not for *him*, of course. But someday some other man might manage to storm the gates that surrounded Alexandra Atkinson. And the rewards would likely be very great indeed.

⁂

After that uncomfortable meeting with Mildred Henderson, Alex let her aunt carry the conversation while they continued down the footpath. As Aunt Winifred peppered Lucien with questions about his time in Paris while also relating her own experiences in the city, Alex couldn't stop thinking of her brief conversation with Mildred. It had been the knowing look in her former classmate's eye that set her particularly on edge.

And you are still Miss Atkinson?

Undoubtedly her aunt and Lucien had assumed it was a dig at her spinster status, but Alex knew the truth. Mildred was needling her quite deliberately about something very different.

Not Mrs. Chisolm.

For though she may not have completed her course of studies at Oxford, Mildred had been there long enough to share a tutor with Alex. And long enough to notice that Alex developed something of a tender for Benjamin Chisolm. Luckily, the idea that her feelings would ever be returned by such a dashing young man was too far-fetched for even Mildred to believe. So the exact truth of the matter was safe. For now. But it was the closest her secret had come to being revealed. And Alex didn't much care for that.

As they grew closer to their starting point, Aunt Winifred not so subtly mentioned a tearoom close by but Alex had reached her limit for socializing for the day.

"I'm afraid I need to return to the office," she said.

"Now?" Aunt Winifred frowned in disapproval. "You don't mean to say you have more work to do at this time of day?"

Given that it couldn't be later than half past three in the afternoon, Alex failed to grasp her point.

"That is exactly what I mean." Alex then turned away as her aunt's frown deepened and addressed Lucien. "You are still coming to the LaSalles' on Thursday?" The question came out far brusquer than was polite, but Lucien simply nodded.

"I will be at Park House at seven thirty."

"Good. I think it will be a productive evening."

Now Aunt Winifred was staring as if she had two heads, which Alex did her best to ignore.

"I look forward to it," Lucien replied.

Alex had the distinct sense he was fighting back a smile, though she failed to understand the source of his amusement. "Would you like a ride?" She gestured up ahead to their waiting carriage.

"No, thank you. I'd prefer to walk so I can get my bearings a little more."

"A fine idea."

Lucien then bid good-bye to Aunt Winifred and tipped his hat to Alex before striding off in the opposite direction. It wasn't until her aunt cleared her throat that Alex realized she had been staring at his back.

Once they were safely ensconced in the carriage, Aunt Winifred gave her a sympathetic look.

"I think we should spend some time reviewing the particulars of courtship etiquette, my dear," she said gently.

"Why? Mr. Taylor behaved like a perfect gentleman."

Aunt Winifred rolled her eyes. "Not him. *You.*"

"Oh." Alex slumped in her seat. "Was I being rude?"

It was an accusation her sisters made sometimes, usually when Alex was simply being honest about their terrible behavior. But if that was the case here, she would feel bad.

"Well, not exactly." Her aunt hesitated. "But you could take a greater interest in him. Gentlemen *like* when you ask them questions, you know. So they can talk about their accomplishments. But you seemed distracted."

Alex lowered her eyes. "I'm sorry."

"Was it seeing that Mrs. Henderson?"

Though she longed to deny it, Alex nodded reluctantly. "I wasn't prepared."

When she looked up again, her aunt was giving her a fond smile. "Yes, well, do keep in mind that might happen quite a bit now that you are moving in society more." Alex failed to suppress her shudder.

Much to her mother's dismay, after Alex had finished at Oxford she refused to have a season in favor of working at her father's firm right away. Thus, she rarely mixed with members of the ton apart from events hosted by her parents—and *they* were snubbed by the most exclusive circles on account of her father being born to a mere gentleman and not another aristocrat.

"But you shouldn't let it bother you quite so much," her aunt continued. "Don't give them your attention. There is power in preparation."

Alex let out a sigh. "What should I do instead?"

Her aunt looked thoughtful. "Whenever I encounter someone I don't particularly like, I ask after them first. Then once they've finished, I say I need to go speak with someone else who is usually across the room." She flashed a sly smile. "I find it easier to end the conversation if I start it. Then I walk away and move on with my evening."

"Really? That works?"

Her aunt shrugged. "Well enough. And it gets easier with practice. But you also have me. Perhaps we should make up a signal and I will come rescue you."

Alex perked up at the idea. "What kind of signal?"

Her aunt tilted her head in thought. "It should be something you wouldn't ordinarily do."

"I can pat the back of my hair." Alex then did the motion. Normally she never bothered to check her appearance once she left her bedroom.

"That is a good one," Aunt Winifred said with a decided nod. "I will keep an eye out during our next outing."

"And I will practice starting conversations. And asking Mr. Taylor questions," she added.

"And *listening*," her aunt replied.

Alex bit her lip and nodded. This was getting to be quite a bit more work than she had been prepared for. But as the carriage pulled up to Atkinson Enterprises and she remembered all that was at stake, Alex was filled with a renewed determination to succeed.

Her aunt pulled back the curtain and gave the building a wary look. "Don't work too hard, my dear. You'll overtax yourself."

Alex laughed as the coachman opened the door. "That hasn't happened yet, Aunt Winifred."

As she stepped down, her aunt muttered something that sounded vaguely like *Don't press your luck*. But when she looked back Aunt Winifred simply waved good-bye. Then the carriage door shut and pulled back into traffic, while Alex was left standing alone on the pavement.

Fourteen

A few days later, Alex once again submitted to the indignities of courtship by allowing her mother and aunt to offer their opinions on her wardrobe. The LaSalle salon was that evening and Lucien was downstairs in the parlor with their father. Alex hadn't seen him since their walk in Hyde Park and thinking of him waiting for her just a few floors below made her stomach flutter.

Alex usually attended the salon on her own, but tonight she needed a chaperone to help sell the legitimacy of her courtship with Lucien. Unsurprisingly, her aunt had not been very enthusiastic about attending a salon dedicated to innovative business ideas, so Father offered to come instead.

"Honestly, darling," her mother said gently, "I think the green suits you best. Much better than that brown thing you were considering."

"Yes, why on *earth* would you even own a gown in such a color?" Aunt Winifred demanded from her spot on the chaise longue in Mother's dressing room.

"Because I like it," Alex grumbled as she tugged on the bodice of her gown. "And at least I could *breathe* in the brown thing."

Her mother let out a dismissive tsk and pushed her hands away. "If you're being this dramatic, I'd say you can breathe perfectly fine.

And stop pulling or you'll tear a stitch and Walters will have to mend that as well."

From her place on the floor, Walters grimaced. She was busy fixing the spot where Alex had ungracefully stepped on the hem earlier.

"Sorry, Walters." Her mother's maid grunted in response. "Could I at least loosen the corset a little?"

Her mother looked appalled by the suggestion. "Whatever for? All you're going to do is sit in a chair and talk about the stock exchange or whatnot."

Alex resisted the urge to correct her. "I'd still like to be comfortable."

"It will ruin the shape," Aunt Winifred pronounced and her mother nodded gravely.

"I don't care," she gritted out.

A perfect figure wouldn't do her much good when she collapsed in the middle of Mr. LaSalle's parlor.

Walters let out a long-suffering sigh. "If you insist, Miss Atkinson."

She might as well have said *It's your funeral.*

Half an hour later, Alex headed downstairs in a slightly looser corset. Though she hadn't noticed any negligible difference in the shape of her gown, Aunt Winifred and her mother acted as if she were now wearing a burlap sack.

They entered the parlor where her father, Lucien, and Freddie were gathered by the hearth. As Alex watched her sister animatedly speak to Lucien while wearing a fashionably cut soft blue gown to great advantage, she was suddenly very glad she hadn't worn *the brown thing.*

But it was the smile on Lucien's face that caused something to tighten in her chest. Something that could not be blamed on her corset. She had allowed herself to forget the very important fact that Lucien was *in love* with her sister. It was an inexcusable oversight.

"Good evening, all," her mother trilled as she glided over to the group. "Freddie, I thought you were going to the Egyptian Hall with the Ericsons this evening to see that fortune-teller."

"Medium. And I am, but I didn't want to miss Lucien," she said with a fond glance in his direction and not at all cowed by her mother's pointed tone. "Mrs. Ericson is simply mad for seances."

Alex realized she was gripping her hands together and forced them apart before plastering a smile on her face.

"Good evening, Miss Alexandra," Lucien said as he turned to her with a short bow. For reasons she couldn't begin to understand, her brain decided that was the ideal moment for the memory of Lucien's quite naked and well-formed backside to pop into her mind.

It didn't matter that her corset had been loosened. She still couldn't breathe. He was wearing the same suit as the night of her mother's birthday party. Some people would be appalled by this faux pas, but Alex didn't care. He looked splendid.

"Good evening," Alex rasped. She couldn't help standing a little straighter as his gaze skimmed appreciatively over her figure.

"We had better go," her father said, checking his pocket watch. Then he turned to his wife. "Have a good night, my dear. Where are you ladies off to this evening?"

"The Foxes are having a little soiree. But I have half a mind to accompany Freddie instead," her mother said with a cross look, to which Freddie simply rolled her eyes.

In Alex's opinion, her sister had been given far too much freedom as a young girl and their parents had long ago given up on any meaningful attempts to rein in her behavior. Granted, Freddie hadn't ever gotten into *too* much trouble—or at least had the good sense to be discreet about it—but now her years of carefree carousing had begun to catch up to her. She was largely considered a flibbertigibbet, and if this engagement with Hank Jr. did not come to fruition, there was a chance she could end up on the shelf right beside Alex.

Unless Lucien steps in.

And why wouldn't he? Especially if Alex made a success of him, which she had every reason to expect he would be. Alex felt her hands tighten again but she forced them to remain by her side as they said their good-byes and exited the parlor.

"You look nice, my dear," her father said offhandedly as he escorted her down the hall to the carriage.

The compliment took her by surprise. "Thank you."

She couldn't remember the last time he said something like that to her. Most of their conversations revolved around the business or whatever irritating debacle one of her sisters found themselves in. For the last few years, Phoebe had been the biggest thorn in his side but they had reached an understanding of sorts over the summer and her engagement to a duke certainly helped.

Now it was Freddie causing him the most grief. Though hopefully this little charade would firmly put an end to that.

"Lucien told me he's staying in Hackney," her father said conversationally as they exited the house. "We could find him something closer, couldn't we? The Albany, perhaps?"

Alex nodded. "Yes. I thought the very same."

"And *I* said I am perfectly fine where I am," Lucien chimed in good-naturedly. "Though I do appreciate the offer."

"Suit yourself," her father said with a shrug. "But let me know if you change your mind. Ah, here's Markham."

Just then, their coachman alighted from the carriage and opened the door. For a moment, Alex wondered if this was at all awkward for him and Lucien. Markham had worked under Mr. Taylor until his recent illness and had enjoyed a promotion of sorts at the expense of the man's health. Would they have even attempted this charade if Lucien's father was still head coachman? Everything would have been decidedly more complicated if that had been the case...

But then Lucien held out his hand and her thoughts scattered.

"Thank you," she murmured as her palm slid against his. Even through the silk of her glove, she could feel the heat radiating off his skin and instinctively shivered.

Lucien frowned in concern as he helped her into the carriage. "Are you cold?"

Before she could assure him that she was fine, her father climbed in behind them and took the seat beside Alex.

As the carriage rocked into motion, Alex turned toward the window. Usually she loved the look of Belgravia in the evening, but tonight the street scenes passed by in a blur of gaslight while her father and Lucien made idle conversation beside her. When they finally turned onto the LaSalles' street, her hands tightened on her lap and her heart fluttered in her chest.

For God's sake, she was still nervous. Well, she wouldn't stand for it.

"Alex." Her father gave her an encouraging smile as the carriage rocked to a stop. "It's going to be fine."

"I know," she said hastily, then flashed him a brittle smile that didn't convince either of them.

Then he addressed Lucien. "Ready for the gauntlet?"

"As ready as I'll ever be," he said with a nervous laugh. Then he looked back at Alex. "Let's get you inside."

Her father chuckled and clapped his hands. "That's the spirit. No sense in dillydallying. Onward!"

They had arrived fashionably late, as her father always preferred to make an entrance, and were led into the drawing room by a towering butler to find the gathering in full swing.

Small groups of people were deep in discussion, some more animated than others, while various gadgets and mock-ups were displayed throughout the space.

There were a few other women in attendance, including Mr. LaSalle's wife, Marguerite.

She immediately spotted them and approached. "I was hoping you would come this evening, Alexandra. And you brought friends!"

Alex then submitted to Marguerite's cheek kisses, which she only allowed because the woman was terribly French and she didn't like to make a scene. "Yes. This is my father, Mr. Atkinson, and Mr. Lucien Taylor. He's just returned from Paris."

Marguerite looked delighted and after greeting her father, began speaking to Lucien in French, most of which was spoken so rapidly, Alex could barely keep up. But Lucien smiled and responded in kind. Alex had never heard him speak French before, and though she was hardly an expert, to her ears he sounded fluent. It was rather attractive.

"I'll go speak to LaSalle," her father murmured by her ear. "You talk Lucien up."

Alex shot him a bewildered look. "But what am I to do?"

Her father arched a brow. "Stay here and be *wooed*." Then he strode across the room, letting out a booming "LaSalle!" as he went.

Alex huffed and returned her attention to Marguerite and Lucien, who were now chattering on like a couple of old friends. Marguerite let out a laugh and threw back her head of dark blonde hair. She was considered very fashionable, but Alex had never paid much attention to her clothing, as Marguerite LaSalle was quite brilliant. Much more so than her celebrated husband, in Alex's opinion. She also harbored a suspicion that Marguerite wrote most of her husband's papers—or at least heavily edited them.

But tonight Alex couldn't ignore her hostess's dazzling cornflower blue gown, nor the way it set off her sapphire eyes—eyes which lingered rather long on Lucien.

Though she would never admit it to her mother, once again Alex was relieved that she hadn't worn the brown thing, otherwise she would have faded into the wallpaper. Now at least she stood a chance of competing with the furniture.

Marguerite managed to tear her gaze away from Lucien long enough to address Alex. "I'm so glad you brought your *friend*," she said, putting a peculiar emphasis on the word.

"Yes," Alex replied. "We have been spending a good deal of time together since his return."

Marguerite raised a knowing eyebrow and looked between them. "Have you? Well, that is wonderful to hear," she said with a genuine smile before turning back to Lucien. "I've long wondered what man would be smart enough to pursue our Alexandra."

Alex's cheeks heated, though perhaps she should not be so surprised at Marguerite's bold comment.

But Lucien appeared nonplussed and merely smiled. "I can only hope I'm smart enough to keep her."

Marguerite grinned. "Oh, I *do* like him," she murmured to Alex and patted her arm before moving on to make the rounds.

I can only hope I'm smart enough to keep her.

It was just a line, but a dashed good one.

Alex cleared her throat. Her cheeks must be crimson by now. "The entire room will know before the evening is over."

And soon the rest of London.

"It's that easy?"

She glanced up at Lucien. He was scanning the room so she let her gaze wander over his profile. "You saw Mrs. LaSalle's reaction."

Lucien turned to her. "She seemed happy for you."

"And also surprised," Alex added. "No doubt Mildred Henderson thought the very same. 'Alexandra Atkinson has finally found a man willing to put up with her,'" she said, imitating the voice of a nosy matron. "It will be the story of the season."

But Lucien only stared at her for a moment, his expression grave. "Is that how you see yourself?"

Her jaw tightened at the softness that had crept into his voice. The last thing she wanted was his pity. She turned away before his eyes could turn limpid. "Come," she said briskly. "Let's look at the displays."

"As you wish."

Fifteen

As Alex led him across the room, Lucien noticed their progress being tracked by a number of eyes. Perhaps she hadn't been indulging in a bit of self-pity after all if simply escorting her to an event garnered this much attention.

Even though Alex had a well-earned reputation for being prickly, this reaction seemed a bit extreme as she was still an attractive, intelligent woman. If this were a real courtship and not a sham based on mutual gratification, he *would* be a lucky man. Hypothetically speaking, of course.

The first display showcased plans for a portable printing press. Alex quickly scanned the documents and frowned. "Hmm."

"What is it?"

She tapped a finger to her chin in consideration. "I don't think this will work."

Lucien stared at the plans but they didn't make any sense to him. He might as well be trying to read hieroglyphics. "Why do you say that?"

She pointed to something that looked like a very small Ferris wheel, or possibly a millstone. "There are far too many pieces here. It will take a number of days just to get it up and running—and that's assuming nothing is lost. What's the use of calling something 'portable' if it is so arduous to put together? Better to work on making it more convenient first, I think."

Lucien furrowed his brow and pretended to have the faintest idea what she was talking about. "Hmm…"

While he tried to formulate a response, a man came up beside her. He was tall and broad-shouldered, with thick, dark hair, and held himself with the kind of innate confidence Lucien had worked very hard to master these last few years.

"Because the inventor hopes that the benefits of such a machine will far outweigh the numerous inconveniences," he said smoothly. Alex glanced over at him and immediately stiffened.

"Or so I've heard," the man added with a charming smile before extending a hand to Lucien. "Hello, I'm Benjamin Chisolm."

"Lucien Taylor."

He squinted in recognition and Lucien couldn't help thinking the reaction seemed forced, like the man was playing a part. "Ah. People have been talking about your supper club. Marvelous idea. They're very popular in New York. I'd love to speak to you about it further, if that's all right." Mr. Chisolm gave Alex an imploring look.

She stared back at him in frosty silence. Lucien wasn't sure if she disliked the man or did not know him from Adam—either was a possibility.

"Of course," she finally said with a terse nod. "How are you?" Though the question itself was friendly enough, Alex's tone was almost accusatory.

Mr. Chisolm looked nonplussed. "Very well. And yourself?"

She lifted her chin. "Never better." Then she released Lucien's arm. "Please excuse me. There is someone I must speak with."

Mr. Chisolm stared after her with a half smile as she stiffly walked across the room and shook his head. "Miss Atkinson doesn't change, does she?"

Before Lucien could answer, the man let out a heavy sigh. "We met at Oxford. I was her tutor, actually."

"Oh."

Then Mr. Chisolm's smile turned rueful. "But she went and fell in love with me, poor thing."

Oh.

"Wasn't the first time that happened, of course. You can imagine what those university girls are like," he said with a chuckle. "Most of them spend all their time with their noses in a book. If a man simply *looks* their way, they think it's true love." He chuckled again, but Lucien frowned. That didn't sound at all like Alex. "Inevitably, I had to let her down," Mr. Chisolm blithely continued. "And she refused to have anything to do with me after that. Then I went off to New York and only just returned last week. But that's all ancient history. I did have a feeling she would be here tonight, though," he added with a knowing little smile that set Lucien's teeth on edge.

"Now then," he said brightly, as if he hadn't just relayed highly private and rather embarrassing information about her to someone he had only just met. "Are you planning to open a supper club here in London? If you're looking for investors, I'm interested."

"Uh, yes," Lucien stammered. Mr. Chisolm then peppered him with questions, which Lucien answered rotely while his mind spun.

Alex had been in *love* with this man? And actually declared herself to him?

It sounded far-fetched, to put it mildly. But then, he was

handsome, charming, and clearly successful. If she were to fall in love with anyone, Lucien supposed it would be with a man like him.

"You won't mention I said anything about our past to her, will you?" Mr. Chisolm asked with the barest hint of concern. "She's clearly still upset and I wouldn't want to embarrass her."

"No," Lucien replied. "Of course not." Though it seemed the man could have avoided that altogether by not saying anything in the first place.

Mr. Chisolm grinned and patted his shoulder, already moving on. "Good lad. Send a note to me at my club, Bedivere's, and we can set up a time to meet next week and discuss things further."

Lucien nodded. "Absolutely."

As Mr. Chisolm left him, Lucien looked around for Alex, but she had disappeared. Mr. Atkinson was deep in conversation with a few older men, so Lucien wandered about feeling like a lost lamb until Mrs. LaSalle gestured to a set of French doors at the back of the room that opened out onto a terrace. "She's out there. I'll keep the others away so you can have some privacy. Enjoy yourselves," she said with a wink, then glided away.

Lucien swallowed and headed outside. Alex stood alone in a dark corner with her arms crossed, staring out at the back garden. Every rigid inch of her bearing seemed designed to ward off others, but Lucien wasn't deterred.

It made her seem less intimidating, to know that even she wasn't immune to youthful romantic impulses and had experienced real heartbreak.

Heartbreak that still clearly affected her years later.

Alex didn't look at him as he approached. "Did you have a productive chat with Mr. Chisolm?"

Lucien paused for a moment, surprised. But then, Alex would have eyes in the back of her head. "He wants to meet at his club next week," he replied as he came beside her.

"Is that so?" she said flatly.

"If you don't want me to, I won't."

She shot him a challenging look. "Why wouldn't I want you to meet with him?"

Lucien stared back at her. "I don't know," he said carefully before gathering his courage. "Do…do you not like him?"

Her shoulders tensed as she huffed a laugh and turned back to the garden. "That hardly matters."

"It does to me," he said after a moment.

"Well, it *shouldn't*." Then Alex whirled on him. "This is business, Lucien," she said with exasperation. "And I expect you to make decisions based on what is best for you without regard for me. Because that is how this works," she added sharply. Her cheeks were flushed and her eyes bright with anger. It was the closest she had ever come to completely losing her cool demeanor. And Lucien was filled with a sudden, overwhelming desire to see that. Very much.

"I understand."

She held his gaze for another moment as the fire faded from her eyes. "Good. We should circle the room once more. Mr. Chisolm isn't your only option."

"He isn't yours, either," Lucien murmured.

She raised an eyebrow. "What's that?"

Lucien pressed his lips together. He didn't want to embarrass her, truly. But if Alex was still carrying around that man's rejection and letting it define her worth, she deserved to know the truth.

"I only meant that you have other options as well. Romantically speaking."

Her dark eyes hardened. "Did he say something to you about me?" Her voice was low and dangerous. He suddenly wished to take the words back, but his hesitation was answer enough. "Benjamin Chisolm is a fine enough businessman," she began. "But you would do well not to trust him with anything else. Furthermore, I would appreciate it if you refrained from making comments about my life, romantic or otherwise. I neither want nor need your sympathy. You are here to perform a service, and I in kind."

Lucien inhaled deeply in a bid to tamp down his frustration. This woman was *impossible*. "My apologies. I didn't mean to offend you with my concern."

If Alex picked up on his sarcasm, she didn't acknowledge it. She simply continued on, forcing Lucien to trail behind her like a chastised puppy. Her complete disinterest in developing even the slightest rapport unexpectedly stung. Perhaps she really was the heartless ice queen everyone claimed. Benjamin Chisolm had gotten the best of her, and now he was left with the scraps.

Upon returning to the drawing room, he automatically held out his arm.

You are here to perform a service.

And by God he would do it. Alex glanced at him and her eyes flashed with surprise before she dutifully slid her arm through his. A kind of instinctual regret began to well inside him, but Lucien pushed the feeling aside and kept his expression impassive. He would perform his role just as she demanded. Nothing more.

෨

Alex spent the rest of the evening in a terrible mood while doing her best to stay as far away from Benjamin as possible. Yet she couldn't help sneaking surreptitious glances at him every chance she got. Objectively, she understood that he was attractive, with his dark hair and above-average height. But there was a sleekness to him now that hadn't been present when they first met back at Oxford. Chisolm family tradition dictated that he, the third son of a baronet, enter the church. But Benjamin developed an interest in the moral sciences, particularly economics. The baronet had not supported his son's academic about-face and cut off his already meager allowance. When Alex met him, he had been a poor student struggling to pay his own way by working as a tutor. Yet he seemed terribly impressed by her immediately, even when she boldly questioned his worship of Adam Smith:

He insists that the free market works best when fueled by the unrestrained pursuit of self-interest, yet he needed to live with his mother for years in order to finish his masterwork.

Benjamin had paused and raised an eyebrow. *I'm afraid I don't follow you, Miss Atkinson.*

Well, I doubt she cooked his food or washed his socks purely out of her own self-interest, Alex had tossed off. *His success was built on the back of someone else's sacrifice. Someone who loved him and, arguably, believed in what he was doing. We can't all live as Mr. Smith, because someone has to do the washing up.*

Alex had fully expected him to dismiss her out of hand, but he only stared at her, while a slow smile took over. That had been the start of it. The connection between them was as undeniable as it was bewildering. But now the qualities that had once drawn her to him seemed snuffed out entirely.

If they were ever there in the first place.

It was an unsettling thought. Alex could allow that she had made a youthful mistake. But it was far more difficult to accept that she had been entirely taken in by this man whose behavior now read as so obviously false to her, even from across the room. It was as if he was looking for something to manipulate in every person he spoke to. Had he always been that way or was this a characteristic born out of necessity? She couldn't for the life of her remember. Nor why she had given him so very much of herself in the first place.

It had been the actions of an entirely different person. A lonely girl away from home and unused to the attentions of men. Alex hated that she had been such a cliché, but there was nothing to be done about it now. She had made her choices and paid a price.

What remained to be seen was what on earth he was doing back in London and at the LaSalles' salon, of all places. They had an agreement. Granted, it had been five years since then, but the terms had been very clear.

I never want to see you again in any *capacity.*

Don't flatter yourself, Alexandra, he bit off. *You aren't the sort of woman men cross oceans for.*

She scowled even harder as Benjamin laughed too loudly at something Mr. Wright had said—and he wasn't very funny. Perhaps the money had finally run out, or the packet of ideas and letters of introduction she had given him were lost. Well, if that was the case it was not her problem. Alex had done everything within her reach at the time to send him off with every advantage. If he hadn't amassed a sizable fortune by now, that was due to poor planning on his part.

But he could still make demands of you.

A few weeks before, Alex wouldn't have been the least bit cowed by any possible threats. How quickly things changed.

"Are you all right?" Lucien asked by her side and Alex forced her gaze away from her former suitor.

"Yes," she said, managing something close to a smile. "Only I'm afraid I'm more tired than I realized."

"Well, you did spend all day at the office," he remarked.

It was true enough, but that didn't excuse her behavior. She didn't deserve his sympathy, nor his understanding.

"I'm afraid I'm not very good company this evening," she said instead.

Granted, she was never very good company. She recalled the easy smile on his face earlier when he was in Freddie's far superior company and a sense of deep, sudden regret bubbled up through her. Oh, what a *mess* this all was. A remarkably stupid idea born out of her own hubris.

"Let's get you home, then," Lucien said gently.

For once, Alex allowed herself to be led, and while Lucien fetched their coats and her father, Marguerite approached.

"Leaving already?"

"Yes, I'm afraid so," Alex said with a tired smile.

Marguerite leaned in. "There was a miscommunication with my supplier and they sent double the amount this month," she murmured. "So you may need to store some of the product for a bit. I will send a note tomorrow."

Alex gave a single nod. "Not a problem."

Apart from running a weekly salon and publishing economic papers under her husband's name, Marguerite LaSalle also imported German-made Dutch caps from a contact in France and, with Alex's support, covertly distributed them to women's groups across the city, as both access and knowledge of how to use such devices was limited. Since Mr. LaSalle was entirely unaware of his wife's activities, Alex occasionally had to store the caps in her room.

"Excellent," Marguerite said with palpable relief. Then she gave her a conspiratorial smile. "I quite like your Lucien, you know."

Alex ignored the urge to explain that he did not belong to her. "I thought Benjamin Chisolm was in America."

Marguerite's eyebrows rose at the abrupt subject change, but then, that wasn't much different from how Alex usually spoke. "I believe he returned to London because his father is ill. You know him?"

Alex had to turn away from her friend's curious gaze. "I'll explain later," she said gruffly. The polite thing to do then was express some kind of sympathy, but Alex couldn't force the words past her lips.

Not for him.

Luckily, Lucien returned then with her father. They all said their good-byes and Marguerite elicited a promise from Alex that she would visit soon with Lucien. Then they stepped into the cool night and Alex released a breath.

"I think that went rather well, don't you?" her father said once they were all in the carriage.

"Yes, very," Lucien replied while Alex managed a grunt.

"Who was that dark-haired chap I saw you talking with, my dear?" her father asked after a moment.

Alex snapped her gaze to him, but there was only curiosity in his eyes. Of course he didn't know, she reasoned. She had been very careful.

"Benjamin Chisolm." She could feel Lucien's gaze on her, but she fought against the urge to glance back at him.

"Ah! I've heard of him," her father said. "He was one of the first to invest in the Sheridan project out of New York, no?"

"Yes," Alex replied tersely. That had been on *her* recommendation—and her money.

"You could do far worse than partner with him, Lucien," her father casually remarked while Alex had to fight to keep the grimace from twisting her lips.

"I will consider it," Lucien answered diplomatically, all while continuing to stare at Alex. She pointedly turned toward the window.

The rest of the drive home was then spent discussing other potential investors and how Lucien could tailor his new business proposal to appeal more directly to them. Normally Alex lived for this kind of strategizing, but she was too distracted by her own thoughts to offer more than a few passing comments and questions.

He returned to London because his father is ill.

Alex refused believe that. It might have been partly the reason, but something else had to be afoot, as Benjamin was always thinking three steps ahead, and prepared to do whatever it took to get what he wanted. She stiffened as those old memories threatened to pull her under, but Alex refused to let her personal feelings affect Lucien's decision. Benjamin was still a successful entrepreneur and this *was* business, after all. If Lucien did decide to partner with him, she wouldn't stand in his way.

It would be just one more reason to sever their connection once this agreement ended.

"What else do you two have planned?"

Her father's question roused Alex from her thoughts.

"The theater next week."

Her father tsked. "That's too far away. Come to the Turners' with us on Thursday."

Alex snorted a laugh. "I am *not* going to the Turners'."

Their neighbors hosted a weekly musical evening largely so their eldest daughter, who possessed more confidence than talent, could make a fool of herself in front of an audience. Alex hadn't gone in years.

Her father looked affronted. "The Turners are delightful!" Then he narrowed his eyes. "And more importantly, Hank Jr. will also be in attendance."

Alex crossed her arms, feeling very much like a petulant child. But she knew what he was implying. The expectations for a courting couple's behavior at such an event would be far different than at a salon. And with Hank Jr. there, the stakes were higher.

"Then I suppose Dierdre Turner won't be the only one putting on a performance," she groused.

"Yes, well, let us hope you are more of a crowd-pleaser than she is," her father returned darkly.

Alex's cheeks heated and she avoided Lucien's gaze. Luckily, they were nearly home, so at least her embarrassment was short-lived. Father then harangued Lucien into accepting the use of the carriage back to Hackney after they were dropped off.

"You aren't cross with me, are you, darling?" Father asked as they made their way inside.

Alex instinctively lifted her chin. "What would I have to be cross about? You merely spoke the truth."

Her father had the decency to look chagrined. "But I could have put it a little better, I suppose. And I do know you are trying your best," he added gently.

The implication being that it was still far from good enough. Alex's shoulders slumped as she handed her cloak to the footman.

"Then I suppose I'll just have to try harder," she said, unable to mask her weary tone. Her father began to speak, but Alex brushed a kiss on his cheek and bid him good night. Then she turned on her heel and headed upstairs. She had heard quite enough from everyone that evening.

Sixteen

As Lucien rode back to Hackney in the Atkinsons' carriage, he couldn't dispel the image of Alex's face from his mind. She had tried to hide the sly glances she kept giving Benjamin Chisolm all evening, but it had been clear enough to him that the man had caught her interest. The reason why it bothered him, however, was less clear. And so what if Alex *did* still have a lingering tender for that man? He had feelings for her own sister, after all. Feelings that were very much a part of his present. And yet, Lucien couldn't help feeling a bit protective of her, especially when Chisolm had been quite clear about his own lack of affection for Alex. Lucien would hate to see her hurt even while he acknowledged that she seemed imperviable to something as pedestrian as *love*.

Still, she had been more quiet than usual on the ride back to Park House and lost in her own thoughts. But while Lucien and Mr. Atkinson discussed potential investors and stratagems, Alex tossed off sharp, insightful comments and pointed questions every so often as if she were flicking off specks of dust. It was, in Lucien's opinion, a stunning performance that would have earned a round of applause in any board meeting. Yet Mr. Atkinson barely seemed to notice or appreciate his daughter's cunning perceptiveness. Did he truly not see what an asset she was to him? What a marvel? The more time Lucien spent with the family, the more he suspected that they did not, in fact, understand what they had in her. To them she was as commonplace as the wallpaper.

Once the carriage arrived at Alain's flat, Lucien made sure to climb out before Markham could open the door. It was dashed odd, having a man he had known since boyhood suddenly wait on him.

"Goodnight, Markham. Thank you for the ride," Lucien said lightly, hoping it might dispel any awkwardness.

But as he looked up at the driver's seat, there was no trace of disapproval in the older man's face.

"My pleasure, Mr. Taylor. Glad to see you are doing well for yourself."

Lucien ducked his head. "I'm trying, at least."

"Your father is very proud, you know," Markham said after a moment. "And we all wish him a speedy recovery."

"Thank you." Given that Markham had been promoted to head coachman on account of his father's condition, Lucien wondered just how much the man wanted him to fully recover if it meant a demotion. But Lucien appreciated the sentiment anyway. "I'm sure I will see you again soon."

"Yes," Markham said with a nod. "I'm sure you will." Then he gave Lucien a little salute before flicking the reigns.

Lucien remained on the pavement and watched the carriage progress down the road. It was not lost on him that if his father had never fallen ill, he might very well have been the one manning the carriage this evening. Or if Lucien had never gone to Paris, he would have followed in his father's footsteps and become a coachman himself.

You need to go somewhere far, far away from here.

And against the odds, Lucien had managed to do it, thanks in large part to his father's generosity. But it was unsettling to realize just how easily things could have been different for him. As well as the impact Alex's words that night long ago had made on him.

Lucien tilted his head back to gaze up at the sky, but only a few of the very brightest stars were visible overhead. It took him a moment to realize that the tightness in his chest was a longing for Bunbury. For evenings by the fire in his parents' little flat while his father read aloud from an adventure story, a warm cup of his mother's *chocolat chaud* in his hands. For a scene he could never return to, no matter how much he wished it.

Lucien brushed his cheek and stared at his wet fingertips for a moment, then let out a surprised laugh.

You're just exhausted. And overwrought.

He had vastly underestimated the toll this deception would have on him. Because he could not afford it. Idly he wondered if Alex was experiencing the same kind of strain but then dismissed the thought. She was used to moving through this world. And she seemed able to control her emotions with an iron fist. No, it could not be the same for her.

Lucien then made his way inside the building and trudged up the stairs to the flat. He was relieved that Alain was working late at the hotel this evening, for Lucien was in no mood to talk with anyone at the moment. He needed to sleep.

⁂

Several days later, Alex found herself in the music room of the Turners' Belgravia mansion glowering as Lucien handed a cup of punch to a beaming Freddie across the room. Tonight's outing was the kind of invitation Alex usually ignored and Freddie delighted in, especially if it provided yet another opportunity to flirt shamelessly with Lucien.

Alex's brow furrowed even deeper as Lucien leaned in closer to listen to whatever drivel her sister was spouting. If he didn't return to her side soon, Alex would have to go fetch him herself even though it went against her every instinct. But otherwise, people might begin to talk. Aunt Winifred had already cast her three urgent looks and she was liable to drag Alex across the room herself if she waited any longer.

This was turning into a mortifying ordeal. At least Alex was upholding *her* end of their agreement. Lucien had left the LaSalles' salon with a stack of business cards in his pocket, but it would be far more difficult to sell their courtship if he made his interest in Freddie any more obvious.

"You know, it might be more effective if you just called Freddie out directly."

Alex snapped to attention and found Will beside her. "When did you get here?"

"Just now. Phoebe's talking to Mrs. Turner." He gestured to her least irritating sister.

"Will you be my second?"

He smiled at the quip. "Even I am not foolish enough to get involved in an Atkinson sisters quarrel."

"We aren't quarreling. Freddie is behaving abominably, as usual. It's a disgrace."

"Hmm," Will said as he eyed the pair. "It looks to me like she's simply talking to Lucien."

Alex huffed. "Yes, but they are standing far too close and she has been monopolizing him for—" She pulled out her pocket watch and frowned. Huh. Seven minutes. That wasn't so bad. She could have sworn it was far longer.

Will tilted his head, awaiting her response. "Well?"

Alex shoved the watch back in her skirt pocket. "Never mind," she grumbled.

"I never thought I'd see the day," he marveled. "You're jealous."

"Absolutely not," Alex said hotly, which wasn't exactly convincing.

"You are."

"Wipe that grin off your face. You look ridiculous. And we're in public."

But the man didn't listen. "I assumed you had come to an agreement with Lucien," he said. "But I never thought you'd have actual *feelings* for him."

She had approached Will with a similar arrangement before he confessed his love for Phoebe. Though she was terribly happy for the both of them, it had certainly complicated things for her.

"I *don't*. This is just a mutually advantageous business arrangement."

"Is that what you're calling it?" Alex shot him her darkest look and Will held up his hands in defeat. "Sorry, I couldn't resist."

"You won't say anything, will you?" Alex couldn't hide the apprehension in her tone.

He sighed. "If Phoebe asks me directly, I won't lie to her. But she seems convinced. At least for now."

"Then I had better go fetch Lucien before he ruins everything."

"Alex," Will cautioned. "You're sure about this?"

"Of course I'm sure."

"Yes, but…" He hesitated. "Things can become complicated when matters of the heart are involved."

"Haven't you heard? I don't have a heart," she said with a laugh that Will didn't return.

He stared at her for a moment. "We both know that isn't true," he murmured.

Will had been a student at Oxford at the same time as Alex. And thus he was the only one who knew about her past with Benjamin. The only one who had seen her at her rawest and most vulnerable. And though he had treated her with nothing but the kindness and compassion she had needed back then, Alex could not stomach being so unguarded in front of another person ever again. They had barely spoken about the business with Benjamin since. That he would allude to it *now* was infuriating.

"And there are other ways for you to gain influence," he added offhandedly. As if she hadn't tried *every other option* she could think of before resorting to a fake suitor.

Alex lifted her chin as she simmered with barely leashed frustration. "What would you know about gaining influence? All you did was manage to be born with a set of genitals that for completely arbitrary reasons are prized above mine and then inherit one of the most powerful titles in the country thanks to nothing more than *fate*."

Will's mouth dropped open, but before she could chastise him some more, Phoebe chose that moment to join them.

"What are you talking about?" she asked with a bright smile. Phoebe had been in a constant, cheerful mood since her engagement. At this moment it was highly irritating.

"Nothing," Will replied just as Alex said, "Genitalia."

He pinched the bridge of his nose and muttered something that sounded awfully like *Dear God, woman*.

"Well, it's true," Alex insisted.

"Funny how your commitment to the truth fluctuates *wildly*," he drawled.

Phoebe let out a long-suffering sigh. "Someone come and get me when you stop speaking in code."

"No need," Alex said crisply as she met Will's eyes. "We're done here."

Then she turned on her heel and marched across the room to fetch Lucien. They had a show to put on.

⁂

Lucien's fingers tightened around the cup of punch as he mindlessly answered Freddie's questions about his time in Paris, while resisting the urge to glance back at Alex yet again. She was still deep in conversation with the duke and Lucien did not want to interrupt them.

When Freddie had first approached him, he was delighted. But the longer he stood talking with her, the more a strange restlessness began to take hold and the harder it was to remain focused. No doubt that was because he could practically feel Alex's gaze boring into his back.

They did need to keep up appearances and she would likely have a few choice words for him when he finally managed to extricate himself from this conversation. But that wasn't the source of his discontent.

Freddie was pleasant as usual and practically dripped with

charisma, but truthfully, Lucien was growing rather bored. Once he would have given his right arm to have her undivided attention. Now though…now he was struggling not to think of Alex, which had been the case for days.

Alex, who wasn't charming at all, and didn't even try to be. Yet Lucien found he *liked* her complete disinterest in giving the usual shallow flatteries—or even standard politeness, for that matter. It was refreshing. Exciting, even. For one never knew what she would say next. And her stoicism, which had so intimidated him as a boy, now gave her an air of inviting mystery.

"And when were you last in Paris?" Lucien managed to ask, fighting to refocus his attention on the woman who had been the object of his affection for nearly half his life.

"Two years ago now," Freddie said. "I went to the Continent with Mother and we had the most wonderful time. She begged Alex to come. But my sister claimed to be far too busy with work." Freddie rolled her eyes, as if this was merely a convenient excuse. "She just doesn't know how to have any fun."

Though Lucien didn't exactly disagree, he *was* supposed to be courting this woman. "She has other good qualities," he replied truthfully.

Freddie's eyebrows rose in surprise, but before she could respond, something caught her eye over his shoulder. "Oh God," she muttered. "Here comes the spoilsport now."

Lucien turned around as Alex marched across the room. Tonight she wore a sapphire gown that was even more becoming than the green one she had worn at the LaSalles'. As their gazes met, her dark eyes narrowed. Lucien couldn't help but smile in return.

"Here you are." He handed Alex the cup of punch.

She stopped abruptly and eyed the cup, as if he were offering her a poisoned apple.

"It's customary to say 'thank you,'" Freddie put in.

Alex shot her sister a scowl and took it. "Thank you."

"My pleasure," Lucien murmured.

Alex turned to him and her mouth curved in the barest hint of a smile.

Freddie cleared her throat. "Lucien and I were just talking of Paris. I told him you've never been, even though Mother invited you."

It almost sounded like an accusation.

"I would have liked to go with you," Alex said. "But I couldn't get away from the business at the time."

"Right," Freddie replied tightly. "Can you *ever* get away?"

"It has been difficult as of late."

"Yes, I can imagine. What with all the tasks you have at the moment." Freddie cast a not-so-subtle glance at him.

The tension between them was so palpable, Lucien nearly tugged at his collar.

Alex glowered, then gestured to the doorway. "I believe your Mr. Ericson has just arrived."

"So he has," Freddie said as she lifted her chin. "I had better say hello before you lose any future stock options."

Then she sashayed away, drawing the eye of nearly every man in the entire room as she passed. Hank Ericson's face lit up so brightly they could have stuck him in a harbor to help guide boats.

"Is everything all right between you two?"

Alex blinked. She too had been following Freddie's progress and turned to him. "Why do you say that?"

"There seemed to be some unresolved anger," Lucien said. "The trip to Paris?"

"Oh. That's how things always are with us," Alex replied with a dismissive wave, but Lucien wasn't convinced. After all, he had quite literally *been* there and was hard-pressed to recall the sisters exchanging barbs with this level of frequency, or animosity. Though Alex had always emanated a cool detachment, Lucien could remember her fierce protectiveness of Freddie when they were young. While for her part Freddie looked up to her eldest sister as if she hung the moon. Lucien didn't know when things had changed or what was at the root of this discord. But neither one of them seemed very happy about it.

"Besides," Alex continued, "Freddie would have hated if I went on that trip. She and Mother spent most of their time shopping and eating."

"Well, it *is* Paris," Lucien pointed out. "What would you have done instead?"

"Visit the catacombs," she answered immediately. Thank goodness Lucien hadn't taken a sip of punch or he would have spit it across the room. "Have you been?"

"God, no," he said. "It sounds macabre."

"Really? I think it's *fascinating*." Her eyes took on a gleam of interest he hadn't seen before. "It is estimated that millions of people are buried there. It shows how insignificant we all are. That even our lives span but a brief moment as time inevitably marches on."

"And that is something that you *want* to see?"

She tilted her head in consideration. "I suppose I find it a kind of comfort. And it helps to put my work in perspective."

Lucien frowned. "What do you mean?"

"That even if I did lose some stock options, it wouldn't matter in the grand scheme of things."

Once again, Lucien was forced to consider the tremendous pressure Alex must be under. And no doubt it was made worse because of the people expecting, nay, hoping for her to fail. She had to prove herself over and over because of her sex. She might be more familiar with this world than Lucien, but that didn't necessarily make it easier for her to navigate.

"I'm sorry."

"No need," she said, back to her usual brusqueness. "I choose to work, even if Freddie thinks I do nothing more than push paper around my office all day. Meanwhile, she has never once bothered to consider how the funds she spends so freely are generated." Then her gaze softened with regret. "I'm sorry. I shouldn't be bothering you with all this nonsense."

"It isn't nonsense. It's your life. And I'm the one who asked," he added.

Alex bit her lip. "Still, I should try harder to be cordial with her. Especially in public."

"That's not entirely your responsibility, though," Lucien said gently. "She could try to be more understanding of your work."

Though he had only spent an hour at her office, it had become perfectly clear to him that Alex did far more than push paper around. He wondered if Freddie had ever bothered to visit her.

"She's hardly the only person who believes that," Alex said

with a dismissiveness that set him on edge. Though hadn't he once thought the very same thing?

"But she's your *sister*."

Alex was quiet for a moment as she scanned the room. "I think it can be hard to see your siblings objectively. So much is based upon the foundations laid in childhood. One has to have the will to rebuild. But I wouldn't even know where to begin," she said thickly.

Before Lucien realized what he was doing, his palm pressed against her shoulder. As an only child, he didn't know much about sibling dynamics. But he could certainly feel sympathy for her. "I'm sorry."

"No need. I'm being silly." Alex blinked rapidly and he had the alarming suspicion that she was fighting back tears. Then she gave her head a firm shake and inhaled. "Now then, I was thinking that you should have some more suits made," she said briskly, back to the business at hand. "For your meetings. I'd pay for them, of course. Though it could be a loan," she added as Lucien began to object. "Please."

He sighed. She was right. If he was to move about in society, he needed more than two suits and he couldn't keep wearing Alain's slightly too short clothing. "Fine. But I *will* pay you back."

She smiled a little. "I know."

Pride unexpectedly flared in his chest. It had been a long time since anyone had believed in him. Including himself. "Thank you."

"There is a tailor not far from my offices that Mr. Potts favors," she continued. "I'm told he does excellent work quickly. I can have an appointment made for you the day after tomorrow. Then you should have at least one new suit ready before next week."

"That would be perfect."

Alex then hesitated a moment. "Why don't you come to my office afterward? I can look over your revised proposal."

"An excellent idea."

"Good. I'll have Potts send a message to you tomorrow with your appointment time. Then come by as soon as you're done."

"I look forward to it."

As they stared at each other, a different kind of tension slowly kindled between them. But this was made of anticipation, rather than old anger.

Lucien realized his hand was still on her shoulder and he slowly drew it back, dragging his fingertips down the bare skin of her upper arm.

She inhaled sharply and goose bumps rose beneath his touch.

Heat pooled low in his belly as desire suddenly bolted through him. Good lord. Lucien *wanted* her.

Alex's petal pink lips parted but just then, Mrs. Turner clapped her hands and announced from the other side of the room that the music would be starting shortly. Alex stiffened and Lucien withdrew his hand, the moment lost.

"I should go sit," she said in a rush and strode away before he could respond.

By the time Lucien crossed the room, Alex was squeezed on a sofa between her sister Phoebe and her mother. Meanwhile, Freddie was whispering softly with Hank Ericson, her not-quite-fiancé, in a corner.

As the rest of the seats were taken, Lucien was left to stand awkwardly beside a bookcase as Dierdre Turner sat down to the piano. He had a fine view of the back of Alex's head, but she didn't even look to him once for the duration of the young lady's performance—and it was quite a long one.

As the minutes passed, Lucien's irritation grew. He had not imagined that sharp intake of breath nor those goose bumps scattered across her flesh. She was affected by him. He was sure of it. Yet Alex seemed perfectly able to control her reaction, like turning down a lamp or shutting a door.

Lucien's fist clenched at his side. He wanted her to feel as bewildered as he did at the moment. As aching and restless for more. He wanted Alexandra Atkinson undone. Because of *him*.

Lucien wet his lips at the idea and it was not lost on him that what he felt for Alex was very different in comparison to Freddie. Rather than the idle yearnings of a lovesick boy, this wasn't based on fantasy. It felt more serious. More mature. A slow but incessant desire gradually picking up speed. And if Lucien wasn't careful, he might lose all control.

The room suddenly broke out into a thunder of applause and he jolted to attention. As Miss Turner curtsied, he clapped along with everyone else. Now that the music was over, people began to mill about the room once more, but he headed straight for Alex. She was still on the sofa caught in the middle of a lively conversation between her sister and mother and not even trying to hide her boredom.

Phoebe brightened as she noticed his approach. "Mr. Taylor! Come sit with us."

Lucien smiled and took an open seat beside the sofa. "I haven't yet had the chance to congratulate you on your engagement."

Phoebe beamed. "Thank you. That is very kind of you to say.

But I am more curious to hear how you are finding London in comparison to Paris."

"Ah, well, I haven't had much time for sightseeing, though I did visit the British Museum for a bit the other day."

"Really? That is Alex's favorite place in London! Did she tell you? I think she must go every week." Phoebe then turned to her sister. "Did you know this?"

Alex met her sister's enthusiasm with a sober nod. "I did."

"I haven't been in years," Phoebe said with a wistful sigh. "Oh! We should all go together!"

Lucien caught Alex's eye and she gave him an apologetic look.

"Only if Mr. Taylor doesn't mind going again so soon," she said.

"Yes," he said firmly as he held her gaze. "That sounds nice. I'm told the Egyptian Gallery can't be missed."

A faint blush stained Alex's cheeks as Phoebe rose. "Wonderful! Let me go ask Will," she said. "I'm sure he would love to go too."

"You will need a chaperone, darling," Mrs. Atkinson called out. "Go ask Aunt Winifred."

"But Will and I can do that," Phoebe said with a wave of her hand.

Her mother raised an eyebrow. "You aren't married *yet*, Phoebe. An engaged couple needs supervision just as much as they do. Likely more," she added under her breath.

"Very well," Phoebe relented and walked away.

"I'm sorry," Alex murmured once her sister was out of earshot. "Phoebe can be single-minded once she gets an idea in her head. I can put her off later."

"Not at all. I'd love to visit again," he replied honestly.

With you.

Though he kept that part to himself. Just as Alex's mouth

curved in a smile, Phoebe returned with the duke in tow. "How about tomorrow afternoon? Aunt Winifred is free then."

"That's a bit short notice," Alex said with a frown.

"I know," Phoebe replied apologetically. "But I'm busy at the school the rest of the week. We're putting on a production of *Henry V* and I need to help with wardrobe."

Alex lifted a brow. "And what of *my* work?"

"Why? Do you have something pressing to do tomorrow afternoon?" Phoebe asked sweetly.

The sisters stared at each other for a long moment, but Alex was the first to break. "Fine," she relented with a huff. "If that works for the rest of you, I suppose I can make do."

"Not to worry, Alex. You'll have all morning to dash the hopes and dreams of London's business elite," the duke put in.

Alex did not look amused by this remark, but Lucien couldn't help smiling as he recalled the crestfallen expressions of the men leaving her office.

"Splendid! Shall we meet out front at two?" Phoebe suggested.

Everyone nodded their ascent and Lucien looked directly at Alex once again. "Until tomorrow, then."

"Yes. Until then," she said, ducking her head like a shy debutante as that becoming blush once again stained her cheeks. Perhaps Alex wasn't as unaffected as he thought. And Lucien was determined to find out.

Seventeen

The next afternoon, Alex alighted from the carriage at Great Russell Street and raced across the courtyard of the British Museum—or rather, as fast as her blasted skirts would allow. She was late, and Alex *hated* being late. But it couldn't be helped. Just as she was preparing to leave the office, Mr. Tompkins, her father's good friend and a key member of the board, had stopped in to see her. That had never happened before. Granted, he only came to ask if Lucien was still looking for investors, but still. It was a welcome development that Alex would have relished if she hadn't also been trying to leave at that exact moment.

Nevertheless, she forced herself to concentrate on him and not the clock. When she finally answered his litany of questions, the man made a not-so-veiled reference to an impending engagement, complete with a shocking eyebrow waggle, and bid her good day.

Alex could have done without the inference, but otherwise her plan was beginning to work perfectly. And if Lucien really did make a success of his supper club, that could only help her own reputation. All in all, it had been a productive morning at the office. Yet the satisfaction she usually felt at a job well done paled in comparison to the nervous excitement bubbling in her belly. But there was no accounting for it.

She had just seen Lucien yesterday.

And she came to this museum all the time.

But not with him.

Alex pushed the unhelpful thought from her mind and mounted the steps.

Aunt Winifred, Phoebe, Will, and Lucien were waiting by the entrance and she could see them between the columns all smiling and talking. For a moment Alex felt out of place, as if she were watching a scene in a play rather than participating in her own life. The uncomfortable sensation came over her every now and again, usually followed by a compulsion to escape. But just then Lucien glanced over and spotted her.

His handsome face split with a grin and he waved. The compulsion immediately vanished, replaced instead with the unfamiliar warmth of acceptance.

Alex felt herself smiling back as she joined the group. "Sorry I'm late," she said in a rush.

"Only by a few minutes," her sister replied kindly.

"Terribly out of character for you, though," Will quipped. "I was considering sending a search party."

Alex rolled her eyes, though she was still smiling. "I was held up by Mr. Tompkins. He stopped by my office to ask about Lucien's supper club."

Will raised his eyebrows. "That's excellent news."

Lucien frowned in confusion. "Who is he?"

"One of our board members," Alex explained.

"And filthy rich," Will added. "If you've already caught his interest, more will soon follow."

"Ah," Lucien replied, looking a little nervous.

"Enough business talk," Aunt Winifred groused.

"Yes, I want to see some mummies," Phoebe said.

"Then see some mummies you shall," Will said gallantly as he offered her one arm and Aunt Winifred the other.

As the three of them entered the building, Lucien offered Alex his arm and she took it.

"I'm sorry about all this," she murmured as they followed.

Lucien tilted his head. "Whatever for?"

"It's more than I expected," she said honestly. "Certainly more than I outlined in the contract."

That had been limited to one social outing a week. But this would be the third.

"It's all right." Lucien then huffed a laugh. "Though I suppose you'll need to revise it again."

"Yes," she said with a nod. "I will do it tonight."

"Alex." He waited for her to meet his eyes. "I was only joking."

"Right. Sorry." She turned away just as his gaze softened, as she had no need to see the pity in his eyes.

Poor awkward Alex.

Luckily, they had entered the Great Court, so Alex pulled away and pretended she was simply taken by their surroundings. Though truthfully, she did not have to pretend very hard. She never grew tired of visiting this mansion full of treasures. It might not possess quite the same grandeur and pomp of the newer buildings she had visited in New York, but she preferred this nonetheless.

As she completed a full turn, she caught Lucien staring at her, a faint smile playing on his lips. "What is it?"

"Nothing," he replied. "I just…I like watching you," he added hesitantly.

Alex glanced around, but no one was paying attention to them at the moment. Aunt Winifred was haranguing a frazzled-looking docent while Will and Phoebe were poring over a map. She turned back to Lucien and he must have read the confusion on her face. He smiled a little wider this time and took a step toward her. Then another.

"Let us look at the map," Alex said briskly and hurried away before he could even respond. She didn't need a map, of course. Alex could probably find her way around the museum blindfolded. But Lucien's attention unnerved her. She could admit that now, as silly as it was. He paid her attention because of their arrangement. Because he was *supposed* to. She would be a fool to look for something deeper.

"I know you are all eager to see the mummies, but I am far more interested in Grecian pottery," Aunt Winifred pronounced as she joined them. "My late husband dragged me to one of those ghastly unraveling parties once. Macabre practice if you ask me. So why don't you go ahead and we will meet by Lord Elgin's marbles in an hour." Then she arched a brow. "I trust you can all behave yourselves in public?"

Will and Phoebe leaned a little closer to each other and exchanged a look sweet enough to give Alex a toothache. It also made her even more aware of Lucien's looming presence. Should she look at him too? Or, worse, flutter her eyelashes? Alex didn't think she could manage that. Lucien was liable to think she was suffering from some sort of apoplexy rather than a poor attempt at coquetry.

But just as Alex had mustered the courage to reach for Lucien's arm, Aunt Winifred simply strode off toward the Greco-Roman room. Saved from embarrassment at least for the moment, Alex let out a sigh of relief. She had utterly failed to consider how awkward it would be to pretend to be courting while in the company of the two most lovesick people she knew. She would need to strategize with Lucien about reasonable displays of affection. Alex could allow for walking arm-in-arm if the occasion called for it and perhaps even some brief hand-holding. But she drew the line at saccharine looks and mawkish nicknames. In her opinion, some things should never leave the confines of a bedroom.

Do not *think of him in a bedroom.*

Yet despite the admonishment, Alex could feel her entire body start to flush.

"Are you sure you're feeling well?" Lucien murmured.

Alex startled a bit, as he was much closer than she realized, and noticed the genuine concern in his face. Then she brought a hand to her cheek, though she very well knew the cause. "Oh, yes. I'm perfectly fine. It's just warm in here. Do you not think so?" She said this all in a great rush and Lucien's look of concern only deepened.

"Perhaps I should take you home. I can flag down a hackney right now—"

"No." The very *last* place she should be was alone in a carriage with Lucien Taylor. "That is, I'm quite well," she added with an enthusiastic smile that probably bordered on derangement. "Please, let's continue." Alex then rushed them toward the Anglo-Roman Gallery.

Will gestured for Alex to enter before him, and she was only too glad to walk with her sister for a bit. She needed to sort herself out and it was difficult to do that while worrying about Lucien.

Phoebe flashed her an easy smile and looped their arms together.

"I stopped by the house earlier today and when I told Freddie about our outing she wasn't exactly pleased," Phoebe said. "I think we could have made more of an effort to invite her along."

Alex scoffed. "Did you not see the *effort* she was putting in at the Turners' last night?"

"I saw her speaking with Lucien for a little while, if that is what you mean. But it looked perfectly innocent to me," Phoebe said. "And besides, you have nothing to worry about on that front. Lucien seems very attentive towards you."

Alex held her tongue, though she longed to reveal the truth to her sister. It would be nice to confide in her.

"Truthfully, I don't think Freddie is very content," Phoebe continued.

"She seemed perfectly happy to me last night," Alex said dryly.

Phoebe shot her a frown. "Freddie always *looks* perfectly happy in company. But I'm talking about a deeper purpose. A life's work."

Alex let out an impatient sigh. "You know very well that she has never shown the least bit of interest in work of any kind. You are coddling her once again, Phoebe. But she isn't a child anymore. And she is perfectly capable of making her own choices."

"Even if those choices go against what you and Father want?"

"I am not making Freddie marry Hank Ericson!" Alex exclaimed rather too loudly. A nearby matron examining a bust of Marcus Aurelius cast her a disapproving look and Alex mouthed an apology before turning back to Phoebe. "How could you think such a thing?" she hissed.

"I know you aren't *making* her," Phoebe allowed. "But you have made your preference perfectly clear."

"Freddie doesn't do anything unless she absolutely wants to," Alex insisted.

"When it comes to most things, yes. I agree. But I don't think you realize how much your approval means. Freddie might not even realize it herself," Phoebe added.

"Oh," Alex said flatly, though she still harbored significant doubts.

"Do you remember how we quarreled before you left for New York?" Phoebe asked after a moment.

"Given that it was only a few months ago, yes," Alex drawled.

Phoebe had accused her of only caring about turning a profit instead of investing in social causes. It was a fair enough point, and since then Alex had taken on more charitable projects, including securing a new building for the girls' school where Phoebe taught.

"Well, it was awful fighting with you," Phoebe continued. "And you know you can be rather . . . intimidating."

Alex pursed her lips. It was true enough. And hardly the first time someone had said that, but it hurt coming from her own sister. Phoebe was supposed to know her better. To understand her in a way others couldn't. "I see."

"It wouldn't surprise me if Freddie felt the same, even though she might not show it."

"And I suppose you want me to be the one to do something about it?"

"Well, you *are* the eldest."

That was also an all-too-familiar refrain. And yet, she could feel the resignation washing over her. "Fine. I will make more of an effort with Freddie. And make sure that she isn't marrying an obnoxious American man purely for my benefit," she added.

Phoebe suddenly reached out and squeezed her hand. "You are a good sister, Alex."

She stared at their joined hands for a moment and squeezed back. "So are you."

Phoebe flashed her a smile then looked around. "Now where did our menfolk disappear to?"

They had reached the entrance of the Egyptian Gallery. Alex followed her sister's gaze, but she was right. Lucien and Will had vanished.

֍

Upon entering the Anglo-Roman Gallery, Alex got caught up in a conversation with her sister. Lucien had tried to keep an eye on her, but then he came upon an old Roman tomb and was thoroughly distracted. When he finally looked up, Alex was nowhere in sight.

"We seem to have lost the ladies," the Duke of Ellis said, suddenly by his side.

It was the first words he had uttered to Lucien directly since they arrived.

Before his unexpected ascension to the dukedom, Will Margrave had been neighbors with the Atkinsons—and a close friend of Alex. Lucien hadn't interacted with the older boy very often, which was something of a relief given that he was nearly as intimidating as Alex. Especially when he was in a lather over something. But as the duke gave him an apprising look, Lucien might as well have been ten years old again.

"Your Grace."

"Don't call me that," he clucked. "Margrave will do just fine."

"Yes, Your—Margrave," Lucien said weakly.

"You're a good sport for coming along today," he continued.

"I like this museum," Lucien answered honestly.

"And Alex?"

Lucien's eyes widened at the rather direct question, but before he could answer, Margrave sighed.

"You needn't keep up the pretense with me," he explained. "I know of your little arrangement. Alex came to me last month with a similar proposition before she knew I had fallen in love with Phoebe."

Lucien stiffened. Alex certainly hadn't mentioned *that*. And he couldn't ignore the absurd bloom of jealousy in his chest. "I see."

"I thought it was a terrible idea then and told her as much." Margrave narrowed his eyes. "My opinion has *not* changed, though I suppose I can't fault you for going along with it. I'm sure she dangled something quite appealing in exchange for your participation."

Lucien didn't care for the man's tone, but he was right. "She promised to find investors for a London branch of my supper club."

"Ah," the duke replied with a thoughtful nod. "Well, you could certainly do worse. And there are a fair number of men who would do a great many things to be associated with Atkinson Enterprises in any capacity." Then he narrowed his eyes again. "You do know she's behind it all, don't you?"

"Yes, I'd gathered that."

"That's not to say that her father contributes nothing. He pulls his weight, of course. And I'm sure the firm would still be successful without Alex, but she is the driving force behind their greatest triumphs."

"A very admirable accomplishment for a lady," Lucien responded.

"It is *because* she is a lady," the duke insisted. "She thinks differently from the rest of them. She doesn't see the world the same way. That is an asset."

Just as Lucien began to respond, Margrave raised a finger. He might not like being called a duke, but he damn well seemed to like acting like one.

"And yet, despite all that, she is not appreciated as she should be. Though she would give me hell if she heard me say this, I am very protective of her. People often misinterpret Alex's demeanor. If she were a man, we would call her stoic. Strong. Principled. Likely, she would be hailed as a genius. Instead, she must be happy with her father's appreciation, admiration from the select few who know the truth, and that great big pile money she has accumulated. But because she refuses to smile and simper at will, she is called cold and unfeeling. So she hides herself away in that office because it is familiar. Because there *she* is the one to make demands."

Lucien felt a flush at the back of his neck at the thought of Alex demanding, well, anything of him. "I'm aware of that," he rasped.

The duke arched a brow. "Are you? Good. And here I was worried because I was under the impression you've been carrying a torch for Freddie all these years."

Now the flush spread to his cheeks. "I didn't—that is, I don't—"

But Margrave waved away his hopeless dithering. "You needn't bother denying it. Obviously Alex knows. Though I don't think she has truly considered all the ramifications involved in choosing you to act as her suitor."

Lucien swallowed. That could refer to any number of things: his personal connection to the family, the veritable chasm between their respective positions in society, *Freddie.*

"But now I've said my piece," Margrave continued. "So then,

why don't you tell me about this supper club I've been hearing about."

Lucien stared at him, thrown by the subject change, until the duke gave a nod of encouragement and he found his bearings. Or at least enough to do his little spiel while they walked through the rest of the gallery.

Margrave listened carefully and made a few polite hums of approval at the appropriate points. "I can see why Alex approached you," he admitted with a trace of reluctance.

Before Lucien could respond to this, Phoebe walked over to them with Alex a few steps behind. "There you are! I thought we had lost you."

"Ah, I'm afraid you won't be able to rid yourself of me that easily, my dear," he said smoothly. The man's entire demeanor appeared to lighten in her presence.

While Phoebe beamed at her fiancé, Alex subtly rolled her eyes. Then she looked to Lucien and he shot her a private smile. A moment of understanding seemed to pass between them, and as the duke moved beside Phoebe, it felt perfectly natural to offer Alex his arm. She hesitated only a moment before she laced her arm through his and they followed a few steps behind the couple.

"I'm happy for them, of course," she began as they entered the Egyptian Gallery. "I'm not so shrewish as that. Only I wish they weren't so very *public* about it all the time. It's growing rather tiresome."

"Entirely understandable."

"Then again, I suppose it's far preferable to the dramatics they both indulged in before they stopped being so dunderheaded."

Lucien chuckled as he stared at the couple just ahead of them. "I find that hard to imagine."

Just then Phoebe leaned her head against Margrave's shoulder and he looked down at her with such fondness that Lucien's heart ached with a strange kind of longing.

"Neither of them were very convincing either," Alex replied dryly. "Both moping about for weeks on end yet refusing to simply *admit* their feelings to the other."

"It can be a difficult prospect," Lucien replied, feeling a bit defensive. After all, he had never declared himself to Freddie.

Alex cut him a glance. "I suppose."

"I understand you approached the duke first about feigning a courtship," Lucien said, deliberately changing the subject.

She turned to him in surprise. "He told you about that?"

"I think he was evaluating my intentions."

Alex huffed. "That's absurd. He knows you're no threat."

Though that was a perfectly true statement, Lucien couldn't help feeling a little offended by her dismissiveness. "Right."

Alex shot him a wry smile. "I'm sorry. Did you *wish* to be a threat?"

"Of course not," he insisted, but her smile only deepened.

"Margrave is overly protective sometimes. He sees dangers where there are none."

"That isn't such a bad quality in a friend."

"No," Alex said on a sigh. "I suppose not."

Another thought occurred to him then. "Who would you have gone to if I turned you down?"

Alex tilted her head in consideration. "I'm not sure. Perhaps one of the fellows at the LaSalles' salon," she said with a shrug that set him on edge. She could have easily aligned herself with an unscrupulous schemer.

The image of Benjamin Chisolm came to him and Lucien's arm tightened instinctively around her own. "You should exercise more caution than that."

She looked up at him. "Goodness, you're as bad as Will! I would have at least discussed any potential candidates with Madame LaSalle first. I'm not quite so naive. Besides, the point is entirely moot now."

"It is," he agreed. And Lucien was thoroughly glad for that. At the very least he might have kept Alex from aligning herself with some duplicitous knave.

Your intentions are hardly selfless here.

No, they were not. But he would not cause any harm to Alex either. Of that he was certain. And yet, he couldn't ignore the fleeting sensation that it was not Alex who was the more vulnerable party in their little arrangement. But it did not matter. Lucien needed this to work. Even if he lost everything in the process. It was a risk he had no choice but to take.

※

Alex was grateful for the distraction provided by the treasures of the Egyptian Gallery, as this conversation had become vexing. Was Lucien really suggesting that she was foolish enough to be taken in by a *scoundrel*? It would be highly insulting, except she couldn't deny that she was rather touched by his obvious concern.

They came to a stop before the colossal statue of King Ramesses II.

"Extraordinary," Lucien breathed. "And I was only here last week," he added with a surprised laugh.

"Yes, but it is hard to grow tired of marvels," Alex said. "I saw parts of his funerary temple in New York when I visited their Metropolitan Museum. Strange to think the pieces are now scattered across an ocean. To parts of the world he didn't even know existed."

Lucien turned to her in surprise. "When were you in New York?"

"The spring. I accompanied Father on a business trip. That was how we met the Ericsons. Hank Sr. and my father got on immediately and they came back to England with us."

In fact, it had been Hank Sr.'s barely veiled comments about Alex's role in the company that had spurred her father's insistence that she find a suitor. But she needn't bother Lucien with that.

"I've always wanted to visit New York," he said softly.

"Really?" Alex hadn't minded the place, but it wasn't until she returned to London that she realized just how much she missed home. "I suppose it's exciting. And everyone is always in a great rush there."

Lucien smiled. "Yes, I've heard that. But it's more the sense of possibility. The knowledge that you can be anything if you try hard enough. Social class doesn't dictate one's path the same way it does here." He seemed to catch himself then and gave her a bashful look.

"Ah, but they have an aristocracy all their own," Alex replied. "Have you heard of Mrs. Astor? The upper class all curry her favor as if she were the queen."

Alex had been introduced to her at some stuffy soiree and they were both left mutually unimpressed.

"My aspirations are hardly so lofty as that," Lucien said with a winsome smile.

"But you would like to go there and try your luck," Alex offered. She couldn't deny that New York didn't seem as beholden to the old guard as London. The people there were more open to ideas and ingenuity, no matter where they might come from. And yet, the thought of Lucien in that bustling metropolis across an ocean made her strangely uneasy.

"Someday, perhaps," Lucien replied, entirely unaware of her thoughts. Then he turned to her with that impish smile. "I suppose I should make a go of it in London first."

Alex forced herself to look away and gazed into the granite eyes of the long-dead Egyptian king. "About that. How is your business proposal coming along?"

She needed to steer the conversation back to something she could control. Something that was safe. All the while she could almost feel his heavy gaze on her profile and warred against the urge to look back.

"I've been working on incorporating the suggestions you and your father made. It will be ready for our meeting tomorrow."

"Excellent." That foolish sense of excitement began to kindle in her belly once more and she moved on to a display of Egyptian jewelry in a desperate bid to snuff it out.

When she had finally looked over every single piece in the display case, she glanced up and found Lucien watching her once again.

"What is it?" she demanded.

The corner of his mouth tipped up. "Nothing. I . . . I like watching you observe things."

"Oh," she said, dumbfounded by this response. Then she forced her brow to relax. She had been practically glowering in her concentration.

Lucien stepped closer. "You sound surprised."

"Well, yes." Alex resisted the urge to step back. "Usually, I'm told I need to smile more." Or people asked what was wrong when all Alex was doing was simply *existing*.

"You were concentrating on the display," Lucien said easily. "It would look rather odd if you were smiling at it."

Her eyes widened. "Yes, exactly."

She couldn't remember the last time someone had seen her so clearly. As they stared at each other, that unique kind of understanding seemed to pass between them once more and Alex was certain she wasn't the only one who felt it.

Lucien offered her his arm. "Come. Let us look at the sarcophagi."

The rest of the visit passed by in a bit of a blur. At one point Phoebe and Will slipped off into a darkened alcove to do God knew what but managed to reappear just before they were due to meet Aunt Winifred. Alex had pulled Phoebe aside and repinned the loose curl hanging down her back.

"Thank you," her sister whispered with a sheepish smile.

Alex frowned. "Tell Will to be more discreet next time, unless you intend to be caught."

"Oh, but that's all part of the fun," Phoebe responded with a cheeky wink and moved to greet their aunt.

Alex stared after her, completely unable to hide her shock. When Lucien approached her with a curious look, her cheeks flushed and she moved ahead.

"Let us see Lord Elgin's spoils, shall we?"

And if he noticed her discomposure this time, he did not comment on it.

⌘

Lucien returned to the flat that afternoon in something of a muddle. He was so lost in thought that he didn't even notice Alain until the man was practically under his nose.

"Where have you just come from? You look as if you were just released from the clutches of some fairy king."

Lucien gave himself a shake. He did feel rather dazed. "The British Museum."

"Weren't you there only last week?"

"Yes, but the Atkinson sisters invited me this time."

"Oh?" Alain raised a brow. "Tell me *everything*."

Lucien huffed a laugh. "There isn't much to tell. We walked around and looked at very old things that don't belong in this country."

"Such a radical!" Alain said with undisguised delight. "I had no idea."

But it was Alex of all people who had made the observation while they were staring at the Elgin Marbles.

An English lord pried them off the Parthenon and we have the audacity to display them as our own.

Lucien's mouth curved up at the memory. She continued to be one of the most confounding people he had ever met. Prickly one moment, understanding the next. Sharp, insightful, and wryly funny.

Alain suddenly snapped his fingers. "Lucien! Where have you gone?"

"Oh, sorry. I was just—"

"Thinking of Miss Alexandra?" Lucien happily shrugged at his knowing tone. There was no use denying it. Alain let out a low whistle. "You are in trouble, my friend. When will you see her again?"

"Tomorrow." Though that was strictly business. Lucien wilted a little in disappointment. At least during their social outings he had the pretense of their arrangement to explain his behavior. But it would be much harder to justify his staring when they were going over his proposal.

He thought again of her adorable little frown as she took in the various displays. How nothing, not even the smallest detail, seemed to escape her notice. Why would anyone *criticize* her for it? He wanted a direct line to that mind of hers. To see exactly what she was thinking of. It shocked him how much he longed to be the sole focus of her attention, even for a little while. Even if it brought him to his knees.

"Ah, then you must make the most of it," Alain continued.

And for one crazed moment Lucien considered asking him about his seduction techniques. But Lucien knew very well that his friend lacked as much experience with women as he did. If Lucien was lucky enough to ever have the opportunity, he would just have to follow his instincts and hope to God it was enough.

"Yes," he said with a decided nod. "I intend to."

Eighteen

Alex tapped her fingers on her desk and let out a huff. She had been going over the same page for a quarter of an hour now, as every time she tried to focus, her mind wandered.

This was not like her *at all*. Neither was this infernal fidgeting. She splayed her palm across the worn wooden surface of her desk and glanced at the small brass clock on the corner. It had been a present from her father to mark her first year with the company. The second hand ticked away. Five fifteen. Lucien would be here shortly.

Alex let out a sigh of defeat and set the report aside for the morning. Then she leaned back in her chair until a throat cleared from the doorway. It was Potts. Goodness, she had forgotten all about him.

"Do you need anything more from me, Miss Atkinson?"

"No, you can go."

He hesitated a moment until Alex raised an eyebrow. "Are you still expecting Mr. Taylor? I can wait if—"

"I don't need a chaperone, Potts," she said crisply. His concern was *wildly* misplaced. And, more important, Alex was his superior.

"Yes, miss," he said sheepishly and gave a short bow before exiting.

With him gone, Alex was properly alone now. The building was always empty at this hour.

Because everyone else has people at home waiting for them.

She frowned at the unexpectedly maudlin thought. It wasn't as if she was going home to an empty house. But then, her parents and Freddie didn't really count. At least, not like that. And they knew better than to wait for her anyway. Alex ate alone in her room most evenings, while the rest of her family was out.

Because that is the way you like it.

And it had been. But now … now Alex wasn't so sure.

She closed her eyes and was met by the same images that had been haunting her for days: Lucien in the Turners' music room dragging his palm down her bare arm while gazing deeply into her eyes. Lucien watching her intently as she took in the marvels of the British Museum. Lucien and his inviting smile. His warm touch. His understanding gaze.

Alex suddenly startled as footfalls sounded outside her office and sat up just as the man himself appeared in the doorway, as if he had been conjured from her thoughts.

"Hello," he said while knocking on the door frame.

"Come in," she rasped, hoping her cheeks didn't look as red as they felt and grateful he couldn't read her mind.

As Lucien entered, Alex realized the only source of light came from the little lamp on her desk. "Sorry." Quite rightly he lifted a brow in question at her odd comment. "It's just so dark in here," she explained. And why did her skin suddenly feel so tight?

For heaven's sake, get ahold of yourself.

But Lucien waved her off as he took the seat across from her. "It's fine with me."

As Alex forced her body to relax, she looked him over. "Is that a new suit?"

The corner of his mouth lifted. "You noticed."

She couldn't help smiling as he preened a little. "It's very nice." Indeed, the charcoal gray suit fit him better than the one he had worn to the museum.

"After the tailor measured me, he said he had a suit already made in nearly the same size," Lucien explained. "The client who ordered it changed his mind, so he was happy to have me take it off his hands. It needed only a few adjustments and I was able to wear it out the door."

The suit showcased his lean form to impressive effect, and Alex had to take care not to linger overlong on his shoulders.

"How fortuitous."

Then his face fell. "I hope that's all right. I know it's more than what we agreed on ..."

"Of course. It's fine. Really, Lucien."

"And I *will* pay you back," he insisted.

"I know." But in truth, she didn't care whether he did or didn't. She was already seeing the benefit of their arrangement.

That was well worth the cost of a few new suits.

"So, then," Alex said briskly. "What have you brought me?"

Lucien looked amused. "You don't waste any time."

"I don't want to keep you," she demurred.

"As you very well know, I've nowhere else to be." Then he flashed her a smile before pulling a stack of papers from his satchel. While he was momentarily distracted, Alex couldn't help smoothing her hair.

As if it would make a difference.

She had worn one of her nicer gowns today in anticipation of his visit, but now she felt silly for bothering in the first place. Lucien didn't see her that way. He couldn't. Moreover, she certainly couldn't even begin to compete with someone like Freddie.

Just as her heart began to sink to the floor, Lucien placed the pages on the desk, then stopped. "Here, let me come closer. Then I can point out the changes I made."

Before Alex could respond, he was out of the chair and by her side. The smell of soap and skin-warmed starch invaded her senses as he leaned over her shoulder to turn a page.

"I added more biographical details here. And outlined the history of the club here."

She cleared her throat. "Good."

"Then I created the one-month timeline, like you suggested."

"Good," she repeated. Alex tried to focus on the paragraph he was pointing to, but her mind felt dull. Sluggish. All she wanted to do was look at him and it took all her concentration to fight against the urge.

"I thought you'd be far more difficult to please than this," he murmured.

Alex straightened against the shiver working down her spine. "I will be. Keep going."

Lucien chuckled then continued going over his changes, but after a few moments Alex didn't really hear the words. Just the sound of his deep voice washing over her. It was so calming. She could listen to him forever.

"*Alex.*"

She jolted in her seat. "Yes?"

Lucien peered at her. "You seem...distracted."

"I am. A little," she admitted. Only then did she realize she was quite obviously staring at his mouth. Alex lifted her eyes to meet his gaze.

"Should we do this another time?"

"No, no," she said hastily.

He rose one dark brow. "Then what is distracting you?"

Her heart beat faster at the amusement in his voice. Was he actually *flirting* with her?

There were any number of things she could have blamed her behavior on: the hour, hunger, the mountain of work that always needed to be done.

But Alex couldn't muster the will to lie. For what would be the purpose? Better to have him reject her outright and put an end to her ridiculous hopes. So instead, she told the truth.

"You."

As she whispered the word, she fully expected him to move back. To explain that she had misread the situation.

"Is that so?" he replied, still holding her gaze.

Alex then noticed the heat in his eyes flaring to life and forced herself to nod. It was too late to turn back now.

Lucien draped his arm across the back of her chair and leaned in closer, slow enough to give Alex time to stop him. To tell him this was a mistake. That it would only complicate their agreement. But Alex again found she lacked the will to stop. She was so *tired* of thinking everything through a half dozen times. Of imagining every possible outcome. Of being the responsible one. The boring one. Everyone else in her life seemed to be at the mercy of their desires at all times. And just this once, she wanted to be too.

As the warmth of Lucien's body enveloped her own, Alex closed her eyes and tilted her head back. Just as Freddie's words muscled their way into her brain.

No one will believe he wants you.

Alex's eyes flew open. Lucien's face was an inch away from her own. His brows rose in question, but they simply stared at each other. The only sound Alex could hear was her own sharp, panting breaths. She still had the chance to save face. To explain this all away. But then her sister would win.

Well, to hell with Freddie.

Alex surged upward and pressed her mouth to his. Her sudden movement seemed to catch him by surprise, but Lucien quickly recovered and pulled her into his arms. As Alex came to her feet, Lucien immediately pressed her backside against the desk.

She kissed him with feverish, searching lips, unable to contain her eagerness as the need for him clawed up her belly, no longer held at bay. Lucien responded in kind, his hands cupping her jaw and adjusting the angle of her face to better suit them. His enticing mouth was soft and warm. She wanted to taste him. As Alex slipped her tongue past his lips, Lucien let out a sharp groan and pulled back.

"Jesus," he panted by her ear as his chest heaved against her own.

She loved how he reacted to her. And Alex, who never had any trouble maintaining control, was suddenly overcome with greed. With the *need* for this man. She nuzzled his neck and caressed his chest. How hard his heart was beating. Then she met his eyes. He was still breathing hard, his eyes like two black orbs. Alex dragged a hand lower while still holding his gaze. Lucien made no move to stop her, even when she grazed his belly, even when she reached the front of his trousers.

She was just about to touch him when he inhaled sharply. Alex paused and shot him a questioning look. "Do you want me to stop?"

"No," Lucien grunted.

Alex smiled. "Good." Then she began to palm him through the cloth, taking stock of his length and girth.

"Quite impressive, Mr. Taylor," she murmured with approval.

He squeezed his eyes shut and moaned. "God, when you talk like that..."

But the rest of his words were lost as Alex leaned forward and gently licked his earlobe. She had never done such a thing before. Had never even *thought* to do such a thing. But in this moment it felt essential. Like she would go mad if she didn't do it. Lucien let out another strangled moan and turned his face toward her, capturing her mouth in a deep kiss that seemed to melt into another and then another, until it was endless. When Alex regained slightly more of her sense, she stroked him even harder and his hips began to jerk upward, as if seeking more of her touch. She was determined to satisfy him and had just resolved to unbutton his trousers when Lucien grunted a curse as his whole body stiffened. It took her a moment to realize what had happened. Alex blinked and looked up, bewildered.

Lucien stepped back, looking absolutely mortified as he covered his face with his hands. "I—I'm sorry."

He had spent in his trousers. He had wanted her so much that he couldn't control himself. Alex supposed she should be disappointed, but she only felt a kind of power surging through her.

"Don't apologize," she murmured. "It's fine."

He let out a hoarse laugh and pulled a frustrated hand through his mussed hair. "It's really not."

"I'm told it can happen," she began matter-of-factly. "Especially if one has not indulged in some time." A straightforward approach seemed the best way to minimize his embarrassment.

But Lucien just scoffed. "Or never," he muttered as he walked around the desk and fetched his satchel.

Alex stared after him, then cocked her head. No. He couldn't possibly mean . . .

"You—are you saying you're a virgin?"

"Try not to sound so surprised," Lucien said sarcastically as he picked up his satchel.

"But, the earring," she sputtered. "The tattoo. *Paris.*"

He shot her a challenging look. "Well? What of it?" Then he stilled as another thought seemed to occur to him. "Are *you* not a virgin?"

Alex lifted her chin. "No." The idea that a woman could be ruined by the very same activity that men were applauded for had always irked her. She certainly didn't shout it from the rooftops, but she wouldn't be shamed by him either. "Does that bother you?"

Lucien stared at her for a moment before shaking his head. "It bothers you, though."

"Nonsense," Alex said firmly. "I'm just surprised."

Lucien's shoulders tightened. "Because of my age."

"Well, no. You aren't that old."

"And yet, most men would have already bedded a *dozen* women."

"I can't speak to that figure," Alex demurred, trying not to laugh as this was clearly a sensitive subject for him. "But I was under the impression that you had an affair with Madame Deveraux, your business partner's paramour."

Lucien's mouth dropped open in shock. "How on earth did *you* hear about that?"

"I hired a private investigator based in Paris look into you," Alex said simply. "Just like I would anyone I planned to partner with."

"A private investigator?" Lucien stared at her hotly. "Don't you think that was a touch excessive?"

Alex shrugged. "It's good business."

"But you could have just *asked* me."

"I wouldn't have known if you were telling me the truth."

"Right," he scoffed. "You had no choice but to invade my privacy because simply *trusting* me was out of the question," Lucien bit off as he picked up his satchel. "It isn't true, by the way. Though I suppose you've pieced that together yourself."

"Lucien—"

"I can't believe I ever thought you—" Then he paused.

"What?" Alex demanded as she came around the desk. "What were you going to say?"

"Never mind."

She put her hands on her hips and stood right in from of him. "You might as well come out with it, since the truth is so important to you," she added, failing to hide the sarcasm in her tone.

Lucien stared down at her, his eyes now black with anger. "You really are as heartless as everyone says," he said with perfect clarity, then turned and stalked out of the room.

Alex had expected those words—it would have been a surprise if he had said anything else—and yet they still struck her chest like a weight. She slouched against her desk as Lucien's angry footfalls receded down the hall. Until the only sound left was her own breaths. Until she was alone once again.

A few days later Lucien nearly tripped as he raced up the gleaming marble steps of The Bedivere Club. London's private gentlemen's clubs had always felt even more absurdly out of reach than the parlors and ballrooms of Mayfair. Yet here he was, entering one of the city's most exclusive establishments. Behind him a line of fine carriages waited out front and it was not lost on him that if fate had offered even a slightly different hand, he might have been among them. A coachman like his father.

You still could be if this doesn't work out.

Lucien grimaced at the unwelcome reminder. He needed to impress Benjamin Chisolm whether or not they decided to partner together. He was respected enough that he could sink Lucien's chances for finding alternative funding with only a few words. And then even Alex's support wouldn't be able to save him.

If you still have it.

But Lucien dismissed the thought as he stepped into the small lobby. A beady-eyed man behind an imposing host's stand gave him a dismissive once-over. "May I help you?" he asked in a tone that indicated the complete opposite.

Lucien knew he didn't quite fit in here, with his non–Savile Row suit, hair in desperate need of a trim, and gold earring. But he was still the guest of a member. And in the end that was all that mattered. "Lucien Taylor to see Mr. Chisolm," he replied, lifting his chin a little.

The host flicked a glance over an open book then arched his brow. "Wait here while I inform him of your arrival," he said reluctantly.

Lucien let out a breath as the host disappeared behind a large oak door, leaving him blessedly alone for the moment. A particularly lurid mural depicting the seduction of Leda by Zeus disguised as a swan took up most of one wall. Lucien turned toward the large gilt-framed mirror hanging on the opposite wall and tried to calm his rattled nerves.

"You can do this," he murmured to his reflection as he adjusted his already straight tie. Then he opened his satchel and considered reading through his proposal one more time, though by this point he had the blasted thing memorized. He forced himself to take a seat instead, but that left him with an excellent view of the mural. Lucien pulled out the proposal and began mindlessly leafing through the pages.

He had been so incensed by Alex's frank admission that he actually stormed out of her office without it. That bloody woman seemed to think nothing of hiring someone to dig into his private life—and they hadn't done a particularly good job if they couldn't determine that the rumors of his affair with Madame Deveraux were just that. Rumors. Rumors spread by Rene to cast blame on Lucien and distract from his own affair with the woman, along with his embezzling.

Lucien had always maintained his innocence, but the truth was no match for a delicious piece of gossip. And certainly no one would believe that Lucien couldn't possibly have bedded the woman because he was still a *virgin*. But regardless of his anger over Alex's actions, Lucien still needed to be prepared to explain why the Parisian supper club had disbanded so suddenly. Chisolm would certainly ask. And he intended to be honest—about the embezzlement, at least.

The morning after his encounter with Alex, the proposal had been delivered to Alain's flat along with a brief note:

Lucien,

Please accept my sincere apologies for last night. I never intended to upset you, but I suppose my intentions are irrelevant.

Here are my notes on your proposal. Best wishes on your meeting tomorrow.

Yours,

Alex

He had stared at that closing for far longer than he would ever admit.

Yours.

Had she meant it? Did she even comprehend what it meant to belong to someone? It seemed like a wildly intimate gesture for a woman who barely bothered to acknowledge most people. Even more so than touching his cock. He immediately began to read through her edits so as not to linger on *that* particular memory. There weren't as many as he anticipated, which was a relief. But as he flipped through the pages, Lucien muttered a curse. She was nothing short of brilliant. Her suggestions, though sparse, were so sharp and insightful that he felt like an absolute idiot for not writing it that way in the first place.

No wonder those employees left her office in near tears.

Lucien then swallowed his pride and incorporated all of her suggestions into his proposal. By the next morning his ego had recovered and he mostly felt a sense of gratitude toward Alex.

Mostly.

"Follow me, Mr. Taylor."

The host's command brought Lucien back to the moment. It was time.

He was led through the heavy oak door and down a dark

hallway that opened into a surprisingly cavernous, wood-paneled room. Floor-to-ceiling windows let in the late afternoon sunlight while a fire sedately crackled away in the massive fireplace topped with an ornate jade mantel. Gentlemen turned out in impeccable suits that likely cost more than the investment Lucien was seeking were scattered about the room talking quietly or reading newspapers. Nearly everyone had a drink in hand. Benjamin Chisolm was seated comfortably near the fire in a forest-green leather club chair but quickly rose once he'd spotted Lucien.

"Hello there!" He shook his hand. "So glad you could meet me here. Did you have any trouble finding the place?"

"Ah, no—"

"Excellent." Chisolm addressed the host, who hovered behind them. "Baxter, get my friend a drink." Then he turned to Lucien. "You'll have one, won't you?"

"Yes—"

"Whatever he wants," Chisolm announced with a lordly wave of his hand.

"I'll have what you're having."

"Good lad," he said with a wink. "A whiskey for Mr. Taylor and another for me. Quickly now, Baxter."

"Of course, sir." The host scraped a bow and scurried off, but not before casting one last look of disapproval at Lucien.

"Sit, sit." Chisolm gestured to the chair opposite his own. "I must say, I'm very excited to hear your proposal. I've mostly been involved in industrial endeavors. But the future is entertainment, or so I'm told. Especially for the middle classes, now that they have a bit of extra money to spend."

Lucien nodded. "Yes, that is one of the groups I hope to aim for." Indeed, that was what had made the club such a success in Paris. It was designed to be accessible to more than only the very wealthy. "When the artists started coming, that was when things really took off."

Chisolm grinned. "I love it. You must have enjoyed some raucous nights with that crowd, I imagine," he added, waggling his eyebrows.

Lucien managed a smile. "A few." He hadn't expected such a blunt comment during a business meeting. "But for me it was work, you know. I never forgot that."

Some of his clients treated his stoic refusal to participate in the festivities as a kind of game and took turns dangling all sorts of temptations before him: liquor, women—men. But Lucien never broke. Though he had desperately wanted to a time or two.

Chisolm gave him a sly look. "Of course. *Work.*"

Before the man could press him further, their drinks arrived. Chisolm made a toast and then gestured to Lucien. "All right. Let's hear it."

As Lucien launched into his little spiel, Chisolm asked him a number of pointed questions. He had come prepared. Luckily, so had Lucien. They spent close to an hour discussing his vision for the business and what he would need to get it started before Chisolm settled back in his chair.

"You've given me much to think about, Taylor. Now we can get down to the *real* business," he said. "Are the rumors true, then? That you're courting Alex—I mean, Miss Atkinson," Chisolm finished with a sheepish grin that Lucien didn't believe for a second.

"Yes. I am."

Chisolm nodded sagely. "Good. Poor girl's a waste sitting on the shelf. Someone should be able to enjoy those charms of hers," he added quietly before taking a sip.

Lucien narrowed his eyes. Chisolm sounded awfully certain about that. "And yet, you turned her down."

He let out a dry laugh. "Well, not at first. But then I found that we weren't…" He paused, as if searching for the right word. "Compatible."

Did this man *really* have the audacity to make such an insinuation? Lucien recalled Alex lifting her chin and boldly pronouncing her lack of virginity. Chisolm had to have been her partner. And the bastard looked damned proud of it.

"I beg your pardon," Lucien demanded. Despite his lingering anger over Alex's invasion of his privacy, he very much wanted to punch this man in his smug face.

"Don't tell me I've shocked you," Chisolm said with genuine surprise. "I took you for a man of the world. And you certainly know Miss Atkinson can fend for herself. No one could coerce her into doing anything she didn't want to do."

Lucien's jaw tightened even while he privately acknowledged this. "Nevertheless, I trust you don't make it a habit of discussing this with people."

Chisolm had the decency to look chastened. "No, of course not."

"Let's move on, then."

The man seemed all too happy to oblige, and as they discussed how Paris compared to London, their conversation moved along with much of its earlier breeziness. But in Lucien's case it was all for show. He left a short while later determined that under no circumstances would he partner with that man. Ever.

Nineteen

lex rubbed her bleary eyes and glanced at the clock. Approximately two minutes had passed since she'd last looked. She let out a frustrated sigh and leaned back in her chair. Workdays never dragged on like this. It was only a little past three o'clock and she was ready to climb out of her skin. Is this how her colleagues felt? No wonder everyone clambered for the doors at the stroke of five. But there was no reason why she should be so distracted.

You know perfectly well *why.*

She frowned at the voice in her head. The theater was tonight. And Lucien was supposed to attend. Though given how they had parted, she wasn't entirely sure he would show up. He had received her note of apology days before, and yet she'd still had no response. Had no idea how his meeting with Benjamin had gone—though that hadn't stopped her from imagining the two men galivanting around London together. Perhaps even sharing a laugh at her expense. But she forced the ugly thought aside. It was beneath her. And there was no good reason why Lucien's attendance should concern her. If he was prepared to end their arrangement because she had engaged in the same business practices as she always did, then so be it. Let him be ridiculous and offended and *on his own.*

Alex pushed back her chair. Enough. If she was going to waste away the afternoon, there were far better places to do it than her office. Trouble was, she couldn't think of anywhere to go. If she went home, her mother or aunt would only pepper her with questions she didn't want to answer. And she couldn't visit the British Museum because it would only make her think of Lucien even more, and that was *not* helpful. Will was in Parliament, Phoebe was at her school, and Freddie in parts unknown…which were all the people she knew. Alex grimaced. How small and dull her life had become. Then, before she could stop it, the thought flitted through her mind for perhaps the hundredth time that day:

I wonder what Lucien is doing?

The near-constant refrain was slowly driving her insane. She didn't *care*. Not one—

"Miss Atkinson."

Alex blinked and turned toward the doorway of her office where Potts hovered with a nervous look on his thin face. She suspected it was not the first time he had addressed her.

She cleared her throat and sat up in her chair, as if she hadn't been caught wool-gathering. "What is it?"

Potts stepped into the room and lowered his voice. "There is a policeman here to see you. Inspector Holland. He says it's urgent."

"You had better show him in, then."

Potts nodded and hurried away.

Well, this was unexpected. She had met the detective inspector last month after he got mixed up in some business with Phoebe and Margrave. He was far too serious, even for a man in his position, and didn't suffer fools. Alex rather liked him.

As Inspector Holland strode into the room, his eyes met hers and he nodded hello.

"Miss Atkinson. Thank you for seeing me."

"Of course. Please sit," Alex said as she gestured to the lone chair before her desk.

As he took his seat, his broad shoulders tightened underneath his jacket. He had the kind of muscular build that was usually found in boxers and sent young ladies into a swoon. And yet, Alex couldn't help thinking she preferred Lucien's lean form.

You are ridiculous.

"I'm sorry to drop by unannounced," he began, entirely unaware of the direction of her thoughts. "But I was in the area and wanted to warn you in person."

Alex tilted her head. "Warn me?"

"I have it on good authority that the criminal known as the Nun has indeed returned to London and was funding Fleur."

"Oh. That. I had forgotten."

Before Will and Phoebe came to their senses and admitted their love for each other over the summer, Will had first thrown over the daughter of his mentor, Lord Fairbanks. The man in turn threatened to name Phoebe as Margrave's mistress in retaliation, so Alex had taken it upon herself to buy up the earl's debts to keep him in line. However, unbeknownst to Alex, Lord Fairbanks had also been involved in a new private gentlemen's club called Fleur with a shadowy Irish criminal—the Nun. When Alex bought his debts, the earl pulled out of the club and then fled the country when he failed to pass a bill that would have targeted woman-owned brothels across the city, while leaving his own establishment untouched.

The inspector's dark brows rose at her blasé admission. "I'm afraid you may be in danger."

Alex waved a dismissive hand and shook her head. "The Nun's

quarrel is with Lord Fairbanks. And last I heard he was hiding out somewhere on the Continent."

The inspector pursed his lips. "Forgive me, Miss Atkinson," he began. "But it was your actions that led to the closing of Fleur. You cost the Nun money and possibly his foothold in the city. That will not be forgotten."

Alex crossed her arms. "What do you want me to do about that?"

"Stay close to home until I arrest him."

"Well, that is unfortunate because I have a business to run," she said dryly. "I also have tickets to the theater this evening."

And nothing short of a meteorite crashing into the city would stop her from attending.

The inspector huffed. "This is serious, Miss Atkinson. The Nun is a dangerous man and he does not appreciate competitors."

"I am not his competitor, Inspector," Alex said. "I simply bought up the debts of a man threatening my sister. That is good business. Perhaps this *nun* person should have found a more solvent aristocrat to partner with."

The inspector blinked. Then his expression darkened. "Is that the defense you plan to use when you are accosted in a dark alley? Or kidnapped and held for ransom? He knows you are a wealthy woman. I've made it clear to Margrave that Phoebe is in danger. Winifred as well," he added with uncharacteristic urgency.

Winifred, is it?

But Alex did not needle him about when exactly he had seen her sister, as the man was obviously in distress. "I am not trying to be flippant," she began, gentling her tone as much as she could. "And I promise to take your concerns to heart. But unless you can provide some kind of evidence that I am a target, I can't very well upend my entire life simply because a criminal who *might* be in London *might* decide to confront me. Besides, this isn't the first time I've angered a man over a business decision."

"The Nun doesn't do your kind of business, Miss Atkinson. He doesn't follow the rule of law and isn't interested in maintaining relationships. He casts people aside once they have served their purpose. And if someone gets in his way, he takes care of them. Permanently." The inspector shoved his chair back. "You don't know who you're dealing with," he growled.

She narrowed her eyes. This sounded personal for him. "And yet, you do."

He avoided her gaze as he stood. "I came to you first as a courtesy," he said, ignoring her comment. "But your father needs to hear this too."

Alex sighed. "Fine. Do as you must." Though she didn't expect his reaction to be much different from her own. "But even if he is in London now, will he be caught? As I understand it, he avoided the police quite successfully for many years."

Inspector Holland paused in the doorway and looked back at her. "Yes, because I intend to do it myself." Then he left the room, but the cold certainty of his words hung in the air and Alex swore she felt a chill.

⁌

The Lyceum Theatre was full that evening for the production of *Cymbeline* and it seemed that nearly everyone wanted to stop by their box to say hello to her parents. Or Freddie. Or congratulate Phoebe and Will, who hadn't arrived yet.

Alex toyed with the emerald bracelet on her wrist as she watched the entrance. Normally she eschewed jewelry, but Mother had insisted it went perfectly with her gown. For once, Alex was grateful for her mother's jewelry box. This blasted bracelet was the only thing stopping her from pacing the room.

"Alex," her mother suddenly hissed by her ear. "You'll damage the clasp if you keep that up."

"Sorry," she murmured and forced her hands by her sides.

Mother's eyes softened. "He'll come, darling. Don't worry."

As she patted her arm, Alex bit her lip. Mother thought she was simply nervous to see her new beau, not because she might have ruined their little sham.

If he had already come to an agreement with Benjamin, he wouldn't need her anymore anyway. Unless she was willing to sue him for breach of contract, there wasn't much she could do to hold him to their arrangement. And she wasn't nearly desperate enough to do that. But the mere thought of finding another man to take his place was exhausting. And unappealing. She wasn't *good* at this courting nonsense. And it irked her to no end. Perhaps Benjamin had been right all those years ago.

I am your only *option, darling. No other man will put up with you.*

Her fingers clenched and she was seconds away from breaking the clasp altogether when a shadow appeared in the doorway.

Alex's chest tightened, but it was only Will with Phoebe on his arm. Her sister was distracted, but Alex's eyes locked with Will's and he must have seen the flash of disappointment on her face. While Phoebe broke off to greet some dowager friend of their mother's, Will ambled over to her.

"A pleasure to see you too," he quipped.

Alex leaned over to give him her cheek. "I'm sorry. I thought you were Lucien."

After giving her a friendly peck, Will pulled back. "He isn't here?"

"Not yet," Alex rasped.

His eyes searched her face. "Is everything all right?"

The soft note of concern in his voice struck a place deep within her belly and Alex had to swallow before she answered. "Yes. Well, no. I don't know," she added miserably.

He began to respond but she shook her head. They couldn't talk about this. Not now. Her sisters were approaching.

"Let me fetch you all some champagne," Will said as Phoebe and Freddie joined them.

"Thank you, my love," Phoebe said with a smile sweet enough to hurt Alex's teeth.

"And do be quick about it, Will." Freddie gestured to her half-full glass. "I'll soon be in need of another."

Alex resisted the urge to frown in disapproval as Will gave a mocking bow. "I am ever at your disposal, Freddie."

Phoebe followed his departing figure before shifting her gaze to Alex. "You're looking well."

"Because she's actually been spending a few hours a week outside the office," Freddie interjected.

Phoebe's lips curved. "With Lucien?"

"He paid her a rather late visit there the other evening," Freddie added with a ridiculous eyebrow waggle.

Alex turned sharply to her. "How did you hear about that?"

But Freddie only lifted a shoulder. "I have my sources."

It *had* to be Potts. Freddie was the only person in the world who could turn that man into a simpering fool. It was damned annoying.

"A pity you don't use them for something useful," Alex groused.

Before Freddie could parry back, their mother interrupted. "Girls," she warned through a tight smile. "We have company. Can you at least *try* to be civil to one another?"

Alex and Freddie exchanged sheepish looks. "Sorry, Mother," they grumbled in unison.

"I must say, I'm quite enjoying being the golden child for once," Phoebe said with a highly irritating smirk after their mother moved on to circulate.

Freddie rolled her eyes. "I think you owe them that after the last few years."

Alex snorted a laugh. At least that was something they could agree on.

Phoebe's insistence on working as a schoolteacher in a rather rough neighborhood while sharing a derelict flat with a colleague had caused their parents an endless amount of worry until she became engaged to Will—and that had only been a couple of months ago.

"But never fear," Freddie continued lightly as she looked around the box. "Alex will reclaim her crown as soon as she strikes a deal with the Ericsons in exchange for my hand and earns Father another million."

Alex pursed her lips at the sarcastic comment while Phoebe cleared her throat, but Freddie simply took a long sip of champagne, seemingly oblivious to the tension she had caused. Or perhaps simply enjoying it. One could never tell with her.

When their father came to join them, Alex let out a sigh of

relief. "Good evening, Bee," he said, giving Phoebe a friendly kiss. "Where is that fiancé of yours?"

"He went to fetch us some champagne, but he should be back soon." Phoebe craned her head as her gaze caught on something else. "Is that Inspector Holland?"

Alex turned around in time to see the man enter their box. "What is *he* doing here?"

"I invited him," their father said.

"How egalitarian of you, Father," Freddie said with a fiendish smile as her eyes locked on the inspector. "I think I'll just go say hello."

"And *I'll* come with you," Phoebe said as she shot Alex a look and took Freddie's arm.

Once they were gone, Alex turned to her father with a raised eyebrow. "The inspector got to you, did he?"

He shrugged. "Holland was so certain that you all were in grave danger that I asked him to come along tonight and see for himself."

"I'm surprised he agreed to that," Alex said. She was mystified as she watched the man tug on the collar of his evening suit, clearly uncomfortable.

"Yes. It didn't take much convincing either," her father replied. "Though now I'm beginning to understand why," he added with a subtle nod.

As Freddie greeted the inspector, he seemed to have forgotten his discomfort and was *smiling*—or at least what passed as a smile for him. Most other people would probably mistake it for a kind of grimace.

Alex groaned. "You'll need to hire another daughter to fend off Holland."

Her father chuckled. "I doubt that. The inspector doesn't strike me as the kind of man to put up with Freddie's nonsense. Besides, Hank Jr. came to me just yesterday to formally ask for her hand."

"Did he?" That was a huge step. Hank Jr. was known around New York as the Slippery Bachelor, for no one could catch him. But it seemed he couldn't resist Freddie.

"I gave my consent, of course," her father continued. "And he seems certain that she will accept him. If he hurries up, we can hold a joint engagement ball for them as well as Phoebe and the duke at the end of the month. Save your mother and me a bit of coin," he said with a wink.

Alex hummed in approval. This was excellent news. Nothing could impede a deal with the Ericsons now. Her plan had worked even faster than expected. Why, both her sisters could be engaged and married within the year. Just as a strange heaviness began to settle in her chest, Lucien finally entered the box.

And all I have is a fake paramour who can't stand me.

Their eyes immediately locked and any relief she might have felt at his appearance dulled considerably at the thought.

"You know, Alex," her father murmured, "you could end your little agreement sooner, if you wished."

She managed to tear her gaze from Lucien. "Why?" she asked sharply. "Did he say something to you?"

"No, not at all."

"Because I do still need his help to convince the board that I can take over one day."

"Yes, but…" Her father hesitated. "I'm worried that you might get hurt the longer this goes on."

Alex let out a laugh that sounded too loud to her ears. "That's absurd."

"Is it?" Her father glanced over at him. "He's a good-looking lad with a sharp mind and plenty of drive. You've a good deal in common."

Alex shook her head. "We're only—" Lord, she couldn't even say they were *friends*. "We both understand the situation," she finished.

He watched her for a moment. "Not everything bends to logic. The heart least of all. And yours is still made of flesh and blood, my girl. Just like the rest of us."

She followed Lucien as he moved through the crowd toward her, all while his gaze never left her own.

"But his heart was spoken for long ago." Alex hadn't realized she'd said the words aloud until her father chuckled.

"Do you mean Freddie?" Alex gave a reluctant nod and his gaze turned thoughtful. "I remember he would follow her around the estate with stars in his eyes. But the affections of boyhood rarely endure the realities of adulthood. And it is rarer still for it to blossom into real, lasting love. Remember that," he murmured before addressing Lucien. "Hello, there. So glad you could join us."

"Sir, my apologies," he said in a rush. "The omnibus I was waiting on took nearly an hour to arrive."

Her father shot her a frown. "I thought you were finding him a flat nearby."

"I did," Alex insisted. "There is one available in The King's Arms."

Which wasn't very far from their offices. She had found it days ago but hadn't had the chance to tell him yet.

He then looked between her and Lucien. "Well, what are you waiting for?"

For him to respond to me.

"That is my fault, sir—"

"Get it sorted by tomorrow," her father insisted. "We can't have you traipsing in from the country three times a week. This won't work."

"Yes, of course," Lucien said hastily.

Just then Aunt Winifred came to her side and murmured by her ear. "Who *is* that large, terrifying man talking with your sisters?"

"Inspector Holland," Alex replied. "He is an acquaintance of Margrave and Phoebe."

Her aunt's eyes gleamed with interest. She didn't look the least bit terrified. "Hmm. I'd better introduce myself."

Alex smiled as her aunt hurried away. It appeared Freddie had some competition from her namesake.

The theater lights then flashed. "You should take your seats," Father said as he gestured to a pair of chairs at the end of the row. "The show is about to begin."

Lucien nodded and dutifully pulled out a chair for Alex.

"Thank you," she murmured as she took her seat. Due to the placement of the chairs, they were a little apart from the rest of her family, though still fully visible to the entire theater.

Because you also have a show to put on.

Alex bit back a sigh and glanced over at Lucien. He was watching her closely, his expression unreadable. She managed a tight smile, but he did not return it before the lights went out.

Twenty

Alex looked absolutely gorgeous in a deep purple gown that perfectly complemented her creamy skin and dark hair. As Lucien took the seat beside her, he caught a whiff of flowery perfume. It was lovely, but he found he preferred her usual scent of ink and paper. Only then did it dawn on him that he hadn't searched the box for Freddie at all. He had seen only Alex.

As the curtain lifted and the play began, Lucien tried his best to focus on the actors onstage, but he kept snatching glances at her profile every few minutes. The delicate slope of her nose, the soft curve of her cheek, the perfectly pointed chin. How had he ever not thought this woman beautiful?

"I take it your meeting with Benjamin went well," she finally murmured without looking at him.

"Why do you say that?"

She was silent for a long moment. "Because I haven't heard from you."

"I'm sorry. I should have sent a response. Thank you. Your notes were very helpful."

"I'm glad," she replied, sounding anything but. "And congratulations. I'm sure your partnership will be very fruitful."

"I didn't—"

"There's no need to be coy, Lucien," she insisted. "You've made a good decision."

"Is that why you looked so surprised when I arrived? You thought I wouldn't come tonight if I partnered with him?" He frowned at the implication. "But we have an agreement."

She lifted a shoulder in response. "Things can change. I understand that."

A few days before, he would have assumed she was indifferent, but now Lucien knew better. She hid so much beneath that cool mask, and he was determined to see it all. He leaned as close to her as he dared, until he could feel the soft warmth coming off her skin. "I assure you, I always honor my agreements," he murmured by her ear. She responded with only the slightest inhalation, but it still made the blood rush to his cock. If this woman ever truly fell apart before him, Lucien wasn't certain he would survive the experience.

He attempted to return his attention to the play for a while, but gave up once again. "Tell me what happened between you two."

She turned to him then and the hesitancy in her eyes was answer enough.

"That bastard," he growled.

"I know what you're thinking," she murmured. "But it wasn't like that."

Lucien shifted in his seat. The sound of her hushed voice only made him grow harder. It was damned inconvenient, as this was a serious conversation. To say nothing of their surroundings.

"Then tell me what it *was* like."

Alex leaned forward to cast a subtle glance past him. "Not here."

As her shoulder brushed his own, a shiver of need ripped through him.

"Is something wrong?"

"No," he huffed and dragged a hand down his face.

She peered at him in concern. "There's a washroom just outside, if you need to be sick."

"I'm not *ill*, Alex," he said with a humorless laugh. "It's you."

"Oh."

The genuine surprise on her face was maddening. Did she really not understand the effect she had on him? One caress from her and he had spent in his trousers, for God's sake.

"I can't stop thinking about the other night. In your office," he added, just to make it perfectly clear.

"Oh," she repeated and turned back to the stage.

Was that a blush on her cheek? It was too dark to be sure.

"Say something," he demanded after a moment.

"I…I can't stop thinking about it either."

Lucien leaned forward, greedy for more. "Despite my less-than-stellar performance?"

Her mouth curved up. "Well, it ended sooner than expected, but it was quite notable before that."

Notable.

Lucien grinned as if she had given him a standing ovation right there.

"And I am sorry," she continued. "About the private investigator. It is our standard protocol, but I should have handled things differently with you."

"No, I overreacted," Lucien admitted. "I'm afraid I was just…a bit out of sorts at the time. Surely you can understand *why*."

Alex shifted in her seat. "Yes, well," she said, clearing her throat. "I wouldn't have been so forward with you if I knew the truth."

"I'm glad you were," he insisted. "But now you must let me make it up to you."

Alex bit her bottom lip, considering. "I don't think that would be a good idea," she said slowly.

"I assure you, I don't lack experience *entirely*." He was suddenly quite determined to prove himself.

"It's not about that."

"Then why—"

But the rest of his words were drowned out by clapping. Lucien blinked as light suddenly filled the theater. It was already intermission and he could recall nothing of the first act. His thoughts were only of her.

Alex looked as stunned as he felt.

Mrs. Atkinson then leaned over her husband to address them. "Alex, come with me. You must say hello to Mrs. Dudley." Then she cast him a knowing look. "You don't mind, Lucien, seeing as you two were whispering together the entire time."

He bowed his head. "Of course not, ma'am."

"Not to worry," she said with a wink. "I'll return her before the next act."

As Alex moved to stand, he placed a soft hand on her shoulder. "We aren't done here," he murmured by her ear.

Their eyes locked for a moment and her heated gaze was the most pleasurable kind of pain. She gave him a subtle nod and departed. Though at first he had not liked the idea of accepting the flat, he was starting to see the appeal of having some privacy. And being closer to Alex.

As Lucien watched her leave, he found the Duke of Ellis frowning at him from across the box. Lucien swallowed as the man approached. Though they had been friendly enough at the museum, Lucien still found him more than a little intimidating.

"Your Grace," he mumbled as he came to his feet. Should he bow since they were in company? Better to be sure…

But before he could, the duke clapped a hand hard on his shoulder. "I told you to call me Margrave."

"Right. Sorry."

"Come with me to get a drink, won't you?"

"Certainly." Lucien let out a relieved laugh. "For a moment there I was worried you were cross with me."

The duke grinned. "Actually I had just remembered the time you stole my clothes by the pond."

Christ. He had forgotten about that. "It was all Freddie's idea," Lucien blurted out. She had *always* been getting him into mischief.

"I'm sure," Margrave said with a laugh. "Remind me never to trust you with a secret. You folded faster than my valet."

Lucien grimaced. It was true.

"I heard my name," Freddie trilled as she came beside them. Her arm firmly held by her not-quite-fiancé.

"Lucien was just ratting you out," Margrave said smoothly. "Remember the time you stole my clothes while I was swimming in the pond?"

Freddie threw her head back and laughed. "Oh, you were *furious*! I think you chased us all the way back home clutching a bunch of leaves to your—"

Hank Ericson Jr. loudly cleared his throat. "Darling, we need to stop by my parents' box."

Freddie blushed and patted his arm. "Of course. Good to see you again, Lucien," she called out as she was firmly guided to the exit.

A dark-haired man with a mustache in the far corner stared after Freddie with the kind of veiled longing Lucien knew all too well. And yet, he felt only sympathy for the fellow. He managed to tear his gaze away long enough to exchange a nod with Margrave.

"Who was that man with the mustache?" Lucien asked once they had left the box.

"Inspector Holland."

"Is he interested in Freddie?"

Margrave shot him a sharp look. "Why do you care?"

Lucien shrugged. "I was just curious," he answered honestly.

Alex had occupied so much of his time lately that he had barely thought of Freddie. The old, familiar ache she usually inspired in his heart felt more like a dull flutter. A genuine fondness for their shared childhood. And Lucien wasn't quite sure how to feel about that. His love for Freddie had been a guiding force in his life for so long, it was a little unnerving how quickly he had set it aside—and that her *sister* of all people was the reason.

Margrave studied him and pursed his lips. "Hmm. Let's get that drink, shall we?"

As they retreated across the hall to a private bar area for those in box seats, Lucien bumped directly into someone. But before he could make his apologies, the large chap stalked away. *Odd*, Lucien thought as he stared after him for a moment.

"Are you coming, Taylor?" the duke called from the doorway and he joined him.

Once inside, Margave ordered them champagne. Lucien accepted the coupe and then lifted it. "Allow me to offer a toast to your engagement."

"Thank you. I am a very lucky man." Margrave's smile was small but genuine. "And might we be toasting you and Alex next?"

Lucien choked a little on a mouthful of champagne and the duke slapped him firmly between his shoulder blades.

"I saw the way you were looking at each other earlier," Margrave continued, unruffled by Lucien's reaction. "And I highly doubt Alex would be able to fake such interest." Lucien's heart fluttered wildly with pleasure. Then Margrave's eyes narrowed. "Frankly, I'm not sure which one of you is in more trouble."

Lucien blinked. "Sir?" The word slipped from his lips before he could stop it.

Margrave stepped closer. "If you hurt her, you will need to go a hell of a lot farther than France when I am done with you.

Lucien swallowed and nodded. "Understood."

"But if she hurts *you*," the duke began as his eyes softened, "know that you can always come to me."

"I appreciate that, but it won't be necessary," Lucien insisted even while his skin prickled with foreboding.

Margrave's mouth curved. "Right. Your *agreement*. My mistake."

Lucien downed the rest of his glass. "There…there is one thing you could help me with," he began.

Good lord, if he was even considering asking this, the champagne must have gone straight to his head.

The duke gave him a curious look. "Well?"

"Do you have any suggestions for making—ah…an amorous encounter better for the other party…"

Margrave's lips pursed, as if he were trying not to smile. "Are you asking me how to pleasure a woman, Taylor?"

The champagne was *definitely* to blame.

"I do have some idea," Lucien protested a little too much. "But…"

"You could use a little advice," Margrave volunteered.

Lucien squeezed his eyes shut and nodded. This was beyond embarrassing, but he didn't want a repeat of the other night and there wasn't anyone else he could ask.

When he found the courage to open his eyes, Margrave had tilted his head, actually considering the question. "While there are any number of techniques one might try, I have found the most important thing to do is pay attention. As closely as you can. Then you will know very quickly when something is working—and when it isn't."

That seemed easy enough.

"But if this is in regard to our mutual friend," he continued, amused, "you could probably just ask her."

"Right," Lucien rasped. The thought of her ordering him about was strangely arousing.

"Oh, and if you find yourself becoming too, erm, overcome, think of cricket. That always helps." Margrave then raised his nearly empty coupe. "Good luck."

Lucien was certain he would need it.

⁕

When Alex returned to the box, Lucien was already in his seat—and her father beside him.

"Now don't get into a snit, Alexandra," Aunt Winifred murmured. "But it wouldn't do to have you and Lucien talking through the rest of the play. You've done more than enough to set tongues wagging. Besides, at this stage it is better to let him miss you a bit."

Alex frowned. "I don't like those kinds of games."

Her aunt chuckled. "Darling, courtship is nothing *but* a game. And trust me, your mother and I know how to win."

There was a thing or two Alex could say about that, given her current status as a spinster and Freddie's slightly scandalous reputation. Even Phoebe's engagement to Will had come about through no parental involvement whatsoever. But Alex decided to hold her tongue and took the seat to the right of her father, who was busy talking Lucien's ear off. She managed to catch his eye and shot him an apologetic look, to which he smiled in return. Perhaps this was for the best, as Alex didn't trust herself to sit beside him for another hour.

You must let me make it up to you.

Oh, she would enjoy that *far* too much. All the more reason to maintain strict boundaries where Lucien was concerned. They had indulged in one lapse of judgment already and she was determined not to repeat the error. Their physical attraction to each other was irrelevant and could only lead to complications. Alex had dealt with such a situation once before and she very much did not wish to repeat the experience.

"When do you plan to see each other next?" Her father's question interrupted her inappropriate train of thought.

"There's a lecture on the latest archaeological practices at the Royal Geographical Society in two days' time."

Her father looked dubious. "Not exactly courtship material."

"It is to me," she said. And more important, it would offer no chance for them to be alone.

"And me," Lucien added.

Alex looked over at him, unable to keep the smile off her face.

Father did not look pleased and was just about to reply when Mother leaned forward from the row behind them.

"Oh, Lucien, do come to the engagement ball next week. We would so *love* for you to attend. Wouldn't we?" she added with a not-so-subtle look at Alex.

"Yes," Alex replied. "We would." She had completely forgotten about the blasted ball. Now she would need to be fitted for an uncomfortable gown, stay up far too late, and make small talk with dozens of people she did not like. She might even have to *dance*. Alex held back a shudder at the thought.

"I'd love to. It would be an honor," Lucien answered just as the lights began to dim once again.

Alex couldn't deny that the thought of Lucien attending brightened her outlook considerably. And that was a dangerous development.

"Now, pay attention," her father hissed, gesturing to the stage. "I paid a lot of money for these tickets and I haven't a clue what's going on."

"Yes, Father."

Lucien shot her another smile and Alex returned it despite the warning gnawing inside her. For whatever this was between them could not be easily controlled. Not even by her. And if she gave in just a little, that would most *definitely* mean trouble.

Twenty-One

Alex glanced at the clock on her desk and let out a sigh of relief. It was well after six, which meant she had made it through an entire day without getting sidetracked with thoughts of Lucien. Tomorrow they would attend the lecture at the Royal Geographic Society, but that was different. There would be no opportunity for them to be alone, and Alex was determined to keep things that way. After all, the whole point of this was for them to be seen by other people. Being alone would be a waste of time.

But as Alex's mind began to drift to thoughts of just *how* they might waste their time, footfalls sounded in the hall near her office. Had Potts left something behind? That wasn't like him. She must have been in a good mood because as Alex quickly sorted the papers on her desk she was ready to tease her usually fastidious secretary about this oversight when the man appeared in her doorway.

"Really, Potts. Did you forget—" But the rest of the words died on her lips.

Lucien.

Alex sat back in her chair. Hard. "You," she breathed, which sounded very much like an accusation.

Lucien quirked a brow at the strange greeting. "Good evening."

"Is something wrong?" Alex practically barked the question.

She was being incredibly rude, but her nerves were in shambles. Why was he here? And *now*? He was ruining everything.

"No. I came to see you."

He stepped into her office and Alex instinctively leaned back in her chair, though there wasn't anywhere for her to go. "But it's nearly dinnertime."

Lucien gave her an amused look and shrugged. "I took the chance that you would still be here."

Alex began to bristle. Was she truly so predictable? But then he held up a hamper. "And wouldn't have eaten yet."

"Oh."

"Since you haven't made it to Paris, I thought I'd bring a little of it to you."

Oh.

"That is … very thoughtful," Alex conceded grumpily.

Lucien smiled and came closer. "I found an excellent bakery while wandering around town earlier," he explained while he pulled a few items out of the hamper and set them on her desk. "The owner is from Marseilles and prides himself on his baguettes, though his patisserie looked very fine indeed. Then he directed me to his favorite cheesemonger—"

Alex bit her lip. No. This was too much. She couldn't bear it. "You shouldn't have gone to all this trouble."

Especially for me.

Lucien paused and his gaze turned inscrutable. "It's no trouble. There," he said with a flourish. "We have bread, cheese, some fruit, and *tarte aux pommes Normande*."

Alex took in the perfectly baked baguette, the wedge of creamy cheese, the apple tart, and the golden pear. "It's perfect," she murmured, then looked at Lucien. "Thank you."

His eyes warmed and he looked proud enough to burst. "My pleasure."

Lucien insisted on serving her first and Alex was forced to wait while he quickly and competently sliced the pear into equal wedges, then selected the best bits of everything for her. The man had even thought to bring a set of plates and napkins, along with a small flask of wine.

It was *really too much.*

"Here you are," he said indulgently.

Alex let out a resigned sigh as she accepted her plate but after only one bite the sigh turned into one of pleasure. It was just a bit of bread and cheese, but dear heavens, it was *delicious.*

Lucien's eyes gleamed. "That good, eh?"

"Yes," Alex said in between bites, which was horribly vulgar behavior on her part, but he only smiled some more.

Lucien then took a bite and let out his own sound of pleasure. "I think the monsieur may actually have been too humble. This is exquisite."

They ate in a pleasant, companionable silence, only stopping to encourage the other to have more of the cheese or bread, or to try it with a slice of pear. Alex had thought it almost too much food at first, but before long they had finished every last crumb. She let out a contented sigh and sat back in her chair. Lucien was staring thoughtfully at the empty hamper.

"What is it?"

He shook his head. "It's only just now occurred to me that I must have kept you from enjoying a glorious multicourse meal with this simple fare."

Alex huffed a laugh. "Hardly. Most evenings I have a tray in my room." Only after she spoke did she realize how pathetic that sounded. "Because everyone is usually out." But that explanation didn't really help either. "And…I prefer it that way," she added with a determined little nod.

Lucien's mouth curved. "I prefer eating alone too. Aside from the present company, of course."

Alex glanced away as her cheeks flushed. "You must think I'm a horrible curmudgeon. Most people would love to dine with my parents or Freddie, while I try to avoid it as much as possible."

It wasn't as simple as that, but Alex didn't know how else to explain it. How could someone love their family more than anything in the entire world and also find them completely exhausting most of the time?

When she dared to look back at Lucien, he was staring at her with a thoughtful expression. "Their hospitality is legendary, and rightfully so," he conceded. "But I can understand the desire for some peace and quiet, especially after working all day."

"Yes. Exactly," Alex said, brightening. "But my family could never see it that way. They always maintained that I was rejecting their company." Simply saying the words was like poking at a sore spot one had forgotten about.

"When I was younger my father always made sure to dine with us as much as he possibly could because he worked so much and he enjoyed it. I think my parents assumed the tradition would continue once I began working for him. But instead…"

Alex pursed her lips, unable to finish.

She was *selfish*. A *spoilsport*. A *stick in the mud*.

Her mind ran through the most hurtful criticisms her family had made over the years while she gripped the arms of her chair, waiting for Lucien come to the same conclusion as everyone else.

"Instead, you needed something different," he said gently. "I'm sorry you've been so misunderstood. And by your own family. That sounds difficult."

Alex swallowed. She must have eaten something spoiled because surely she was hallucinating right now. That was the only explanation.

Lucien peered at her. "Alex, did you hear what I said?"

"Yes. I did. Only I…"

He smirked. "Don't believe me?"

"Something like that." Alex managed a small smile in return, but it was time to move the subject away from her. "Now, why do *you* prefer to eat alone? A rather strange preference for a man who ran a supper club," she said archly.

Lucien chuckled. "Well, maybe 'prefer' isn't the right term. But I'm used to it." Alex gave him a questioning look and he shrugged. "Born out of necessity, I suppose. My parents both worked long hours. Having supper together, the three of us, didn't happen very often."

"Oh." Alex felt like an idiot—and a selfish one at that given that it had been her own family that necessitated the separation in the first place. "I'm sorry. I wasn't thinking…"

But Lucien waved a hand. "It's fine. I have very fond memories of sitting at the table in the kitchen of Atkinson House eating my supper as my mother doled out instructions to the staff. It was like watching a symphony conductor."

The late Mrs. Taylor had run her kitchen with the kind of quiet mastery Alex couldn't help but admire even as a young girl.

"She was an impressive woman," she said. "And a genius with a pastry bag."

"Yes," he murmured.

Lucien's gaze warmed so much that Alex felt the urge to look away. She did not deserve his esteem for simply speaking the truth. "You must miss her very much."

He nodded and glanced away. "Every day, even after all this time. But Paris helped with the grief." Then his eyes fixed on her again and she was bewildered to find his gaze even more intense than before. "I suppose I owe you my thanks for your encouragement that night all those years ago. I'm not sure I would have left without it."

"I'm sure you would have," she said readily.

He cocked his head and smiled. "You're too modest."

As her heart began to flutter, she had the most disconcerting realization: Alex wasn't bewildered. She was *nervous* again. But that was impossible. She had known Lucien since he was in short pants. She had seen him cry at least a dozen times. Once over a sandwich he had dropped on the ground. No. It was ridiculous that such a person could make *her* feel like this.

"Did you enjoy Paris?" she asked, attempting to direct the conversation toward safer waters.

He nodded. "Very much. It was an education in…life."

"I'm sure. You must have learned a great deal about cooking," she added, relaxing a little. There. Cooking. A much safer topic. No doubt he could speak for *hours* on the subject.

But Lucien paused a moment before answering. "Among other things," he said in a low, suggestive tone as he slowly moved around the desk toward her.

Alex arched a brow. Was he actually *trying* to fluster her now?

She was a little offended he thought it would be that easy. Ignoring the ripple of warning moving through her, Alex tilted her head. "Is that so? Do tell."

Alex had never backed down from a challenge before, especially one issued by a man. Like hell would she start now.

But Lucien's eyes only sparkled. "I may be a virgin," he began as he stopped directly in front of her. "But Paris isn't exactly a nunnery."

She nodded, as if this were a perfectly normal thing to say. "Right."

"And while I may lack experience, I'm not without an imagination. And, I confess, I have spent quite a lot of time lately imagining you."

"Have you, now." She tried to sound stern. In control. But even she couldn't hide the tremble in her voice.

Slowly, Lucien placed a palm on either side of her until she was boxed in between him and the desk. Then he leaned closer and lowered his voice.

"Would you like me to show you?" As he held her gaze, his eyes warmed with something that went beyond mere desire. It was a kind of knowing, like she was being seen, *truly* seen, for the very first time. She forgot that this had started as something of a challenge for her. Lucien was completely serious.

"Just say the word, Alex. Yes or no. This is entirely your choice."

She had no doubt that he would stop if she asked. At any point. And that knowledge made the last of her nerves fade away.

"Yes," she gasped, suddenly breathless. "Yes."

⁊℃

Oh, the things he would do to make her say *yes* again.

And again and again.

Lucien straightened while keeping his gaze firmly on her face. He had learned that Alex's expressions were subtle and fleeting, but they were there all the same. One only had to watch. And lately Lucien had been watching her a great deal.

The duke's advice echoed in his head:

The most important thing to do is pay attention. As closely as you can.

He would make up for his lack of experience with consideration. His hands encircled her waist and she inhaled a sharp breath as he drew her to her feet. Alex dressed for the office like a particularly dowdy schoolmarm, yet it fanned his desire far higher than the scantily dressed dancers in the most notorious corners of Paris ever had. He flexed his fingers against the fine fabric of her skirt.

She began to take off her spectacles, but Lucien caught her wrist.

"No. Leave them on."

"Don't tell me you've been imagining *those* as well," she said archly.

Lucien grinned. "Is that so unbelievable?"

"Only as much as the rest of it." She stuttered a little as he pressed his lips to the delicate flesh of her inner wrist.

"Surely I don't need to explain that you are a desirable woman."

He did not add that her romance with Chisolm proved as much.

Her eyes flashed with uncertainty. "But you want—" Then she clamped her mouth shut.

Freddie.

Her sister hovered like a ghostly specter over them. And though Lucien longed to deny it, that would be disingenuous given that his long-held affection was the very reason he stood here in the first place. And no doubt Alex would be insulted by such a bald-faced lie.

So instead he settled for the simple truth: "I want *you*." Then he pressed his mouth to hers with an urgency that was all too real. Alex gasped against his lips and drove her fingers through his hair, bringing him even closer. Lucien had to grip the edge of the desk with one hand to keep his balance.

He couldn't believe he had ever thought her cold and unfeeling. The woman was a whirlwind. Or a summer storm that rolled in without warning. But Lucien had come prepared.

Their kisses turned deeper as Alex opened her lips to welcome his tongue. Though he might not have much experience with the rest of it, Lucien was a man who dearly loved kissing and Alex matched his enthusiasm. She caressed his shoulders before palming his upper arms. Lucien instinctively flexed under her touch and she let out a purr of approval.

Lucien dragged his lips along the smooth column of her neck. "Tell me what you want," he said hoarsely by her ear.

Alex met his eyes. "I rather liked what you were doing."

Lucien immediately continued. He nibbled the flesh just below her ear and Alex arched against him. "Oh God," she whispered.

He nearly melted at her words. Then he did it again. Harder. This time her response wasn't intelligible but she gripped the nape of his neck and held him there. Lucien smiled against her skin and obliged. Then he deeply inhaled.

"I love the way you smell," he growled. "Like fresh ink and paper."

Alex rasped a laugh. "So, like an office?"

Lucien shoved the chair out of the way and set her on top of the desk, then pressed the tip of his nose to hers. "A very *appealing* office."

She gave him a coy smile and smoothed her palm down his chest. "Take off your jacket."

He had never removed an article of clothing so quickly. Her eyes glinted with humor as her hands continued to stroke his front. One began to wander a little lower, but Lucien halted its progress. "Another time," he said as he dragged his hand down the length of her thigh. "I have something to prove today."

Alex tilted her head. "You're so certain there will be another time?"

Oh, but he *loved* when she teased him.

Lucien licked his lips and leaned in close once more. "I intend to convince you I deserve the opportunity," he murmured by her ear and heartily enjoyed her responding shiver. He scattered broken kisses across her neck and jaw while he found the hem of her skirt. She then shifted in place and together they hiked up the swathes of dark fabric.

His breath caught at the sight of her black silk stockings. A length of fine embroidery wound up the side of each leg. Lucien squinted and looked closer. Then he smiled. They were tiny pink rosettes set on a green vine. He *never* would have expected such whimsy from her. Lucien looked up and found Alex watching him closely. He ran a finger along the length of one thigh. Even softer than he imagined. "How adorable."

Her cheeks turned nearly the same color as the rosettes. "Years ago my sisters started giving me embroidered stockings for my birthday as a joke. But I've fully embraced the novelty on my own now," she said with a smirk.

Lucien wondered what other delightful objects he would find on her stockings.

If you get the chance.

He silenced the thought and kissed her. Hard. Time to prove himself.

She wrapped her arms around his neck and let out a soft moan. Lucien slid a hand up her thigh and stopped to caress the band of skin where her stockings ended. Alex moaned a little more and gripped him tighter.

"Show me," he rasped. "Show me how to please you."

"Higher."

He immediately obeyed and cupped her through the soft cotton lawn of her drawers. She was so impossibly hot.

Alex canted her hips against his hand. "More, Lucien."

He found the slit in her drawers and pressed two fingers inside. Then let out a guttural curse as he grazed her flesh. She was so wet. For *him*. He began to stroke and pulled back to watch her face. Alex had closed her eyes but then he felt her fingers on his wrist.

"Like this," she murmured, directing him higher, and began making slow circles with his fingertips.

As he followed her lead, the change was immediate. Her eyelashes fluttered and her breath quickened. He pressed a little harder and she let out a very rewarding gasp.

Her head fell back and she tilted her hips a little higher. He wrapped his free arm around her waist and guided her down onto the desk until she could comfortably lean on her elbows.

Suddenly she gripped his wrist and looked him directly in the eye. "Don't stop."

As if he even could.

Lucien moved his fingers a little faster and her eyes fluttered shut again as she began moving her hips against his hand. Faster and faster until she cried out and her whole body tensed. She was absolutely mesmerizing. Lucien had barely recovered from this display when her trembling hand covered his own and guided him toward her entrance. She shot him a desperate look.

"I need more."

He nodded and pressed a finger inside her channel, then another. She was even hotter and wetter than he could have ever imagined. "Oh God, Alex," he groaned as she tightened around him. He began to pleasure her with his fingers and she let out another sob.

Her hands gripped the front of his shirt. *"Lucien."*

He pressed a hand against the front of his trousers. The urge to fuck her was nearly overwhelming. He had *never* felt this tempted before.

Alex let out another gasp and shuddered. He could feel the orgasm rippling through her wet heat. Then her eyes flew open and she gave him a look of such raw intensity that he felt impossibly exposed.

"Please," she begged, reaching for him. "Please let me."

Her gaze softened and Lucien was completely at her mercy. In that moment she could have asked anything of him and he would have crossed the fiery pits of hell to give it to her. He gave a breathless nod and she practically tore his trousers open. His aching cock sprung free from his smallclothes and Alex gripped his length. She began to pump him, gently at first until he urged her to go harder.

"I won't last," he gasped.

"I don't care," she said, working him even faster.

Within another moment he let out a guttural roar and bent over

Alex as he let out the strongest release of his life. His hands pressed onto the desktop and he shoved against her hand, mindless with a pleasure that went on and on. He hadn't even had the wherewithal to avoid spending on her, but Alex didn't seem to mind. She only drew him closer and stroked his back in slow circles.

I'm not sure which one of you is in more trouble.

The duke's ominous words echoed through his addled mind, and Lucien let out a weak laugh he hoped didn't sound as desperate as it felt.

Him. It was definitely him.

Alex wiped off her glasses and held them up to the light. They had gotten rather foggy during their intimacies. She cast a glance at Lucien as he pulled on his jacket. He had been avoiding her gaze ever since they finished, and she was trying very hard not to be disappointed.

"May I ask you a question?"

He finally looked at her and for a moment wariness flashed in his eyes. "Certainly," he replied as he straightened the lapels of his coat.

"*Why* are you a virgin?"

He let out a surprised laugh. Alex knew she was being forward, but it seemed within her rights to at least ask.

"I was busy running a business," he said with a shrug.

Alex blinked. "But you must have had opportunities."

Lucien looked uncomfortable. "I suppose. Eventually. And I don't need to remind you that I was a rather…awkward youth. That didn't disappear overnight."

"Fair enough."

"And just because I had opportunities didn't mean I wished to take them. Or at least, take everything that was on offer," he added.

"Huh."

Lucien arched a brow. "You sound surprised," he said drolly.

"Well, yes. I am. It's just…that's not what I've been told about men."

He opened his arms. "And yet, here I am." Then his gaze sharpened. "What about you? I hardly need to point out that *your* behavior is unusual."

"It isn't unusual, it's not *approved*," she said hotly. "Women have fleshly desires the same as men, yet we are shamed for it."

He nodded vigorously. "It's similar to how I'm made to feel shamed."

"Except no one would ever call you ruined," she pointed out.

Lucien deflated a little. "You're right."

"But I agree that you shouldn't feel ashamed," she added. "I'm sorry if I made you feel that way. It's only that you—"

"What?" he prompted.

"Well, I'm sure you could have whomever you wanted."

Lucien watched her closely, his expression grave. "Not quite."

Alex winced.

Freddie.

In the heat of their encounter she had completely forgotten about his deep, impossible love for her sister and their stupid arrangement. Why had she *ever* thought this was a good idea?

"I know there are men who think nothing of bedsport," he continued. "But I always wanted…" He paused and let out a sigh.

He didn't need to finish the thought, though. Alex understood.

The dreamy look in his eyes said enough. He wanted to be with someone he truly cared about. Someone he loved.

She recalled the image of him crying furious, heartbroken tears in the hedge all those years ago, along with the look of enchantment on his face as he stared at Freddie in the gig just weeks before. Anyone else would have seen the beginning of a grand love story, yet Alex had only thought to separate them. What kind of person did that make her?

The villainess.

Alex suddenly felt ill and in need of a bath. Though it would take far more than a single tub of water to rid herself of this feeling of disgust.

"Anyway," Lucien continued with a shake of his head. "Perhaps I've been too precious about it." Then he fixed her with a look. "And you?"

"I didn't give it much thought one way or another, to be honest," she said. "Not until the opportunity to bed a man presented itself."

"Benjamin Chisolm."

Her cheeks burned with that old hurt. That resentment. She looked away. "I thought I loved him."

"That is understandable. I'm sure he was very charming."

Alex chafed against his gentle tone and turned back to him. "I wasn't some cow-eyed idiot who lifted my skirts over a few pretty words." Then she narrowed her eyes. "Is that what he told you?"

Lucien shook his head. "No. Not at all. He said he was your tutor and that you had feelings for him." He cleared his throat. "Feelings that weren't…reciprocated."

Alex's immediate reaction was to laugh. She almost would rather Benjamin had told Lucien the truth. Or a closer version of it. But then a darker, uglier thought occurred to her. She inhaled a shaky breath. "And you believed him without question because of *course* that was the most likely explanation."

Lucien's brow furrowed, but he didn't deny it. "I—I didn't… that is—"

Heat gathered behind her eyes while the familiar taste of rejection clawed up her throat. Damn him for making her think he actually understood her. And damn her for *ever* entertaining such a stupid idea.

"Because I couldn't have possibly been the one to end things, is that it? After all, a woman like me would be lucky to have an offer from a man like him," she practically growled.

"Alex. No," he protested weakly, but his crimson cheeks gave him away. Then he let out a sigh and dragged a hand down his face. "I'm sorry. I did believe his story, but I never thought for even a moment that you would have been *lucky* to have him."

She softened a little at the incredulousness in his voice, but she crossed her arms against the urge to accept his apology. Alex didn't owe him her forgiveness. Not yet. "All right, then."

He began to rub his palm in slow circles over her shoulder and her eyes fluttered shut. His touch felt so warm and comforting that she was sorely tempted to lean against him. To let someone take care of her for just a moment. "Why did it end?"

She opened her eyes and mulled over the question before answering. "I expected to work for my father after I left Oxford," she began. "Benjamin did not agree. He wanted me to support his career at the cost of my own. And use my connections to help him, of course." Her jaw tightened as she spoke, but she pushed on. "We argued about it. Frequently. When it finally became clear to him that I would not give in, he threatened to go to my father to force my hand."

Lucien dropped his hand and looked properly shocked. "That fiend."

Alex shrugged. "He was hardly unique. Very few men are willing to cast their own dreams aside to support their wives. But I was too young and naive to realize that at the time."

"Did your father ever find out?"

Alex shook her head. "Only Will knows the truth. He took care of Benjamin."

"By offering him a ticket to America," Lucien supplied.

Alex flashed him a grim smile. "Along with a few other things to help him find his feet. My allowance at the time couldn't cover the entire cost." Then she turned away. "After that I promised myself I would never rely on anyone else ever again."

"But there are some things we all need that can't be bought, Alex," he murmured.

Her shoulders tightened and she neatly stepped away from Lucien. She had indulged in enough self-pity for one evening. "Not me." Then she looked back at him. "I've made sure of that."

Lucien looked dubious but did not press her on this. "Why do you think he's returned to London?"

Alex relaxed a little, grateful for the subject change. "Marguerite said his father is ill, but I doubt that is the whole truth."

"Don't you think it's odd that he wants to invest in my business?"

"No, because it's a good idea."

"Alex," Lucien began, shaking his head. "You can't expect me to ignore your past with him. The man had barely said hello before he started telling me all about you."

"And as I told you before," Alex insisted. "You shouldn't let personal feelings interfere with—"

"Not if I don't *trust* him," Lucien countered. "Believe me, if there is one thing I've learned from running the supper club it is that a person's character matters."

Alex pressed her lips together. She didn't know what else to say. If Benjamin did end up making Lucien the best offer, she wanted him to take it. She wouldn't be an obstacle to his success.

"You'll only be hurting yourself if you reject him simply because of me. And I don't need your pity."

"I do *not* pity you, Alex."

"But you...you feel *something*."

"Yes, I do," he said plainly. "And that matters."

The admission should have sparked joy in her, but Alex only felt miserable. "Not in business."

He stared at her for a moment before letting out a scoff. "Right," he said as he pulled on his jacket. "My mistake, then."

As he gathered his things, every part of her cried out in protest. *Wait.*

But Alex stamped down the feeling. Buried it with all the others she did not indulge in. Better for him to be disappointed with her now than later on anyway.

He did not look at her again before he stormed from the room. And Alex was alone once more.

Twenty-Two

*L*ucien stifled a yawn with the back of his hand as he entered the lecture room of the Royal Geographical Society. It was only a few minutes before the discussion started, but most of the attendees hadn't taken their seats yet and instead milled about the room happily chatting with one another. Lucien looked for Alex's stiff form, but his heart sank. She wasn't here. He quickly took an empty seat at the back and braced his elbows on his thighs. If she didn't come tonight, he needed a plan.

He had left Alex's office the night before convinced that she was the most maddening, impossible woman he had *ever* encountered. Their exchange echoed in his head as he stormed into Alain's flat, while he stripped down to his smallclothes, and as he scrubbed her scent from his face and body. Then he flung himself onto a chair and glared up at the ceiling.

After all, a woman like me would be lucky *to have an offer from a man like him.*

Lucien let out a groan and pressed the heels of his palms against his eyes.

Maddening, impossible, and irritatingly *insightful*.

For until the truth of her past with Chisolm left her lips, it had been all too easy to imagine her as the wounded party. As the lonely, heartbroken young woman burying herself in work to forget the pain of rejection. This realization stripped the undeserved anger from his bones. But it was the certainty in her words and bearing that left him tossing and turning for most of the night.

Because it was proof that he wasn't any better. That he saw her just like everyone else.

And for that Lucien was thoroughly ashamed of himself.

I thought I was in love

But *had* Alex loved him? Was she even capable of the emotion? She spoke of intimacy the same way she talked of stock portfolios and investment capital. Lucien had wanted her to rage at him. To tear off that mask of cool indifference. But he knew the exact moment he lost her.

I don't need your pity.

He pinched the bridge of his nose as his irritation began to rise anew. If only Alex were *here* he could try to—

"Mr. Taylor."

Lucien glanced up in the direction of the mildly disapproving voice and locked eyes with Alex's formidable aunt.

She came.

He scrambled to his feet and bobbed his head. "Mrs. Bailey," he said while trying to cast a furtive glance behind her.

In response, the older woman let out an exasperated huff. "Alexandra will be here in a moment. She is in the hallway speaking with Mrs. LaSalle."

Lucien gave a distracted nod and glanced eagerly toward the doorway. "Good. Wonderful. I'm very glad she is here."

Mrs. Bailey narrowed her eyes. "Yes. I wanted to speak with you before she returns. About your…courtship."

The hesitation in her voice drew his full attention.

"Madame?"

"I was a great fan of your mother. She made her way in the world through a mixture of talent and sheer will I couldn't help but admire."

"Thank you—"

She held up a hand. "Let me finish. Your father, however, always struck me as being more concerned with finding new ways to sneak in a few more chapters than excelling at his job."

Lucien was sorely tempted to point out that there weren't very many ways to excel beyond performing the task of driving Mr. Atkinson around, but he held his tongue. Besides, Mrs. Bailey wasn't exactly wrong, as finding new ways to read more was one of the chief driving forces of his father's life.

"Now, I may be a spoiled old woman, but I am not a snob. I don't care that your father is the coachman and your mother was the cook. Not if you truly care for Alexandra. I say all this because I have not yet decided which of your parent's traits you have inherited: the drive of your mother, or the opportunism of your father. And I am *quite* interested to see which wins out."

Lucien cleared his throat and nodded. He understood her skepticism, even while finding it deeply insulting.

"My niece is very dear to me," Mrs. Bailey continued. "And while she would be mortified if she knew I was saying any of this to you, I know how it can feel to be a woman out of step with society. The endless whispers, the deliberate exclusions, the outright lies. She has experienced all of it and bears it with more grace than anyone I know. But while her independence is one of her best qualities, a certain amount of loneliness can follow, if she isn't careful."

"She doesn't seem very lonely to me," Lucien said, in an attempt to defend Alex.

But Mrs. Bailey shook her head in frustration. "I'm not speaking of *now*, but years in the future. Her sisters will marry soon. They will have families of their own. And some day even *she* won't be able to spend all her time in that blasted office!" Mrs. Bailey punctuated this with a little stamp of her foot.

He glanced around the room, but her outburst seemed to have gone unnoticed—that, or people were polite enough to ignore it. A large gentleman was watching the both of them from across the room and just as recognition began to kindle in his mind, Alex entered and his thoughts scattered. As their gazes tangled, she stopped short and a look of hesitance crossed her face. This uncharacteristic display of wariness struck a place deep within him and brought a single thought to the surface. He didn't want her to feel unsure. Ever. Especially about him. As the corner of his mouth curved in greeting, Alex's dark eyes fixed on it.

Come here, Lucien tried to say. *Stand beside me.*

After a moment, she took a halting step forward. Then another. His smile widened just as Mrs. Bailey tapped his forearm with her fan and he was obligated to tear his attention away from Alex. She gave him a smug smile and leaned closer.

"I, for one, am dearly hoping drive wins," she murmured before turning to address Alex. "There you are. Take my seat. I've just spotted a gentleman I haven't seen in many years and must accost him immediately about this oversight."

Alex obeyed her aunt's command and dutifully moved to the chair beside Lucien, which she took without looking at him. He held back a sigh and sat down. This was going to be difficult.

"I was worried you wouldn't come tonight," he said after a moment.

Alex swallowed and lifted her chin but kept her gaze firmly in front of her. "You should know by now that I always honor my business agreements, Mr. Taylor. No matter what."

Lucien's first instinct was to retreat, but he resisted. "Business agreements," he repeated slowly, letting his tongue linger on the words. It felt as silly as it sounded.

When he didn't say anything more, Alex reluctantly turned to him. "That's what this is," she insisted. "Or have you forgotten?"

He stared into her eyes, watching with relief as her pupils grew. Lucien might not be certain of much where Alex was concerned, but he knew she was attracted to him. "No, I haven't forgotten. But I do think I have misunderstood."

Just as her brow furrowed in confusion, a man with a large gray mustache approached the lectern and began to introduce the speaker. Alex gave Lucien another wary glance before facing forward.

⁓

Alex barely heard a word of the hour-long lecture, which was a pity as she had been looking forward to it. Instead, her mind turned over the words Lucien had muttered half to himself just before the lecture began.

I do think I have misunderstood.

Misunderstood *what?*

When the roar of applause filled the room, Alex nearly jumped out of her seat. She looked around in a daze before joining in and caught Lucien shooting her a knowing smile. Alex frowned in return. She didn't like this feeling he brought out in her. It was as if she were standing on a small, slippery rock. One wrong move and she would fall.

Alex had come here tonight prepared to endure his company for the sake of appearances, and fully expected his enthusiasm level to match her own. But then he had smiled at her when she entered the room. The kind of private little smile she had seen her parents exchange hundreds of times. One that spoke of a kind of intimacy that had always remained a mystery to her, until now.

It had brought her to a complete stop, yet she still felt the floor shift beneath her feet.

Do not *fall.*

Despite this admonishment, it still took her a moment to recover herself enough to move. And still he smiled, watching her with an unfamiliar kind of interest that was both intoxicating and terrifying. It was something of a relief when her aunt distracted him enough that she could continue unobserved.

Now, though, his attention had shifted away from the speaker to her once more.

Alex focused even harder on the empty lectern. "Fascinating, wasn't it?" But this attempt at levity failed and the words came out strangled. Tight. Affected.

"Very."

She cleared her throat at his deep murmur. And *why* must he continue to watch her? The man very well knew what she looked like. And yet, she could practically feel his gaze wandering over her cheek, the slope of her nose, down her neck—

"Alex," he prompted.

She turned to him then only in a vain attempt to hide the blush fighting to escape her collar and raised an eyebrow, as if everything were perfectly normal between them. As if his fingers hadn't been inside her, urging her toward release. As if she hadn't stroked him to completion in her own office.

This man.

As she met his eyes, full once again of that damned spark of understanding, the weight of all that had passed between them suddenly pressed down on her.

He wasn't the first man she had been with. But he was the first man—the *only* man—who had considered her pleasure. That was the problem. Technically, Benjamin took her virginity—which she believed to be a social construct designed to control women anyway—but her first taste of true intimacy was with Lucien. He had seen a side of her no one else had. A side she normally kept carefully hidden away. Because it signaled uncontrollable need. Dependency. Recklessness. All the things she abhorred most.

"May I speak with you," he continued. "Privately?"

Yes.

Alex shut her eyes against the nearly overwhelming urge to accept his offer. To allow herself to be spirited away to some dark corner. And then...

She forced her eyes open. The balance of power had shifted between them. And it had to be remedied immediately.

"I'd prefer we stay here," she said carefully.

Lucien's brow wrinkled with concern rather than irritation. "All right. Would you care for any refreshments?"

Alex nodded. Her throat felt lined with sandpaper.

Lucien smiled at that and rose before offering her his arm. Must he always be so *polite*? She took it reluctantly and allowed him to guide her to the next room, where a large bowl of punch and plates of shortbread were laid out. He handed her a glass first, before taking his own, then gestured to the shortbread, which she declined.

Aunt Winifred was nearby, talking with an older man that must be her erstwhile friend. She caught Alex's gaze and nodded in approval. No doubt Aunt Winifred wouldn't mind if she and Lucien slipped away somewhere. There were likely a half dozen empty rooms in this place. Perfect for a quick tryst. Alex forced the wayward thought from her mind and took a sip of punch, then grimaced.

Lucien chuckled. "It does leave something to be desired."

"Did no one taste this after dumping an entire sack of sugar into the bowl?"

"An appalling misuse of sweetener," he quipped, flashing her that private little smile once more.

The corners of her mouth trembled with the urge to return it. "Your Gallic sensibilities must be horribly offended. Let me apologize on behalf of the British inclination to over-sugar anything."

The smile turned into a grin. "Ah, but you forget I have the audacity to be half English. An unforgivable flaw of which I was often reminded."

"Oh heavens, I can only imagine," she said with a laugh. A *laugh*.

And all while Lucien watched her with those dazzling eyes of his. Then he took another sip of the terrible punch and winced. "God, it's even worse the second time."

Another laugh burst from her, even louder than the first, and Alex slapped a hand over her mouth as a few people cast inquiring looks in their direction.

Get ahold of yourself.

She removed her hand and straightened her shoulders, attempting her usual formality. "I assume you didn't wish to talk to me about the punch."

Lucien glanced down and shook his head. "No. I wanted to apologize for my behavior yesterday." Then he looked up, his eyes filled with remorse. "You were right. I made a number of assumptions about you and it was difficult to accept my own thoughtlessness."

Alex felt her heart skip several beats. She shouldn't be so affected by this simple admission. After all, she *was* right. And yet, how often had anyone—least of all a *man*—admitted it with such simplicity? Such lack of hubris?

"Thank you," she murmured. "I appreciate you saying that."

The corner of his mouth lifted and he leaned a little closer to her. As she inhaled a greedy lungful of his scent, her eyelids fluttered. Would he ask to speak with her privately once more? Alex wasn't sure she possessed the strength to say no a second time.

"Then we are friends again?"

She snapped to attention. He was giving her a hopeful, open look that called to mind that long-ago night when she had found him by the hedge, his boyish face streaked with tears.

You really think I could leave this place?

"Yes. Of course. Friends." Alex looked away as she swallowed the bitter tang that filled her mouth. *Friends.* "Excuse me. I need to freshen up." Then she left without another word.

❧

Alex remained in the powder room for as long as she possibly could before her aunt would come looking for her. She stared at her somber reflection in the gilt-framed mirror and pretended to fuss with her hair, though there was no one else around she needed to convince.

Friends.

It wasn't until he said the word that she realized just how very much she did *not* want to be Lucien's friend.

Friends didn't yearn to feel the heat of their bodies pressed together. Or kiss each other. Or spend an inordinate amount of time wondering what the other looked like naked.

At least, not any friend she had ever had.

Alex certainly never thought about Will that way. Even when she proposed to him.

No. These feelings for Lucien were decidedly *un*-friendly.

So stop being a coward and tell *him.*

Alex sighed and leaned her forehead against the mirror's cool glass. She could accept that he was attracted to her. But would her pride allow her to accept being second in his heart to Freddie?

"I don't know," she whispered in the quiet of the room. She hated this feeling of weakness. Of uncertainty. She had felt this way once before and had resolved never to put herself in such a position ever again.

Only one option remained. She must tell Lucien how she felt and exactly what she wanted. Master this desire before it consumed her.

She stepped out into the hall and marched toward the lecture room with a newfound determination. But she hadn't taken more than a few steps before an all-too-familiar voice called out from behind her.

"May I have a word, Miss Atkinson?"

The chill that ran through her brought her to a halt.

Though his voice was as smooth as silk, she well knew it was more a demand than a question. For Benjamin never took "no" for an answer. Except once. And Alex had paid for that quite dearly.

She turned around and cast him her most withering look. The one that reliably made grown men cower. "What do you want?"

But he only smiled as he strolled toward her. "Come now. Is that any way to greet your first love?"

Alex rolled her eyes. "You are nothing of the sort."

"If that's what you need to tell yourself to carry on, so be it." He gave her a smug little smile that turned her stomach.

Good Lord, how had she *ever* been attracted to this man? Alex longed to give her younger self a much-needed dressing-down for falling for such shallow charms. She lifted her chin. "You know very well that I am involved with someone."

"Yes, the boy," he said with a dismissive flick of his hand. "That's what I want to speak to you about, actually."

"Well, I don't want to speak with you at all. About *anything*." She then turned on her heel and continued back down the hallway. No doubt Benjamin would interpret her utter disinterest for hurt, but she didn't care.

"Oh, I think you will want to hear what I have to say very much, Alexandra."

She hesitated at the warning in his voice and couldn't help looking over her shoulder. Benjamin remained in the same spot, but the look he gave her brought her to a complete stop.

He knew. She didn't know how, but he *knew*.

She faced him and crossed her arms. "Out with it, then. I must return before Mr. Taylor begins to worry."

Benjamin chuckled as he approached her.

"I had my suspicions from the first. But it wasn't until I had a very interesting conversation with your sister at the Langhams' last week that I became certain that this was nothing more than a farce."

Alex's mouth went dry. "I don't know what you mean."

Benjamin tilted his head. "Don't you? Admittedly it took a few generous cups of Lady Langham's famous punch to get anything out of the chit, but once I mentioned you and your little paramour, she was all too willing to express her…let's say, 'skepticism,' over the pairing."

Alex swallowed.

"I knew you could be ruthless when it came to business, Alexandra, but I never thought you would stoop so low as to keep your own sister apart from her true love."

"I have done nothing of the sort," she said coolly.

"That's not what Winifred thinks," he said with a shrug. "In fact, she's rather torn up about it, poor thing."

Alex stepped closer and pointed her finger directly against his chest. "You're *lying*."

He merely raised an eyebrow. "Are you certain of that?"

Alex pursed her lips. She wasn't, actually. But given their past, it was a reasonable assumption. "What do you want?"

"I've been trying to arrange to meet with Lucien again, but the lad's been rather evasive. I can't help but think you've put him off me."

"I absolutely have not." That, at least, was true. "Perhaps *you* need to make him a better offer."

Benjamin seemed to consider this, then shook his head. "Hmm. No, I don't think so. Actually, I think he should accept my new offer. Unfortunately for him, it isn't as good as my original offer.

But it does come with the assurance that I won't ruin his reputation and yours by spreading some rather nasty rumors."

Alex didn't know why she was so shocked. She should have anticipated something like this since the moment he appeared in the LaSalles' salon.

"You're threatening to blackmail me *again*?" She let out a bitter laugh. "I thought you would have come up with something better by now."

Benjamin raised his hands up in a helpless gesture. "I stick with what works. And this approach has served me well in the past."

Alex gritted her teeth against the knowing look he gave her. She wasn't sure what angered her more: that she was being swindled by this man yet again, or that the whole of society was convinced he possessed some kind of unparalleled business acumen. Though perhaps having absolutely no morals *was* the best way to get ahead.

"Why are you really back? Did something happen in New York?"

Benjamin flicked a glance at his nails, as if the question was terribly boring. "Oh, the usual. A few bad investments. A lean year in returns. A failed romance and a very irate husband," he added with a sly look.

Alex rolled her eyes. "And now you need money."

Then he met her gaze. "I need a guaranteed success. Quickly."

"And you came to me of all people?"

He tilted his head, considering her. "You have good instincts. When it comes to business, at least. And besides, you owe me."

"I absolutely do *not*," she huffed.

His eyes narrowed. "We would have been married for years by now if you hadn't been so stubborn."

Alex couldn't hold back the incredulous laugh at the thought. "You are making a very big leap there, Benjamin."

"Then give me this and I won't do something worse," he said. "Like go after your company."

Alex's breath caught. "You wouldn't."

"Only if I have to," he murmured.

A heavy weight seemed to crash over her then and she let out a sigh. She was so bloody *tired* of dealing with people like him. But what choice did she have?

On impulse Alex grasped his hands. "Will you promise to make a success of him?"

She had never pleaded with anyone before. At least, not since she was a child begging Lucien's mother for one more slice of cake. That she was now doing it on behalf of the same woman's son was not lost on her. "Please, Ben," she whispered. "If you ever cared for me, even just a little."

He frowned and for a brief moment she caught a glimpse of something that looked very much like concern. "Of course." He then pulled his hands from her grip and smoothed his cuffs. "That's the best way to make real money anyway. And it *is* a good idea." He paused and gave her a considering look. "Frankly, I'm surprised you didn't want to invest in it yourself."

She let out a little huff. "I don't want to go into the food business."

"Why not? I know you helped with that proposal. It has your mark all over it. And your ideas were sound. Inspired, even," he added reluctantly. "You can't tell me you're happy sitting in an office marking up other people's ideas all day."

"I'm good at it."

"Yes, I know," he said with a dry laugh. "But doesn't it get terribly boring? I never thought you would still be working for your father all these years later. What happened to helping women open their own—"

"Stop," she bit off, forgetting for a moment the power this man held over her. "We're done here." But for once Benjamin did as he was told and shut his mouth. "And I'll speak to Lucien," she continued, her voice as thin as a reed. "You'll hear from him soon."

Benjamin gave her a complacent nod and looked at his feet in an appropriate expression of shame, even if it wasn't entirely felt. Either way, she should be pleased. As promised, Lucien would come away from their agreement in a better position than he started. And despite everything, she did believe Benjamin would use all his resources and connections to make the business a success. But most important, she could put an end to this courtship farce with him. Though it would be difficult, if not impossible, to sway the board without Lucien, Alex couldn't go on like this. She would have to think of something else. But in the meantime, her life could go back to normal.

No more interminable evenings spent in theaters or ballrooms, gasping for breath in a too-tight gown, trying to convince everyone around her that someone actually wanted to be with her. She would confess nothing to Lucien and had no desire to play the villain. If he and Freddie still wanted to be together so badly, then let them. Alex would not stand in their way anymore. The Ericsons be damned. And then everyone would get what they wanted. It was a perfectly Shakespearian ending.

But as Alex walked away, regret began to slowly churn inside her until she forced it to stop. Until she felt nothing but the numbing embrace of apathy. Then she forced her lips into a smile and entered the room.

Twenty-Three

As soon as Lucien caught sight of Alex entering the room, he made his excuses to the gentleman who had been talking his ear off for the last fifteen minutes. About what, Lucien couldn't even recall. His only thoughts had been for Alex. Namely, what he would say to her and, more important, what she would say in return.

He weaved through the crowd toward her, unable to stop a genuine smile from spreading across his face. But as Lucien grew closer, his step faltered. Alex looked pale and drawn, while she clenched and unclenched her hands with a kind of nervous tension Lucien had never seen from her before. Then she turned sharply to him. As their eyes met, Lucien knew. She was going to end this tonight. End it now.

He could feel the smile fall away from his lips and his steps begin to drag. But there was no avoiding this. Nothing he could do to change her mind.

Lucien shoved his hands in his pockets as he moved beside her. "Well, then. Have you something to say to me?"

She cleared her throat and stood a little straighter, as if her puffed-out chest was a kind of armor. "I believe our association has come to its natural end."

He let out a dispirited laugh at the primness in her voice. This woman who had fallen apart from his touch. "Oh, do you? Funny, I signed a contract that says otherwise."

Alex's eyes briefly fluttered closed. "I am voiding our contract."

Lucien licked his lips. "On what grounds?" He forced his voice to remain steady. Controlled. "You know damn well I haven't broken your morality clause."

"I do."

Her soft reply only angered him further. "Then *why?*" he said through gritted teeth.

"Benjamin spoke to me just now. He is very keen for you to accept his offer. And I think you should take it," she explained calmly, slowly. As if he were an unruly dog that needed to be brought to heel. "He's a bit sore that you've been avoiding him, though, so it will be less than you originally discussed—" Lucien barked a laugh. "But," she continued with a silencing look. "I will make up the difference."

"Absolutely not," Lucien scoffed. "Forget the money, I don't want to partner with him on principle."

"But—"

He turned his whole body toward her. "I told you I don't *trust* him," he hissed.

"You must," she urged. "He will ruin your good name if you don't. And I—I won't be able to protect you."

Lucien stared into her pleading eyes. "Is he threatening you?"

Alex glanced away. "It's…complicated." Then she shook her head. "I'm so sorry."

"Whatever for?"

"I really did want to help you. But now all I've managed is to force you into a business relationship."

He took her arm. "You haven't forced me into anything."

She let out a sigh. "Lucien, if you don't partner with him, he will ruin your reputation."

"Then let him. What do I care if—"

"And my sisters." At his silence, she continued. "If it were just myself, then so be it. But Phoebe already has enough to deal with becoming a duchess and Freddie is one scandal short of being blackballed by society. I can't... I can't *do* that to them. No matter what I may want."

"I see," he murmured after a long moment, taking some comfort in the way her body visibly relaxed under his touch.

"Good," she said with a nod. "I did make him promise that he would make a success of you."

Lucien let out a dry laugh. "Well, that's a relief."

"And I will look over your contract. You won't be bound to him forever," she added, pressing her hand to his forearm for a brief moment.

Lucien stared at the spot before lifting his gaze to her face, where she watched him anxiously. Was this how she expressed affection? In contracts and legalese and business dealings? Was she trying to communicate her regard or was he simply looking for a scrap of meaning anywhere he could find it, like a hungry beggar in the doorway of a banquet?

"What about the board? Don't you need me?"

But Alex shook her head. "I'll think of something else. Or perhaps taking on the Ericsons as clients will be enough to prove my acumen once and for all."

Suddenly a white-hot urge snaked through his veins. The urge to take her firmly by the shoulders and refuse to let her go. Not until she said something that couldn't also double as recorded minutes from a board meeting. Something *real*. As real as everything he felt for her. Everything he had wanted to say. But he could still say them, couldn't he?

Do it, then. If you're so sure she'll want to hear it. That she'll fall into a swoon over you.

But instead Lucien kept his mouth shut. Kept all those pretty thoughts and feelings tucked safely away. Because of course Alex wouldn't swoon. She probably wouldn't even blink. He was Lucien Taylor, the son of the cook and the coachman. He had been lucky she ever thought to bother with him at all. Even if it had only been a ruse to keep him away from Freddie.

God, *Freddie*.

What Alex must think of him, claiming to be in love with her own sister but then gladly taking her favors. He was a cad. A walking embarrassment. Not even when he boarded the train to London with little more than the clothes on his back had he felt this pathetic.

She was right. Their association had come to an end. And not a moment too soon.

"All right, then. If that is what you think is best," he said woodenly. "Consider our contract terminated. It was nice doing business with you, Miss Atkinson." Then he gave her a stiff, short bow and walked out of the room.

※

Alex scanned the ballroom of Park House, taking in the array of guests enjoying her parents' hospitality. A month before, she would have been very pleased by the turnout—from a purely business-minded perspective, of course. Personally, there were only a handful of people here that she could stand, and she was related to most of them. But as her aunt had sagely noted, Will was a duke and dukes were expected to invite a certain kind of people. Alex did note with pleasure that Phoebe had also invited all of her fellow schoolteachers, along with Inspector Holland, who somehow looked even more uncomfortable here than he had at the theater. She had exchanged a congenial nod with him earlier before he slunk off to hold up a wall.

Now though, Alex took absolutely no pleasure in noting the attendance of various captains of industry. For no matter how hard she looked, the one face she truly wished to see was not to be found among this crowd. It had been a few days since she ended things with Lucien. A few days since he walked out of her life without a backward glance—not that she deserved one anyway. After they parted, she had walked blindly around the lecture hall until Marguerite found her and guided her to Aunt Winifred. If they spoke on the way back home, Alex couldn't recall a word.

When she woke the next morning, she went straight to the office and worked until her eyes ached. Then Alex did the same thing the next day, and the next. Work had saved her before when she needed to forget Benjamin and it would save her once again. She was counting on it. Then this cursed engagement ball interrupted her schedule. And if it had been for anyone other than two of her favorite people, she would have made some excuse. But that wasn't possible for Will and Phoebe. And if the last few weeks had taught her anything, it was that Alex needed to keep the few people she loved very close.

Just as her throat began to tighten with emotion, someone who inspired the very opposite feeling approached.

"Alexandra! I was hoping to see you here."

It was Mildred Henderson.

"A reasonable expectation, given that it is my sister's engagement ball," Alex said dryly.

Mildred let out a laugh, as if she had made a joke, and gestured to the nondescript man beside her. "This is my husband, Mr. Thomas Henderson."

"How do you do," Alex replied and wondered what on earth had made Mildred leave school early to marry this man. He seemed perfectly average to her. "I did not realize you knew my sister, or the duke."

"We are quite good friends with Ellis," Mildred said, using Will's title, which Alex knew he absolutely hated and indicated that they were not, in fact, anything remotely close to *good friends*. "He and dear Thomas were at school together."

At the mention of his name, dear Thomas gave a short bow and shot her a hesitant look. "I asked my wife to introduce us, actually."

"Oh?" Alex said. That was genuinely surprising.

"The duke speaks very highly of your expertise," he began. "And I—"

"Yes," Mildred gracelessly interrupted him. "Dear Thomas is interested in investments and he is under the impression that you have some knowledge in that area." She laughed again. "But I told him it is your *father's* company."

"Darling," the man said tightly as an embarrassed flush stained his pale cheeks. "Miss Atkinson works there as well."

"Oh, of *course* she does," Mildred replied with a dismissive wave of her fan.

Alex began to suspect it was dear Thomas's willingness to be bullied by Mildred that had been his greatest attraction. She almost felt sorry for him.

"Is that delightful Mr. Taylor here this evening?" Mildred asked while craning her neck. "I have not seen him."

"No," Alex said. "He is not."

When it was clear she would not say anything more on the matter, Mildred pouted. "I am sorry to hear that. But chin up. There is still a little time left for you to find a husband."

Alex did not reply to this remark and instead turned to Mr. Henderson, who looked absolutely mortified by his wife's rude behavior. A pity he didn't attempt to do anything about it.

"Come by our offices next week, if you wish. I am there every workday."

The man broke into an eager smile that changed his demeanor entirely. "Thank you. I will."

"Lovely to see you again, Alexandra!" Mildred trilled as she all but dragged him away.

Alex rolled her eyes in good-bye.

I am there every workday.

It was the truth, yet for some reason the thought caused a sinking feeling in her chest.

Before Alex could ruminate on it any further, Phoebe hurried over in a cloud of gold chiffon. Mother really had outdone herself for Phoebe's ballgown. Even Alex could tell that it was beyond exquisite. "Did you hear the news? Freddie is engaged! Hank Jr. proposed last night with the largest diamond I have *ever* seen."

Alex blinked. Whatever relief she might have once felt at the news barely registered now. "Oh. That's good," she managed.

"I know I wasn't very keen on their relationship before," Phoebe began, "but she did seem happy when she was showing me the ring. Imagine, we could all be married within a year," she said with a grin and then looked around. "Where is Lucien?"

"He isn't coming." And even though Alex made sure to sound controlled, some of the sorrow must have slipped in, for Phoebe immediately turned to her with concern.

"What's happened?"

Everything.

Alex cleared her throat. "I ended things," she said with a decided nod that must have looked as ridiculous as it felt.

"When?"

"Three days ago."

Phoebe shook her head in disbelief. "But…*why?*"

"I don't want to get into it now," Alex insisted. "This is your party and you should be celebrated accordingly. And please don't say anything to Will. No one else knows yet. I told Mother and Father that Lucien was ill and couldn't come tonight."

Though that excuse wouldn't work forever. Her father was already growing suspicious but had been too distracted with ball preparations to press her further. But after tonight, that would no longer be a distraction.

Phoebe put a hand on her shoulder. "Alex, I'm very sorry."

Her throat tightened at the sympathy in her sister's voice and Alex was sorely tempted to tell her the truth.

It wasn't real anyway.

But she couldn't manage the words. "It's for the best," she croaked instead.

Phoebe turned away as Will called to her from the dance floor. The orchestra had just struck up a waltz. "Oh, I wish I could stay with you, but—"

"Don't worry about me," Alex said with a wave. "Go enjoy yourself. I'll be fine."

And she would be. For Alex was always fine. But fine wasn't the same as *happy*. She understood that now. All too well.

Phoebe shot her one last look before she joined Will. Freddie and Hank Jr. were also among the other dancing couples and as they swept past, the light of the chandelier caught on the ring and sparkled.

Phoebe was right. It was massive.

A smile played on her lips. Perhaps this would be all right. Perhaps Freddie would be happy in New York with Hank Jr. And if she wasn't, well, now she could have Lucien.

Alex stepped away from the edge of the dance floor until her back touched the wall. Until she was shrouded in shadows and would not draw any more attention. Phoebe was mostly right. She and Freddie would both be married within the year, and Alex sincerely wished them every happiness. She had played at courtship, and that had been more than enough for her. Alex was cut from a different cloth and she needed to stop trying to fit in where she did not belong. Tomorrow she would go back to the office and do what she did best. Do what she was made for.

Twenty-Four

*L*ucien stared up at the top floor of Atkinson Enterprises. It was well after six and only Alex's office window flickered with dim light. He had made it through a long, excruciating week without coming here. Every time he felt the urge, he set his thoughts to something else. *Anything* else. But now he had a reason. A very good reason.

Chisolm had sent Alex his contract two days ago. She should have returned it by the evening. And yet, she still had it. At first, Lucien had worried. Perhaps Alex had fallen ill. Or maybe someone in the family was in distress. But now that he was here on the street corner seeing the evidence to the contrary before his very eyes, Lucien felt only anger.

She was the one who had orchestrated this deal. *She* was the one who had insisted that Chisolm was Lucien's best, nay, only option. And now she kept him waiting. But *why?* Lucien couldn't fathom the reason. Simply because she could? Because she enjoyed toying with him? How dare she. How *dare* she.

He would march up there and give her a piece of his mind. That was not how you treated someone. Even someone you *hadn't* been intimate with. But the fact that they had and yet she still treated him with such utter indifference only made his blood run hotter. Lucien had just stepped off the curb when a man came out of the shadows and slipped into the building. Lucien stopped short. He hadn't gotten a good look, but the man seemed strangely familiar. Frowning, Lucien continued across the street and tried to place him. It wasn't until Lucien entered the deserted lobby that it came to him: It was the large, shifty-looking fellow he had seen at the theater. And again at the Royal Geographical Society. And now he was here, long after the rest of the staff had gone home for the day.

Everyone except Alex.

Concern blunted his anger and Lucien moved faster, his heels clicking along the pristine marble floors. He reached the bottom of the staircase and spotted the man just as he disappeared down the hall on Alex's floor. Lucien's stomach turned as he raced up the stairs, determined to catch up, and was suddenly very thankful that London's omnibuses were so unreliable that he had taken to walking most of the time. He was only slightly out of breath when he reached the top and entered the hallway. The man was a dozen paces ahead of him but immediately turned around. Lucien paused and swallowed. The intruder was much taller than he had appeared from across the street. And far larger. He had a bulbous crooked nose and scarred cheeks. It was the face of a man who had seen more than a few fights.

But Lucien only lifted his chin. He wouldn't back down. He couldn't. "What are you doing here?"

The man cast an apprising look over him, then smiled. It called attention to a long, ugly scar that ran diagonally across his mouth. Lucien didn't even *want* to know how someone got a scar like that. Or how they survived. Rather than answer his question, the man clenched his fists by his side, cracking each knuckle as he advanced on Lucien.

Lucien took a step back and held up his hands. "I don't want any trouble," he said, hoping to distract the man for as long as possible.

"Leave now," he growled. "Or else you will indeed find more trouble than you can handle." Lucien responded by putting up his fists. The man's ugly smile only grew. "Fancy yourself a hero?"

"Something like that."

The man scoffed. "Never did care much for the heroes. Always preferred the villains, myself," he said before throwing the first punch.

Lucien neatly ducked out of the way. He was absolutely no match for this man, but he had learned a few things about fighting from his burly French cousins. The first was to run away—but barring that, one must avoid being hit for as long as possible. Let the aggressor tire themselves out.

"Alex, get out of here!" Lucien shouted as he moved nimbly out of the man's reach.

The next was to shout for help. Loudly and often.

"Shut up," the man growled as he lunged for him again.

Lucien spun back. "Alex! You're in danger," he shouted again, even louder. God, he hoped she could hear him.

After avoiding and shouting, there was nothing left to do but throw a punch. Ideally, to the soft parts of the body. Lucien quickly ran his eyes over the man's towering form. The bastard didn't seem to have any soft parts. Lucien raised his fists once more and resumed a fighting stance.

"That's it, boyo," the man growled. "Show us what you got."

Lucien took note that the man spoke with an Irish brogue. It seemed like an important detail, if he survived.

He threw a false punch with his left and rammed his fist into the brute's stomach. It was a perfect execution of the maneuver. Under different circumstances, Lucien would be quite proud of himself. However, the man's torso appeared to be comprised entirely of solid muscle. He let out a soft grunt but otherwise seemed unaffected.

Damn.

The man grinned and crooked two fingers at Lucien. "Come on, lad. Let's see you try that again. But give it some heft this time."

Lucien rolled his shoulders. He had used all the heft he had. "What do you want with Miss Atkinson?" he asked. Time to employ a little distraction.

"Not your concern."

"Wrong." Lucien punctuated this with another punch that clipped the man's jaw and quickly stepped back. "She is my concern."

The man shook his head and gingerly touched the spot. "You're not half bad for a runt, but you've wasted enough of my time."

Lucien's eyes went wide as the man advanced on him. He had clearly just been toying with him. Lucien backed up a couple of steps before the man landed a solid punch to the gut that brought him to his knees.

"*Alex,*" he called out again, far weaker than before. The man then hit him square in the jaw and Lucien saw stars. He fell heavily onto the carpet and blinked. After a moment he tried to push himself up.

"Stay down, boyo," the man said before delivering a swift kick to his side.

Lucien coughed as a fierce pain bloomed across his middle.

"Stop fighting it or I'll kick you again," he growled.

But Lucien wouldn't give up. Not while Alex was in danger. He would push through the pain for as long as he could. Just as Lucien managed to roll onto his back, someone shouted at them from down the hall.

"Get away from him."

Slowly, he turned his head just in time to see Alex marching toward them with a dark look on her face and something in her hand. Like some avenging queen. Lucien smiled weakly at the thought. She had come to save him. Then everything went black.

Alex had forgotten about the pistol in her desk. When she first started staying late, her parents had practically forced the weapon on her. She refused right up until they made it a condition of her employment, so she grudgingly learned how to use it from a retired army friend of her father's. Then she separated the bullets from the pistol and safely locked it all away in her drawer. Until she heard Lucien shouting her name.

Alex would have come sooner, but her hands were shaking as she loaded the gun and it took a few tries. But as soon as she set eyes on Lucien laid out on the carpet, his face twisted with pain, a strange kind of calm took hold of her.

She raised her arm and pointed the pistol at the large, ugly man standing beside Lucien's crumpled form. "I told you to get away from him," she said coolly.

The man puffed out his sizable chest and looked her square in the eye, but Alex didn't even blink. She had absolutely no qualms about shooting this great brute, and as she cocked the pistol, he seemed to realize that.

Rather than challenge her, he bolted down the stairs. Alex was momentarily stunned. "That *coward*." She had half a mind to run after him if not for Lucien.

Alex rushed over and knelt beside him. She gently placed her palms on either side of his battered face. His cheek and lips were already starting to swell. "Lucien, look at me."

He groaned and opened his eyes. It wasn't ideal, but at least he was awake. "Oh, you great fool. *Look* at you," she chided.

Lucien gave her a bloody-lipped smile. Then he mumbled something that sounded like "My heroine." Alex's heart lurched but now was not the time to indulge in maudlin emotions. He needed medical attention immediately.

"Wait here. I'm going to call for help."

Lucien mumbled something in the affirmative and tried to nod before closing his eyes once more.

Alex hurried over to the telephone booth behind the main reception desk and demanded the operator send the police and a doctor. Then she returned to Lucien's side and cradled his head in her lap. She began to brush her fingers lightly through his hair and he nestled even deeper against her.

"What were you even doing here?" she whispered, not expecting an answer.

But his eyes slitted open for a moment. "To see you," he murmured. "I came to see you."

Alex let out a sigh as guilt filled her chest. Guilt mixed with anger. She hadn't listened to Inspector Holland's warning and now her stubbornness had hurt Lucien. For that, Alex could not forgive herself.

"I'm so sorry." As she bowed her head, a tear slipped down her nose and landed on Lucien's bruised cheek.

"Please, don't cry," he said as she wiped it away. Then he grasped her hand. "It's rather terrifying."

Alex laughed despite herself. "Is it, now?"

"Unnatural, really," Lucien continued as his eyes fluttered closed once more. "Like seeing a dog riding a bicycle."

Alex laughed louder through her tears. "Or the queen in her dressing gown."

But Lucien didn't respond to her quip. His chest rose and fell, though his breathing was labored. Once Alex was sure he was unconscious, she cried even harder.

She had no idea how much time had passed before she heard faint voices shouting. Reluctantly, she left Lucien and hurried down to the lobby, where two policemen were waiting. They identified themselves as Officers Clement and O'Connell and together they carried Lucien downstairs. Then they laid him on one of the lobby sofas just as the doctor arrived. He was an older man with curling white hair and an air of competence that set her slightly at ease.

While he saw to Lucien, Alex told the policemen as much as she could, though she couldn't help stopping every few moments to pepper the doctor with questions.

The exasperated man finally shot her a quelling look. "Madam, I must insist you cease speaking and let me evaluate your husband!"

Alex didn't bother to correct him. She just dutifully clamped her mouth shut.

"You say you've been in contact with Inspector Holland?" Officer O'Connell asked. He seemed to be the senior and had taken charge of the scene.

"Yes," Alex said distractedly. She was unable to look away from

Lucien's still form laid out on a lobby sofa. He hadn't regained consciousness even while they were moving him. And every minute that passed, her worry grew.

"All right," Officer O'Connell continued. "He will be informed about this incident. In the meantime, we will have a look around the neighborhood, but chances are this fellow is long gone. Is there someone we can notify for you?"

Alex finally managed to meet the man's eyes. "Uh, yes. My father. Though I'm not sure anyone is home at this hour."

The officers exchanged a look. "I can see you both home safely in our vehicle, while Office Clement stays here and takes a look around."

"Thank you," Alex said.

The doctor then approached them. "Well, he's certainly been knocked about, but nothing seems to be broken. I'll wager his ribs are bruised, though. Best thing is to let him rest as much as possible."

Alex let out a sigh of relief and nodded. "Of course."

"And someone should watch over him tonight," the doctor added. "On account of the blows to his head and the possibility of internal bleeding."

"I will," Alex croaked.

The older man frowned. "You need to rest as well, madam. This has been quite a shock. If you exert yourself anymore, I fear you will fall into a swoon."

At any other time, she would have given the doctor a piece of her mind.

I have never once swooned and do not intend to start now.

But she didn't possess the will to challenge his backward

assertions at the moment, so instead she managed a smile, or something close to it.

"Thank you for your concern, Doctor," Alex said. "Your expertise is much appreciated."

She must have sounded convincing, for the man preened a little before collecting his fee and shuffling off.

Once he was through the doors, Alex's smile fell. She would call for the family physician as soon as they got home and confirm the diagnosis.

Then she abruptly turned to the waiting policemen. "Shall we be going?"

Officer Clement, who hadn't said a word since he arrived, cracked a smile and nodded. "Yes, ma'am."

They then loaded Lucien into the back of the police wagon before Officer Clement left to assess the scene.

"I trust this will be the only time you get to ride in one of these," Officer O'Connell joked after Alex insisted on staying with Lucien.

"Unless I met that brute again," she muttered with cold certainty.

The man's eyebrows rose. "I'll pretend I didn't hear that, ma'am," he said as he touched the brim of his helmet and shut the door.

⁂

The ride home proved to be interminable, as poor Lucien let out a pitiful little moan every time they went over a large bump. He still hadn't regained consciousness and Alex was nearly out of her mind with worry when they finally arrived at Park House.

As soon as Officer O'Connell opened the doors of the police wagon, Alex leaped to the ground and raced up the front steps. Munson must have been watching from the window, because the door immediately swung open. No doubt he was positively scandalized by the sight of a police wagon in front of the house.

Indeed, the venerable old butler looked rather pale. "Miss Alexandra!"

"There's no time for hysterics, Munson," Alex commanded as she moved past him. "Ready the blue room. Mr. Taylor is not well. And call for Dr. Mosley."

But Munson was distracted by Officer O'Connell carrying a limp Lucien up the front steps.

"Munson!" Alex clapped her hands and the butler snapped to attention. "*Now.*"

"Yes, Miss Alexandra." He nodded. "Right away."

"Is anyone else at home?"

"No. Your parents and Mrs. Bailey are at the Turners'."

Alex relaxed a little. Then they weren't far. For once she was grateful for the Turners and their musical evenings.

"Send a note to them. But be *discreet*," she said. "And my sister?"

Munson hesitated. "Miss Freddie is … out."

Alex narrowed her eyes as he hurried away, calling to the footmen as he went. Freddie was up to something, but it would have to wait for later. Alex then turned to Officer O'Connell as he entered the doorway. "Can you make it up the stairs?"

He lifted Lucien a little higher. "Of course. This fellow's as light as a feather."

Alex couldn't help smiling. She would have to tease Lucien about that later.

If he ever wakes up.

But Alex pushed the awful thought aside. "Follow me."

She marched up the staircase and down the hall, doling out

orders to every member of staff she came across: bandages, hot water, a tea tray, and refreshments for Officer O'Connell.

Everyone dutifully nodded and scampered off, but Alex couldn't ignore the curious looks on their faces. This would be the talk of the neighborhood before sunrise.

Well, at least her family wasn't here. Alex didn't think she could handle answering their incessant questions at the moment.

"Here we are," she said once they reached the blue room. It was the guest room closest to her own, just down the hall, and named for the light blue toile wallpaper and matching linens. Her mother had never found a surface she didn't immediately want to cover in toile. But since Father didn't share her love of the print, it was relegated to only this room.

Alex turned on the bedside lamp and pulled back the bedcovers. Officer O'Connell laid Lucien down and Alex immediately set to work removing his shoes. She wanted him to be as comfortable as possible. Once his shoes were off, she worked on his coat. Lucien groaned a little as she slipped it from his shoulders and Alex winced.

"I'm so sorry," she whispered and tried to move more slowly.

Eventually, she was able to remove the garment and she eased him back against the pillows. Alex let out a sigh and closed her eyes until someone behind her cleared their throat.

"If that's all, ma'am, I will be on my way," Officer O'Connell said.

Alex turned around sharply and blinked. She had forgotten about him. "Of course," she said briskly as she got to her feet. "Thank you so much for your help. Cook will make you something, if you're hungry."

But Officer O'Connell shook his head. "That is very kind, but not necessary. It's my job to help." Then he nodded at Lucien, tucked in bed. "He'll be all right. Lucky to have a woman like you fussing over him."

Alex looked down as her cheeks flushed. "It's my fault this happened to him in the first place."

"I'd say it's the fault of the fellow who attacked him," Officer O'Connell said. "But don't worry. Inspector Holland will get to the bottom of this. I've served for a long time and there is no one else I'd want investigating a case than the inspector."

Alex managed a small smile. "Yes, he is very good."

Officer O'Connell shot her a knowing look. "You didn't hear it from me, but he's the most honorable detective on the force. Remember that."

Then he gave her a nod and left the room just as a maid came in with the supplies she had requested.

Alex swallowed past the lump in her throat. "Thank you, Sadie," she rasped. "You can set that all down right here."

"Munson said the doctor is on his way."

"Send him up as soon as he arrives," she said, just barely holding on to her stoic veneer.

The maid bobbed her head and closed the door gently behind her.

Alex immediately set to work pouring the warm water into a bowl and wetting the corner of a cloth. She then eased down beside Lucien and began to clean the dried blood from his face. But her guilt wasn't kept at bay for long. After she had cleaned most of the blood from Lucien's jaw, she dipped the soiled cloth into the bowl and wrung it out, then set about cleaning the rest of his poor bruised face.

If only she had *listened* to Inspector Holland and taken more care. Was it so terrible to stay home while he sorted things out? Did she really value her own safety and the safety of those around her so little?

Alex's lower lip began to tremble. How foolish she had been. How careless. If Lucien suffered any permanent injury, she would never forgive herself. Just as hot tears gathered in her eyes, a soft knock came at the door.

"Come in," Alex croaked as she set the cloth aside and hastily wiped her face. The door swung open, but it wasn't Dr. Mosley who hurried into the room. It was *Freddie*. Relief swept through her while Freddie's shocked gaze raked over Lucien.

Then she turned to Alex. "Oh, my dear," she said as she rushed to the bedside, her face softening with concern. "What on earth has happened?"

Alex opened her mouth to respond then promptly burst into tears.

Twenty-Five

*L*ucien cracked one bleary eye open and groaned. Everything seemed to hurt to varying degrees: his head, his chest, his entire *face*. He gingerly rolled onto his back as memories came to him in scattered bursts: that awful man landing a solid punch to his jaw, Alex calmly threatening the man with a gun, then, confusingly, Lucien being carried up a staircase. But by whom? Worst of all was the image of Alex crying beside him. Lucien remembered wanting to comfort her so desperately, but the words hadn't come before he passed out once again. He hadn't felt this out of sorts since the morning after the first—and last—time he let his cousins take him out drinking.

He tried to open his other eye, but it was too swollen to be of use. God only knew what he looked like. He groaned again. This time because he felt so pathetic.

A rustling came from just out of his line of vision but Lucien didn't have the strength to turn over again. Then he heard someone yawn. A *female* someone.

"Hello?" Lord, he sounded nearly as bad as he felt.

"You're awake!" Freddie then leaned over the side of the bed, flashing him a sunny smile that immediately fell. "Oh, Lucien, you look awful."

He briefly closed his good eye. "Yes, I imagine so, given I feel awful."

"Let's get you up," Freddie said as she helped him into something resembling a seated position. Then she handed him a full glass of murky liquid. "Here. You're supposed to drink this as soon as you wake. Dr. Mosley's orders."

Lucien eyed it warily. "And he is?"

"Our family physician. Another doctor looked you over back at the office, but Alex wanted a second opinion. All right. Drink up. It's to help the pain."

Well, in that case…

Lucien accepted the glass and obeyed. It tasted awful, but he would endure much worse if it made him feel even a little better. When he finished, Freddie took the glass and set it on a tray.

"Would you like anything to eat?"

Lucien nodded and Freddie tugged on the bellpull. She was dressed in a plain white muslin day gown with her hair pulled back in a simple knot. He wasn't used to seeing this side of her and it wasn't very long ago that such a discovery would have been mesmerizing. But now…now he felt nothing more than a sense of comfort. The kind one enjoyed when in the company of old friends.

"How long have you been here?" he asked.

Freddie shrugged and sat back down in the bedside chair. "Only a few hours. I was reading but dozed off. Alex was up with you for half the night until Mother forced her to go to bed, which she *only* agreed to do if someone else would watch over you. The doctor was concerned you might be concussed," she added.

Lucien vaguely recalled an elderly man prodding him. "I thought I was dreaming," he said with a frown.

Freddie smiled. "You cried out a few times. Apparently you bruised some ribs as well."

Lucien skimmed his fingers along his injured side and winced.

"The doctor said they would be quite tender for at least a week. The only thing you can do is rest."

"How—how is Alex?"

Freddie hesitated. "Badly shaken up," she murmured. "I don't think I've ever seen her cry. Not even when we were children. She blames herself for what happened."

Lucien was stunned. "But *why?*"

"I'm not sure. She wouldn't say much to any of us." Then Freddie frowned in confusion. "What were you even doing there? Alex said you had both decided to call things off."

Not both.

But it was hardly the time to mince words.

"I wanted to speak to her about my business proposal," Lucien admitted. "When I arrived, a man slipped inside just ahead of me. And I remembered seeing him hanging about in a couple of other places before. I think he's been following her for some time now, waiting for the right moment."

To do *what* remained unknown.

Freddie hugged her shoulders and shuddered. "Well, it was very brave of you to confront him like that."

Lucien shook his head. "It was stupid."

"That too," Freddie said with a smile.

"But I couldn't just leave her alone," he explained. "Of course, that was before I knew she had a pistol on her."

"Alex is full of surprises." Freddie chuckled before her expression turned curious. "So. You went to speak to her about a business proposal at eight o'clock at night?"

Lucien glanced away. "I was hoping she would…that we might…"

Freddie leaned forward a little. "Yes?"

He sighed and sank farther down against the pillows. "Has anyone ever been able to convince Alex to do, well, anything?"

"Not to my knowledge," Freddie said dryly. "She is quite sure of herself. I suppose that's what has made her so successful. But it can have its drawbacks." Lucien grunted in response.

"Don't give up on her," she suddenly urged. "Not yet. We Atkinson women can be a stubborn bunch, I'll admit. But we have our good qualities too. Even Alex."

Lucien turned toward her. His eyelids had started to feel heavy. "I wasn't planning on it."

Nor did it feel like much of a choice at the moment. He needed to try to get through to her, at least once. Or he would regret it for the rest of his life.

Freddie nodded with relief and sat back in her chair. Lucien's languid gaze landed on her hands. He frowned and tried to focus. Whatever had been in that liquid was damned powerful. It was becoming a struggle to keep his eyes open. Then he realized what had caught his attention: Freddie was wearing a massive, sparkling diamond ring.

"When did you get that?"

She followed his gaze and quickly folded her hands together. "Oh. A few days ago. It's nothing," she added.

Even in his grossly impaired state, Lucien could tell she was acting strangely. "Why ever would you say that?" he slurred. "Don't you like it?"

If Lucien had the means to put a jewel of that size on a girl's finger, he would certainly expect her to be *happy* about the blasted thing.

She bit her lip. "Can you keep a secret?"

Lucien nodded. "Of course." Then he tried to mime locking his mouth with a key, but it looked more like an aborted wave.

Freddie glanced toward the door, then leaned closer. "Last night I went to…"

But the rest of her confession was lost as Lucien closed his eyes and floated away into a deep, heavy slumber.

❦

Alex sat up with a start. She had only intended to sleep for an hour—two at the *very* most—but based on the light streaming through the sides of the curtains it was far later. She let out a sigh and rubbed her eyes.

I knew I shouldn't have accepted that cup of tea from Mother.

It must have been laced with a sleeping draught, though Alex did acknowledge that she felt significantly more refreshed. Her body clearly needed the rest, but it was preferable to *not* be drugged by one's mother.

Alex let out an idle yawn as she turned to the small clock on the nightstand and squinted at the face. Then she let out a gasp.

It was nearly noon.

Alex leaped out of bed and quickly washed up. She was still in her clothes from the night before, but didn't bother to change. There wasn't any more time to waste. She stepped into the hallway just as Freddie was closing the door to Lucien's room.

Alex charged straight toward her. "What are you doing?"

Freddie held a finger up to her lips. "He just fell asleep."

"Oh." She came to a halt. "How—how is he?"

"He'll be fine, but he needs to rest." Freddie hooked her arm through Alex's and began to lead her down the hall. "Come downstairs with me. You should eat. Doctor's orders."

"All right." She must still be feeling the effects of the draught given that she didn't have the energy to resist.

"Don't worry," Freddie soothed as she patted her hand. "We'll check on him in an hour."

"All right," Alex repeated, though she did cast a mournful look at the closed door.

Suddenly a memory of a very small Freddie leading her along in much the same manner came to her—along with a similar feeling of surrender. Only then it was so they could go build a castle or play with her dolls.

Freddie could be quite persuasive under the right circumstances.

"Is anyone else at home?"

"Mother is napping and Father is at the office. But I am under *strict* orders to keep you away."

Alex let out a huff. "That is the absolute last place I want to be right now."

"Hmm," Freddie replied as they entered the parlor.

Alex broke away to take her usual seat closest to the door while Freddie rang the bell for tea.

"I don't suppose you and Lucien had the chance to talk before he was pummeled," she asked as she took the chair across from Alex.

"No. I didn't even know he was in the building until I—"

Heard him calling to me.

Her heart clenched. Lucien had engaged a man twice his size to give her the chance to escape. Alex wasn't certain he would be alive right now if she had left him behind. She cleared her throat in a bid to keep her emotions at bay and looked down. "He was very brave."

Alex could feel her sister's eyes on her, but she had already broken down in front of her once today. A second time would be excessive.

"You both were," Freddie murmured just as a maid entered with the tea cart followed by Mrs. Drummond, their London housekeeper and Mrs. Holloway's older sister.

"Hello, ladies. How are you feeling, Miss Alexandra?"

Alex managed a weary smile. "I'm fine, thank you."

"I'm very glad to hear it. You gave us all a good scare last night."

"I'm sure," Alex replied and moved to pour the tea, if only to give her hands something to do. And somewhere else to look other than in Mrs. Drummond's concerned face. "Does Mr. Taylor know about Lucien?"

Mrs. Drummond sighed. "No. I was hoping poor Lucien's condition would improve a little before I sent word to my sister."

"He seemed better when I spoke to him," Freddie offered. "He's still very sore, poor thing, but nothing a good long rest won't fix. The doctor said he should be able to return home in about a week."

Shocked, Alex looked at her sister. "A *week*?"

Freddie shrugged. "That's what he said. Maybe even a little longer, depending on how he heals." Then she narrowed her eyes. "Is that a problem?"

"No," Alex said quickly. "No, I just didn't—oh, *blast*."

She hadn't been paying attention and overfilled her cup. Now tea was getting everywhere.

The housekeeper politely ignored her very unladylike curse and began mopping up the mess. "Allow me."

"Sorry, Mrs. Drummond," Alex mumbled.

"Not a problem, Miss Alexandra. Might I suggest a drop of whiskey? I've found there's nothing better for soothing the nerves," Mrs. Drummond said with a wink.

Normally, Alex would feel compelled to insist that her nerves were *just fine*, but today she waved a hand. "Yes, why not."

Mrs. Drummond flashed her a smile and nodded. As the housekeeper headed for the liquor cabinet, Freddie arched a brow.

Alex rolled her eyes. "Don't tell me I've finally shocked you."

"In the last day you've cried in front of me, said you didn't want to go to the office, and now you're drinking in the afternoon." Freddie ticked off each item on her hand. "Yes, I'd say you've suitably shocked me."

Alex huffed a laugh while Mrs. Drummond returned with the whiskey bottle and poured a generous drop into her teacup. "I suppose that is a rather surprising trifecta."

"I would have thought hell would freeze first." The housekeeper abruptly cleared her throat. "Apologies for my bad language, Mrs. Drummond," Freddie said. "My sister and I are both a little out of sorts today."

Mrs. Drummond tried to look stern, but a smile pulled at her lips. "Will there be anything else?"

"No, thank you," Alex said, but then Freddie called her back.

"Send word to Dr. Mosley and tell him Lucien woke about an hour ago, had the medicine he left, and fell asleep again. He'll probably stop by later anyway," Freddie added airily. "But I know he wanted to be notified when Lucien woke."

"Of course, Miss Winifred," the housekeeper said with a nod and left the room.

Alex bit the inside of her cheek and mentally chastised herself for feeling envious over Freddie taking charge of the situation. She should be grateful to her sister for taking over when she had been too exhausted to stay up. She *was* grateful. But oh, how Alex wished she could have been there when he woke. Instead, he had been greeted by the image of Freddie, looking fresh-faced and angelic in her simple white gown. She could picture his smile of relief, even now. But just as Alex's stomach began to tighten, she took a long sip of tea.

"Alex," Freddie prompted. "He will be *fine*," she said with certainty. "Don't worry."

Alex was swamped with guilt over her unkind thoughts. "I know," she bleated, not sounding very certain. Freddie gave her an encouraging smile and patted her hand. But before Alex could castigate herself any further, someone knocked softly on the door.

Mrs. Drummond entered with a worried look on her face. "Sorry to interrupt," she began. "But an Inspector Holland is here. And he said it is urgent."

Alex set down her cup and hurried to her feet. Just the distraction she was looking for. "Of course. Show him in."

She smoothed the front of her dress and patted her hair. Now she regretted not taking the time to change. Alex wasn't used to having even a hair out of place, but it was too late for that.

"You look fine," Freddie grunted. "It's only the inspector."

Alex turned in surprise at the dismissive comment and found Freddie slouching with her arms crossed.

Strange.

But Alex didn't have the chance to ruminate on this any further before Inspector Holland appeared. Only then did Freddie bother to sit up—and reluctantly, at that.

"Thank you so much for coming here," Alex said as she shook his hand. "I know how busy you are."

Freddie muttered something under her breath that Alex couldn't quite make out. The inspector cast her a quick glance before addressing Alex.

"I would have come sooner, but Officer O'Connell suggested it had been a late night. I thought I would give you both time to recover."

"Hello, Inspector," Freddie said curtly.

"Miss Atkinson," he said with a brief nod before turning back to Alex. "Is there somewhere we could speak in private?"

"Why don't we go to my father's study—"

"No need," Freddie said briskly. "I have some things to attend to. *Lovely* to see you again." Though her tone indicated quite the opposite. Then she marched out of the room with her nose stuck in the air.

Alex was bewildered. She had been certain Freddie would make a nuisance of herself in front of the detective, as usual. She turned to him and shook her head. "I don't know what's gotten into her."

But Inspector Holland's gaze was fixed on the doorway while his hands were clenched in fists at his sides. Then he quickly recovered and turned to her. "I'm sure it's nothing to be concerned about."

Alex furrowed her brow. "Yes," she said slowly, then gestured for him to sit.

Inspector Holland looked relieved she didn't press him further, and Alex filed that away in her mind to ruminate on later. They had far more important things to discuss at the moment than the reason for Freddie's sour mood.

Once alone, Alex gestured to the tea service. "May I offer you a cup of tea?"

"No, thank you." Then he leaned forward and clasped his large hands together. "I'd like you to tell me exactly what happened last night," he said, getting right to the point. It was a quality Alex could appreciate.

"Certainly. But didn't one of the officers tell you? I gave them a full statement last night."

The inspector nodded. "Yes, but I'd still like to hear it from you. Particularly regarding anything you can remember about the man who assaulted Mr. Taylor."

Alex then related exactly what she'd told the officers: She had been working at her desk when she heard Lucien's shouts. After loading the pistol, she charged down the hallway and exchanged words with the assailant. The inspector's lips twitched in an amused smile when Alex described their exchange along with her shock when the man ran off.

"Well, you did have a gun," the inspector pointed out.

"I suppose that put me at an advantage."

"Describe him for me."

Alex took a sip of tea as she pondered this. "Tall. Most definitely over six feet. Well-built, but he seemed older. Like he was past his prime. He had dark eyes but I couldn't see his hair color as it was hidden under his cap. But he also could have been bald."

"Anything else of note?"

"He had several scars on his face, including one across his mouth."

The inspector's jaw tensed ever so slightly. "Thank you, miss. Atkinson. That is very helpful," he said. "Is Mr. Taylor available?"

"He's asleep at the moment, but I can try to wake him."

Inspector Holland shook his head. "That won't be necessary. I'm sure he needs to rest. I'll speak with him another time."

Alex tilted her head. "Then . . . you know his attacker?"

"Given your description, I'm quite certain it's an ex-boxer named Gerald O'Hara. Went by the name of Gorgeous Gerry back in his fighting days." Alex let out a snort and the inspector raised an eyebrow. "It was meant to be ironic."

"I'll say," she muttered.

"He's also a known associate of the Nun," Inspector Holland continued.

Alex let out a breath. Though she had assumed as much, having her suspicions confirmed only deepened her guilt. "What happens now?"

Inspector Holland's dark eyes gleamed. "Are you willing to testify against O'Hara in court?"

Alex didn't hesitate. "I will do whatever it takes to ensure nothing like this happens again to anyone I—" She stopped abruptly and swallowed. "Anyone I care for."

The inspector watched her closely. "Of course."

Love. She had been about to say "love."

Inspector Holland was still talking, but Alex didn't hear a word. Her mind was a whirl.

"Miss Atkinson," the Inspector suddenly prompted and Alex's gaze shot to his face. "We can continue this later, if you need to rest."

Alex sat up a little straighter. "No, I'm fine. Please continue."

"As I was saying, I am building a case against the criminal

known as the Nun and his associates. But very few people are willing to speak against him for fear of retaliation."

"What is the difference?" Alex shrugged, unconcerned. "I'm
already a target, as you can see."

"Yes, but I'd wager that after last night the Nun expects you to
be scared. Likely, that was what O'Hara was sent to do in the first
place. Pummeling Mr. Taylor was just a bonus," he added.

Alex's blood began to boil. "Well, then he has made a *sizable*
error," she pronounced.

Inspector Holland pursed his lips as if he was trying not to smile.
"I can't tell if you're one of the bravest women I've met, or simply the
most reckless. Your sister Phoebe presented a similar conundrum."

"I suspect it's a mixture of both," she said with a weary sigh.
"I will take more care, though. I can promise you that. My sisters
and I may be reckless on occasion, but we all have healthy sense of
self-preservation."

Alex had meant it as a lighthearted quip, but Inspector Holland's face noticeably darkened. "Then I suggest you have a word
with Winifred, given that *her* sense of self-preservation appears to
be missing entirely."

Alex tilted her head. "What happened, Inspector?"

He avoided her eyes and rose to his feet. "Just…keep an eye on
her. I will send word when I have something. In the meantime, I
suggest staying close to home as much as possible. And do not go
anywhere alone."

"Understood," she said with a nod. "I mean it this time."

As the inspector put on his bowler hat, he grumbled something
under his breath that sounded an awful lot like "*Finally*" and left
the room.

Twenty-Six

Over the next few days, Lucien slowly recovered in the comfort of the Atkinsons' home. Freddie and Mrs. Atkinson stopped by at least twice a day, sometimes with Mr. Atkinson in the evenings, while Mrs. Drummond brought up most of his meals. At Lucien's request, she hadn't told her sister the extent of his injuries so as not to worry his father. Only that he'd had an accident and was recovering at Park House.

He passed the long hours of the day by picking through the stack of mystery novels Mrs. Atkinson had foisted upon him or playing checkers or cards with Freddie. He had never asked about where she had been the night of his encounter, and she never brought it up herself.

Instead, Freddie now wore her diamond ring with pride and casually mentioned potential spring wedding dates and flower arrangements, all while complaining about Phoebe's utter lack of interest in planning *her* wedding in December.

"Thank heavens she has Mother and Will deciding everything for her," Freddie said. "Otherwise, Phoebe would have to get married in the parlor with flowers from the back garden."

She then shuddered for comic effect, but that didn't sound so bad to him. But while Lucien much appreciated the company, there was only one person he truly wished to see.

Alex came by on his second evening there. He had just woken from a long, drug-induced slumber to find a shadowy figure watching over him from the foot of the bed.

"I wrote to Benjamin earlier," she began without preamble in her usual formal tone. "I said that you have fallen ill and would be indisposed for the time being but reassured him that you are still fully committed to your partnership. I will write him again in a few days."

Lucien didn't give a fig about Chisolm and tried to tell her so, but the words came out garbled. As he struggled to focus on her, Alex whispered something before ducking out of the room. It took Lucien's sluggish mind a few moments for the meaning to sink in:

I'm so sorry.

Freddie tried gently prying a few times, but Lucien didn't have the will to discuss his situation with anyone other than Alex. He did learn that she was staying close to the house under Inspector Holland's advice, but otherwise she kept her distance.

Every few hours, Lucien forced himself out of bed and walked around the room. Each day, he was able to walk a little longer. By his fourth day at Park House, he could walk down the hall and back without assistance. By the fifth, he could manage the stairs, though ascending was considerably harder.

"You mustn't push yourself," Freddie warned as she accompanied him back to his room. "Don't think we're in a hurry to have you leave."

Lucien sighed and gently rubbed his aching ribs. "I know. But I'm so *sick* of sitting in bed staring at the wallpaper. I see those French peasants when I close my eyes at night."

Freddie chuckled. "Yes, the toile is a bit much in that room. I'm surprised Alex put you—" She stopped abruptly as something seemed to dawn on her. Lucien gave her an inquiring look. "I only meant that usually guests stay in the bedrooms on the floor above. The blue room was our old nanny's quarters, so it's closest to Alex's bedroom."

Lucien was silent. He hadn't known that. This whole time she had been mere steps away, and yet he never saw her.

"I see," he replied evenly. "I suppose…I suppose it was more convenient to put me in there that night."

His heart sank as he spoke. Alex wasn't a sentimental fool like him. She made decisions driven by simple logic. And her continued distance proved that.

Freddie studied him. "We can move you to another room, if—"

"*No.*" The word came out far sharper than he intended. "That won't be necessary," he added more gently. "I think I need to spend more time out of bed, that's all."

"Mmm," Freddie hummed. "As long as the doctor approves."

Lucien rolled his eyes. He was damned tired of needing that man's approval for everything. "It's fine as long as the pain doesn't worsen."

She patted his arm. "I'm sure you know best."

Lucien let out a dry laugh. He wasn't sure about anything these days.

On the sixth day, he felt considerably stronger and the swelling on his face had gone. There was still some faint bruising around his eye and jaw, but Lucien thought it made him look rather roguish.

The day passed in the usual manner: He took a turn around the back garden with Mrs. Atkinson, played several rounds of cards with Freddie, and gossiped with Mrs. Drummond over his midday meal. Dr. Mosley had come again and was pleased with Lucien's progress.

"You're well enough to return home tomorrow. Though between us fellows, I can tell the lady of the house you need another day or two," he added with a sly look.

Lucien gave him a puzzled frown. "Pardon?"

"There's no need to play coy with me, young man." The doctor chuckled. "When I was your age I'd have done much worse to stay so close to my fiancée. We've been married forty-two years now, and I swear it has gone by like that," he said with a snap of his fingers.

"Congratulations, but I'm not engaged to anyone," Lucien grumbled.

The last thing he wanted to hear about was this man's felicitous home life.

Both of Dr. Mosley's bushy white eyebrows rose considerably. "Oh. My mistake. I just assumed—"

Lucien huffed. He was getting quite tired of people's assumptions. "Assumed what?"

"I've known Miss Alexandra her whole life," the older man began. "I've seen her through every childhood sickness. Every injury— though granted she didn't have many of those," he digressed until Lucien gave him an exasperated look. "The point is," Dr. Mosley continued, "I've never, *ever* seen her as distressed as she was the night they brought you here."

Lucien blinked. "Oh."

"Yes," the doctor said with a laugh. "*Oh.*" Then he rose and put on his hat. "She's an interesting woman, Alexandra. Isn't one to suffer fools, I gather."

"No, she isn't," Lucien agreed.

The doctor arched a brow. "Luckily, you don't strike me as a fool. Try not to prove me wrong," he said with a wink and left the room.

Lucien let out a sigh and tilted his head back against the pillows. That remained to be seen.

That evening Freddie and her parents went to dine with the Ericsons, ostensibly to discuss wedding plans. Lucien joined Mrs. Drummond in the servant's hall for a light supper, then headed back to his room. As he made his way down the hall, a soft light flickered under Alex's bedroom door. Lucien paused, momentarily struck by the urge to knock.

No. If Alex wanted you, she would just come out and say so, he thought morosely.

Lucien shuffled off to his room and settled into a chair to read another one of Mrs. Atkinson's novels. But every few sentences, he would glance at the door and wonder if she was still in her room. Freddie had mentioned they were all taking Inspector Holland's warning seriously by staying close to home and never going out alone, but then, Alex had never been one for following orders. Perhaps she had taken the chance to slip away for the night. Which meant she could be in danger at this very moment. Really, it was Lucien's *duty* to check on her.

He snapped the book shut and stood.

As he stepped into the darkened hall, a golden light spilled out from under her door.

Lucien wasn't sure if he was relieved or disappointed. Then irritation won out. He stalked down the hall, or as close to it as his still tender side allowed. Before he could think twice, Lucien knocked on her door. He'd had quite enough of this. If she intended to hide from him indefinitely, then she would have to say it to his face. Lucien began to knock harder as Alex pulled the door open.

"Good heavens! What is it—" She stopped abruptly and stared at him in shock for a moment before her brow furrowed with concern. "Do you need the doctor?"

"Uh…" Lucien replied, distracted. Alex's hair was down. *All* of it. He couldn't stop staring at the mass of dark waves that hung over her shoulders and down her chest.

She was also dressed for bed in a silk wrapper thrown over a white nightgown. Lucien's gaze wandered lower, where the tips of her toes peeked out from the hem of the gown.

This was a mistake.

"I should go," he choked out and turned to leave while pressing a hand against his trousers. One glimpse of her and he was already half hard.

A *horrible* mistake.

"Wait," she called out, her voice unusually weak. "Please, Lucien."

That brought him to a stop. He was useless when she begged for him.

This isn't sexual, you idiot.

Indeed, as Lucien turned around to face her, Alex only looked… guilty.

He cleared his throat and lifted his chin. "Yes, what is it?" He aimed for a cool formality and hoped she didn't glance below his waist. Alex joined him in the hall, then shyly bit her lip.

Goddammit.

Lucien shifted in place. Why did this woman have such an effect on him? "What is it?" he prompted.

Alex's eyes widened a little at his sharp tone. "Could we speak for a moment?"

"Fine. Speak, then."

She glanced around. "In my room?"

Lucien knew he should say no. There was no one upstairs. No reason they needed more privacy. And yet…

His chest tightened. "Certainly." The word came out like a growl.

Lucien extended his arm toward her bedroom and followed Alex inside. He had expected her room to be like her office, stark and empty, but this was nearly the opposite. The high walls were covered in a beautiful dark floral wallpaper, the details of which he couldn't make out in the firelight, while a thick paisley rug covered most of the floor. Shelves filled with books and other bric-a-brac lined an entire wall, while a gilt dressing table took up space by a bed dressed in a deep red coverlet. It was rich and regal and also quite *cozy*. As Alex moved by the hearth, his gaze caught on her lovely profile lit by the flickering fire. He watched her for a long moment, then let out a sigh of defeat as he shut the door behind him.

Dr. Mosley had been mistaken. He really was a complete and utter fool.

🐏

The door shut softly behind Lucien but Alex still couldn't make herself turn around. Couldn't make herself face him and see up close the evidence of her own hubris. She had spent the last few days burying herself in work, only leaving her room in the dead of night when she was certain Lucien was asleep and she could check on him without having to explain herself.

But perhaps that was a mistake. She had grown so used to seeing him unconscious that it had been quite a shock to find him at her door and very much awake.

"Alex," he said, his deep voice suddenly cutting through her thoughts. "Look at me."

She swallowed a whimper and forced herself to turn around, her hands clasped tightly at her waist. He was closer than expected and as the firelight from the hearth played over his face, Alex stared at him greedily, eagerly. The bruising around his jaw was much improved, now a faint yellow instead of that horrible purple and blue. He took a few steps toward her and though he still walked with a limp, it was far less noticeable than it had been just two days earlier when she caught sight of him with Freddie in the back garden.

"You're moving better," she noted.

Lucien frowned in confusion. "How do you know that? I haven't seen you at all."

Blast.

Alex opened her mouth, but she couldn't make herself say the words. Make herself admit just how pathetic she had become.

But Lucien still seemed to understand. He moved closer and closer, his eyes fixed firmly upon her face, until he could tuck a lock of hair behind her ear. It took every bit of her strength not to press into his touch like a cat.

"Why do you insist on hiding away, Alexandra?"

Her breath caught. Alex had never particularly liked her full name. It sounded too grand. Too regal for a woman like her. A woman who didn't know how to properly interact with anyone. A woman who preferred an empty office to a ballroom. A woman who was quite terrified of the emotions coursing inside her.

"Because," she murmured.

"Because you think it is easier this way," he offered.

She glanced down, which was answer enough.

He gave his head a slow shake and clicked his tongue. "But don't you know how magnificent you are? How much we all wait for just a glimpse of you so that we might gain a bit of your attention."

She let out a choked laugh that sounded more like a sob. "I think you are still concussed."

He smiled at her then, that bright brilliant smile that lit up her entire body. "I very well may be, but that doesn't mean I'm not also right." Alex started to object, but he held a finger to her lips. "I've spent a week in this house interacting with every single person here except for you. And yet it is your name that is always on everyone's lips. Your counsel, your knowledge that everyone seeks. I've seen enough to know that *you* are the steady, beating heart of this family. And much like the body, a family can't function properly if its heart is missing."

"Lucien—"

"It's true," he insisted. "Every word of it."

As he brushed his thumb gently along the curve of her cheek, Alex was shocked to realize she was *crying*.

"Sorry." She pulled away and immediately wiped at her cheeks. "I don't know why I . . ."

"You don't need to apologize for that," Lucien said as she trailed off. "For anything."

"I absolutely should," Alex insisted as she stepped back. "It's my fault you were nearly killed."

But Lucien immediately followed. He would give her no quarter. "Given that you weren't the large man who pummeled me, I think your fault is misplaced."

"But I—"

"*No*, Alex," he interrupted. "I won't let you take this on as well. You are already carrying far too much." She very much wanted to challenge him on that, but then Lucien slid his hand around the nape of her neck and began to gently massage the muscles there. "See? You're so tense."

Alex's head tilted back at his touch as warmth spread down her neck and over her shoulders.

"There. That's it," he murmured in approval.

It was shocking just how *good* this felt. How easy it would be to sink into the feeling and forget everything, but she forced herself to stay focused. "Why . . . why did you come here?" she managed to ask after a moment.

"Isn't it obvious?"

Alex slitted her eyes open at the amusement in his voice. "No."

Lucien leaned in until his lips brushed the shell of her ear. "I came here to be properly ruined. By you."

At some point Alex had pressed her palms to his chest and now her fingertips flexed against the firm muscle beneath.

"Lucien," she said in a terrible attempt to sound disapproving. "You aren't well."

"Then how come I've never felt better than I do at this exact moment?"

She pulled back to meet his eyes. "Because in addition to being concussed, you are delusional."

He grinned in response and Alex felt it all the way down to her toes. "Why don't you let me worry about that and you focus on my deflowerment."

Alex huffed a laugh but when she began to step back, Lucien's hands clasped firmly around her waist. The heat of his palms immediately sank into her skin.

"Tell me you don't want me and I'll leave this room," he said, leaning into the crook of her neck once more. "And never bother you again."

Before Alex could even begin to formulate a response, her traitorous body pressed against his lean form.

"It…it would be a mistake," she said weakly. *Miserably.*

He pressed a tender kiss against her hair. "And yet, I have it on very good authority that Alexandra Atkinson doesn't make mistakes."

Alex let out a long, tortured sigh, then turned her head to meet his gaze. She didn't have the will to deny him. Not now. "Fine. Get on the bed, you impossible man."

"With pleasure." He shot her a grin before practically bounding across the room—or at least as fast as his injury would allow.

She followed him at a more sedate pace, though internally her heart was galloping. Was she *really* going to do this?

Lucien waited for her by the bedside and as he extended his hand, she saw that his eyes were full of hope and anticipation. And need.

Oh, most definitely.

As their palms slid together, she felt the same jolt of electricity that had shot up her arm all those weeks ago. Now she understood, without a doubt, that it had been mutual attraction. He drew her close and tilted his head to kiss her, but Alex began unbuttoning his shirt instead.

Lucien let out a soft chuckle. "Right to it, then?"

The corner of Alex's mouth twitched up. "I want to see what state you are in before we begin."

"Ah. And here I was hoping you simply found me irresistible," he quipped.

Alex's hands stilled on the last button and she met his gaze. "I do." Just as his eyes began to darken, she looked back down. "I wouldn't be doing this otherwise."

Though Alex still harbored a number of doubts, she could silence them for at least an evening. And, if nothing else, she would make sure Lucien left her bed with a thorough education in several ways to pleasure a woman.

Together they slowly removed his unbuttoned shirt and she brushed her fingers lightly over the lower ribs on the left side of his body. Like his jaw, the bruising there had faded from purple to yellow. He inhaled sharply as she continued to touch him.

Her eyes darted to his face. "Did I hurt you?"

"No," he said tightly. "Quite the opposite."

Alex smiled as she looked away again and continued her inspection. "What did Dr. Mosley say?"

"That I'm fit as a fiddle and in prime fighting shape." At Alex's disapproving frown, he covered her hand with his and brought it to his lips. "He told me to take it easy, but that I'm healing." Then he kissed her fingertips. "It will be fine. I'm just a little sore."

"I should be on top, then," Alex said with a nod. Lucien froze and looked at her through lowered lashes. "That way you won't have to move too much," she added.

"Yes," he rasped. "I gathered that."

Then he dropped her hand and began removing his trousers.

Alex followed his lead and took off her wrapper. Lucien's eyes followed her every movement, and he nearly got tangled in his trouser legs as he tried to pull them off.

"Careful or you'll bruise your other ribs," Alex laughed as she prevented Lucien from tumbling over entirely.

"I'm afraid it will take more than another bruised rib to stop me," Lucien said as he kicked off his trousers and sat down on the bed.

Just as he reached for her, he stopped. "What…what about protection?"

"I assumed you would withdraw," she said matter-of-factly, to which Lucien audibly swallowed. That had been Benjamin's preferred method during their first few encounters.

Lucien let out a strangled laugh. "You might be overestimating my abilities on that front."

Alex paused to consider this, then remembered the cervical caps currently in her possession. "Oh!"

Then she hurried over to the closet and threw open the doors. After rummaging around for several moments, she pulled out a packet and disappeared into the en suite bathroom to insert the cervical cap.

When she emerged, Lucien was still on the bed but eyeing her closet. "Should I be concerned that you have such a large collection of prophylactics in your bedroom?"

Alex lifted her chin and crossed her arms. "Only if you take issue with a woman managing her reproductivity."

"No," he said quickly. "Not in the least."

"Madame LaSalle and I help distribute them to women's groups across the city," she explained with a smile, putting him out of his misery.

"Ah," he said, visibly relaxing. "Let me stress that I have absolutely no issue being with a woman of experience, but I was already feeling woefully out of my depth."

"You have nothing to worry about on that front," she said as she moved toward him. "I assure you."

"Still, I know I . . . I can't possibly measure up to Benjamin."

Alex was willing to wager her entire personal fortune that Benjamin had given very little, if any, thought to her pleasure. "You do not need to worry about that at all."

"That is most encouraging," Lucien said, then grunted as she straddled his lap.

"I will admit our time together was not *entirely* without pleasure—"

"I am less thrilled to hear that," Lucien cut in.

Alex smiled at his petulance and pressed him down onto the bed. "But, and this is the important bit, so listen closely: He never made me feel as good as you did with only your fingers."

"No?" His wide-eyed hope filled her with such fondness she nearly lost her breath.

Alex leaned in until the tips of their noses touched. "Not. Even. Close."

Lucien responded by capturing her mouth in a deep, insistent kiss. "Good," he rasped. "I want you to forget him entirely by the end of tonight."

She threw back her head and let out a throaty laugh. "Please do."

His hand cupped the back of her neck as he brought her toward him for another lush kiss.

"I have been wondering how you're so good at kissing," she admitted once he finally released her.

He shot her a sly smile. "I don't have quite the same qualms about kissing as I do for the other bits," he said as he began to leave a trail of kisses down her neck. "And it seemed that Paris was a good place to learn how to kiss properly."

Alex laughed again as she craned her neck back to offer him better access. "Lucky me, then."

"I'm very glad you think so," he said as his hands slid along the exposed flesh of her thighs where her nightgown had ridden up to pool around her hips.

Just as that ache began to build between her legs, Alex shifted and began to unbutton the front of his trousers. Lucien said nothing but he stared at her face with an intensity that was nearly overwhelming on its own. Then together they pulled his trousers down past his hips. She took him in hand then, and though he was already impressively hard and hot, she stroked him a few times for no other reason than to hear the surrendering gasp escape his lips.

"Alex," he panted. "*Enough.*"

She smiled. "Very well."

He caught her eye and his hands tightened on her hips. "You know what I want."

She rose on her knees and positioned him at her entrance. As soon as the tip of his erection brushed against her overheated flesh, Lucien let out a hiss and squeezed his eyes shut.

Alex paused, holding herself still as she stared down at him. "Shall I continue?"

He let out a pained nod and gently tugged at her hips. Slowly, so slowly, she began sliding down, down, down until finally he was in her to the hilt. She gasped in surprise at how he filled and stretched her. How *good* it felt to have him inside her.

She began to rock her hips, chasing that flutter of pleasure at her apex, and Lucien let out something that sounded very much like a whimper.

"*Alex*," he murmured and dug his fingertips deeper against her flesh.

She moved a little faster then, finding a rhythm that caused the flutter to bloom. She let out a gasp and leaned her head back.

"Look at me," Lucien suddenly commanded. Alex had been so focused on what she was doing that she hadn't noticed his heated stare. As their gazes tangled, the intimacy of the moment nearly overwhelmed her but she fought against the urge to look away.

"You are so beautiful," he breathed.

A different kind of warmth bloomed in her chest and she smiled down at him. "Touch me. Please."

Lucien nodded eagerly and together they pulled the nightgown off her overheated skin and his warm hands immediately closed over her breasts. Then she showed him how to fondle her nipples just the way she liked as a new wave of pleasure crashed over her. He began thrusting upward and it felt like stars were gathering behind her eyes.

"Harder, Lucien," she gasped and he readily obliged, both with his thrusts and with his fingers. Alex let out a gasp, then moved her hand to the sensitive bundle of nerves and began to touch herself. She was close now. *So* close.

Lucien let out a reedy curse. "Alex," he said, his voice sounding both rough and weak at the same time. "I *can't* last. Not when you're doing that."

She failed to hold back a smile. "Then we'll just have to come together."

Lucien threw back his head and pumped into her even harder while Alex rode him until her orgasm suddenly crashed over her in a blinding light. Alex's deep moan seemed to push Lucien over the edge. As he came inside her, the feel of his hot seed filling her set off a second, deeper orgasm and Alex saw stars. White hot pleasure fanned out through every limb and it took several moments for her to fully come back to herself.

Well, that had *certainly* never happened with Benjamin.

She collapsed on top of Lucien, laughing at the thought, while he bound her in his arms, holding her with a fierce tightness she had never experienced before.

Twenty-Seven

She was dazzling.

The persistent thought would not leave Lucien's addled mind and mirrored the rhythm of his racing heartbeat. Alex's cool command in bed had been intoxicating to watch and made the moment she fell apart all the more satisfying. Though Lucien knew he owed a great deal to her explicit instructions, he still couldn't help feeling absurdly proud that she had found such pleasure in his body.

He gave her one last squeeze, reveling in the sensation of their sweat-slick skin pressing together, then released her.

"Oh God," she said with a start and scrambled off him. "Have I hurt you?"

"No, not at all."

She watched him closely and Lucien basked in the concern in her dark eyes. "You're certain?"

He cupped her flushed cheek. "Entirely." Then he slowly dragged his fingertips down her jaw and the column of her throat, lingering along the lines of her collarbone. "In fact," he began, "we could do that again very soon."

Her eyes went wide. "Already?"

"Oh, yes," he assured her as he continued to drag his fingertips along the silky skin of her shoulder. Alex shivered under his touch and his cock began to stiffen. "I'm quite certain I was made to do nothing but pleasure you."

Alex let out a surprised laugh and smiled. "I'm sure you have a few *other* uses."

"Well, I'm not interested in finding out."

"Come here," Alex murmured as she pulled him closer.

This kiss was slower and more deliberate, but no less arousing. Lucien sank his hand into her thick mass of hair and cupped the back of her head, pulling her even closer, until there was no space between them. Her lips parted on a gasp and he thrust his tongue into her mouth, which she accepted with an eagerness that shot straight to his cock.

This woman was a marvel. A wonder. All that cool control she presented to the public hid a veritable fire just below the surface. And Lucien wanted nothing more than to watch her burn. How he loved that this side of her was a secret only he knew.

Chisolm was either a liar, an idiot, or both for ever letting her go. He should have been on his knees begging her to stay, willing to make any concession to keep her. But his fumble was Lucien's gain.

"Alex," he panted by her ear. "I want you again."

"Yes," she said with a furious nod and began to move onto her side, but Lucien stopped her.

"No. I want you under me this time."

Her brow furrowed with worry. "You're sure?"

"It will be fine. And I'll stop if it isn't." Then he cupped her breast and sucked her rosy nipple into his mouth.

Alex arched beneath him and parted her thighs, as if she was helpless to resist. Though Lucien very well knew this woman did absolutely nothing she did not want to do, that made her submission that much sweeter. He continued to lavish each breast with his tongue until Alex's hips were thrusting against him, and he was certain she was on the brink.

"Lucien," she panted.

He smiled down at her and took a moment to enjoy the sight of Alexandra Atkinson completely undone for him. Her cheeks and chest had flushed a deep pink, while her hair was splayed across the pillow like a tangled halo. She dragged a hand through his hair and stared up at him with eyes so dark they were nearly black.

"*Please.*"

Though technically she was the one begging for him, Lucien was completely at her mercy. He fit his aching cock to her entrance and nearly spent himself when he felt her warm, wet heat. He gritted his teeth and began to ease slowly into her. Somehow she managed to feel even tighter in this position.

Lucien had to shut his eyes, lest he become overwhelmed too soon.

"Yes, that's it," she murmured and pressed her palms against his backside, urging him on faster, and Lucien let out a startled gasp as he slid fully inside her.

"Oh God," she panted weakly and he forced his eyes open.

Lucien took in a shaky breath and began to thrust into her.

"Harder," Alex commanded after a moment and her fingertips dug into his flesh.

"Yes, Miss Atkinson," he replied.

Alex let out a throaty laugh that turned into a cry of pleasure as he obeyed.

She raised her hips and he felt her smooth legs wrap around his back. The sensation nearly overwhelmed him. Lucien tried to shut his eyes again in a bid to last a little longer, but she was too beautiful, too alluring, and he simply couldn't look away.

"Touch yourself," he rasped in between ragged thrusts. "I want to watch you come beneath me."

Alex's hand immediately snaked between them and he watched in rapture as she brought herself to pleasure in just a few strokes. She tightened around him and began to cry out but the rest of the moment was lost to him as he followed her into bliss. His release seemed endless, even greater than before, and he shuddered above her, leaning on his forearms to keep from crushing her. But then her hands smoothed up his back and pressed him down upon her lush, welcoming body.

Lucien didn't know how long they lay together like that. Her panting breaths fanned out across his neck and shoulders and her heart thundered beneath his own.

It couldn't have been like this with anyone else. It could only be like this between the two of them. He was certain of it.

Eventually their heartbeats slowed and Lucien moved off her.

They said nothing, just stared into each other's eyes. Did he look as limpid and lovesick as she? He most certainly felt that way. He pressed a gentle kiss to her lips and turned away to adjust the pillow behind him. Then he felt her fingers tracing a spot on his right shoulder.

His tattoo.

"When did you get this?"

Lucien lay back down on his stomach to give her a better look. He liked the feel of her nimble fingers skating over his skin.

"A couple of years ago. One of my cousins was getting married so we all went out and got roaring drunk. Then we ended the night in a tattoo parlor."

"You didn't!"

He smiled at her scandalized tone. "Oh, we did. But I was one of the lucky ones. The parlor also specialized in piercings and another cousin left with a gold ring through the tip of his penis."

Alex sat up with a start and Lucien rolled over onto his back with a grin. She looked properly appalled. "That's terrible!"

Lucien shrugged and folded his hands behind his head. "He claims his wife likes it, so I suppose it was worth it."

Alex let out a surprised laugh as she pulled up her knees and wrapped her arms around them. "My goodness, men are stupid creatures."

"I won't argue with that." The position made her look younger, more vulnerable, and Lucien felt a surge of protectiveness for her.

Then she rested the side of her head against her knees. "What does your tattoo mean?"

"It was something my mother used to call me. A French term of endearment. It literally means 'My little cabbage.'"

"That's very sweet," she said with a smile that made his heart feel like it might burst in his chest.

"I was teased mercilessly for it for weeks afterward," he admitted. "But it was the only thing I could imagine wanting to have on my body for the rest of my life."

"You made a good choice," she murmured, still watching him with those dark doe eyes. Then she lifted her head and scanned his torso. "You feel all right?"

"A little sore, I'll admit. But it was worth it."

She blushed and glanced away but he could see her fighting a smile. "You shouldn't sleep here. The maids will see you in the morning," she added unnecessarily.

"Right." It was the most sensible course of action. As no matter how independent Alex was, it wasn't good form to bed the daughter of his host. And yet, Lucien still felt disappointed. He threw back the covers and rose.

Alex pulled on her wrapper and helped him find his discarded clothes. Then he dressed.

"We will need to talk about this tomorrow," he said with as much authority as he could muster.

Alex nodded and met his gaze straight on. "We will." Then, before he could think twice, he wrapped an arm around her waist and gave her a deep, thorough kiss. Alex sank against him as if she had lost her ability to stand, and Lucien took that as a good sign.

When he finally pulled back, she blinked up at him in a daze. "Sleep well," he murmured.

She nodded slowly. "You too." Then she leaned against the door frame as Lucien shuffled down the darkened hallway.

He looked back when he reached his room and she was still there, watching him. He gave a little wave and she smiled before shutting her door.

Given the length and strenuousness of their bedsport, Alex should have slept soundly that night. But instead she lay awake for hours going over every detail of their encounter. She had not known it could be like that between a man and a woman—no, that *she* could be like that. But Lucien brought out a playful tenderness she had not indulged in for years. And the more Alex ruminated, the more the pit in her stomach grew and the louder her doubts sounded. Sometime close to dawn she finally drifted off into a fitful, restless sleep that provided little relief from her thoughts.

Hours later she awoke with a start on the edge of a dream in which Lucien's lean form hovered above her while he whispered filthy things into her ear. Alex sat up and shook her head in a bid to strike the appealing image from her mind, but that did nothing for the warmth still pumping through her veins. The very real *happiness* she felt. She threw back the covers and rang the bellpull as she stalked to the en suite bathroom.

Alex couldn't wait for the maid, so she turned on the taps of the bathtub. She still smelled him on her skin, her sheets, in her hair. That had to be why she dreamed of him. Why she could still feel his arms around her, still feel him inside her. The bottom of the bathtub was barely full of water but she threw off her wrapper and climbed in. Then she picked up the bar of soap and the sponge and got to work scrubbing him off her. She needed to be able to think. To focus on anything other than him.

Eventually the maid arrived and helped Alex wash her hair and dress for the day. Afterward, Alex sat at the dressing table while Millie styled her hair in a chignon. She was doing her final check when Alex cleared her throat.

"And is Mr. Taylor about?"

They was the first words she had uttered that morning. Millie met her gaze in the mirror and surprise briefly flashed across her face. But she was too well trained to let it linger.

"Yes, miss. I believe he is out in the garden with Miss Winifred."

Alex instinctively clenched her hands on her lap then forced them apart. "Thank you. That is all, Millie."

The girl then bobbed a curtsy and left the room.

Alex gazed at her reflection. Lucien had called her beautiful last night. Said she was like the sun. But all she saw was a somber woman of indeterminate age who looked incredibly tired. For a moment she was very tempted to steal the rouge Freddie kept secreted away in her room, but for what purpose? To what end? A bit of cosmetics wouldn't change things. Things she had no *wish* to change, she stubbornly reminded herself as she shoved the chair back. Enough of this. Alex had already wasted too much of the morning on maudlin thoughts. If she left now, she could still have a productive day at the office.

Her stomach chose that moment to growl loudly in protest. Alex let out a sigh. Fine. She would eat first and *then* go to the office. She headed downstairs full of purpose and was relieved to find the breakfast room empty. Trays of food were on the sideboard and she made a plate without really taking notice of the food. Alex had always liked this room. It was warm and cozy and offered a fine view of the back garden. Her mother once shared that the wallpaper was a print called the "Strawberry Thief" because it depicted a bird feasting on the fruit from a garden. Alex liked looking at it. The colors soothed her and gave her something to focus on while she ate. But just as she moved to sit, her gaze was caught by two figures outside. It was Freddie and Lucien coming into view. They were walking side by side, though Lucien was still limping just a bit. But whatever pain he might be feeling, that didn't keep the grin off his face. Freddie was chattering away animatedly and his eyes were riveted to her. Then she began to laugh and he joined in. If they had been two strangers that Alex happened upon in the park, she would have assumed they were a very happy young couple.

Something curdled in her chest and she set the plate heavily on the table. Even though her appetite had entirely vanished, she sat down in a chair. It wasn't that the scene surprised her, exactly. Alex knew very well that Freddie and Lucien had a connection that long superseded whatever had developed between them these last weeks. But to see it so clearly before her eyes was different. Was *undeniable*. She could allow that perhaps Lucien did think Alex was beautiful. And she could not dismiss the passion they had shared last night. But was that enough to sustain a relationship? Alex was very aware of her limits and they ended far before she could get anywhere close to Freddie's natural effervescence. It seemed the height of folly to expect Lucien to simply forget about the girl he had loved for so long in favor of her older sister who possessed absolutely none of her qualities.

Alex swallowed as a bitter taste filled her mouth. She needed to leave. Before she had to face either of them. But as she rose from her chair, she heard voices just outside the room and in another moment the door swung open and there they were, still laughing and chatting away like a couple of old friends. Because they *were* old friends. Alex was used to feeling out of place among other people. But it had never bothered her before. Now, though, as she waited for the two of them to notice her presence, she was gripped by something hot and ugly. It twisted low in her belly, winding its way up around her heart then squeezed until it felt like she couldn't take a deep breath. For a brief moment Alex thought she might be dying and had to grip the back of the chair.

You aren't dying, you idiot, the voice in her head chastised. *You're* jealous *of them.*

Jealous. The thought struck her like a fist just as Lucien's eyes met her own. And even though she could plainly see the warmth in his gaze, it wasn't enough. Alex couldn't handle this rush of feeling inside her, too strong and fast for her to control. She couldn't allow herself to get swept away any more than she already had. So she tightened her grip on the chair and met his gaze head on.

֍

"There you are," Freddie trilled just over Lucien's shoulder. "We were about to send for Dr. Mosley to attend to you. I don't think I've ever seen you sleep past nine outside of this week."

Alex did little more than grunt in response. She looked more stiff and drawn than usual, but Lucien was willing to bet she had slept even worse than he had. It had taken every bit of self-control not to go right back into her bedroom last night. Well, tonight he would not make the same mistake.

"Good morning, Alex," he said easily as he rounded the table and approached her, unable to keep the idiotic smile off his face. He was just so blasted *happy*. Even Freddie's stories about her French fencing instructor had sent him into a fit of giggles outside. He moved to press a kiss to Alex's check and felt her flinch. Very well. She wasn't used to displays of affection in front of company. Lucien would act accordingly in the future.

"Good morning," she murmured and seemed strangely hesitant.

He glanced over at Freddie, who was giving them a knowing smile. He returned it and pulled out the chair beside Alex. "We've already eaten, but I'm happy to keep you company."

"And I will give you both some privacy," Freddie said with absolutely no subtlety.

While out on their stroll, he had all but confessed that he and Alex had spent the night together and she had been terribly excited for them.

Alex said nothing but her gaze followed Freddie as she retreated. Once the door of the breakfast room swung shut, Lucien took her hand in his and nuzzled her neck. "Did you miss me last night? Because I missed you terribly."

"Don't," Alex said as she slipped out of his reach.

Lucien gave her a frustrated smile. "Really, Alex. Freddie is gone and your parents are both already out for the day. I saw them leave myself."

"It isn't that."

"All right," he said easily. He could endure the ice queen act if that was what she needed until she grew more comfortable. "I thought we could go to Madame Tussauds today. Freddie said the new exhibit is great fun."

She turned away. "I have to go to the office."

"Oh. Well, then perhaps tomorrow?"

"Lucien, *no*."

Something about her tone caused the hairs on his neck to rise. "Look at me." Her lips pursed, but after a moment she reluctantly turned to him. "What is going on?" he asked. Though even as he spoke the words, he knew. He could read her so well now.

"Lucien," she began in a placating voice, but he shook his head.

"At least have the decency to be honest with me," he demanded. "You certainly don't hold back with anyone else."

He watched her swallow and look away, her pale face gone ashen. If he were a better man, he would have left then. The message was clear enough. But Lucien wasn't leaving until she looked him in the eye and ended this. Until she said the words.

"I am sorry if last night confused things for you," she began. "But this doesn't change anything."

He let out a harsh laugh that sounded foreign to his own ears. "Are you joking? This changes *everything*."

She turned back to him then and as her dark eyes narrowed on him, he suddenly regretted his earlier desire. "It was only intercourse, Lucien. I thought you understood that."

Intercourse.

Leave it to Alex to use the least romantic term possible. But maybe she was right. And Lucien *had* misunderstood. An embarrassed flush crept up his neck. "I am not so untried as that. And you very well know it was more."

"It was—"

"Tell me it was like that with Chisolm," he demanded. "Tell me it was *ever* like that with him. The man you supposedly *loved*. The man you intended to *marry*."

Only when Alex looked up at him with wide eyes did he realize he had stood and knocked the chair over. Lucien inhaled through his nose and grappled with the anger coursing through him. He wasn't used to losing control like this. Even when he learned of Rene's deception, that his entire business was ruined, he had felt more disappointed than *angry*.

"I don't want to talk about Benjamin," she said, frustratingly calm. "He has nothing to do with this situation."

"This *situation*," Lucien parroted. "You mean us."

Alex flexed her jaw. "There *is* no us. There never was an us. It wasn't real."

Lucien turned away with a huff and placed his hands on his hips. "I knew I shouldn't have let you break the contract." If he just had a little more time to show her—

But now Alex was out of her chair, staring at him in challenge. "You didn't *let* me. There was no further use for it once Freddie became engaged."

"Oh? And what of the rest of it? What of the company? The *board*?"

She lifted her chin. "That is no longer your concern." It was her cool demeanor that grated the most, he realized. The way she always seemed to occupy a higher plane than the rest of them, where she wasn't troubled by such pedestrian concerns as *feelings*. And perhaps, at one point he might have truly believed it. But now it was too late. She had let him see too much behind the mask.

"You're afraid," he said, like it was an accusation. "You're afraid to actually feel something real. Something you can't control or write into a contract or buy out."

"I feel guilty about what happened to you," she allowed. "Because of my negligence."

"Do you know why I was there that night? Have you even once considered it? I went there for *you*," he said. "To ask you to give us a real chance."

Alex stared at him for a long moment while her face remained carefully blank. "Well, that would have been a waste of time," she finally said. "I would have just sent you away."

Her words cut him to the quick and managed to hurt more than all those punches and kicks to his body. Yet he smiled at her then, through the pain. And it must have looked as deranged as it felt, for she shrank back a little. "It was eight o'clock on a Friday night and you were still there," he said. "Why? What possible reason could you have for being there at that time?"

Alex shook her head but did not answer.

Lucien took a step forward and leaned in. "Because that is all you have. Because your life is *nothing* without that office and those papers." He pulled back and shook his head. "And you deserve it." Then he turned on his heel and headed for the door.

Lucien did not wait for her response and did not look back. If he couldn't have her, he could at least have the last word.

Twenty-Eight

Alex returned home that evening later than ever before. She had stayed in her office reviewing contracts and marking up reports until the words swam before her aching eyes and her back felt as stiff as a board. Until she reached her limits, both physically and mentally. Then she rode home in a daze, her mind blessedly empty of thoughts and recriminations.

At this hour she expected her family to either be out or abed and she sent up a silent prayer as she stepped into the quiet entryway and gave her cloak and gloves to the sleepy-eyed footman. Then she padded up the stairs toward her room, too tired to even ring for a tray. It wasn't until she had closed her bedroom door, turned up the gas lamp, and begun unbuttoning her bodice that she noticed someone in the corner.

Freddie tugged on the lamp beside her with a well-timed dramatic flair and, even in her addled state, Alex was willing to bet she had practiced the motion at least several times.

"I've been waiting *ages* for you."

Alex didn't even try to hide her tired sigh as her gaze traveled over her sister. She was in her nightgown and slippers with a book on her lap. Alex narrowed her eyes. "With the light off?"

But Freddie merely lifted her chin in challenge. "No, I heard your carriage out front and set the scene."

Something about this proud admission made Alex's lips twitch with amusement, but she wasn't in the mood for Freddie's inquisition. "Can we leave the bevy of accusations for tomorrow? I'm really quite tired."

Freddie set the book aside and came to her feet. "I'm not here to accuse you of anything."

"No?" Alex couldn't hide her surprise.

"I came to see if you are all right."

Well, this was not what she had expected. Somehow that was almost worse. "I'm fine," she insisted even as her shoulders hunched.

Her sister tilted her head. "It would be understandable if you weren't."

"You're speaking of Lucien, I assume," Alex said primly.

Freddie huffed a laugh. "You don't need to pretend with me. I *know* you're devastated."

"I assure you, I am not," Alex began. "We had an agreement. If you don't believe me, ask Papa. He can confirm everything. Whatever you saw, it was only an act. A mutually beneficial arrangement that has come to its natural conclusion." She finished this little speech with a decisive nod.

There. Now that it was all out in the open, she wouldn't have to continue with this farce and play the part of the jilted woman.

"Oh, Alex," Freddie sighed and shook her head. "You poor thing."

"It's *true*. Ask Papa," she repeated, hating how desperate she sounded. "He'll tell you we set it up."

"For heaven's sake, I know that," Freddie snapped. "It was terribly obvious you were up to something at Mother's birthday. And while I was furious in the beginning, neither you nor Lucien are that good at acting. Especially *you*."

Alex opened her mouth, then closed it. She could hardly deny that.

"But then, after seeing you together that night at the theater," Freddie began. "Well, I understood why—" She broke off and shook her head. "It just made a kind of sense. That's all."

"And yet you told quite the opposite to Benjamin Chisolm," Alex said with far more bitterness than she would have liked.

Freddie's face blanched and she looked down. "Yes. I'm sorry about that. I'll admit I was feeling rather pitiful that evening. When he pestered me about you and Lucien, I eventually made some unkind insinuations."

Alex pursed her lips. So Benjamin had been trying to sniff them out. That put Freddie in a better light than the version he had told.

Then her sister glanced up and her gaze sharpened with curiosity. "At the time I thought he was just being a nosy gossip. But if he actually brought it up to you, that's rather forward. Especially for a mere acquaintance," she added in a suggestive tone.

"So you aren't mad at me for Lucien anymore?" Alex said instead.

Freddie sighed and mulled over the question. "I *do* like him," Freddie said. "But not that way. And certainly not after seeing you together."

Alex let out a dry laugh. "Am I really so repelling to you?"

"No," Freddie drew out the word. "But I am quite certain I would have come to the same conclusion even without your interference."

"Congratulations, then, on realizing you are in love with your fiancé," she said dryly.

Freddie's gaze darted away and she shifted on her feet. "About that…"

"Oh, Freddie." Alex pinched the bridge of her nose.

"Just—just listen," her sister said with a petulant little stamp of her foot. "I was fully prepared to marry Hank Jr. Was even looking *forward* to it. But then I…"

"Met someone?" Alex offered in the silence that followed. "If you don't love Lucien," she continued, "and you don't love Hank Jr., then it stands to reason that someone else has captured your interest."

"You make me sound hopelessly fickle," Freddie said crossly.

"*Are* you?"

Freddie swallowed and stared at a spot on the rug. "Perhaps I was before. I can admit that. But this…this feels much different," she murmured. Then she looked to Alex. "That's why I came here. Because I can't just stand back and watch you throw away your chance at happiness. Most people don't ever get to experience what you have with Lucien."

"Freddie—"

But her sister grabbed her hands then and gave them an urgent squeeze. "If you feel even a quarter of what I feel, you need to take this chance. Lucien *loves* you, Alex. I saw it yesterday with my own eyes. The man is truly lost to you."

It took a few tries but Alex finally swallowed past the lump in her throat. "That may have been the case when you saw him, but he feels very differently now. I am quite certain."

She then tugged on her hands but Freddie would not let go. "Are you?"

Alex had to turn away from her pleading gaze. "It doesn't matter anyway. He's gone."

"He hasn't disappeared off the face of the earth, Alex," Freddie pressed. "Go after him."

"Absolutely not." She still had *some* pride left.

"And you will let him go? Just like that?"

"It is for the best," Alex said with finality.

Freddie flinched. "That is a coward's excuse," she bit off with such vehemence Alex wondered if this mystery suitor hadn't used the very same reason with her.

"Perhaps," Alex allowed. "But it is also the truth. I wouldn't say that if I didn't mean it."

Freddie released her then and took a step back. "I don't think I've ever felt sorry for you before," she murmured.

"I find that hard to believe. Most of London feels sorry for me."

Ice queen. Spinster. Heartless shrew.

How many times had she heard those words, and not once had they ever bothered her. Until now. Because they must be true.

But this time her sister had no sharp retort. No snappy rejoinder. She only looked at Alex with undisguised pity. "I hope you can live with yourself, then. Knowing you let your chance at love slip away. I know I couldn't."

Alex turned to the hearth and stared at the flames, trying to find the words to explain. To assure Freddie that she had no regrets about Lucien. That she was confident in her decision. But when she finally looked back, Freddie was gone.

❦

After Alex irrevocably ended things between them, Lucien left Park House and went straight to Alain's hotel to ask for a job. The only place available at the moment was as a kitchen grunt, someone to peel potatoes and chop vegetables and clean dishes. It was well beneath his experience, but Lucien was desperate so he took it on the condition that he start the following week. He needed to see his father first. The condition was granted and Lucien left for Bunbury on the early train the next morning.

He needed to reassure his father that he was well on the mend and also get an update on his own health. Lucien didn't *think* Alex or Mr. Atkinson would retaliate against his father, but it was better to be prepared. Now that Lucien was merely hurt instead of hurt and angry, he regretted his parting words to Alex. He couldn't make her want to be with him and it was stupid to assume that their lone night together would be as earth-shattering for her as it had been for him. He felt like the naive, immature lad Alex must see him as. He wished he could be as controlled as she was, but Lucien simply didn't have the stomach for it. Better to live life with his heart on his sleeve than locked up in a box somewhere.

He departed the train and as he descended the platform, the parallels between today and his last visit to Bunbury were not lost on him. How much had changed in a handful of weeks. But this time there was no Freddie to offer him a ride, so Lucien made the two-mile trek to Atkinson House on foot. He almost wished he had missed Freddie the first time too. That he had never renewed his acquaintance with her and thus never lost his heart to Alex. As he rounded the bend in the road and the large Georgian mansion came into view, Lucien came to a stop.

No, despite the very real pain in his chest, he could not regret what had happened. Then he let out a helpless little laugh. It had taken him *years* to move on from Freddie and that had been entirely one-sided. It stood to reason then that he would be pining for Alex for the rest of his life. He let out a resigned sigh, adjusted the strap of his battered satchel, and continued on. So be it, then. He was used to torch-bearing.

When Lucien finally arrived at the carriage house, he was surprised to see his father not only out of bed but waxing the landau with smooth, vigorous strokes. He glanced up at the sound of Lucien's footsteps, and then his face broke out into a wide smile.

"There he is!"

Lucien had sent a message ahead of his arrival, but he truly had not expected his father to be up and about. As his father gripped him in a tight embrace, a weight Lucien hadn't even known he was carrying floated off his shoulders.

"Hello, Father," he murmured. "I'm so glad to see you."

His father pulled back and gave him a worried look. "What's happened, Lucien?"

Lucien shook his head and glanced down as the words seemed to get caught in his throat.

I've failed again.

And this time, it really did feel like the end of the world.

His father clicked his tongue. "Let's get you inside. Mrs. Holloway brought over a basket with all your favorite treats and I'll make us some tea."

A little while later, they were seated in the flat's cozy parlor drinking cups of Assam tea and Lucien was tearing into a still-warm scone.

"You look much better," he said.

Indeed, his father's face had filled out and the dark circles under his eyes were entirely gone. He was still thinner than he had once been, but no longer alarmingly gaunt.

"Thank you. I've been feeling better. You, however, look awful."

Lucien let out a dry laugh and took a sip of tea. "Getting the stuffing kicked out of yourself will do that." No sense in hiding the truth any longer, now that they were both on the mend.

His father did not look amused. "Yes, it certainly will, but you have the look of a young man in the throes of heartbreak."

Lucien carefully set the teacup down and ignored the comment. "You knew about my injuries, then?"

His father watched him for a moment before answering. "Not initially, no. But once you were up and about Mrs. Drummond admitted how bad it was."

Lucien was quiet as he took in this information.

"Now what about Miss Atkinson?"

"It's over."

"She called it off?"

Lucien let out a bitter laugh. "Of course."

His father crossed his arms and continued to give Lucien that assessing look. "But you still care for her."

He considered telling his father about their arrangement, saying that it had all only been for show. But he didn't have it in him to lie anymore. Because even if it had started that way, that wasn't how it had ended. Certainly not for him, anyway.

"I do," he murmured, unable to meet his father's eyes.

"And there is no chance of a—"

Lucien snapped his gaze up and gritted his teeth. "*No.*"

His father raised his hands in supplication. "All right, all right. I only wanted to be sure."

Lucien slumped back in his chair. "Sorry. I didn't mean to be cross with you. But I can't talk about it."

About her.

"Fair enough," his father said with a nod. "What about work? Can we talk about that?"

"Please. Tell me what you have been doing."

Lucien then listened as his father related the gradual reassumption of his duties. "I don't think I'll ever return to the London property," he continued. "But from what I hear, Markham is doing a bang-up job."

"He is," Lucien said. "But is your position secure? I've been worried about you."

His father waved a hand. "Oh, I'm fine. I still have a few more working years left in me. And when I do retire, I have my pension and some savings."

Lucien leaned forward. "But will that be enough for you to live on, especially if you can't stay here in the flat?"

"Yes. Certainly. Your mother and I made provisions."

"But the money you gave me for Paris," Lucien pointed out. "I know how costly it was. And I want to assure you that I will pay you back every last cent. In fact, I'm starting a new job next week and—" He broke off as his father suddenly looked very guilty. "What is it?"

"Nothing," his father said briskly. "Tell me about your new job. Is it the supper club?"

Lucien frowned, unconvinced. "No. I…I've given up on that. I'm working in the kitchen at Alain's hotel—"

"But you hate working in kitchens."

"Yes, but I need the money, Father," he said with exasperation.

The guilty look returned. "Not for me, I hope."

Lucien let out a sigh and dragged a hand over his face. Were all parents this impossible? "I do want to be able to help you, especially after what you did for me."

"I should have told you much sooner," his father said, almost as if he were chastising himself. "But I didn't think you would take things this far."

"Told me *what*?"

His father reached out and patted his hand. "You don't need to worry about me, Lucien. And certainly not about money."

"But Paris," he insisted. "You must have used all your savings to send me. And if I had any idea of the cost then, I wouldn't have let you!"

His father stared at him for a moment. "I didn't use my own money, Lucien. Not a cent."

Lucien shook his head, confused. "Then how…"

"She made me promise never to tell you," his father said matter-of-factly while studiously avoiding Lucien's gaze. "That I should allow you to think it was me. I objected, naturally, but what choice did I have? You're right. I could never have afforded to send you to that school. It would have cost me everything. But I wish I could have—"

"Oh my god," Lucien said as he sat back in his chair.

You need to go somewhere far, far away from here.

Alex was the only one who had seen him that night. The only one who had known just how wretched and broken he had felt.

"It was her. All this time."

His father finally looked at him and gave a solemn nod. "I thought Miss Alexandra must have told you. That it was what brought you together."

"No. She never said a thing."

"I don't think she intended to deceive you," his father offered.

But Lucien just laughed. "Certainly not."

He was willing to bet Alex had forgotten all about her generous act. And even if she hadn't, she wouldn't have told him, if only to keep him from feeling indebted to her.

"I'm sorry," his father said. "I should have told you, but you know how she can be."

Despite everything, Lucien's lip curved at the thought of a younger Alex haranguing his father into submission.

"I'm sure she was rather terrifying," he replied. "And yes, you should have told me."

His father gave a sheepish nod. "Do you at least feel better now?"

Lucien laughed again at the hopeful look in his father's eyes. "Perhaps a little," he allowed.

About you, anyway.

"Then I should tell you that there is another reason why you shouldn't worry so much about me."

"Oh?" Lucien said drolly as he poured out another cup of tea. "And what is that?"

His father was suddenly unable to keep from smiling. "Mrs. Holloway and I are to be married."

Lucien froze holding the teacup. *Married.*

"Are you upset?" his father asked, suddenly anxious.

Lucien considered the question and shook his head. "No. I'm not."

"Good," his father said, visibly relieved. "And you know, I will always love your mother."

Lucien smiled. "Yes, Father. I know," he answered honestly.

"Mrs. Holloway inherited a little cottage in Kent from an aunt. And we will live there once we both retire."

"I'm glad."

His father then cast him a look. "There is also a bedroom for you…"

"In case I remain a poor bachelor," Lucien finished, attempting to make a joke that didn't quite land.

"I only meant that there will always be a place in my home for you. No matter what. You are still very young, Lucien," his father continued. "And you are smart and hard-working. You will achieve much in your life. I am sure of it."

"Thank you, Father. I appreciate that."

Now, if only he had that much faith in himself.

Twenty-Nine

Alex kept her grueling schedule for the next several days. Every morning she arrived promptly at eight and worked straight through until five. If it were up to her, she would have stayed even later but Father insisted she could no longer stay in the office alone, so she left with him. But once at home, she took a tray in her room and worked for a few more hours. Then, when she could barely keep her eyes open, she collapsed and slept like the dead until it was time to wake up and do it all over again. She barely saw her family, aside from her father during the carriage ride home each evening, as he was usually too busy entertaining clients during the workday. He knew that things between her and Lucien were over but had the good grace not to press her on it. A board meeting was scheduled for the end of the month and Alex was meant to announce their new partnership with the Ericsons and, she hoped, garner enough support to ensure her future as the head of the company even without Lucien by her side. But now the thought failed to ignite even the slightest spark of excitement in her. She simply didn't care anymore. It just felt like another task in an endless list. Alex probably would have continued on with her schedule indefinitely until there was one meeting she absolutely could not cancel.

She slipped away from the office during the lunch hour to meet Marguerite in the mews of Park House and give her the box of cervical caps she had been storing.

"There is one packet missing," Alex admitted once the box was safely loaded into Marguerite's carriage, then pointedly avoided her friend's curious gaze.

"Well, I cannot blame you for that," she said with a throaty chuckle. "I hope you made good use of it."

"Marguerite!" Alex was far too shocked by the comment to maintain her composure.

But the woman merely shrugged in her ever-so-French fashion. "Life is not all about business, Alexandra. You need to indulge in a little bad behavior. And what a man to indulge with," she added with a little sigh.

If the situation had been different, Alex would have loved to gossip about Lucien with Marguerite. But the thought of everything they had *indulged* in only made her feel, well, sad. The emotion must have shown on her face because after a moment Marguerite's brow furrowed with worry.

"What is it, my dear?"

Alex had to clear her throat before she could get the words out. "Mr. Taylor and I have parted ways."

"Oh. Oh, I am *very* sorry to hear that," she said as she grasped Alex's hand.

She shook her head furiously as her nose and eyes began to prickle. "It's fine. Really. I'm fine." She would not shed any more tears over Lucien. And especially not here. Marguerite's horse was staring at her and the air smelled of cabbage.

"But it would be understandable if you weren't," she said kindly.

Alex bit the inside of her cheek and inhaled deeply until the feeling passed. "I will be," she said with something approximating her usual tone. "When is the meeting?"

"Tonight at seven in Whitechapel. Can you come?"

Alex usually assisted Marguerite in distributing the caps, and it was during these meetings that they learned of potential women-owned businesses to invest in, but she didn't have the will today. She had already deviated enough from her schedule and needed to get back to the office. It was the only thing keeping her from falling completely into despair. "I can't this time. I'm sorry. But do let me know how it goes."

"Yes, certainly. And we will meet soon, yes? At the salon next week?"

"Perhaps." But it was likely she would miss that too. She certainly didn't want to cross paths with Benjamin again. "I should get back to the office."

"Of course," Marguerite said. "Do take care of yourself. You are looking quite pale."

Alex managed a brittle smile. "I will." Then she retreated into the house. Time to get back to work.

Alex returned to Atkinson Enterprises to find the office in a state of absolute chaos. Workers rushed around like headless chickens, bumping into one another and dropping sheafs of papers while her father roared at someone in the conference room. Alex kept her head down and continued on to her office, but Potts had abandoned his post. Rather than trying to flag someone down, Alex decided to wait for the chaos to come to her and returned to her desk. Consequently, she did not have to wait very long. Within a quarter of an hour, her father stormed into her office with Potts scurrying behind.

"Alexandra, where the *hell* have you been?"

"I had lunch with Madame LaSalle," she replied coolly. "Has something happened?"

Her father let out an incredulous laugh. "Happened? The company is under attack!"

"What do you mean?" she replied, trying to stay calm in the face of his near hysteria.

"The board. They're calling a meeting tomorrow to challenge *me*. That blasted upstart Chisten—"

"Chisolm, sir," Potts cut in.

Alex's stomach tightened. *No. It couldn't be.*

"Whatever his name is, I don't care," her father railed. "Apparently Tompkins is an old family friend and he convinced him to retire and give him the seat. But Chisolm's been sneaking around for *weeks* now talking to the other board members about mismanagement and failed dividends and all kinds of rot."

"Well, it isn't true," Alex said simply. "Nothing has been mismanaged. And profits are up as usual. He has no case."

Her father paused and gave her a look that caused Alex's blood to run cold. "Leave us, Potts."

When they were alone, he collapsed into the chair across from her. "That isn't the worst of it. He's called your role in the company into question and spooked the other members."

"What role?" Alex shot back as a sudden rush of anger flooded her veins. "For all they know I sit here twiddling my thumbs all day. I don't have any power. I'm not even on the board." Which, frankly, had long been a point of contention. But her father had always maintained it was better for the company to minimize her public-facing role as much as possible.

"Chisolm maintains otherwise. Says *you* are actually running the company and that I am just a figurehead."

"But you aren't," Alex insisted, though that was splitting hairs.

"The rest of it is not too far off the mark, though," he said, then gave her that look again. "Alex, do you know him?"

She pressed her lips together and wished very much that she could melt into the floor. "He was my tutor at Oxford," she said reluctantly. "I…I may have told him about my original idea for investing in businesses."

"Oh, for God's sake," her father cursed. Then he let out a hysterical laugh. "He knows everything, then."

"And what if he does? It's his word against yours."

"That may be all it takes. Then they can boot me from the board and put Chisolm in my place. And I'd wager that's *exactly* what he is after. What happened, did you jilt him?" He had meant it as a joke, but Alex immediately looked away and her father cursed again. "What the *hell*, Alexandra."

"It was a long time ago," she insisted. "And he's been in America for years now. I never expected him to do something like this. He was supposed to invest in Lucien's company."

Her father scoffed. "Well, that didn't work so I guess he chose option B."

"What do you mean?"

"Lucien isn't opening the supper club," he snapped. "He's been in Surrey with his father. Did you really not know?"

Alex shook her head. She had buried herself in work specifically to shut out any word about Lucien. But if that was the case, then Benjamin's motives made a little more sense. "He needs money. Chisolm, I mean. We agreed that he would be the lone investor in the supper club."

Her father narrowed his eyes. "Did he threaten you?"

Alex had never heard her father growl before. "Yes," she murmured.

"For God's sake, why didn't you tell me?"

Alex looked up at him and blinked. His face looked pained. "It never occurred to me," she answered honestly. "I took care of it myself." Like she always did with everything. And that had never bothered him before. But Alex kept that to herself. Her father pinched the bridge of his nose and sighed. It was the first time he had ever looked haggard. Alex felt a deep pang of regret. "I'm sorry. What can we do?"

"The meeting is tomorrow at nine. I've already sent word to Lucien. He should be there in time."

Alex balked. "Whatever for?"

"Because the world still thinks you are courting," he said exasperatedly. "And tomorrow we will tell the board that you are engaged, which hopefully will instill a little bit of confidence in our leadership."

"You can't," Alex said, now feeling like a headless chicken herself.

Lucien here? Tomorrow?

"It is the only way, my dear," her father replied sadly.

She sat back in her chair, stunned. Why on earth would Lucien ever agree to do this?

"Come along," he prompted. "We need a plan of attack. The very future of this company depends on it."

That was at least something she could fight for.

❦

After finding Alex pacing in her room that night, her mother insisted on giving her a sleeping draught, which she reluctantly accepted, if only because it was nearly midnight and her thoughts were still awhirl.

"I am sorry about all this," her mother said as she poured out the dose after first making Alex get under the covers. "I know your father meant well by insisting on hiding your true role in the company, but it has not done either of you any favors."

Alex dutifully accepted the glass and swallowed the pungent liquid with a wince. "I didn't realize you disapproved."

"I told him he shouldn't feel so beholden to catering to the base impulses of the board," her mother explained. "Let the ones who disapprove of you leave and good riddance. You've proven yourself over again and again. And they would have seen that if your father had only let them. But instead he downplayed your accomplishments and your role into something more palatable for the masses." Then she hesitated. "I've often wondered why you went along with it."

"I didn't know there was an alternative," Alex said, more petulantly than she wished.

Her mother tilted her head. "I've never known you not to approach a problem without examining it from every possible angle. You give no quarter in any other area of your life, which is one of your great strengths." Then she pressed a hand to her cheek.

"But you have always treated your father with kid gloves. Even as a girl."

Alex swallowed thickly and glanced down. "I just…I wanted to help him. As much as I could."

My brilliant girl.

And she liked feeling special, especially in a world that treated her with such contempt.

"He can take this, Alexandra," her mother insisted. "And if he fails tomorrow, he has only himself to blame."

Alex let out a humorless laugh. "Even if it is at the hands of the man I jilted?"

"Men have done much worse," she said with a wry smile. "The point is, your father will be fine. *You* will be fine."

"Well, I certainly won't work for that man if he does take over the company."

"No," her mother agreed. "But it might not be such a bad thing for you to leave, either."

"No other firm will have me."

"Then strike out on your own. My goodness, you have spent *years* now drafting fail-proof business plans for other people. I imagine you are quite able to do it for yourself." Alex bit her lip as she considered this. "But we don't need to talk about all that now," her mother continued. "First you need to rest."

The draught had already started to take effect and Alex's eyelids grew heavy. She had barely managed good night before she drifted off to sleep.

Thirty

Alex awoke early the next morning admittedly refreshed, but with a stubborn pit in her stomach. She could barely stomach more than a cup of coffee for breakfast until Aunt Winifred practically force-fed her a bun.

"No one ever triumphed on an empty stomach," she said with a firm nod.

Alex was in no mood to argue and soon enough Father hustled her out the door. They barely said anything on the ride to the office, both too lost in their own thoughts.

The mood in the office was just as grim and almost violently subdued compared to the day before. It reminded Alex of a funeral, though she supposed it was, in a way.

The death of the company.

"Come this way," her father prompted, interrupting her morose thoughts. He guided her to the conference room. "Chin up," he murmured as they turned the corner.

Alex did as he commanded while fighting against the instinct to shrink back. A dozen men milled around the hallway waiting for the proceedings to begin, and she recognized many members of the board. Men she had known since she was a child, and who had known her father even longer. For some of them had been on the board of this company since Grandfather had been in charge. For the first time, she was struck by the duplicitousness of it all. The sheer greed. When would they ever have enough? But then a gentleman stepped aside and she saw Benjamin in full view.

Before Alex even knew what she was doing, she charged straight up to him, her father heedlessly calling for her to stop. For his part, Benjamin made no attempt to hide. He simply met her gaze.

"Why are you doing this?" she hissed.

"I told you," he said calmly, glancing at something behind her. Probably her father frothing at the mouth. "If I couldn't invest in the supper club, I would be forced to take drastic action. And here we are."

"You've been planning this for *weeks*," she shot back, but Benjamin only shrugged.

"I needed a back-up plan. And when Mr. Tompkins mentioned his seat on the board, I made a suggestion. The rest was remarkably easy." Then he narrowed his eyes. "I truly had no idea your father was hiding your contributions."

"I'm not *hiding*," she protested.

"Nevertheless, he did you a disservice," Benjamin continued. "But not to worry. I am not so closed-minded as the rest of these fellows. When everything settles, I would be happy to take you on as an advisor."

Alex scoffed and stepped back in disgust. "I would never work for you."

But Benjamin only shrugged. "Suit yourself. I suppose you'll have more time to practice your needlepoint and watercolors. All those feminine pursuits you always turned up your nose at. Make yourself a good little wife for Lucien Taylor. Ah, there he is now."

Alex turned and her gaze immediately tangled with Lucien's. They stared at each other for the space of one heartbeat, until her father took his arm and led him inside the conference room.

"This won't work, by the way," Benjamin said by his ear. "But it's a good effort. *Very* romantic."

Alex cast him her most withering look. "As if you would know anything about that."

She then stormed off, his dry laugh following in her wake.

When Alex entered the conference room, Lucien was already seated at the table. Her father waved from the other side of the room where they were to sit and watch the proceedings. As Alex passed, Lucien shot her a glance and gave her a small smile. Alex did her best to return it, but she was so nervous that it must have looked more like a grimace.

"They're going to start by summarizing Chisolm's accusations," her father murmured by her ear as she sat next to him. "Then Lucien will speak on my behalf. I've already denied everything, but I thought this could help sell the idea that he is to be my successor, and he's far more popular than I am at the moment."

Alex gave a single nod. It was a sound strategy. "Fine."

"And then there will be a vote."

She balked. "That's *it*?"

Her father nodded. The fight seemed to have left him, and Alex hated seeing him so resigned. "That's it."

This was appalling.

She looked over at the conference table as the stragglers were all taking their seats and her eye caught Benjamin's. He had the nerve to actually *wink* at her before sitting down.

Alex growled under her breath.

"I am very tempted to give that boy a good thrashing," her father said.

"He isn't worth it," Alex replied and crossed her arms.

As the meeting began, her gaze kept wandering to Lucien. He was staring at the speech her father had given him, and speaking to himself, likely memorizing it. Alex found herself riveted to the movements of his mouth as he formed the words with his full lips. A shiver went down her back as her unruly mind recalled the feel of those very lips on her mouth, her neck, her—

"Here we are," her father muttered and Alex blinked.

It was time for Lucien to speak. She shifted in her chair and forced her focus to return to the meeting.

He tapped the papers on the tabletop and cleared his throat. "I have been asked here today to speak on my experience working with Atkinson Enterprises, both as a client and as a future member of the family." Alex didn't think she had imagined his hesitation on that last part and her cheeks heated in mortification. "I am supposed to assure you all that I plan to take on a very involved role in the company upon my wedding to Miss Atkinson and help usher Atkinson Enterprises into a bold new era. That you are all in good hands thanks to my stewardship. And that the lies spread by Mr. Benjamin Chisolm about Miss Atkinson's outsized role in the company are merely a shameful attempt to frighten shareholders and gain control of the board himself." Lucien then paused. Alex looked up to find his gaze fixed firmly upon her.

"But I am not going to do that."

"I didn't write that," her father grumbled, sounding more confused than concerned, and the entire room broke out into murmurs.

"Instead, I am going to tell you why Atkinson Enterprises does not need me."

"I didn't write *that*, either," he said more urgently now.

But as he began to rise from his seat, Alex placed a hand on his arm. "Wait."

He shot her a frustrated look but obeyed and sank back into the chair. Meanwhile, Potts had appeared and was handing out papers to everyone in the room. When he reached Alex, he gave her an encouraging smile and for the first time in twenty-four hours, Alex felt something close to relief.

Beside her, Father snatched the paper from Potts. "What is this supposed to be?"

But her secretary merely tilted his head. "You'll see."

Alex scanned the paper and frowned. It was a list of businesses they had invested in. How on earth was this supposed to help? She looked back to Lucien but he was watching the room, waiting until everyone had a paper. Then he continued: "Before you is a list of every business Miss Atkinson single-handedly championed, often clashing with her father and even more than a few of you. Yet these companies have all proved to not only be highly profitable but in a few cases revolutionary in their industries. At the bottom of the page is an estimate of the total profits generated by Atkinson Enterprises' founding shares in these companies. As you can see, that is a substantial total and it is all due to Miss Atkinson's visionary thinking."

Alex was frozen in shock. She could do nothing, say nothing, only watch Lucien as he defended her so beautifully. So *publicly*. He turned to her then, as if he had heard her thoughts.

"If my presence in this company is truly the only thing keeping

Mr. Atkinson in charge, then I will stay. Happily, I might add. But know this: I will consult with Miss Atkinson on every single decision, every single move I make. The truth is you don't need me. Because you have her. And she is by far the most valuable person here. Thank you."

All hell then broke loose as the board members began lobbing furious accusations at each other—and especially at Benjamin, while Lucien just sat back in his chair, taking it all in.

"By God, I think he's done it," her father whispered and reached for her hand, but Alex needed to get out of there.

She quickly stood and slipped from the room without looking at anyone. She needed to go to her office. There she could think. There she could—

"Alex. Wait!"

She stopped in her tracks and turned to face Lucien. He too stopped a couple feet before her. His handsome face full of concern.

"I…I just wanted to make sure you're all right," he said awkwardly.

Adorably.

"I'm fine. I wanted some air."

His gaze stayed fixed on her face. "I'm sure. I had no idea you would be at the meeting."

Alex startled a laugh. "Oh, I'm sorry."

"No, that isn't—" He took a step toward her, then appeared to remember himself. "I'm *glad* you were. I meant every single word. It is the very least of what you deserve."

Alex had to look down. His earnest expression was too much for her battered heart. "Why did you come?"

She forced the question past her lips. She had been wondering since yesterday. What had her father possibly offered to make him return here? To defend her, of all people?

He was quiet for a long moment, then he stepped closer until the toes of his shoes came into view. "Because you needed help. And I wanted to pay you back."

She looked up sharply. "For what?"

"Cooking school. My father told me," he added at her confused look.

"Oh," she said. "That wasn't necessary."

Lucien let out a surprised laugh. "Alex, you changed my life. Why did you not *tell* me?"

Alex frowned. Wasn't it obvious? "I didn't want you to feel beholden to the family."

Or me.

"So instead you let me think you were some heartless ice queen all these years?"

"I *am* a heartless ice queen," she insisted rather stubbornly.

He smiled at that and took another step. "Perhaps an ice queen. But not heartless. Not at all," he murmured. "There is another reason why I came here today."

"Oh?" Alex rasped as Lucien tucked a stray lock of hair behind her ear. It took every ounce of strength not to lean into his hand. "What is it?"

Just as Lucien opened his mouth, the conference door burst open and her father came barreling out. "Where are they? Where is— oh, there you are!" He came rushing over, his face full of joy. "You did it! We did it! They voted Chisolm down! We keep control!" He slapped Lucien on the back and the two men gave each other hearty congratulations. Suddenly, they were surrounded by what felt like every employee in the building, all celebrating, as if the end of some great war had just been declared. Alex took it in as if at a distance. She was happy for Father, of course. But she could not muster this level of enthusiasm. Not for this, anyway.

Alex stepped back from the crowd and leaned against a wall, where she was joined by Potts. She gave him a sly smile. "When did Lucien find the time to tell you to put that list together? I thought he only returned last night."

He looked affronted. "It was my idea. I simply told him about it this morning right before the meeting began."

Alex smiled even wider. "Very good, Potts."

"Thank you, ma'am. But I just gathered the figures. You did the work."

Eventually, the ecstatic celebration became a slightly more subdued one and her father came looking for her. "They've voted Chisolm off the board too, which means there is an open seat. I nominated you, and I think we have the votes, but we need to act now."

It was the kind of recognition Alex had wanted for years. With a board seat, she would have more control over the direction of the company. "I need to speak with Lucien."

"What, now?"

"Yes," Alex said and left her father standing there looking agog while she wound through the crowd. Someone had broken out the bottles of champagne they kept on hand for important clients and the atmosphere had become festive. She eventually found Lucien backed into a corner by the lobby secretary. But as soon as he saw Alex, he politely excused himself and rushed over to her.

"Hello," he said happily. "Did your father tell you the news? They want to give you a seat on the board."

She gripped his lapels to steady herself as someone bumped her from behind. "Can we go somewhere to talk? It's too loud here."

Lucien nodded and Alex led him through the crowd and down the hall into her office.

"Alone at last," Lucien quipped with a smile as he leaned his hip against her desk.

As he stared at her expectantly, Alex could feel her nerves beginning to buzz and shoved them aside. She needed to get this right.

"I couldn't see it before," she blurted out.

Well, so much for that.

She inhaled a calming breath and focused her thoughts. "That is, I couldn't see how you would fit into my life," she tried again. "I was so scared of changing anything. Because I thought I needed it. Because all I have ever done or have been valued for was work. My sisters are beautiful and charming and talented at a dozen different things. But I am good at business. And for a long time, that was fine. That made me happy. Until you came back and everything changed. Then I thought I could stop it. That I could remain the person I had been before you—" She broke off as her voice cracked.

"But the truth is, I *miss* you. So terribly. I miss those stupid little outings that we were forced to go on and whispering through a play and going to the British Museum. I want to do more of that. More of *everything* with you. I've done nothing but work for the last week and I realized that I absolutely hate it," she said with a laugh. "That I don't want to fit you into this life. I want to *change* my life to fit you."

His hand rested on top of hers. "Alex..."

"What was the other reason?" she demanded. "Why you came here."

His gaze burned into hers and Alex didn't think she would ever find the will to look away. "Because I've fallen in love with you, Alexandra Atkinson," he said. Just as Alex's heart began to soar, Lucien continued: "And I want to court you."

Alex tilted her head, confused. "But…you already have."

He gave her an indulgent smile. "I mean properly, this time. For real."

Alex considered this. Briefly. Then shook her head. "No."

Lucien's eyebrows rose. "No?"

"No," she said firmly. "I don't care for courtship. It's a waste of time and there are too many ridiculous rules."

"Oh." Lucien looked deflated. "I see. I understand—"

"I think we should marry instead."

His eyebrows rose again. "Really?"

"Yes. If you'll have me."

He pulled her into his arms then, laughing. "You *scared* me, Alex!"

"I'm sorry." She smiled against his shoulder. "I didn't mean to."

Then he pulled back. "I'll think of a way for you to make it up to me."

"Please do."

And just as they were exchanging a smile far too wicked for a place of business, her father interrupted them. "Come on, Alexandra. The board is waiting!"

"No, thank you," she said.

Her father tilted his head, as if he had misheard. "What do you mean?"

Then she turned back to Lucien. "I quit. Give the seat to someone else."

Her father stood there gaping at them. "I...I don't understand."

Alex managed to tear herself away from Lucien and took her father's hands in her own. "I want to thank you for everything you have ever done for me. But it's time for me to move on and do something else."

He looked so pitiful in that moment that Alex felt her heart wrench. "Are...are you sure?"

At another time Alex might have been swayed to take back her words, to do whatever it took to make her father happy. But not now. Not any longer. He was a grown man and perfectly capable of running this business without her.

Alex nodded and glanced at Lucien. "Quite a bit more than that." Then an idea struck her. "What about Potts? No one else knows my job as well as he does, nor the way I think. He would be an excellent replacement."

"I'll consider it," her father said reluctantly, but Alex knew that was just for show.

She pressed a kiss to his cheek. "Thank you, Papa." Then she looped her arm around Lucien. "There's one more thing. We need your blessing."

He looked between the two of them. "You do? You mean...it's *real* this time?"

Lucien squeezed her arm and smiled at her. "Yes, sir. Entirely real."

Alex grinned back at him. "And for the rest of our lives."

Her father clapped his hands and let out a happy shout. "Oh, but this is wonderful news! Though your Aunt Winifred will be cross that she didn't have a hand in it."

"She will recover," Alex said.

"And your mother will want a double wedding."

"Absolutely not." Then she gentled and turned to Lucien. "Unless that is what you want."

He chuckled. "Heavens no. Something small."

"And private," she added.

"Why not the church in Bunbury?" her father suggested. "So that Mr. Taylor might easily attend?"

They both looked at him and then each other, and in that moment it was decided. A small, private ceremony at the church in Bunbury.

"That sounds perfect," Alex said. And for the first time in her life, she was genuinely excited at the prospect of attending a wedding. How very convenient that it was her own.

Epilogue

December 1896
Park House
London, England

The ballroom of Park House was nearly bursting with guests for Phoebe and Will's wedding breakfast which, given it was now well after dark, had spilled over into more of a wedding supper. Alex stood with Lucien by the edge of the dance floor, taking in the happy couple as they waltzed for what must have been the sixth time that evening.

"Do you wish our wedding had been like this?" Lucien murmured by Alex's ear.

"Of course not," she replied, instantly repelled by the idea, then met his gaze. Lucien had been her husband for almost two months now, yet she still hadn't grown used to the feeling. She woke up most mornings worried it had all been a dream until she saw him sleeping soundly beside her. No, this was real. This was her life. "Our wedding was perfect for *us*."

He gave her a slow smile and drew her even closer to his side. "I agree."

They had taken her father's suggestion and married in Bunbury only two weeks after Alex's proposal so as not to encroach on Phoebe and Will's wedding date. The preparations had been simple out of necessity: autumn flowers from the garden at Atkinson House, a decadent chocolate mousse cake made by the cook based on a trusted recipe Lucien's mother had developed, and a small guest list of only family and very close friends. And, to her mother's great disappointment, Alex wore a gown she already owned that was not white. It was, however, the same gown she had worn the night she propositioned Lucien in the summer house at his request.

"That was the night it all began for me," he had admitted. "The night I began falling in love with you."

It was harder for Alex to pinpoint exactly when her feelings had crossed over into this all-encompassing love, though she expected it was around the time when Lucien became more interesting to her than work.

Since leaving Atkinson Enterprises, she had partnered with Marguerite LaSalle to create an investment firm that focused exclusively on women who had been turned down by banks and other firms. They offered interest-free loans for smaller businesses in addition to funding larger-scale ideas and inventions. The firm handled everything from neighborhood laundries to a company that produced a dishwashing machine for home use.

At first Lucien had been all too happy to assist Alex in this new endeavor but lately he had been talking with Alain about reopening the supper club or at least a modified version of it at the hotel. The newlyweds hadn't yet found time for a honeymoon, but they intended to visit Paris in the spring. Alex was very much looking forward to visiting the catacombs and also meeting Lucien's relatives. She had even resumed her long-abandoned French lessons in preparation. She and Lucien had whiled away many an evening practicing increasingly scandalous French phrases by the fire in the parlor of their small, elegant townhouse in a sleepy little square not far from Park House.

"Do you think we can slip away now?" Lucien murmured as he subtly nuzzled her ear.

"Yes," Alex said with a smile. "We've shown our faces here long enough."

Lucien gripped her hand in his own. "And we can always blame our absence on being newlyweds ourselves."

"Excellent point."

But just as they made their way to the exit, they were intercepted by Inspector Holland, looking as stern as usual. "May I have a word, Mr. and Mrs. Taylor?"

"Inspector. I didn't know you were here," Alex replied.

"Their Graces were kind enough to invite me," he began. "But I only just arrived."

"I see. Well, we were just on our way home. Can't it wait?"

The inspector's eyes narrowed. "Afraid not. It involves the Nun."

"*Him* again," Alex grumbled. She was growing quite tired of that man interrupting her life.

"I think we should hear this, my dear," Lucien said gently.

Alex crossed her arms. "Very well."

They moved to a secluded corner of the room where they would not be disturbed. "Gerald O'Hara was brought in last night," the inspector began. "He was arrested during a raid of an illegal boxing ring that he has been running."

"Why, that's excellent news," Lucien said enthusiastically as he turned to her, but Alex was still watching the inspector's face closely and knew there was more to come.

"And?" she asked.

"He admitted to following you on orders of the Nun, but when we visited his alleged headquarters, the place was empty. The man seems to have vanished."

Alex frowned. "What does Mr. O'Hara know?"

"Apparently not much," the inspector replied. "He claims he never even met the Nun in person."

"And you believe him?"

The inspector gave her a level look. "For the time being. As I understand it, that is largely how the Nun operates and why he has so effectively evaded capture all these years. Very few people know what he looks like."

"But why was he at Alex's office that night?" Lucien asked.

"Mr. O'Hara maintains that he did not think Mrs. Taylor would be there at that time of night," the inspector explained. "He had been instructed to look for any information related to her business activities and insists that he would have left once he realized she was still in the office." Inspector Holland then addressed Alex with a smile. "I am beginning to think the Nun is more of an admirer of yours rather than a threat."

Alex snorted. "If he is so interested in understanding my business acumen, he would be better off making an appointment."

"You take this too lightly, Alex," Lucien grumbled. "I don't like it."

"Well, it's no matter anyway," she said. "The Nun is gone and I no longer work for my father."

"He will return though," the inspector replied darkly. "That is the only thing I am sure of. You still need to take care. *All* of you."

Alex opened her mouth to respond, but Lucien cut her off. "We will, Inspector. You have my word." He then gave Alex a pleading look. The one she hadn't yet been able to resist and she let out a sigh.

"And mine," she said.

"There you two are!" Freddie suddenly cried out from behind them. "Don't think you can slip out without saying good-bye—" She froze once she saw the inspector with them.

"Miss Atkinson," the man said flatly, but even Alex noticed the way his entire form seemed to tighten in her sister's presence.

Interesting.

Not long after Alex and Lucien's wedding, Freddie had called off her engagement to Hank Jr. and returned the massive diamond ring. Alex hadn't been terribly surprised, only that it had taken her so long to do so.

"I knew it wasn't right," Freddie had explained. "But I didn't want to distract from your wedding."

However, since then she seemed more unhappy than ever. Yet every time anyone tried to talk to her about it, she insisted she was fine.

Now Freddie stared at the inspector with a strange mixture of hostility and interest.

"We were just leaving, actually," Alex said in a bid to keep her sister from boring a hole into the man's forehead.

Freddie didn't even look at her. "And what are *you* doing here?"

The question sounded much more like an accusation, yet the inspector appeared entirely unbothered. "I had some information for your sister. And I was invited," he added, arching a brow.

Alex and Lucien exchanged a look, but he seemed just as bewildered as she was.

"May I speak with you privately?" Freddie asked.

Alex was certain the man would deny her, but just before the silence could grow even more excruciating, the inspector nodded. Just once.

Freddie didn't wait a minute longer and strode toward the hallway.

Alex frowned as the inspector trailed after her. "I have half a mind to follow them."

"Oh, let them be," Lucien said. "The house is full of people. And the inspector is a good man. He wouldn't do anything improper."

"It isn't him I'm worried about," Alex replied.

But Lucien only chuckled. "If you interfere now, it will only prolong the inevitable. You must let them work it out themselves. Whatever *it* may be," he added.

Alex turned to him then. "I suppose you're right."

"You don't say that very often," Lucien said with a grin as he led her toward the coatroom. "Let that be the last word on it."

Alex rolled her eyes even while she fought back a smile. "I suppose I can indulge you just this once."

"And here I was hoping you would indulge me quite a bit more when we got home," he said with a very obvious eyebrow waggle as he handed Alex her velvet cloak.

"You really are the most incorrigible man," she said with a laugh. "If I had known you were like this, I might not have proposed to you."

But her husband only grinned wider. "Oh, it is *all* because of you, my dear. You have been a terrible influence on me," he said with a wink. "And don't you ever think otherwise."

"I might need a thorough demonstration of just how terrible,"

Alex murmured as they walked down the long hall toward the front door.

"Well, I will be very happy to oblige you, madam," he replied, tugging her closer to him. "As I am quite unable to deny you a thing."

Alex turned to him then and pressed a hand to his jaw. "I think that is a particular malady we both suffer from."

Lucien covered her hand with his own and kissed her palm while his eyes burned into hers. "Then we had better get home and hope the cure is a nice long stay in bed."

Alex chuckled. "I don't think there is a cure for this, my love."

Lucien tucked her arm through his as they continued down the hall. "And thank heavens for that."

I would be remiss if I did not mention that the setup for this book was largely inspired by the 1995 remake of the classic film *Sabrina* starring Harrison Ford and Julia Ormond. Why that version and not the original with Humphrey Bogart and Audrey Hepburn? Because in 1996 I rented it from Blockbuster for reasons I can't remember and then proceeded to watch it *many* times over a weeklong period. When I was thinking about Alex's book, it seemed like a delicious twist to have the gender roles reversed, and it was great fun to revisit a premise that has lived inside my head for so long.

The character of Alex was also informed in part by the lives of many overlooked women of the Victorian era, including the economist Mary Paley Marshall, who was among the first group of women allowed to attend Cambridge University and sit for the Moral Sciences Tripos. But while in my book Alex ends her relationship with her economics tutor, Paley Marshall married hers: the economist Alfred Marshall.

While for many years Marshall championed both the education of women in general and of Paley Marshall in particular, later in life he would become an outspoken opponent of women attending Cambridge even while Paley Marshall became the first female economics lecturer at the university. He would also disavow the book they coauthored, *The Economics of Industry*, and claimed it was mostly his wife's ideas (ideas commended by John Maynard Keynes, no less). For her part, Paley Marshall continued to support her husband's career, likely at the expense of her own, and never publicly spoke against him. She taught at Cambridge for more than twenty years.

Acknowledgments

I feel like I always thank the same handful of people when I write my acknowledgments, and it really is such a gift to have their steady support. I could not write my books without them. Thank you to my family, especially my mom and my mother-in-law for taking good care of my girl each week. Thank you to Elizabeth for reading an early draft and sending emotional-support texts. Thank you to my friends for reminding me that I have a life outside of my Word documents. Thank you to YY Liak for the gorgeous cover. Thank you to Junessa Viloria and the team at Forever for their enthusiasm for this story. And my heartfelt thanks to all the readers, booksellers, and librarians who continue to champion historical romance both in person and online.

About the Author

Emily Sullivan is an award-winning author of historical fiction set in the late Victorian period. She lives with her family in New England, where she enjoys taking long drives and short walks, and she always orders dessert.

You can learn more at:
EmilySullivanBooks.com
Instagram @PaperbackLady
Pinterest.com/ESullivanBooks